Dust Up at the Crater School

Dust Up at the Crater School

Chaz Brenchley

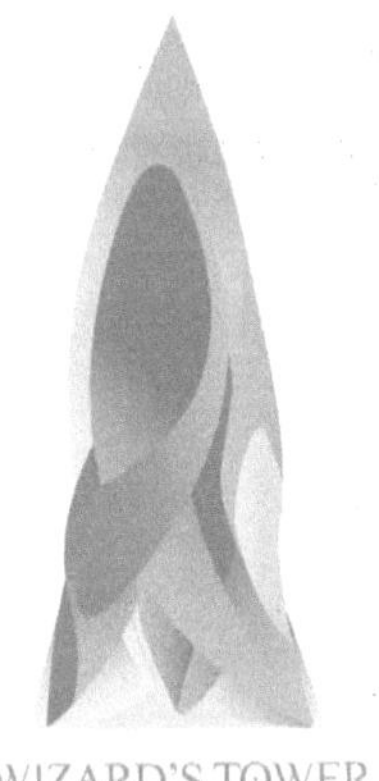

Wizard's Tower Press

Trowbridge, England

Contents

CHAZ BRENCHLEY

In loving memory of my mother
Vera Joyce Brenchley, née Grant,
who read Chalet School books herself in her childhood
and was thus pretty much solely responsible for me.

Praise for Dust Up at the Crater School

"Only in the laboratory of Chaz Brenchley could the British school story be lovingly sutured together with the Old Mars of the pulps, animated with the crackling static of a planetary dust storm, and sent lumbering down to the village. No — **skipping** down to the village, with a beret, and a paper bag full of bulls'-eyes, and a wholesome desire to excel at lacrosse."

Francis Spufford

Praise for Three Twins at the Crater School

"What a brilliant wheeze, to transplant a girls' school story to a steampunk Martian colony. Chaz Brenchley performs a pitch-perfect quantum shift that's full of plums. If you're a fan of Brent-Dyer or Brazil or Blyton, you will love Three Twins at the Crater School."

Val McDermid

"All the earnest charm of a British boarding school story, plus aliens! I wish I were a Crater School girl."

Marie Brennan

"Three Twins at the Crater School is splendidly full of peril and charm. It calls forth very particular memories of books and mountain schools and the adventures of teenage girls."

Gillian Polack

"In a past that isn't ours, in a world of aether ships and an Eternal Empress, the Crater School embodies all the values, passions, high jinks and adventures of the classic girl school stories of the first half of the twentieth century. For every fan of The Chalet School, Malory Towers, Dimsie or the Abbey Girls, this is a guiltless pleasure."

Farah Mendlesohn

"Who would have thought an English boarding school story and a science fiction adventure mashup would work so spectacularly? This is a one-sitting page-turner!"

Sherwood Smith

"The British Empire has met its match in Chaz Brenchley's Mars. Mysterious aquatic aliens have transported humans to the Red Planet by means unexplained, and the Brits, willingly taking on the colonizing of this new world, establish themselves well. The Crater School brings to mind the rigidity of Aubrey Upjohn's Malvern House, the rowdiness of Stalky's Coll, and the resourcefulness and sheer heart of St. Trinian's. Brenchley had me at 'British girls' school on Mars.'"

Jennifer Stevenson

"If Angela Brazil and Edgar Rice Burroughs had decided to write a story together, Three Twins at the Crater School might have been the delightful result. Friendship, family ties—good and bad—and schoolgirl shenanigans set against the backdrop of a Mars straight out of early science fiction makes for exciting and yet cozy reading. I was especially intrigued by the hints of alternate history—the deathless

Queen Victoria, a Great War fought between Britain and Czarist Russia—there's much to explore here, and I sincerely hope there will be further instalments."

Marissa Doyle

"In this inventive combination, Brenchley offers readers an entertaining opportunity to revisit the school stories and planetary romances of days gone by. Along the way, he interrogates the assumptions and attitudes of those books and their era with charming ruthlessness. Highly recommended."

Juliet E. McKenna

"A rollicking good read from start to finish! Move over, Enid Blyton, there are new girls at school—they fight monsters!"

Ellen Klages

"Twins we will never forget and cool Mars creatures."

Miranda and Talia, age 9

CHAPTER ONE

An Unexpected Pupil

The news was all over school, running like wildfire through corridors and dormitories, greeting each batch of new arrivals almost before they'd taken off their hats and found their friends.

Rowany de Vere—Rowany, of all people!—had made a mull of her Oxford entrance, and was back unexpectedly at the Crater School for an extra year of coaching before she tried again.

"Not that she can be Head Girl again." Thus Lise Harper, stoutly, to her particular crew. "We've never had the same Head Girl two years running, and I don't suppose we ever will. It's, it's against all tradition. And besides, it's Melanie's *turn*." Melanie Fitzwalter had been Rowany's deputy for the last year, as well as Games Prefect and head of Stokes House. Lise was a Stokes girl, loyal to a fault; and a sportsman through and through; and, above all, a devoted supporter of Melanie's ever since her first term. Melanie had been in the Middle School in those far-off days, but she'd taken the gawky hopeful Junior under her wing for reasons neither one of them had ever been able to explain. She'd taught Lise not to fear the hockey ball, however hard it came; and how to strengthen her backhand, how to guard her stumps, how to pull an oar. Now Lise was a Middle herself, and still Melanie's most passionate defender, come what may.

Her listeners on this occasion were her own cohort, a group that formed last term and was already widely known as the Crew. Double twins, no less, and sundry other original sinners: they were eyed admiringly by their juniors, warily by authority, askance even by their own tribe. Where the Crew led, trouble was likely to follow. Fun first, but trouble after.

The Crew was well accustomed to Lise's passion, and generally paid it no more heed than it was worth. This time, though, they were all more or less in agreement.

"Of course Melanie should be Head Girl," Tasha decreed, from where she lay sprawled on Levity's bed with her head in Tawney's lap. "It's not just that she's been waiting for it, she's *trained* for it. A whole year's apprenticeship, as Rowany's deputy. It rubs off, that Rowany-ness. Melanie's almost as much on the ball as Rowany ever was. More's the pity."

"Just as much!" Lise declared, inevitably.

"Well, perhaps," said Tawney the peacemaker, "but I'm sure she learned it from Rowany."

"You're sure that who learned what from Rowany?" The voice was none of theirs, but instantly familiar to them all. They disentangled themselves from each other and scrambled to their feet, feeling vaguely that a mannerly gesture might somehow help an indefensible situation; then one by one they lifted their gaze to confront the mild and curious expression of the very person they'd been discussing.

Crater School prefects were legendary, of course, for being exactly where you didn't want to find them, and for hearing exactly what you wouldn't want them to know. Even so, this was an extreme example, and seemed particularly unfair. This might be Melanie's own house, and of course she was on duty and on alert the first day of term, but still! Didn't she have anything better to do than go prying about, listening at the doors of dormitories that were supposed to be empty at this time of day...?

In fairness, not one of them supposed that she had really been eavesdropping. She'd heard voices and just come marching in, no doubt about that. Just in time to catch that last remark. Oh, why hadn't they at least thought to close the door...?

"Tawney? You were saying?"

Tawney cursed her fate, wondered what terrible punishment lay in store, and stood mute, staring at her shoes.

After a long, long silence, Melanie surprised them all with a chuckle.

"Oh, very well. I'm not going to pitch you into a row on the first day—and I can't very well, given that the remark was certainly not intended for my ears, however happily it found its way there. But try to treat this as a lesson, people. Gossiping about others is a social crime at best, and doing it where you can be overheard is downright foolhardy—and in school, wherever you are, you can always be overheard by someone. It's bound to get back to your, to your gossipee, so don't do it, there's good children."

"T'isn't gossip if it's news," muttered Tasha. "Is it?"

"That, my dear Tasha, is a fine line and you're better off not trying to tread it. Especially where it concerns your seniors. You'll hear officially what you need to know. Beyond that, anything personal is down to other people's judgement, whether they choose to tell you. Now: I know that you all like to live in one another's pockets, and you haven't seen each other in an age and there's a lot to catch up with—some of which might authentically be called news, Tasha, yes—but this isn't the best day to be disregarding rules wholesale. Only two of you belong in Stokes at all, and those two shouldn't be lolling about in their dormie in mid-afternoon. Twins—both sets—you're in Jopling, aren't you? In one dormitory, yet? I can't imagine what fevered brain thought that was a good idea—"

"—That was Miss Leven," Tasha murmured, just sufficiently *sotto voce* that Melanie could pretend she hadn't heard it—

"—but don't you have work you should be getting on with there?"

"Please, Melanie," Jessica said, in her role as the slightly newer Abramoff, hence not quite so tainted in her reputation, "we were all unpacked already, as we didn't go home this hol and neither did the Mishtwins, so Miss Peters said she thought it would be better for everyone if we just got out of her hair."

"Out from underfoot," Rachel interrupted, "is what she said exactly."

"In other words, you were making such a nuisance of yourselves that your own housemistress flung you forth. Sent out of your country for your country's good, eh? And you decided your best plan was to come down and make a nuisance of yourselves in Stokes instead. I see. And is the same true for you, Pete?"

"Well,"—the shortest, youngest, newest and fiercest of the Crew screwed up her face in a terrible scowl—"I didn't get flung out of Greenaway. But I didn't need to unpack, and there wasn't anything to do, and I didn't have anywhere else to go, so..."

"I see," Melanie repeated, a little more gently this time. Pete had lost both parents, she knew, and was effectively homeless until her uncle guardian found work and a place to settle. The Crater School had a tradition of taking in orphans—there was hardly a school on Mars that did not— and making self-reliant women of them, but Pete was a

challenge even here. In half a term she had not settled to
school strictures; she was still more boyish than otherwise,
in Melanie's estimation; and her only friends, the older
girl knew full well, were here in this room. "Well, I can't be
doing with you all hanging around in here, even if the rules
allowed it, which they don't. Even on the first day of term,
Levity, no. I have you and Lise on the list for unpacking
at five o'clock, which gives you two hours to fill; why don't
you all raid the practice lockers, go down to the cricket field
and play all-against-all? On the outfield, please, not on the
pitch; that's sacred, and Mr Marks would have my ears for his
collection if I let you kids tear it up before the first match of
term. And mind you pad up properly, batsman and wicket-
keeper both. I don't want to be explaining bruises or worse to
Sister Anthony. If anyone comes by to ask what you're up to,
tell them I sent you. As a punishment. Understood?"

"Yes, Melanie," seven beaming faces acknowledged.

"Good. Go on, then; scram. And mind you're back in
time, you two. Don't keep me waiting."

Once she was safely out of earshot, as the Crew scrambled
happily downstairs towards two unexpected hours of their
favourite pastime, one triumphant voice murmured, "See? I
told you! *Definitely* rubbed-off Rowany, that was..."

Some foundations—if rumour is to be believed—are only
too glad to see the back of their founder, however soon or
late it comes, that happy day. Not so the Crater School. The
school's onlie begetter had been Mrs Mackenzie for some
years now, but she was still and always Miss Tolchard within
these stone walls, and still welcomed with open arms by
staff and pupils alike whenever she chose to come across the
water. Indeed, on one never-to-be-forgotten Speech Day, she
had been apostrophised from the stage—in front of parents
and dignitaries—as "Beloved Matriarch," which the school

would certainly never let her forget, although the guilty girl had long departed.

Her marriage to the famous doctor—whose own great project was the Sanatorium the other side of the lake, where he and his team studied and treated all the various and peculiar diseases unique to the Red Planet—had necessarily called a halt to her position as Headmistress of the Crater School. Nevertheless, she was still its founder and still its owner, and she kept an interest far greater than financial. She always liked to visit at the start of every term, to meet whatever new girls there might be, and to talk over whatever challenges the school knew it would be facing.

It was her custom to telephone before she came. This particular day—being the start of Michaelmas Term, after the long holiday, when most new girls would arrive to begin their school career—Miss Leven had been expecting her predecessor's call all day. It hadn't come; and so after dinner she had shared a cup of coffee in the staff room and then excused herself to her own study, where there was more paperwork awaiting than she cared to consider.

She had barely worked her way into it before she was interrupted by a peremptory, not to say insouciant tap at the door. Frowning, she lifted her head; the door opened before she could speak, and her visitor stepped lightly in.

Unwelcome vanished in a moment from Miss Leven's face. She rose to her feet, holding her hands out in delight. "Evelyn! I had entirely given up on you tonight."

"Meaning, I know, that this is a ridiculously late hour to be calling. Nevertheless, here I am, casting myself upon you all unprepared."

"Is Mac away again?"

"He is. And he made me promise not to row myself over to see you, with the merlins being as turbulent as they are; so I'm dependent on the good offices of a doctor with a car, or else the public steambus. Young Penberthy was kind enough to bring me this evening, as he has a dinner engagement with your Miss Calomy, down in the town. I'd wager he has more on his mind than dinner, too," she went on pensively.

"Oh, don't tell me I'm in need of a new art mistress! Again!"

"Well, of course she may refuse him—but I'd start casting about, if I were you. Those two seem quite set on each other."

"Oh, they are, there's no question about it, bar the one he hasn't quite popped yet—but I did hope he might hold off for a few years."

"Oh my dear, did you really? When were the young ever in anything other than a hurry? Ed engaged me in earnest conversation as he drove me down tonight, wondering if I might be able to construe 'Seize time by the forelock' as a Latin aphorism. I gathered that he had tried *Carpe diem* for size and found it inadequate to his needs. He was afraid she might think it had something to do with fish."

"Oh, lor'! That poor boy! What did you tell him?"

"To trust to his English tongue, of course, and his native sense of timing. He needs no more."

"No, you're right, of course—and he is a charming lad, and they will do very well together. And we will be left in the lurch again. That's the trouble with your wretched Sanatorium, it attracts so many extremely eligible bachelors. And of course Mars needs wives and children, but it needs single women too. How else are those children, or the girl-children at least, to be educated? Sometimes I come over all heretical, you know, and think that we shouldn't be so quick to let our teachers go, just because they've decided to get married. Babies don't always follow on the instant—and there are nannies and nurseries in any case, children needn't be a bar on a woman's career."

"Why, Peggy Leven, you're a radical! A revolutionary!"

"Of course I am. I have to be. We need different customs and different solutions, this far from Home. The old ways aren't always the best ways, not for us. Not on Mars. You wouldn't like to come back, I suppose?" Miss Leven pierced her friend and employer with a gimlet eye. "Say two or three days a week, just to see how you like it?"

Miss Tolchard laughed gaily, even as she shook her head. "I'm sorry, Peg, it can't be done. I told you, there's a ukase against my rowing over, and Mac can't spare a driver to be running me back and forth. Besides, I don't want to be that much away from home, while my own children are young. Oh, I know they'd be perfectly fine without me—but the same is not true in reverse."

"Which is why my revolution will never happen, I know. Very well. Let us set radicalism aside as a lost cause, fit only for arguments in Oxford quads, and turn our minds to other matters. I'll ring for another cup, so you can share this pot of Mrs Bailey's excellent coffee"—she suited the action to the word—"and I'll ask the maid to make up your usual room, shall I? Or is Edward Penberthy expecting to collect you and take you home again?"

"Not he. I couldn't do that to the child, provide a period to his adventure. He'd have felt himself under curfew all evening, watching the clock, wondering how late he could make me wait. No, I told him to focus on Miss Calomy tonight; and yes, I'd be very grateful for a bed. I know I shouldn't have sprung myself on you like this, all unannounced, but—well, the opportunity was quite sudden, and he was very eager to be off. It seemed a shame to pass up the chance. I'll have breakfast with your new girls in the morning, if I may. Any originals amongst them?"

"Not that I've noticed," Miss Leven said. "They seem a very normal group of girls, for a wonder. And every one of them a Junior; not a single older applicant this term, so we've no need to be squeezing an extra girl into a form or a dormitory that's already settled."

"That must be some relief, after last term. How are those two wicked ones settling in?"

"Which two? They're all wicked, at that age. Oh, I know who you mean: half-term's unexpected arrivals. Jessica Abramoff is the perfect Crater School girl, let me tell you: mischievous and inventive, just the way we've always liked them. She's a good influence on her sister, too, despite everything their parents may believe. Little Pete Thorogood, on the other hand—well, I'm not sure we're doing her any good at all."

"Pete?—Ah yes, she's the girl who's more than half a boy, isn't she?"

Miss Leven smiled. "That's one way to put it. And she does *not* want that proportion changed, thank you very much. We've never had any time for fussy young ladies, and Pete is the very model of that self-reliance that we try to teach our girls, that they're sure to need at some point in their future lives—but, oh *dear*, Evelyn! She's like something out of the Wild West—or no, better, she's like one of our own pioneers from a hundred years ago. She has a genius for anything mechanical, and for hard work too, so long as she thinks it worthwhile. She can coal and fire a boiler, or strip a motor to its component parts, then put it all back together again and leave it running sweeter than before. She's a deadly shot with a catapult—or a cricket ball, come to that— and she can't wait to show off her prowess with a rifle as soon as she's allowed to. But she has the heartiest contempt for what she calls schoolbook learning, and her opinion on evening frocks does *not* bear repeating. Given her druthers, she'd live in overalls all week and Sunday too."

"Yes. When I encountered her, I remember, she had an oil-smut on her nose and a live sandroach in her pocket.

Which she was all too pleased to show me. To be fair to the infant, I don't believe she was trying to shock me; I think she expected me to find it as fascinating as she clearly did herself. She led me to understand that she meant to keep it as a pet. I presume that was not allowed?"

"Indeed not! A female heavy with eggs? We'd have been overrun in no time. Her dormitory prefect confiscated it instanter, and took it to Miss Hendy. Who might herself have preferred to keep it, if I'm honest, but she was prevailed upon to release the creature, at some significant distance from the school. Miss Hendy and Pete are somewhat in sympathy with each other, I believe—but not alas enough to induce the child to spend any time at her studies. Practical lessons are meat and drink to her, but paper and ink are poison."

"She's hardly our first to feel that way," Miss Tolchard said meditatively. "Remember when Melanie was new, and sports were all in all to her? If she couldn't chase it or hit it with a stick, she didn't want to know."

"True for you," Miss Leven laughed. "And I'm not sure she's really changed, in her heart of hearts. She's consented to go to a training college, to study human physiology and health—but only so that she can come back here and be a better games mistress. I'd best warn Miss Whitworth, she'll be needing to find a husband herself in four or five years, just to make room. Melanie will not be denied."

"She'll be an asset, when she comes—but yes, all the better for some training and experience elsewhere. Will she go Home?"

"She'll have to. She can't get that training on Mars, it doesn't exist. Female sports? Far too frivolous a notion, my dear. Even now. We remain a pioneer culture at heart. Women can labour all the hours God sends, but only on the farmstead; we still struggle with notions of women in the workplace, where men are meant to be. Games for women is something further yet, beyond imagining. Like education for women."

"And yet, here we are," Miss Tolchard murmured, long familiar with this particular argument.

"We are; but—"

The maid came in just then, with fresh coffee and a cup for the visitor, and a plate of dainty biscuits. Miss Leven sent her off to make up bed and fire in the guest room; and when she was gone, Miss Tolchard picked up a new thread.

"Speaking of women's education, what of Rowany's?"

"What indeed?" Miss Leven returned. "She's presented me with a list of what she needs, but I don't know how we're to achieve it. To be sure, we have most of that knowledge amongst the staff, but how any of us can spare the time to teach her, with the standard timetable as full as it is..."

"Oh, that's easy," quoth Miss Tolchard. "You don't teach her anything; you point her at the books she needs, and instruct her to teach the brightest of her juniors. That way everybody benefits. She'll absorb what she needs, under the pressure of having to pass it on; her victims will thrive under her tutelage; and your staff will find their burdens at least a little lifted."

"Evelyn Tolchard! I can't use her as an unpaid member of staff!"

"That's Evelyn Mackenzie to you, and I'll thank you to remember it—and of course you can."

"In these walls, my lady, you are and will always remain their blessed Miss Tolchard, Mac or no Mac—and how on Mars could I justify that, when her father's paying full fees for her extra year?"

"The results will speak for themselves. You know yourself there's no better way to learn a thing than to teach it to someone else. And it won't hurt the girl to take on a little responsibility alongside. At the moment she thinks she has it easy this year, with nothing to do but learn. What say we send for her now, and break it to her? She won't be in bed yet."

"You really are the wickedest woman. No, let her have her night among her own clan, being a schoolgirl once again, all unexpectedly. You can break it to her after breakfast. And I'll be interested to know what she tells you in return, of the truth of all this. I know the story I've been told, which is not the story we are telling the school; and I know fine well that what I've heard is not all there is to it. There are layers within layers here."

"There are—and they're probably best left undisturbed," said Miss Tolchard, who had had Rowany as a house-guest for the last few days before term began, and knew more perhaps than Miss Leven, and was uncomfortably obliged not to share it. "But I'll tell you what, we might turn the tables, too. We could have your Pete instruct Rowany; I know 'practical engineering' is on that list of hers. Set it up as a club, and let Rowany and anyone who's interested learn at the feet of the master. That'll make the child feel a part of this school, quicker than anything else I can think of. By the way, what is her baptismal name? I cannot believe that her parents actually called her Pete."

"The seal of the confessional, my dear; I am seven-times-seven sworn not to say. No, not even to you. Pete she is and Pete she will remain. Despite our best efforts. Oh, that uncle of hers may be a dear and I do wish him all the best, but he has so much, so very much to answer for..."

CHAPTER TWO

The Powers That Be

"Come along in, my lambs, and don't be shy. If the Crater School has taught you only one thing in all these years, it should be to step boldly through any doorway that's open to you."

That was a frightful slander on a beloved institution, which had taught them all far more than that; but Melanie said it with a smile, and came to the door herself to usher the two newcomers through. She well remembered how big a step it seemed, that first time you came into the Prefects' Room by right, by appointment from the Head.

"Welcome to your new home," she said breezily. "I know that you both know it intimately already, from many a summons in your wicked years—but this is where you belong now, and I do have to say that we're delighted to have you. Sit yourselves down here, where we saved you two seats together, take a crumpet and a cup of tea, and we'll get down to business..."

In truth, Melanie thought, she was talking for her own comfort as much as that of the two new appointees. The Prefects' Room had been her home for a year and more, with this last step up from Games Prefect to Head Girl long predicted, almost expected—and even so. She was finding it a higher and a harder step than ever she'd anticipated. Before this, she'd always had Rowany to turn to in moments of crisis or self-doubt. Rowany had remained those few months older, those few inches taller, that one term senior as they progressed together through the school. It seemed as though they had been friends for ever, and colleagues too: colleagues in mischief first, and then in authority, little by little as older wiser heads deemed them ready for it. And now Rowany was—well, not gone exactly, but no longer what she was, in a strange way no longer senior. Melanie had her place, and was obliged to occupy it, and it all felt very wrong indeed.

Still: the burden was hers to carry, even if it came without rewards. She would be a poor creature indeed, who clam-oured for prizes at the first hint of responsibility. No one had ever justly called Melanie a shirker. She seated the newcom-ers, with another encouraging smile; then took her place—hers at last, not Rowany's!—at the head of the table. And felt all eyes turned to her, and met them all with as much grace as she could manage; and said, "Well, then. As the first order of business, I'd like to introduce our two newcomers, and welcome them to the Prefects' Room. Yes, Mary, I know that we all know them both perfectly well already, but that's really not the point. We don't keep minutes of prefects' meet-ings, but nevertheless: a formal introduction is called for, I believe. I know I had one, and so did you, for I was there. So: without further ado, *if* I may," glowering around the table to make entirely certain of it, "ladies, let me make known to you Fidelis Carpenter and Arie Bunker, our two newest recruits to the, the prefecture."

Arie blushed. Fidelis frowned and visibly had to swallow down a protest, *that's not what that word means*. It wouldn't take long for her to overcome a natural shyness and give her innate pedantry full rein, here as she did in class and out, with staff as freely as with juniors.

"As you know," Melanie went on, speaking firmly over the rising murmur of welcome, "every prefect takes on a particular job. We've not had the usual wholesale turn-out this year, so I don't need to assign tasks all round—unless anyone's unhappy with what they were doing last term?"

No one spoke up, so she went on, "Very well, then. Obviously I can't be Head Girl and carry on with games at the same time, there aren't enough hours in the day; but equally obviously, we have a perfect candidate to step in to that role. If she's willing. Alis, will you be Games Prefect?"

Alis gazed at her with a mutinous twinkle in her eye, and said, "Captain."

"I ... beg your pardon?"

"I'm honoured to accept, of course, but I want to give the job a new title. I think 'Games Captain' sounds more appropriate, don't you?"

"What she means," her friend Marina said lazily from her seat at Alis's side, "is that her father's a naval captain and her brother's headed the same way, *after* being Games Captain at his own school, and she doesn't want to be the only member of the family without a captaincy under her belt. You'd best look out, Felicity, for she'll want the Pioneer captaincy as well. She'd like to be Captain Captain Rasmussen. Then her whole family would have to salute her."

"That's slander," long-limbed Alis said equably. "Besides which, won't you be bumped back down to Vice Captain, Felicity, now that our beloved Rowany has returned in disgrace?"

"Let me answer that," Melanie said quickly, before one of Rowany's many fans around the table could decide to take offence, "because the answer is a simple 'no'. Rowany won't be resuming captaincy of the Pioneers, any more than she'll be Head Girl again. Miss Leven did ask me to be clear about this if the question came up at all, because we all need to be clear with the rest of the school: Rowany's here just to study this year, to make up whatever deficits Oxford saw in her. She's, how shall I say it, outside the hierarchy now? Of course she's still Rowany, with all that that implies; but she has no official position in either school or house, and no official duties either. We can't look to her to step in, if things get out of hand; we can't ask her to substitute for any one of us."

"That's barmy," Elise van Buren said bluntly. "Given how the kids are all in awe of her. Why waste that power, when we have it to hand?"

"Because Miss Leven expects us to generate our own power, I suppose," Melanie said. "Without being dependent on Rowany, any more than we are on the staff. We have to stand on our own feet now, and having Rowany around is ... a complication. Not that she's not welcome—but she's not a prefect either, and we may as well accept that first as last."

"She's been given her own room in Jopling," Marina confirmed. "Which is a thing unknown hitherto. I imagine it's meant to reinforce that notion of her as a being apart, neither fish nor fowl. Can we call her a red herring, and be done? I well know the pleasure of lingering over a hot crumpet, but I have to practice; I've a lesson first thing in the morning, and Mr Fellenor will *not* love me if I don't have my bowing sorted out. Mahler is *most* peculiar to me," she added wistfully. Marina's violin was thought likely to spread her fame across the province and further yet—but that meant work, and the school did all it could to keep her at it. Miss Leven was known to have hesitated before offering her the prefectship, for fear that even a little authority might prove a distraction from her true calling.

"Yes, of course," Melanie said hastily. "With Alis stepping up to be Games Prefect—oh, very well, Games *Captain*, if you must—that leaves her job as Staff Prefect vacant. Fidelis, can

I ask you to take that on? It doesn't mean much in the way of extra work, and you do get choice insights into the ways of the Staff Room."

"I think I can do that," Fidelis agreed carefully, "if Alis will brief me on all the ins and outs?"

"Depend on it, my child," Alis said, with an airy wave of her hand. "Actually, I have it all written down, to make sure I didn't forget anything. I'll pass my notebook on, like ancient wisdom."

"Excellent," Melanie said. "Thanks, both. That leaves you, Arie—and actually we have a task new-minted that should be right up your street. Miss Leven hinted to me that we don't take enough care of our little people, so I thought we'd best make them an official job. I'm not sure about the title yet—'Juniors Prefect' just sounds odd—but would you be prepared to keep an eye on the Junior School, and try to defray trouble before it has to come to us officially? You know what they're like, with their cliques and wars and upsets."

"I do—and of course I will, I'd be glad to."

"Thanks, then. To be honest, I think what really happened is that the staff noticed you were doing that already, and felt it ought to be officially acknowledged. Well, that's that, people. Is there any other business, or may I release Marina to her fiddling?"

"I suppose it's no use my proposing that we create another new job, with the express purpose of crushing all wickedness out of the Middles," Elise said with a gleam in her eye, "and co-opt Rowany for the position, in direct defiance of Miss Leven and her edict? Rowany has to do *something* with her time, apart from study; she might as well let us make use of her."

"Absolutely no use at all, no." Those very words were on the tip of Melanie's tongue, along with *didn't I already tell you so?* and other scathing comments—but in fact it wasn't she who said them. The voice came from the doorway. Somehow nobody had noticed the interloper, standing there without so much as a by-your-leave. Now that they'd seen her, they couldn't understand their own heedlessness; she was inherently hard to overlook.

The entire Crater School prefectorial body rose to its feet as one person, and shrieked, "Rowany!"

She flinched under the weight of that outcry, looked back over her shoulder in an exaggerated manner, stepped across the threshold and closed the door carefully behind her.

"Hush, my children, hush. You sound like a gaggle of fourth-formers at their reckless worst. Do you want to bring the staff down upon you in their wrath? Because, let me tell you, I do *not*. I'm not even supposed to be here. Indeed, I'm strictly forbidden. Strictly," she stressed, drawing up a chair to the table as though by right and reaching a long arm for the last remaining crumpet.

"Yes," said Melanie, as the room settled. "We've been told all about that. No duties, no responsibilities. We're not even supposed to ask you for advice. So what, may I ask, are you doing here?"

"Can't a girl drop in for a friendly chat with her—what are you? Not forebears. Afterbears? Erstwhilebears?"

"Not in the middle of a prefects' meeting, she can't. And don't tell me you didn't know what we were about. That door was closed for a reason; if you'd knocked, we'd have told you to go away, sight unseen."

"Which is exactly why I didn't knock, for I wanted to speak to you. To all of you at once, and in private, which is why I'm breaking in on your meeting before you scatter to the four winds. So: will you send me away again with my tail between my legs, or will you listen?"

There could only ever be one answer to such a question. "Go ahead," Melanie said, striving to remember that she was Head Girl here now and nominally in charge. It was harder than ever to keep that in mind, with Rowany actually in the room. How Oxford had ever contrived to say "no", or at least "not now", to her was beyond Melanie's imagining; certainly she could never do it herself. "We're listening."

Indeed, they could have heard a pin drop, had anyone been so distracted as to be playing with one. In fact they were motionless, riveted: what on Mars was Rowany going to tell them?

She smiled around the table, all too aware of their weighty attention; then she said, "So here I am, and I know it's going to be difficult for everybody having me around, so I did want to say sorry for that. And to promise you that I won't make a nuisance of myself. You people run the school now—yes, you do, Mary, far more than the staff do; only think about it for a moment and you'll see that—and I'm determined not to interfere. Melanie's in charge, not me. Miss Tolchard and Miss Leven both have been quite clear about that. It was a condition of their taking me back for this extra year, that I focus on my work and not the school. I'm to be—semi-detached, is how Miss Leven put it. I am in the school but not quite of the school, is what Miss Tolchard said.

"All that said," she said, "I am still myself: which means that I am a Craterean through and through, whatever Authority dictates. I am no longer officially one of you, but to some extent that leaves me more free to help you, without actually infringing on the strictures of the staff. I do mean to buckle down and study hard this year—but I can see ways that we can play that to your advantage, if you choose to make use of me. For example, I don't believe you can have come this far without someone's mentioning the Middles...?"

The first full day of term was never anything approaching a normal day at the Crater School. To be sure, there were classes, and a timetable; but all day long girls would be called out of class in batches, house by house, for unpacking. Others had to go to the San for vaccinations, if their health certificates weren't up to date. Actually trying to teach a lesson was hopeless. Instead, mistresses contributed further to the chaos by sending girls hither and yon on errands, running to the Stationery Prefect for supplies or to the Library Prefect for textbooks. They appointed classroom monitors, or else staged elections according to their whimsy. If their mood was mean—and no mistress was ever reliably sunny-tempered on the first day of term—they might give a test on holiday tasks that of course no self-respecting schoolgirl had tackled yet, or on something random that they just felt girls ought to know: the early history of the colony or provincial administration or something equally appalling. Sometimes Miss Hendy would set a dozen plants in pots around a long table, and challenge a class to identify them all, with prizes for the best guesses and the absolute worst. Often, by mid-afternoon, the staff had entirely had enough of trying to instruct or entertain a teeming classroom of hopelessly over-excited girls, and would simply send them out to the playing-fields to run off their excess energy.

It was no surprise to Rowany, then, that the whole school seemed noisier and busier than usual, even while absolutely no learning was going on. The corridors were hectic with messengers dashing this way and that, their arms heaped high with books or ink-bottles or exercise paper; and every single one of them—or so it seemed to Rowany—eyed her sideways with a mix of curiosity and pity, even while they greeted her courteously. No one stopped to chat. To be fair, there never was time on the first day of term; and she was so much older, so very much senior, most of them would have shrivelled at the very thought of a casual chat with the legendary Rowany de Vere; and even so. She thought that every single one of them was struggling against a desperate need to know exactly what had happened, and the terrible impossibility of asking.

Sighing inwardly, she left the Castle as soon as she could manage it. Not that that helped, particularly. The broad gravel path leading down to the boarding houses was just as busy. She had half a mind to seek the shelter of her own room, but that was no good either. The chances of reaching sanctuary without being called aside were slim; one needn't be officially a prefect to help with the chaotic ceremony that was unpacking. Besides, she had not been raised to hide from the face of adversity. She walked past Jopling House without a sideways glance.

Which left her with the inevitable question of where she was actually going, where indeed she could go now that hiding was off the table.

There were the playing-fields, with a casual game of cricket going on already, and someone organising relay races of outstanding complexity. Running around held its attractions—but she was years older than any of those girls, and if the object was to avoid being stared at, then petitioning to join one group or the other was quite out of the question.

On she went, then, seeing nothing in her future but a solitary walk, far from the madding crowd—until her mind was suddenly and startlingly changed for her, by a noise arising from the shrubbery ahead.

No, not a noise: a *sound.* That was more polite. And not just any sound: it was music. What was more, it was music that she recognised, that she'd danced to more times than she could count. Just, she'd never heard it before as a duet for violin and trumpet...

She might not be Head Girl any more, she might not be any kind of prefect, with any kind of authority at all; but none the less, she was still Rowany de Vere. She stepped forward with all the boldness of untold generations of military ancestors, and not a few Martian pioneers besides; and smiled beatifically upon the tunesmiths, until their music died away in a squawl and a splutter that no one from Ireland to here could have known as "King of the Fairies".

"Hail and well met, twins," she said easily into the dreadful silence that followed. "Indeed, twin twins, I might say. Where are your better halves?"

The single glance they threw at each other in that moment, one Mishkin and one Abramoff, told Rowany much that she was curious to know. Mischief was afoot, beyond question.

Still: she *wasn't* Head Girl, *wasn't* a prefect now. Truly, it was none of her business. She forged forward determinedly: "Well, never mind; I can trust each of you to speak for your twin too, I think. Jessica, Tasha," she added, just so the younger girls were clear that she was quite clear herself about which twins she had to hand. "I have a kindness to ask of you, if you will."

The two blinked nervously. Jessica laid her fiddle down carefully on a convenient bench; Tasha shook spittle out of her trumpet, and eyed Rowany with the wariness of long experience.

It was too hard, not to laugh. So she did, a broad wholehearted peal, which made Tasha scowl and Jessica blanch.

Recovering, Rowany said, "Relax, you young idiots—and do tell me what you're up to, before I get around to asking favours. I'm just an adjunct now, remember, I couldn't put you in trouble if I wanted to. No one ever accused me of telling tales, even when I was newer than you are, Jess."

"We're not doing anything wrong!" Tasha said hotly. "We're, we're pre-emptying trouble, that's what we're doing."

"Possibly pre-empting," Rowany murmured helpfully. Tasha looked doubtful. "No, but do go on. In what way are you pre-emptying trouble?"

"Well, we're both in orchestra, and you know we always play on First Day? For the dances?"

Of course she knew. It was a hallowed and much-loved tradition that after supper on their first evening back, everyone helped to clear all the tables to the side, so they could have dancing up and down the dining hall.

"Well, last term Miss Llewellyn was really rude about our playing," Tasha continued. "She said we raised a, a right cacaphony."

"Cacophony, probably," Rowany offered.

"That's what I said, cacaphony. And Jess wasn't here then, so she doesn't know half the music; so I said I'd help her practise, not to give postage to fortune."

"Hostages—no, never mind. That was very good of you, Tasha," and never mind the peculiar racket that violin and trumpet had made together. She wasn't about to mention any such thing. "I'd heard you played a pretty fiddle, Jess; I'll look forward to hearing more of it tonight. But that's not why I wanted to talk to you, obviously. Am I right in thinking that you both—I mean, all four of you—were brought up speaking Russian at home?"

Jessica nodded hesitantly. "Along with other languages, I mean. English, obviously, and Hindi and Malay and all sorts. But our grandparents were old-school Russians, and didn't really speak anything else—so yes, Rachel and I have it fluently."

"Us too," Tasha confirmed. "Grandparents again, mostly, though our parents too would talk Russian as often as English. Sometimes I think they did it deliberately," she added, with all the naivety of fourteen, "just to make sure we kept up."

Rowany was sure that they did exactly that, but decided not to say so. "Well," she said heartily, "this couldn't have fallen out more conveniently—because it so happens that I stand in desperate need of coaching. Russian is one of the languages that Oxford has chosen to demand of me, and honestly, I have barely more than a smattering, and of course there's no one on the staff here who can coach me. The Crater School doesn't offer it at all. So would you and your twins be willing to take me in hand, for an hour or two a week of Russian conversation?"

The two younger girls stared at her, and then blankly at each other. Rowany sternly suppressed an internal giggle, and added hastily, "Of course you will need to discuss it with your other halves before you agree, I entirely see that. But do talk it over and let me know, will you? Because truly, I stand in dreadful need."

Waiting for their awkward nods and inevitable reassurances, of course they'd talk it over with their sisters and tell her the verdict as soon as might be, Rowany allowed herself briefly to forget that she was no longer a prefect. These two might indeed have been inspired to practise, before tonight's dancing—but to do so out here, beyond the playing-fields? Nothing within school grounds lay further, except the sculpture-garden. And now she was no longer speaking, she became aware of rustlings and whisperings, among the greenery of that secluded space. Jessica and Tasha had been notably reluctant to explain where their twins had gone; *not very far*, Rowany interpreted. Indeed, the likelihood was high that all the Crew was within call and spying on her now. That raucous music might well have been doubling as a watch-signal, its sudden cutting-off the warning that trouble approached.

What on earth could they be up to, on the first day of term, that needed such secrecy and such careful guard? Rowany had no right to ask, and no reason to wonder; it simply wasn't her place any longer. And yet, she remained merely human, still more than less a schoolgirl; curiosity was a fierce flame in her heart. A flame that would burn late tonight, long after weary Middles were in bed...

CHAPTER THREE

The Light in the Demon's Eyes

In class or out of class, time at the Crater School was as strictly regulated as the canonical hours in a monastery, or so generations of girls had been heard to complain.

In truth, their time was measured out as carefully as their meals. Work was balanced against leisure, exercise against rest. After supper on a typical schoolday, everything was calculated towards calming excitable minds to bring them in tune with tired bodies and nudge them gently towards a warm and welcoming, welcome bed.

First Night was anything but typical, of course, and normal methods would avail them nothing. Wise heads had taken a coarser and more direct path from the beginning, which tradition had now absorbed. Nothing could speak peace to a girl's mind on her first night of term, back among her friends with a thousand things to say; but brisk and vigorous dancing could at least exhaust her body, so that sleep should come willy-nilly.

That was the theory, at least, though the girls by and large never knew it until seniority and responsibility made things clear that had been cloudy before. Levity was still too new to school to have an inkling. One term here had taught her what was meant to happen at every bell, but she had barely troubled her head as to why. No staff would be so mean as to set prep on the first day back, so the whole school was at a loose end, and might as well dance. That was reason enough.

She danced, then, with a will, making eightsomes with the Crew and whomever else was going spare, foursomes with all her friends in various combinations, pairs with any available twin when she couldn't have Lise. It was a point of policy, almost a point of honour that neither set of twins should ever dance with themselves. Besides, one of each set was in the orchestra tonight, so there was almost always one or the other going spare.

Even so, and despite the fun of hurtling up and down the dining hall to Strip the Willow or The Gay Gordons or The Bridge of Athlone, Levity kept an urgent, almost a frantic eye on the clock, willing this hour to be over even while she was enjoying it so much.

Eight o'clock, and the Juniors were sent away to prayers and bed, and she could hardly bear the suspense. Eight-thirty, and at last it was the Middles' turn to thank the orchestra and the supervising prefects and skip away towards their separate houses. They should have had nothing on their minds now but those little rituals that absorb any girl in her last few minutes before lights-out and sleep. If the Crew muttered significantly to each other before they parted, per-haps that was only loyal friends on their first day re-united, not wanting yet to say goodnight. If only one person in particular took note, perhaps it was because only one person had good reason, which she had not shared with anyone else.

Perhaps one was all it took.

Her mouth tingling with the very particular flavour of arrowmint toothpaste, Levity took unusual care over her cubicle curtains, making sure that every edge overlapped, so that no one could peep in accidentally. They'd have to part the curtains on purpose, and nobody would do that now; visiting was strictly prohibited in these private minutes before bed. Safe from being overlooked, then, she flopped down determinedly onto her knees beside her bed.

Nightly prayers were a custom here, she had learned, that girls were trusted to observe unsupervised. That kind of trust is a double-edged blade, and either side could cut you to the quick, so it was a custom that they all kept, to some extent. Sometimes—often—somewhat skimpily on her part, Levity was willing to confess, at least to herself.

Tonight, though, she had more reasons than one to be scrupulous. In part, it distracted her from what would come later, and any distraction was welcome just now; but more immediately, and far more importantly, she had a real grievance to lay before the Almighty. A bone to pick.

Her not-very-much younger sister Charm had been sick all through the holiday. She'd missed all the fun of house-hunting, up and down the canals; she'd been too ill to celebrate her own birthday; there had even been talk of moving her to the Sanatorium across the water, where the finest doctors on Mars fought day in and day out to defeat the worst of Martian diseases.

It hadn't come to that, quite. Instead a doctor from the Sanatorium had come to her, and poked and prodded and pondered, and finally decreed. It wasn't marsles, or the marthambles, or the Red Rue. She had a case of Felliton's Incongruence—"It's atypical," he said, "because she's so young, which is why it's taken us so long to spot it"—which should be perfectly treatable, now that they knew.

Nevertheless: "She's missed the holiday," Levity grumbled to God, "she's missed her own party, and now she's missing the start of term. Mamma has her in the new house, and I know she's going to get better now—but isn't this enough? What did Charm ever do, to lose so much? She's only a kid," said with all the blithe maturity of fourteen, securely a Middle, gazing across a vast gulf to the distant shores of thirteen and the Junior School. "Let us have her back, before she misses anything more."

Too well-trained to bargain with Providence, it occurred to her belatedly that she was hectoring instead—but so be it. Mamma had always said that the Empire's relationship with God reminded her of nothing so much as the school bully demanding money with menaces.

Satisfied that she wasn't really *quite* that bad, this particular scion of Empire rose from her knees and spent a surprising amount of time tidying her cubicle, hanging her dressing gown as they were always told to, "so that you can find it in the dark," setting her slippers just so and her outdoor shoes beside them, neat enough for a military inspection.

"Now then, you people, aren't you ready *yet*?" That sudden voice was their dormitory prefect, Betty; and if she sounded less patient than normal, that was because the housemistress always held a gathering for Stokes prefects on the first night of term, and the longer her young charges kept her away, the less time Betty would have with her favourite staff.

"You'd best get into bed right now, whatever the state of your cubies," Betty went on brusquely, "for I'm turning the lights off in three—two—one..."

Various squawks met her announcement. Levity herself scampered to her bed, slithered between the sheets and was the very picture of innocent, obedient girlhood—had anyone cared to look—before the room was abruptly plunged into darkness.

Half an hour later she was still lying there in the same pose, still wide awake and breathless with anticipation, when someone did in fact part her curtains, sidle through and grope their way to her bed.

The briefest possible flicker of a torch, and a hand touching her shoulder: that was the signal agreed upon. Levity's long legs were out of bed almost before her mind had caught up with them, she was so tightly wound for this.

Lise the torch-bearer moved out of the way on silent feet. Well-drilled by regular fire-practice, Levity found shoes and dressing gown in the dark. Then—drilled in this instance by wicked co-conspirators—she pushed pillows down beneath her blankets and bashed them into something that might reasonably be taken for a Levity-shape, by a dorm prefect coming back late and in a hurry for her own bed.

Out of the cubicle, out of the dormitory; down the corridor and down the stairs and out of the back door of the drowsy house, into the brisk night air.

There were lights in Miss Hendy's rooms, the sound of laughter drifting from an open window. Still no time for talking; they tiptoed down the gravel path till that house and all the houses were behind them, and ahead lay only the playing-grounds and this bisecting path, that drove forward into darkness.

Lise and Levity were holding hands now, just to keep together. If their breath came short, it was only because they were fighting to keep down the exultant giggles, oh yes. Most certainly yes. They had achieved the greater part of their night's adventure, the most difficult aspect, the escape. Before them lay only fun and frolics now.

Onward, onward. Along the path: past the en-tout-cas netball and tennis courts, past the hockey pitch that would turn now to its long summer duties hosting second-eleven and inter-house cricket, to the cricket pitch proper with its sacred square—

And here was a flash of controlled torchlight, aimed at their feet, and a murmur from the dark beyond.

"Where have you two *been*? We've waited an age."

"That's not true, it can't be," Lise said placidly. "Your bedtime's the same as ours, so you couldn't have got away any sooner than we did."

A Mishtwin's high, clear laugh: was that Tasha, or Tawney? It hardly made a difference, here and now. They were all ghosts tonight, shadows of their daylight selves. Ghosts in sturdy dressing gowns, proof against the night.

Levity shivered despite that, and decided that she didn't want to think about ghosts. They weren't here to scare themselves, they were here to feast and frolic.

"Are we the last, then?" she asked.

"You are. Let me just count heads, though, make sure nobody's wandered off."

It was good Pioneer practice, especially in the dark. They took it for granted that Tasha meant it literally, going around the circle tapping heads one by one as she counted aloud..

"...Five, and six, and I make seven." The stars were bright enough to show her tapping her own head in conclusion. "One Crew, present and correct, in all its constituent parts. We could row six-handed, with Pete for cox. Who's captain?"

"Not you!" was the common chorus.

"Not after the hash you made of that trumpet fanfare at the dance," her twin added scathingly.

"It was a glorious tribute to a fallen hero," quoth haughty Tasha. "It was supposed to die away in a cadence of sorrow. As it did."

"It died away because you ran out of puff, and we all know it. Anyway, never mind that now. I vote Lise for captain, because she's been here as long as anybody—which means us, really; all the rest of you are new, and should give way before our wisdom—and besides, Lise's level-headed and won't lead us to catastrophe. I've heard Miss Leven herself say so. Well, not that bit about catastrophe. She doesn't know about that."

"I hope not!" Lise said emphatically. "Not that I'm leading you anywhere except into the sculpture garden. Who else has got torches?"

Four spears of light sprang into being at the word, all of them aimed directly at her face.

"Well, don't dazzle me, you—you goops! Point them at the ground, so that we can see to walk. And for everybody's sake, don't flash them around too much. Light travels a long way at night, you know. We'll be safe enough once we're in the grove, it's too leafy to let anything leak out—but then even, turn the torches off once we have the candles lit. You do remember where we left them, yes?"

"*Now* I remember why Lise's never allowed to be captain," Tasha muttered rebelliously.

"Captains are supposed to be bossy, that's the point. Now for pity's sake be quiet, and come along..."

By torchlight, then, down into the shadows of the sculpture garden, where twigs and branches reached out malevolently to clutch at you, where the going was soft underfoot—according to Rachel, whose father bred racehorses—and mysterious shapes half-glimpsed really were the imps and faeries, the faces and the unicorns they seemed to be in the sudden flash of an errant torch.

There was no such thing as ghosts, of course—but even so, Levity thought she might perhaps prefer this place in daylight after all.

Still, you couldn't have a midnight feast at midday; you had other places to be at midday, and lunch to look forward to. And being a little uncomfortable, a little uncertain, even a little nervous was probably all part of the fun; and she was fourteen and far too old actually to be scared of the dark, even a little bit.

Rachel struck a lucifer, making shadows that jumped alarmingly.

"Someone remind me where we put all the candles," she said. "I think I just ruined my night-sight, all I can see is dazzle."

Jessica laughed, tucked her arm through her twin's and guided her to where a candle waited in a jam-jar liberated from the art room, at the foot of a tall twisted wrought-iron elf. Once that wick was safely lit, they moved on to the next, in the arms of a squatting toad; and so on around the garden, until the whole grove was washed in a soft yellow light and it seemed as though every tree and every sculpture sheltered its own small bottled flame like an offering.

Almost every sculpture. By common consent, they made no offerings to Old Gaunt. He was the hollow trunk of a tree that had grown and lived and died right here beside the pond. Some cunning hand had cut and carved at him until now he was a louring face, girl-tall and menacing, with a gaping mouth that looked wide enough to eat you whole. It was good Martian sense to be a little afraid of Old Gaunt, even in daylight. No girl would go near him; it was held to be unlucky to mention his name anywhere within his hearing, which given the size of his ears meant anywhere on school grounds. When Tawney had suggested bringing a blanket to throw over him, to hide their doings from his black gaze, she had only been half joking, half at most. No one had taken her up on it, but secretly Levity thought they all wished one of the others had.

No candle for Old Gaunt, then; he must glower at them from his own private darkness. Still, with all the other candles placed high and low in their protective glass, the whole grove was bathed by a warm steady glow.

"Time for eats," Tawney said contentedly. "Drag out the goodies."

The goodies had been left beneath a bench, in two stout cardboard hatboxes that Pete had raided from the Greenaway attics days ago, before the start of term. Nothing had been left to chance: this was to be the best-organised midnight feast ever.

Lise lifted lids, and crooned over the contents. "Proper Dutch sardines, and rye bread to eat them on, already in slices, with butter for those who want it. Cheese and biscuits; no grapes, it's not the season, but apples and chutney. Pork pies and sausage rolls, *with* mustard. Scones and cream and jam. Where are the knives and forks and napkins?"

"In the other hamper," Tawney said, scorning to describe anything so grand as a mere box, "with the lemonade and the cakes. We have done ourselves proud, people. Does anyone want to say grace, before we fall to?"

By the looks on all their faces, everyone thought that somebody else ought to, but no one wanted to step up and do it themselves. This was somehow a little too illicit to ask for the blessing of Providence; and yet, it wouldn't quite feel right without. They gazed a little blankly from one to another—and then gasped and turned and stared, as a voice came from behind them.

More than a voice, a new light: a wicked red light, shining from Old Gaunt's eyes. And the voice came from his mouth, hollow and sepulchral; and it said, "Who speaks of grace? Who dares? Who is it dares to speak of grace, in my accursed dominion?"

A bare minute later, the Crew had at least stopped screeching, and had almost stopped running. They were just staggering to a slow, bewildered halt in the middle of the cricket pitch where they were forbidden to be at any time, never mind in the middle of the night. Staring at each other in the darkness, and reaching to hold hands. Realising that those hands were empty because they'd left their torches behind, every single one of them. Beginning to feel ashamed of themselves, because girls of their acquired years and wisdoms really didn't believe in ghosts and ghouls and creatures of darkness. Even beginning to wonder if the bold thing wouldn't be to go back, to investigate the source of that terrible voice and that eerie spectral light—except that they had left all their torches behind, and not one of them was bold enough to blunder back in darkness, no.

Which meant there was nothing for it but to abandon all their plans, their delicious feast and that delicious feeling of trespass that came with it. To creep to their separate houses in a miserable silence, tails between their legs, and only hope to make it back to their separate beds uncaught and unsuspected...

A t about the same time, Old Gaunt released another, far more normal sound, if it is normal for a vast and terrible carven face to gurgle like a much-amused schoolgirl.

In the light of all those candles, a pair of feet emerged from his capacious mouth, clad in school-approved outdoor shoes. They were followed little by little by the rest of Rowany de Vere, as though she were being unswallowed, inch by squirming and seemingly everlasting inch of her.

At last, an athletic wriggle brought her free. For a little while she just lay sprawled there on the grass before him, like a cast-up and rejected sacrifice, whooping and gasping with laughter as no sacrifice ever has. Then she pulled herself together, hauled herself to her feet and dusted off what felt like buckets'-worth of leaf-loam, twigs and insects such as a hollow trunk is likely to collect.

"Earwigs! Euh!" she muttered, detaching one from her collar and tossing it savagely to the carp that waited in the water. One last shake of her long person, one last raking comb of her fingers through her hair, and she turned to examine the abandoned feast by the light of a torch covered with red crepe paper.

"Well, well," she murmured joyously. "How very *Nellie Martin*! And so much lovely food; we simply mustn't let it go to waste, like the ship-boys' dinner in that old and shocking song. I shall gather it all up like the virtuous girl I was raised to be, and take it where it belongs. Which would be the Prefects' Room, if I were still a prefect; but of course I'm not. Neither a member of staff, by any stretch of the imagination. Lost and found, lost and found: we need a third alternative. For tonight, I suppose my own room will have to do. Tomorrow—well, confiscated perishables have always counted as a finder's fee, unless judiciously claimed. And I don't see any of those little wretches coming forward to confess to this. Not any of this, their illicit feasting nor their tremulous running away. I hope they get back to bed safely, though. It would be a shame to lose their feast *and* their liberty, in one fell swoop..."

CHAPTER FOUR

The Funeral Baked Meats

"**P**lease, is Miss Leven here?"

Actually Lise could see perfectly well that she was, but it was always polite to ask. The staff were sticklers about that, along with many other equally fatuous wastes of time—almost as bad as the prefects, the staff could be—and here on their own territory, at the very door to the Staff Room, it was as well to be punctilious.

Even when your eyes were bugging almost out of your head, when an unexpected sense of outrage was building inside you like a boilerful of steam and you thought you might explode with the unfairness of it all, it was still important not to put a foot wrong. Even more important, perhaps. If Miss Tattersall took offence and decided to read her the riot act, then a lifetime's training might not be enough to keep Lise's tongue civil in response. And she really did need to do that, if she were to achieve what she'd actually come here for, rather than merely pitching herself and all the Crew into trouble beyond trouble, an unimaginable row.

"Miss Leven? Why, yes: as a matter of fact she is. But why would you be looking for her here, child?"

"Please, I did go to her study and ask," as any girl was entitled to do between tea and supper, "and Miss Pengelly said that she was here." Gorging herself, apparently, on ill-gotten gains. Lise could hardly bear to wait until she could assemble all her friends and appal them with the perfidy, the greed, the—the downright *front* of their headmistress and all her staff.

And the prefects too, they were all assembled here and clearly having a whale of a time; and of course Rowany was with them, though she was neither prefect nor staff but something in between. Indeed, Rowany was eyeing Lise from across the room, with a marginally disturbing gleam in her far-seeing eye.

A gleam in her eye, and a cake-fork in her hand.

"L ise, dear? Were you looking for me?"

"Oh—oh, yes please, Miss Leven." At least the headmistress had had the grace to leave her plate behind her. Even so, Lise found it hard to drag her thoughts into order, never mind to trot out all her well-rehearsed arguments, under the pressure of so many eyes and so many murmuring voices. That laden table, which seemed to be laughing at her entirely.

"Shall we go somewhere quieter, where we can be alone? Come along, Lise. I happen to know that the coaching-room is free at the moment."

Of course it was; all the staff who might have been using it were gathered here, feasting on other people's tuck. Still, Lise went without a word, following Miss Leven down the corridor to a small, cosy room that held a desk and two chairs, a shelf of books and papers and not much more. Perfect, for intensive one-to-one tuition; it didn't even have a window to be distracted by.

Meanly, Lise hoped that Rowany would find herself spending many an hour in here, this coming year. And struggling every moment. She had no proof, but she needed none; she was suddenly sure beyond question that Rowany had been the source of all last night's woes and losses.

"Well now, Lise." Miss Leven took one of the chairs, and gestured her towards the other. "What can I do for you?"

"Please, Miss Leven, it's not for me, not really. It's for Levity." And having said so much, of course she had to say more; so she took a slow breath, stifled all her mutinous thoughts and went on carefully. "Levity's never been at school before, so she doesn't really understand what's right. She doesn't know to ask for things. We've told her, but she still won't. Either she thinks we're pulling her leg, or she's scared that you might say no and that would be worse than never asking at all, never hoping; so..."

"So you've taken it on yourself to ask on her behalf?" Miss Leven finished for her, when she seemed to have run herself entirely aground.

"Yes, please, Miss Leven."

"And what is it that you think Levity should be asking for, exactly?"

"An exeat. For Saturday." Lise said it all in a rush, just to get it out there.

"My dear child, term's barely begun! You've only been here twenty-four hours."

"Yes, but no. Levity came up sooner," Lise explained carefully, as though Miss Leven couldn't possibly be aware of that, "so that her mother could focus on nursing Charm; so she hasn't seen her sister for a *week* already, and I know she's really worried about her. If she could just go down for the day, I'm sure it would make all the difference to both of them."

"That's a very kind thought, Lise, and it does you credit. She couldn't possibly be allowed to go alone, though. You do realise that, don't you?"

"Well, um, yes." No Middles were ever allowed off school premises alone; that was inherent, absolute. "Of course I'd be willing to go with her, I'm still her sherpa even though she's been here a whole term now. I expect I always will be. And, um, if maybe the rest of her *particular* friends could come...?"

"Oh, no. I am not wishing the whole Crew on Levity's poor mother, uninvited. However, I think perhaps we might do better. As it happens, I spoke with Mrs Buchanan this morning on the telephone. Charm is recovering by leaps and bounds, it seems, and she's desperate to be back amongst us. I do feel that such eagerness should be rewarded, so long as her doctors agree; so, *if* she doesn't go backwards through the rest of this week—and I do mean if, and only if—then I think we might hope to welcome her back at the weekend. On Sunday, say. If so be that her sister and a select few of her friends had gone down on Saturday and stayed overnight, then they might bring Charm back between them, don't you think?"

"Oh, Miss Leven! That would be ... marvellous!" It often happened in conversations with the headmistress that a little pause crept in between one word and the next, where a girl might need to scramble for another word instead. The whole staff was weirdly down on natural schoolgirl vocabulary, and Miss Leven was the worst of them all. She had a way of lifting an eyebrow and saying nothing at all, that could leave you stammering hopelessly for *minutes* afterwards.

"Well, let me speak again with Mrs Buchanan, before gratitude overwhelms you. I wouldn't wish house guests on her without at least a word of warning. And it can't just be Levity and her immediate chums, either; I couldn't countenance sending a cohort of Middles out without a consort. Oh, don't look so stricken—I don't mean to burden you with a mistress.

I can't spare one anyway. Nor a prefect, if it comes to that: not over the first weekend of term, when no one has settled down to comfortable habits yet. No, I think in all fairness it will have to be Rowany."

Nobody was about to risk a treat of such magnitude by making a fuss, based merely on what Lise had seen and reported, the whole authority of the Crater School making merry on their stolen bounty. Besides, nobody wanted to admit—hardly even to themselves, let alone each other, never mind any semblance of Authority—that they might have been scared away from their fabulous feast by some stratagem. If it was a trick, that was worse than if it had genuinely been the spirit of Old Gaunt. And if it was *Rowany*, then, well—

Well. Nobody was going to mention anything. And they thought—or at least hoped—that Rowany was too much a gentleman to do the mentioning herself, in a gloating kind of way. And even if she made herself horrible all the way down and all the way back again, even that wouldn't matter too dreadfully much, compared to the glory that lay between. There was nothing more rare, almost nothing more legendary than an overnight exeat from the Crater School; and to win it for four of you, and in the first week of term—well, Lise was almost floating on the effervescence of her own achievement.

Levity still seemed uncertain, as though she didn't dare to believe it for fear that the whole outing might yet be snatched away from her, sister and all. Saturday had dawned cloudy, with spatters of rain, and she had worried all through breakfast that a storm might confine them to school. Then the wind had cleared the sky in short order, and she had worried that perhaps a gale was coming, which would disrupt the running of the train or stall all traffic on the canals and so prevent them from getting anywhere. But an hour later the

air was still and deliciously warm; the school was ten minutes' walk behind them and too far away—they hoped!—to
call them back; they could see smoke rising above the roof
of the funicular station, like a promise that the train was
steamed up and ready for them. And, which was more, Rowany was being her properly charming self, and the whole day
promised to be delightful.

The train-ride down was never speedy. One time—heading for Mr Messenger the dentist with half a dozen other
pale, silent victims and a mistress-escort who had given up
on them all and was reading a book—Lise had been driven to
counting the clicks of the mighty gears beneath the engine as
it ratcheted its backward way down towards their doom.

This journey was nothing like that. No one was suffering
anything other than the pangs of extreme excitement; there
was no exasperated adult overseeing them, only Rowany,
whom half of them had known and adored all their schooldays, however monstrously on-the-ball she might have been
in her prefect years; and nothing lay ahead of them but a day
and a night of pleasure and discovery.

Levity and Rachel had the window-seats on one side of
the compartment, as by right. This whole outing technically
counted as Levity's treat, for all that Lise had arranged it;
and besides, the journey was still comparatively new to them
both, so of course they wanted to see out. Lise and Tawney,
who had travelled up and down countless times already,
were happy enough in the middle seats, even if they did lean
over their friends' shoulders all the way down to point out
this landmark or that, where they'd seen an imago harried by
an eagle and where the shepherd-boy had tried to race the
train. "That was exciting, because he fell—off that rock there,
I think it was, trying to leap right over, the great idiot—and
he was obviously hurt, so Miss Harribeth let us pull the com-
munication-cord to stop the train..."

Rowany had a window on the other side, but didn't seem too interested in looking out of it. Of course, she must know the scenery by heart by now. Lise said that, in an aside, and Rowany laughed. "I suppose I do. Tell you what, let's test it, shall we? We'll play I-Spy, out of this window behind me—but I won't actually look. We'll see if I can remember the landmarks as they come, before they're gone, with no more help than the clues you choose to give me."

I-Spy was properly a game for little kids, of course—but none of the Middles was above joining in cheerfully when Juniors were playing, and this sounded like fun. Besides, when did anyone ever have the chance to beat Rowany at anything?

Not these girls, never yet: not at tennis, not at ping-pong, not at cards or bingo or chess or marbles. They couldn't outrun her, outthrow her or outthink her. Some said grouchily that she had the Devil's own luck, but Lise was inclined to believe that Rowany was simply better than everybody else. Taller and older helped too, of course, and those were undeniable; brainier had never seemed in question either, until this term and her unexpected return from Oxford in defeat.

To that long list of ways that Rowany outshone a normal girl, apparently they'd need to add that she was more observant too, and with a better memory. Landmark after landmark went by behind her and she guessed them all, with no more clue than the initial letters: "HM, Tawney? Oh, that must be Holman's Mound; we should be passing through its shadow any second... Yes, there we go. Who's next? Levity? Something beginning with S, you say—my money's on the seagulls over Barrow Brook. Well, I suppose we should call them canal gulls, really. They're a long, long way from any ocean. Remind me to tell you later why we have so many utterly useless British birds on Mars, if you haven't heard the story already; it's a good one. Who's next...?"

A dozen times they tried to trip her up, and a dozen times they failed. At last she offered to play with her eyes closed, after Rachel had accused her of taking hints from the view through the opposite window. It was at that point that Levity shrieked, "Oh, I know! We're not really playing I-Spy at all, are we? It's, it's, it's Kim's Game!"

"Of course it is, in a way," Rowany agreed placidly. "And with that blinding revelation, the game comes to an end, and Levity wins a bulls-eye. The rest of you had better take one too; peppermint sharpens the intellect, I'm told." She produced a charmingly sticky bag from her pocket, and passed it around. "Now, we'll be there in five minutes. Who needs me to reach down their overnight cases for them?"

The very question was an insult, of course, and a deliberate one. Four outraged young ladies—young *Martian* ladies, with all the length of leg that that implies—stood as one, and lifted down their own cases from the overhead rack, while Rowany sprawled at her ease and laughed at them.

Indignation can rarely outlast a bulls-eye, though, and these were particularly scrumptious examples of their kind. By the time the funicular drew to a slow halt at its familiar platform and the station master yelled "Terminus!" to one and all, the Middles were firm friends with Rowany once again; and that was before Levity slid the window down and leaned out at a perilous angle to work the handle of the carriage door.

Somewhere on the platform, out of sight to all but her, a voice shrieked, "Levity! Over here!"

Startled, Levity craned around—and her foot slipped on the shiny linoleum compartment flooring, and the door swung open beneath her so that she was carried out over the platform, folded double through the window and squawking mightily. Lise shrieked, to see her in such peril; she might as easily fall forwards and crack her head as fall backwards and break her leg. For a moment it seemed that fall she must, one way or the other. But then Rowany of the long arms reached out, caught hold of the door and drew it closed again. As soon as they could reach her, Lise and Tawney between them seized hold of Levity by sundry parts of uniform or girl and hauled her bodily back through the window and into the compartment.

Once they'd set her on her feet, Rowany gripped her by the shoulders and looked her up and down.

"All serene, youngster?"

"I—I think so. Thank you." The pale cheeks flushed suddenly, and Rowany grinned in response.

"Steady, now. Don't burn yourself to a cinder; you'll make me look bad, if I have nothing to hand over but the ashes of embarrassment. We've all done mad things in our time, Levity. Though that was tolerably spectacular, and in front of half the town. Who was it yelled at you, anyway—your sister?"

Levity nodded awkwardly, mumbling, "They're down by the ticket barrier..."

"They were, I should say. Here they come now."

And there they were indeed, right outside, pulling the door open again now that it was free of dangling schoolgirls: the striking Isobel Buchanan, reaching in to catch her elder daughter in a hug and positively lift her out of the compartment, kicking and squealing in protest; and Levity's slightly younger sister Charm, lurking in her mother's shadow and peering shyly up at all these older girls.

Privately, Lise thought that Charm looked worse than Levity had in that immediate moment after Rowany's rescue: grey and washed-out like an ageing dishcloth, all stark green eyes and purple shadows. Still, the doctors said she was on the road to recovery, well enough to come back to school; and doctors ought to know. Besides, it didn't do to stare.

Lise waited calmly until Levity had done with her mother's embraces and moved on to her sister's; then she collected Levity's overnight case and her own, and stepped down to the platform.

Rowany of course had gone before her, to shake hands and say, "It's good to see you again, Mrs Buchanan. After the excitements of last term, I confess I had hoped for a quieter visit this time, but—well. Welcome to the Crater School. I fear it's a moveable feast."

Mrs Buchanan laughed gaily. "And all the more welcome so. What's life without a little excitement? Thank you for rescuing my eldest. Again. And speaking of moveable feasts, I understand I am to see rather more of you this term? In a tutorial sense?"

Rowany's face twisted, as though she would rather not have talked of this just now, with just this audience; but she said, "Yes, if you can bear it. Miss Calomel says you have a better collection of prints and plates than the school does; and you have the artist's eye besides. Oxford says I need a coach, to develop my observational skills."

That was news to Lise, as it would be to any Middle who'd suffered under Rowany's all-seeing eye. Supposedly she was talking about art rather than real life, but even so, it seemed strange. More than strange, it seemed peculiar.

Now wasn't the time to wonder, though. Mrs Buchanan had turned from Rowany to her, and the two twins crowding down behind her.

A slow smile and, "Let me see, now. You're Lise, of course, there's no forgetting that face; you've the look of the Plains in your eyes, my dear. The far horizons leave their mark. You two, though—well, you'll be Tawney, of course, and you're Rachel. Yes?"

"Yes," the twins agreed in unison, with a shared chagrin. It was Tawney—of course!—who went on, "I suppose Miss Leven told you, which of which twins were coming down?"

"Not at all. I just know one face from another, even when they're copies. Now: everyone got all their bags and baggages? No coats left behind, no books, no sweets? Off we go, then. Everyone bring their own, and we shan't need a porter. We're only walking down to the canal anyway, it's no distance at all."

"Oh, Mrs Buchanan—are we going on a boat?"

"Indeed we are, Tawney. It's the only practical way to get about, I find. You'll see why, when we come to Willowbank. I'd have thought the name should be clue enough; has my errant daughter not told you every detail of our new home?"

"Truly not, Mrs Buchanan," Lise put in quickly, before either of the more heedless twins could offer the same denial more baldly. She knew perfectly well that Levity hadn't wanted to talk much about the house, because she'd left Charm lying deathly ill there and every mention was necessarily a reminder. The last thing Liv needed now was to have that truth exposed. So, "We're all excited to see it; not knowing what to expect is a part of the thrill. I don't think any of us anticipated going there by boat, though."

"Except Miss Button-lip up front there," Rachel said, picking up her cue and nodding at Levity's back as though she'd been deliberately holding out on them. "But is there truly no road at all?"

"Oh, there's a bridle-path to the stables behind the house. You'd be in clover, Rachel; your people keep horses, don't they? You could ride back and forth to town in all seriousness, just as our forefathers must have done. But I have four legs to take care of already," Mrs Buchanan went on, with a fond glance at her two daughters walking arm-in-arm ahead. "I'd sooner not commit to four more. These are quite enough trouble on their own, thank you."

"Not so much now that they're at school, surely?" Rowany suggested. "We must be soaking up a fair proportion of that trouble on your behalf. Speaking of which, I'm charmed to see that you put Charm in her school uniform today."

"Not my doing; she insisted. She wanted to feel like one of you, she said, poor little mite. She's hated missing out on these early days of term. She's sure that her friends are having all the best fun without her, and by the time she gets up the hill term will have started in earnest and it'll be all work and no play."

"At the Crater School? It's hardly likely. Oh, I know what she means, and she's right, of course—the first days of term are unique, and routine is already settling in. But her friends are wild to see her, I can tell you that much; I am burdened with many messages, even though we're taking her back with us tomorrow. I'm sorry I couldn't bring any of her own special gang down with me, but Juniors aren't allowed out on trips without a mistress, and I didn't quite count."

"Oh, never worry about that. She's quite thrilled to have an escort of big girls. It makes her feel important. Besides which, her sister is all she ever needs or wants, in her heart of hearts. You all brought Liv to her, and are thus blessed beyond all mortal women... Now then, people!" Mrs Buchanan clapped her hands, largely for her daughters' attention, as the path they'd been following down from the station brought them out onto the canal bank. "That's our skiff there, with the picnic-basket in the bows. I thought we could eat on the water, before we pull for home. There's a big ship supposed to be coming through the locks at noon, and I know you'd like to watch that if she's on time... What's that, Tawney? No, indeed: there is in fact a sail, but we shan't be raising the mast today. Charm isn't allowed to take an oar, she has to sit up front and guard the picnic-basket from the rest of you marauding starveling creatures; between the rest of us, though, we'd be a sorry crew if we couldn't pull a few short miles. Even against the current, such as it is. Rowany, will you take stroke?"

"I will, if you'll take bow, Mrs Buchanan. Then you can keep watch on us all, and Charm doesn't have to stand guard because you're between us and the hamper and can fend off any raiding party. Which means she can take the tiller, and cox if we need it. How's about it, Charm? Want to be in command of the boat?"

Of course she did, though she didn't quite believe it. She glanced uncertainly from face to face, seeing nothing but nodding approval wherever she looked, and it still needed more than her sister's nudge to have her take her place in the sternsheets. Not until everyone else—including her mother, and worse, including Rowany!—had stepped aboard and was sitting to their oars and looking to her, not until then could she board in her turn, settle with the tiller under her arm and stare around helplessly at all the waiting faces.

No Crater School girl would ever willingly leave another stranded. They were all of them ready to pitch in; it was only that Lise was first to speak. "Would you like me to cast off, Charm?"

Charm flushed a vivid red, because of course she'd been about to give the order to row off while the skiff was still moored to the bank, and of course everyone knew it. She nodded mutely. Lise grinned at her and hopped out of the boat again to attend to the mooring ropes fore and aft, while Rowany said, "Did I ever tell you about the time my father gave me my first driving lesson? I'd taken his precious Hispano-Suiza half a mile down the driveway, excruciatingly slowly and blurting steam all the way, before he and I both realised that I still had the handbrake on."

Trust Rowany, Lise thought, coiling rope as she stepped aboard again. That girl could always make you feel better. Or worse, when the occasion called for it. She could make you feel an absolute worm if she wanted to. Hopefully those days were behind her now. Behind them all. Not a prefect and not a mistress, she should never find herself standing in authority over the Crew again...

Which had of course not stopped her from stealing their midnight feast and feeding it to the staff and prefects. That was still a black mark against Rowany, in Lise's scrupulous judicial heart. She didn't mind scoldings or punishments, if you got caught breaking rules, but she did hate to be mocked; and seen from here, that whole episode seemed like the basest mockery, from first to last. Old Gaunt coming to life, forsooth...!

Still: that was a school affair, and here they were, out of school and free on the water. Charm caught stubborn hold of her confidence after that false start and soon had them scudding upstream on this little side-channel, pulling lustily against the slow current. The town flowed by steadily on either hand—grain store and flour mill, loading docks and lumber yards: to Lise it always seemed like seeing Terminus from behind, with all its workings exposed , like the innards of a clock—until they came to the junction with one of the two major canals that met here.

Here was the massive lock system that connected the higher canal with the lower; and here as promised was a great cargo vessel about to descend. Rachel murmured, "Quinquereme of Nineveh," and Rowany laughed.

"Apes and peacocks, Rachel? More likely pig-lead and ironware and cheap tin trays. Though I daresay there might be cedarwood or sandalwood, from the new plantations."

They weren't the only people who had turned out to watch. There were idlers on the bank, and a dozen other small boats on the water, tied up well out of the way.

Charm spotted a mooring and guided them in; Lise jumped out as self-appointed rope monitor and tied up bow and stern. Then they all settled down to a delightful picnic, each keeping one eye on the high-sided ship as she manoeuvred through the open gates of the upper lock while the other eye watched plates appear in steady progression from that promising hamper.

Sardines, with bread and butter; cheese and biscuits, apples and chutney; pork pies and sausage rolls; scones and cream and jam...

It was their midnight feast all over again, a deliberate conspiracy between Rowany and Mrs Buchanan, it must be. They were being laughed at all over again!

CHAPTER FIVE

"Lev's Livitated, I Mean, Liv's Laminated..."

Isobel Buchanan was a little puzzled, and a little irritated. The picnic should have been a treat for everyone, and it had gone subtly wrong somehow. She couldn't quite put her finger on it, but there had definitely been something amiss ever since the basket had been opened and unpacked. No one had said a word, but that was half the trouble; fourteen-year-old girls should not be so unnaturally silent. Nor cast such speaking glances at each other, or such savage glares at one of their own.

Whatever her status, Rowany was still emphatically a Crater School girl, still sporting the uniform as proudly as any; and—whatever her status, however nearly grown-up she might appear—Isobel was inclined to blame her for that uncomfortable meal as clearly as her juniors did. The menu had been entirely of Rowany's design, expressed in a telephone conversation yesterday. Isobel had enjoyed putting it all together, assuming that these were favourite foods among her daughter's set. Now, having seen the outright indignation so poorly suppressed, she suspected it had been some kind of joke, and was indignant on her own behalf.

Even now, with the lock and the picnic some miles behind them, the girls were rowing raggedly, distracted by their tempers or their grievance. Well, there was at least something Isobel could do about that.

"Charm!" She hailed her younger daughter, all the length of the boat from bow to cox. "Take out your watch, and call the stroke at thirty to the minute. It'll be good practice for you, if you ever want to cox in races."

Isobel herself had won her blue in the Oxford Ladies' number seven seat, on choppy water that famous year when both boats sank after crossing the line at Mortlake. Oxford had never fallen below thirty-six that day, and beat Cambridge by a canvas; but thirty would be an effort for these youngsters, as much as they could manage. A mile or two of pulling hard and fast should haul them back into a decent frame of mind. Exercise was always her first and best solution, when girls turned awkward. It's just too much work to keep a sour temper when you're straining every muscle, especially in a team with others depending on you; and the golden rush that follows will wash away any last trace of the sullens.

I sobel had her wish, just as she'd expected. A mile down the canal, all the girls were pulling in harmony, grunting with effort as they kept the boat skimming over the water. From her seat in the bows she could only see her younger daughter's face, but she was confident that Charm's frown of concentration was a reflection of every girl's, except perhaps for Rowany. That girl was pulling well within herself, so far as Isobel could judge; but her juniors were giving their all, absolutely at their limits.

Satisfied, Isobel watched the bank for landmarks. Another mile, and the Waterman's Arms went fleeting by. That was her signal. She called out, "Ease off, girls. Take your time from stroke. Rowany, bring us down to twenty-four, if you will, and then to eighteen. You've all worked hard enough; we can idle the rest of the way. Charm, put up your watch and keep an eye out for the willow-stand. You'll have to steer us in, remember."

Charm had not forgotten. The crew might be relaxing at their oars, breathing hard but pulling easy and grinning right and left, as though there'd been some victory achieved—which perhaps there had, though Isobel thought it all her own—but not their cox. Charm still had that look of intense focus, all the world on her narrow shoulders as she twitched the rudder-strings this way and that, as she watched the canal-bank mistrustfully, as she called her crew back to order: "Steady now... Let her run. Starboard, ready—three strokes, on my order: one! two! three! Mum, you might want to duck..."

She'd made the turn so briskly, the hanging branches of the willow that watched the water-gate did indeed brush their fingery leaves over Isobel's neck, in a slightly eerie welcome. The boat had enough momentum that they could do no more than touch Lise's blazered shoulder as she passed, which she hardly seemed to notice. Then the boat was clear of the canal's current and the willow's shadow both, into home waters, their own quiet pool.

"All oars, paddle! One, two, three! Let her run now. Oars inboard. Port side, stand by..."

The boat drifted up to kiss the jetty and come to a slow, swaying, perfect halt. Charm remembered to take the stern rope with her as she stepped ashore; Isobel did the same at bow, and here they were.

Isobel wanted to hug one small daughter, who had done a difficult thing calmly and confidently under experienced and critical eyes. She wouldn't do it, though, in front of all these bigger girls. Instead, she gave Charm the best reward she could think of: "Charm dear, why don't you show our guests around the house, while Levity and I sort out all this baggage," the picnic-hamper and the girls' night-cases still cluttering up the boat, "and decide who's sleeping where?"

Of course she already knew who would be sleeping where, and of course all the girls knew that, Charm none better; but her beaming smile outran all duplicity.

Cox once more, with all the pleasures of that role and none of the responsibilities, she said, "Of course, Mamma, I'll be glad to. Here where we've tied up is what Mamma calls our mirror pond, she's going to set sculptures all around the banks to overlook the water; and here's where we go into the house. It's properly the back door, I s'pose, but it's the only one we use to come and go. There's no road at the front, only a bridle-path, and we don't keep a horse, so a boat's the only way, really. Liv and I can have canoes, Mamma's promised; maybe even for Christmas, as it's going to be a hot one this year..."

"...And down here—well, it's the cellar, obviously, but Mamma likes to call it the Ossuary. You'll see why when I turn the light on—there! To be honest, I didn't *quite* like to come down here when we first moved in, before we had the 'lectricity connected, because it's all really rather creepy by lamplight."

"I should say it would be." Rowany gazed in amazement at the cellar walls, where long-extinct native Martian monsters hung in fossil form, embedded in red rock for millennia untold, until some human hand came to quarry out this simple space and bring them all to light.

"I must say, Charm, your mother has an absolute gift for finding the perfect place to suit your family. This house is lovely, from top to toe."

Any compliment to the head of a family is of course a compliment to all the family, and Charm took it as such, bashful and delighted. And given that it came from the erstwhile Head of School, hero to all her cohort—well, briefly Rowany felt embarrassed at such an easy score.

She reminded herself firmly that it was only practice, only good practice for what was to come; and tucked her arm through Charm's and steered her back towards the cellar steps, saying, "And now that we've seen all the joys of the house, from top to toe, what say we corral your mother and your sister too, and have them show us the gardens? I know you've been in charge of those, while you were sick at home here, so it's best if someone else acts as guide, to spare your modesty."

"In charge" might be running things a little high, but Rowany was very aware of how sick Charm had been. It showed yet in her pallor and her tight-stretched skin, every bone of her face to view. Food and air and company would fix that, now that the doctors had given her a clean bill of health, and she was sure of all three in the constant rioting rumpus of the Junior School; but for now it could do no harm to cosset her a little. This was Charm's weekend, and no one knew that better than Rowany.

The younger girl leaned on her arm a little more than Rowany liked, climbing those stairs. She had led them traipsing all through this angular, unpredictable, interesting house, talking all the way; that was likely more exercise, both for her body and her tongue, than she'd had since the disease had laid her low. And it came after a long day on the water, which she must have found tiring in itself. Rowany tucked the slender arm more firmly through her elbow, and led on in search of their hostess.

Five minutes later, Charm was ensconced on a garden bench in the warm sunlight, with a glass of cool lemonade in her hand and a spectacle before her, as her schoolmates competed in a hectic round of jungle croquet.

The garden had no formal lawn, and almost as many corners and unexpected spaces as the house itself. Each girl had been sent off with her own hoop, to place it wherever she liked while the others hid their eyes; only Charm knew where each had been set. Now they were sending their balls wildly in all directions, in a fevered hunt for hoops. Sometimes one or another would appeal to Charm, was she getting warmer or colder; sometimes two or three would collude, to trade information. Everyone kept their own count of strokes, as both Isobel and Rowany had declined to referee.

Instead, those two worthies had removed themselves to the kitchen, from where they could watch through a window while they peeled and chopped vegetables for dinner.

"I foresee imminent breakdown, squabbles and calamity," Isobel said cheerfully.

"Not they," Rowany contradicted. "Not today. They're playing up, for Charm. It's all theatre, not sport at all."

"Ah. Perhaps you're right," Isobel acknowledged, as Rachel tried to take an impossible shot by climbing into an oak tree, lying full-length along a branch and swinging her mallet from there, once it became clear that there simply was no legal stance at ground level. "Well, we'll leave them to it, shall we? You and I need to talk, I gather."

"Well, Miss Leven thinks it would be helpful. Her actual word was 'providential', I believe."

"Was it, indeed? I'm not often mistaken for a higher order of being. But finish up with those carrots and come into my studio. We'll look at a picture or two, and see what we can see…"

One brisk, demanding, revelatory hour later, they were perhaps both relieved to be interrupted by a rather breathless Middle.

"Yes, Lise? What is it?"

"Please, Mrs Buchanan, could somebody come? Lev's livitated, I mean, Liv's laminated, I mean—oh, please just come?"

The child seemed halfway between laughter and alarm. She was hardly the first to find herself there, after having to do with one or both of Isobel's daughters. Isobel simply sighed, gathered Rowany with a glance—*whatever this is, you'll probably want to see it, if only to report back later, to the staff or to your own cohort*—and followed the twitching, fretful Lise.

Not out to the front, where they'd left the girls at their game, in the long easy gardens with nothing but fields beyond and the endless Martian desert after those. Some imp of mischief had brought them to the back, to the pool; and to that stand of hoary old willows between the pool and the canal; and—

—And there were those wicked girls all in a group and staring upward, even Charm who was supposed to be resting quietly and not getting excited. This was the exact opposite of that, and Isobel was disposed to be cross with every one of them, but most of all with her elder daughter. Levity certainly should have known better. No, she did know better. What she should have done was corral her mettlesome friends, and—

But Levity wasn't among them, wasn't anywhere in sight at all. For a moment, Isobel's heart was in her mouth. Surely the idiot child hadn't tried *climbing* a willow? Root and branch, those old trees were not to be trusted. Isobel had told them so, time and again. She pictured bright-haired Levity scrambling up in all her heedless youth, betrayed and falling, tumbling headlong into the water. Both her girls swam as readily as they walked—but what if a nymph had been by? These were marginal waters, barely within Charter territory; a nymph could appear anywhere, but was almost likely here.

No: Lise would have said, if a nymph had come. And the girls wouldn't be looking upwards, with their backs to the water. Knowing this crew, they'd probably be squabbling with the creature in fingertalk. Or jumping into the water after it.

So Isobel looked up in her turn—and saw her errant daughter, though she couldn't quite believe it.

One tall narrow wing of the house ran along the poolside, reaching almost as far as the willows. At the near corner, a bare flagpole thrust up from the eaves, standing ten feet taller yet—and clinging to that pole was Levity, and how she had come there without actually levitating was more than Isobel could imagine.

Suddenly, Rowany was all Head Girl, official status notwithstanding. "Explain this to me," she rapped. "Sharply, now."

"Well, we—we saw an imago go over," Rachel muttered.

"It was really low, Mamma!" Charm put in her contribution. "And I thought it was signing to us with its feelers, like a nymph would—"

"Even though you knew better?" Isobel said, on a sigh.

"Yes, Mamma, even though—and Levity thought, if she could get closer she'd be able to see better, and it could see her, and see her signing back..."

"She thought she'd get *closer* to an *imago*, so it could *see* her *better*?" Possibly not even an imago could bite more deeply than Rowany's voice.

"It, we thought it was talking to us," Charm insisted quaveringly. "We always talk to nymphs, and they're dangerous too..."

A naiad counts ten over a nymph, and no one knows how much an imago counts over a naiad. No one has survived an imago. No one. That was legend, to be sure—but it was a legend that every Martian child was weaned on. A nymph would kill and eat you; a naiad would destroy your village entire; an imago—well. A nymph lived to grow, to survive, to become a naiad. A naiad lived to lay eggs, to raise nymphs, to grow old and wise and become at last an imago. An imago lived to fight and fly and lay eggs of its own and so die, vivid and hectic, there and gone. It didn't eat or grow, it had no interest in you as food. It didn't speak or sign, in any form that humankind could fathom. It would kill you anyway—for the sheer wonder of it, some said—and go on about its brief chaotic business, undelayed.

"Well. Never mind that for now. Just tell me, somebody— however did my daughter get *up* there? She never climbed that wall."

"N-no, Mrs Buchanan." Lise, being as matter-of-fact as she could manage, in the circumstances. "She climbed the willow, and then used that long branch there—the one that nearly reaches the house, you see it?—as a, as a kind of spring, swinging up and down on it until she could jump across the gap."

"It almost looked like the tree tossed her up," Charm said, sounding properly in awe of her big sister.

"I ... see." Isobel knew that she still saw with an Earth-born eye, despite all her years on Mars. That was a significant element in her success here, that she could tell the story of the Red Raj from an outsider's point of view, untainted by sentiment or prejudice. Just now, though, it meant that she looked at the distance from tree to roof—from tree-branch to daughter—and couldn't suppress a shudder, even knowing as she did that gravity was lighter here, that willow was whippier, that impossible leaps and hazards were taken for granted by her impossible, hazardous children.

"And—and how does she propose to come down again, do you suppose?"

Levity's friends and sister all looked similarly blank. In other circumstances, it might have been funny.

"I'm, um, fairly sure that I could make it up there, the same way that Liv did?" Tawney offered, a little doubtfully.

It is even possible that Rowany's lip quirked a little at that, before she said, "And then there would be two of you, equally stuck? Thank you, Tawney, but no. I don't suppose it's occurred to any of you that what she's clinging to up there is a flagpole, and that where there is a flagpole, there must at some point have been a flag?"

More blank and bewildered looks. Rowany sighed, and went on, "Where there has been a flag, there must have been a means of raising and lowering it. If you look, you can see that the halyard comes down below the roof, and is tied off to a cleat beside that window there. A little thought might suggest that by opening the window, one would be able to hoist the flag of one's choice from the security of the room beyond—or, indeed, to help a dangling schoolgirl find her footing on the windowsill, and eventually inside… No, Charm, stay where you are! You too, Rachel. With Mrs Buchanan's consent, I'll go up myself and bring Levity to safety."

"Yes. Please, Rowany. If you would. I think that must be the little boxroom, at the end of the upper passage…" Isobel's voice sounded faint, even to herself; she couldn't take her eyes off her daughter on that precarious perch.

"Consider it done. You others, *stay here*." Her voice promised awful consequences to anyone who disobeyed. Whether or not she had the actual authority to follow through on that, the Crater School girl had not yet been born who could disobey Rowany in this mood. Even Isobel was a little awestruck, even under the weight of her anxiety. She supposed that Rowany had not intended to include her in that command—but nevertheless, even if she'd wanted to follow, she wasn't quite sure that her feet would have taken her.

Long legs carried Rowany swiftly through the house and up narrow, winding stairs. Here surely was the passage, and there the boxroom: empty as so much of the house was, because the Buchanans' nomadic lifestyle had left them with few goods to call their own. Three quick strides brought her to the window; one swift tug threw it upward in its frame, and she could lean out and peer about.

There was the cleat, convenient to her hand; and the halyard drawing her eye upward to where the flagpole was rooted in its bracket just below the gutter; and just above it, yes, there was Levity. Or the toes of Levity's shoes, at least, poking out.

"Levity, can you hear me?" Rowany deliberately kept her voice low, not to startle the girl.

She seemed startled enough anyway, her face appearing suddenly beside the foreshortened pole, blinking down owlishly, both hands clinging tight.

"Rowany?"

"Yes, of course. Now, holding on to the pole is a good idea. If you sit down at the roof's edge there, keeping good hold, and let your feet dangle over, I can guide them down to this sill, and—"

"No."

"I beg your pardon?"

"Not yet, not now. You come up here. It'll be easy from there, you can do that. I'll help."

"My dear child, why on earth—?"

"The imago," Levity said briefly. "It's coming back."

CHAPTER SIX

The Imago, and What Came After

For a moment, Levity wondered if Rowany meant to snatch her bodily from the roof and haul her through the window by main force.

But no: the tall girl's hands caught hold of the stone gutter rather than Levity's ankles. A heave and a twist, and Rowany positively *eeled* up onto the roof. She found the gutter secure enough to stand on, much as Levity had before her, and came swiftly to her feet. One hand gripped the flagpole, while the other arm came around Levity's shoulders, companionable and supportive and infinitely reassuring. One wouldn't dare to fall, once Rowany had taken hold. It would be impertinence.

"Now, kid. Where's this imago of yours?"

She wasn't fooling Levity for a moment. Her casual question was quite belied by the haste that had drawn her up here. Nevertheless: it was like a challenge laid down, and Levity felt a duty to respond in kind.

She lifted a finger and pointed along the canal, away from town. "There, see it? It followed the water down, but now it's coming back."

Rowany was used to seeing an imago from below, from far below, when she saw them at all. She looked instinctively for the familiar cross-shape, something like a dragonfly on an unthinkable scale—and of course couldn't see that at all. What she eventually did see was head-on and almost at head height to her now, almost that low: a blur of wings and a cylindrical body between. Impossible to tell how long it was, foreshortened as it came; too easy, far too easy to see the claws and pincers in silhouette against the tawny sky, the needle-sharp legs hanging like a fringe beneath.

Too late to scramble back down to the window now. It was growing at astonishing speed, swifter than anything she'd ever seen airborne. She tightened her grip on Levity and considered the notion of simply throwing her off the roof. Her friends were clustered so close below, they'd give her something of a soft landing. And then perhaps Mrs Buchanan could drag all the youngsters inside, heedless of broken bones, before the imago had finished up here with Rowany. That would be a way into school legend, should she want one. Just think what the Juniors would make of that tale, with one of their own as witness...

Of course she didn't do it. She only stood there, shoulder to shoulder with Levity; and—somewhat to her surprise—the imago didn't rip them apart in a frenzy of blood and horror. It seemed to stop rather in mid-air, just a short distance from the house, from them. A determined girl could make that leap, perhaps—though not with Rowany's hand so tightly clenched about her collar, just in case.

The imago hung there, motionless now except for its frenzied wings. Rowany could hear the hum of them, feel it almost at the roots of her teeth. And then, foolishly, Levity started to sign to it, as though it were a nymph. Everyone knew that imagos—no, *imagines*, that was the proper plural—couldn't sign. No one actually knew why, but common consent said that they lost the rational mind of the naiad they had been, in the metamorphosis. An imago was all instinct, fight and flight; what did it need of words, of thought, of intellect? The creatures were called merlins in all their forms, nymph and naiad and imago, precisely because this reversion was like living backwards, going from wisdom to mindlessness.

And Levity signed to it anyway, because what else would any Martian girl do, come face to face with doom?

—And the imago signed back.

Loosely, almost clumsily, as though it barely remembered the forms or how to shape them; but there was no doubt about it. Its antennae moved as though it were a nymph, as though it had things to say, a message to pass across this narrow space between it and them, this great broad gulf between merlin and humankind.

It signed, and the two girls stared.

Levity said, "Hold on to me," and let go of the flagpole.

"What are you doing?" Rowany snapped, even as she shifted her grip, finding a swift way to wrap both arms about both Levity and the pole, to anchor them as firmly as she could manage.

"I need both hands to answer." Said as though it was obvious—as of course it was, if Rowany had only been thinking straight. Even though Levity had no useful answer to make to the imago, only *You have led me into the dark, and there is no food here*, which was almost the first sequence any child learned and almost the most used since the colony's earliest days, a swift shorthand for *I'm sorry, I don't understand*.

The imago took its time, seemingly, to decode that; then it lifted its antennae and replied, with the same signs that it had used before. And then it was gone, blurring away downwater so swiftly that even Rowany's sharp sight lost it sooner than she could quite believe.

"*Wind like stone*," Levity muttered, "*and the rock and the air the same thing*. What on Mars can that mean?"

"I think it's a question," Rowany suggested, disliking the doubt in her own voice. "*When the wind is like stone, how can we tell the ground below from the air above?* Perhaps it's philosophy," she added, even more uncertainly.

S he said the same thing again later, after she and Levity both had scrambled back into the boxroom, where they'd been met by a frenzy of schoolgirls and a profoundly anxious parent.

"I mean," she went on when things were calmer, "if the imagines are going to break two centuries of silence, it does have to be for something profoundly meaningful, doesn't it? They're not going to stop and tell us that the milk is off. This might be a truly significant moment."

"Which would be splendid," Mrs Buchanan said drily, "if we could only understand it. Perhaps someone with more knowledge of the merlins or a deeper understanding of fingertalk can make head or tail out of this, for I confess I can't. At any rate, you two will have to report it. I'm sure the Bureau of Native Affairs will be interested, if only because it's the first time we've ever known an imago to say anything at all."

Then she chased the other girls out, to spend some little time having a forthright talk with her daughter and the erstwhile Head of School, about the utter folly of stopping to chat with a passing imago, however fascinating its discourse. And then it was time for dinner, during which she imposed an absolute ban on further discussion; and after that they played ridiculous parlour games until she sent them all off to bed. "Yes, I know it's early; but Charm needs her sleep, and

you've all had quite a day of it. Rachel might as well stop trying to swallow those yawns. She'll set you all off, I know—but
that only makes my point for me. Go on, shoo. I want some
grown-up talk with Rowany in any case. I'll be up to check on
you in half an hour, so make sure you're all in bed and lights
out, please, before I come."

In fact it was Rowany who went up forty minutes later,
willing to play either sympathetic fellow or stern adult as
needed for any wakeful girl. The large attic had been fitted
out as a Middles Dormitory *pro tem*, with even Levity for-
saking her own room to sleep in with her friends; Rowany
climbed the stairs half expecting to find a riot at the top, or at
least a busy conversation in the dark.

Only silence greeted her, though, the thick silence of a
room full of sleepers. She shone a wary torch on each bed,
just to make sure, but none of the girls so much as twitched.

"Asleep?" Mrs Buchanan asked, when she returned to the
drawing-room.

"That, or very solidly pretending. I'm not easy to fool, and
I believed them."

"Good. They need it, one and all, after so much excitement. We won't wake them in the morning, either; let them
lie in till they wake themselves. Or each other, more likely.
You look like you could use your bed yourself, young Rowany."

"No, no; I'm—"

Rowany's protestations were sabotaged by a yawn wider
than any of Rachel's. Mrs Buchanan laughed and ushered
her through to the kitchen. "A mug of cocoa and up the stairs
you go, young lady. Yes, yes; you can take it with you. I'm
fairly sure I can trust you not to spill. You know where your
room is? Good, then there's no more to be said. Sleep in as

late as you like, tomorrow; if the girls need herding, I'll see to it myself."

Those were the words and that was the thought that Rowany took up with her, her mind wrapped around them as her fingers wrapped around the warm sweet-steaming mug: the lure of sleep and the promise of no disturbance, no duties in the morning, nothing to get up for.

Which was why she was all the more startled to be roused almost before daylight could find its way in through her curtains, and not by her hostess. It was Levity who woke her: Levity wrapped in a dressing gown and still a little damp about the edges, Levity who wouldn't explain anything but hustled Rowany towards the bathroom and her own ablutions with an urgency that was all the more imperative for being conducted in whispers.

"Be quick, Rowany, do. Then go downstairs to Mamma. I've to wake the others and see to Charm, so there'll be a rush for the bathrooms in a minute, and it'd really be a help if you were done already."

No one could bathe at quite that inhuman speed, whether or not they understood what was going on. Crater School training stood Rowany in good stead, though, and there was barely a queue outside by the time she relinquished the precious bathroom.

She dressed in a hurry, determined at least to have the news before her juniors did. Down in the kitchen, she found Mrs Buchanan preparing a vast breakfast.

"What can I do to help?" asked practical Rowany. "And what's the why of all this rush, and—and why's it still so dark? The sun's surely up by now..."

"If you step outside, you'll see," Mrs Buchanan replied grimly.

Rowany did just that. She stood on the back doorstep and gazed at the sky, and was startled twice over; and came back indoors conspicuously more thoughtful than she had stepped outside, if not actually wiser.

"Have you ever seen the like?" Mrs Buchanan demanded, even as she passed Rowany a loaf of bread and a knife, and set her to making toast. "You're native-born, I know, so you've a few years more of this under your belt than I do."

"Yes and no," Rowany said carefully. "That sky, the rim of shadow on the eastern horizon that even the sun can't penetrate—oh, yes. Any Martian can tell you that's a dust storm coming. But the rest of it, so many birds flying west, great flocks of them, and all so silent, so intent—no, I've never seen that. I've never heard of that."

"Not just the birds, either," Mrs Buchanan said. And then, in response to Rowany's blank look, "Have you forgotten the imago already?"

"Oh." Almost she had, in the morning's mysteries. "Goodness. Do you think...?"

"*Wind like stone,*" her hostess quoted. "*Rock and air the same thing.* That's how my daughter understood it. Does that sound like a dust storm to you? A bad one?"

"I think your daughter understood it better than I did. Philosophy, forsooth! I should be ashamed. But the merlins don't ordinarily show any interest in dust storms. Nor in us."

"Nor do all the birds of the sky ordinarily black out the heavens this way. Whatever's coming, Rowany, I don't believe it's ordinary. Which is why I want everyone up and on our way, as soon as may be. You and I can scull, while the girls eat breakfast on the water. If we don't go now, we'll have no chance of reaching school before the storm hits."

"We?" Rowany repeated, a little stupidly.

"Yes. Of course I'm coming with you, all the way. It's that or keep you all here, and I'm not supplied for a mob. I couldn't feed you. There's no flour to make more bread, and these are the last of the eggs. Heaven only knows when we'd be able to get into town again, if a really bad storm closes in on us. I'm not risking that. We'll make a dash for school and safety, where you all belong, and if necessary they'll just have to put up with me too."

It took longer than anyone quite liked, to see a gang of excited Middles and a querulous invalid packed and in the boat and tolerably settled. Nevertheless, inside the hour they were on the move. It felt perverse to Rowany to be pulling easterly, when both the current below and the endless streams of birds above were urging them westward. She and Mrs Buchanan plied two oars each, with the girls squeezed in between. Charm had the position of honour in the stern again, but that was more honorary than useful. It was a long straight pull, with no other traffic on the water; no need for a cox for miles yet.

Toasted egg sandwiches and flasks of tea were sovereign against morning chill and tension both. Soon enough the girls were demanding to help row. Work would be better than sitting idle, so a swift rearrangement put them all in yesterday's seats. Every bone in Rowany's inveterately Martian body was urging her to pull harder, to set a faster pace, to hurry, hurry, hurry!—but she held them to a steady twenty-four strokes a minute, figuring it best to hold something in reserve. No telling but that the funicular might be off already; the stationmaster would never risk his precious engine out of its shed in a dust storm. If so, they'd face a long hike to the crater and a steep climb up to the school on the rim. Or they'd just have to find somewhere to stay in town, till the storm blew over. That was more likely, come to think of it. With so much hurry in her, and her younger daughter still so frail, Mrs Buchanan would never let them tackle the distance on foot. Only Charm could see the coming weather, and Rowany wasn't about to set a bad example by peering over her shoulder when all her focus was needed to maintain a steady stroke, but she was already full of misgivings about this whole adventure.

At last Charm hauled on the tiller-ropes to steer them off the main canal and into the Town Cut. Another few hundred yards—with both tow-paths bizarrely empty and the water too, the only boats to be seen lifted out and turned hull-up on the banks—and here was the mooring for the funicular station.

"No, don't tie up," Mrs Buchanan said, as her two daughters prepared to do just that. "Everyone take your own oar ashore, and come back for your bags. ... Now, Rowany. You and I can lift her, I think. If we leave her on the water she'll be swamped when the storm hits, and I don't fancy diving to recover her."

She was right, of course. All those other grounded boats made sudden sense; a hull full of rock-dust would sink beyond question, and need a major operation to recover her.

On Earth, two people might have struggled to raise a boat of this length; in Martian gravity, with a hull of springy high pine, it was an effort but not a strain. They lifted the boat between them and turned her over to lie like a turtle-shell above her nested oars.

"All set, girls? Charm, take my arm. And off we go. The station's just a step from here."

It was; but the sky was a peculiar shade of brass, the sun was no more than a streak beyond the haze, a strange sour wind tugged at their clothes and there was no sign of smoke rising above the station roof. Rowany's forebodings settled into her heart as a grim reality.

Nor was she being unduly glum. The path brought them to the station portico—and there was the stationmaster, just winding a heavy chain about the iron gates.

"I'm sorry, ladies," he said, "there'll be no trains today. Going up to the school, was you?"

"We were hoping to, yes," said Mrs Buchanan a little wearily, already seeing how impossible it was. "They are expecting us; I telephoned, first thing."

"Ah, and you can't call again. The lines are down already. It's always the top that catches the worst of these storms early. I couldn't get through to my mate at the rim, to say that we're not coming. He'll know, mind." *And so should you have known*, his frown said as he eyed the group of anxious girls.

"There's always the pony trail," Charm said hopefully. "We could ride. Couldn't we, Mamma?"

"No one would hire you horses, lass, with this lot on its way," the stationmaster said, as kindly as he was able with one eye on the sky and half his mind obviously elsewhere, the other half wishing to dash off and join it. "No, you find yourselves somewhere in town to hole up and batten down. The Temperance Hotel would take you, though likely they're full already, so many strangers are finding themselves caught here. The Navigation's really not the place for young ladies. I'd try the vicarage myself, if I were you, ma'am. Not that they'll have room either, but they'll know where people can be billeted. The Reverend's wife is everybody's port of call, times like these."

That would mean a blanket on the floor in the church hall, Rowany suspected gloomily, pressed in among a hundred strangers. They'd manage, of course they'd manage; but there would be no comfort in it, no privacy and precious little fun.

Just then, though, she heard the imperative toot of a steam-whistle behind her. That hadn't come from the funicular track, and no one would be flying an airship in this wind, with the promise of worse on the way. Which only left one choice, one way to turn.

Accordingly, she turned to the road—and there was a familiar and beloved vehicle, Dr Mac's great Armstrong Siddeley steamcar. That wasn't Dr Mac in the driving-seat, though, behind all the wheels and levers. It was a much younger man. For a moment, Rowany didn't recognise him in her confusion.

Then Charm squealed, "Dr Ed!" and squirmed away from her mother, trotted down to the roadway and practically threw herself into the young man's arms.

She was quite right, of course. That was Edward Penber-thy, one of the junior doctors at the Sanatorium. Presumably, he was the young genius who had—eventually—diagnosed the condition that had taken such toll of Charm, and coaxed her back to health.

He was being watchful of her, even now. Teasing her, sticking his tongue out to provoke her into doing the same, feeling the glands beneath her jaw before he tucked her casually under his arm and turned to her mother.

"'Morning, Mrs B," he said casually. "Wondered if you might like a lift up the hill, as you have all this mob to see home?"

"Indeed and I would," she agreed, a little breathless with gratitude. "But—how in the world did you know?"

"Ah, as to that, I believe Miss Leven telephoned from across the lake. The chief spoke himself. He's a sucker for any tale of abandoned striplings and maidens in distress, as I'm sure you know. As soon as he understood that you'd be stranded here with no train to fetch you up and a major storm on the way, he ordered steam-up in the car."

"I still say we could ride," pony-mad Charm murmured wistfully to his elbow.

"I'm sure you could, maggot, if you could find horses—but not as quickly as Rowany could walk it, and that wouldn't be quickly enough. We'd find your dust-stripped bones halfway up the crater wall after the storm is over, and that would make us sad. Come on now, in you get. Mrs Buchanan and the maggot here can sit in front with me; the rest of you heap your cases on the rack and pile in. It'll be a squeeze, but you're all willow-wands. You'll manage."

"Do they really think the storm's going to be that bad?" Mrs Buchanan asked, as she helped lift cases onto the back of the gleaming vehicle.

"We have patients who remember the Great Dust, back in '87, when the whole planet was engulfed for six months. No one's quite saying this is on a par with that—but this is what it looked like on its way, they do say that. And the birds fleeing, they haven't seen that since then. Everyone thinks we're in for the long haul. It's why the chief was so keen to see you all fetched up safe—including you, Mrs B. He says that isolated house of yours is no place to sit this one out."

"As it happens, I agree with him," she said placidly. "But what would you have done if I didn't, if I insisted on going home again? Stripling?"

Dr Penberthy grinned, quite unabashed. "That's exactly what the chief said. But I pointed out that if it's as bad as everyone thinks, there's always the chance that even this beauty won't make it back all the way; and his place is in the San, come what may. He owes it to the institution, to stay put. Besides which, I added haughtily, the maggot here is my patient, so her care naturally devolves onto me; and where she goes, I reasoned, you would go, willy-nilly. Rachel, Lise, you two are stokers, all right? Hurl some more redcoal into the boiler, and we'll be away."

Nothing actually happened quite that quickly. Despite his bantering air, he was a careful and punctilious custodian, of vehicle and passengers both. He settled mother and daughter on the broad bench seat—with Charm conspicuously on the driver's side, where he said she could help sort out the levers for him, if he got himself lost—and oversaw his young stokers at their work, locking down the furnace door himself once he was satisfied that they had steam enough for the long climb home.

Four Middles and Rowany made a squeeze indeed, even for the Armstrong Siddeley's capacious back seat; but they squoze together cheerfully enough, with barely a grumble about elbows and eyes. Then Dr Penberthy lit the naphtha headlamps—"for we can't be too careful, however good the seeing is just now down here, and I wouldn't choose to do it in the dust"—and climbed aboard at last. He was careful still with his checklist; "It's Dr Mac's pride and joy, this beast, and he'll be livid with me if I dent it. So you doublecheck me, will you, Charm?"

"Only if you call me maggot," she replied, wrinkling her nose at him.

"Only if you promise never to dry behind your ears. Very well, then, maggot: onward! Pressure high, brakes off—and away we go!"

The magnificent vehicle eased out of the station yard like an old wise horse, in no kind of hurry. That couldn't last. One glance at the sky was enough to tell anyone that, be they anxious young doctor or mother with an eye—two eyes—to the future or heedless schoolgirl with no mind for anything but the present, and the more adventure the better.

Even before they had left the town behind them, Dr Penberthy was cranking up the steam. Trains no doubt could run faster—but not on the funicular line. Here the car had a significant advantage, as the coach road that led up to the Sanatorium was well made and well maintained. It was longer, though, in sheer distance, curling around to the further side of the great crater before climbing to its height in a series of dizzying switchbacks. And even once they reached the rim, they would still be half the crater's circumference shy of the school, and that road was far less smooth or easy to drive in the best of weather.

Rowany gazed at the darkening sky with an ever-increasing sense of dread, and willed Dr Ed to drive this thing faster.

CHAPTER SEVEN

"Wind Like Stone, and the Rock and the Air"

The coach road wound back and forth in an endless run of zigzags as it climbed. Charm sat in the front, with her mother on one side and Dr Ed the other, and focused very hard on not feeling carsick. Steamcarsick. It was a familiar feeling, but was it even a word? She could ask Miss Peters when they got back to school. If they ever did.

She wanted to close her eyes, because that sometimes helped her feel better. She couldn't do it, though. Dr Ed would think she was frightened, either by the long drop down to the plain below, that grew deeper with every swooping turn, or else by the building storm.

It really wasn't fair. She was never travelsick any other way—like any right-thinking Martian girl, she delighted to be out on the water, sailing or rowing or chugging along in a steam-launch; and trains were still fun, and she yearned to go up in an airship—but cars and charabancs always made her feel ill.

It didn't help that being sick all the holidays had left her feeling so weak and trembly. Nevertheless: she was not going to disgrace herself, today of all days, in front of Dr Ed and her sister's friends. She just wasn't.

Nor, of course, was she going to close her eyes and snuggle in with Mamma. She did feel very clingy still, despite really wanting to be back at school too. That was almost the worst of being ill, that the world went on without you and you had to miss so much. Every day she'd had letters, from Liv and from her own friends, but it wasn't the same. She had ached to be back at the Crater School, while at the same time all she really wanted moment by moment was to be lying on the sofa with a rug across her knees, a book in her hand, a glass of lemonade at her side and Mamma always within call...

Maybe that was a sign of how sick she'd really been, that she wanted two impossibly different things at once. Never mind. She'd had one, and now she would have the other. This might be her last chance to snuggle with Mamma until half-term, and she couldn't take it. Not with Liv and her friends—not with *Rowany!*—sitting right behind her. And she couldn't close her eyes, because Dr Ed would misunderstand. And she couldn't conceivably be carsick, because everything and all of them together.

So she stared straight ahead, through the steamcar's windscreen, watching the storm build.

If there was anything to be scared of today, she thought, it wasn't the climb or the long steep drop to the valley floor. That was always there, and they had a good road beneath them and a splendid heavy car to carry them and Dr Ed to drive it. They could hardly be safer—if it weren't for the storm.

The storm changed everything. Everyone knew scary stories about whole communities buried in a bad storm, ships lost on the canals, travellers vanished and never seen again. Dust seemed so harmless, but dust and wind together could be lethal. Dust would blind you to the world, of course, but it was more than that. Dust could clog an engine, and leave you stranded; dust could fill the ridges in your tyres and make the road dangerously slippery beneath you. If it caught you out in the open, with no shelter, dust on the wind was like sandpaper and razors, eating through clothes and skin together, eating flesh from bone and then grinding away the bone itself until there was nothing left of you, nothing at all...

Charm had never been out even on the fringes of a storm before this. It was fascinating and horrifying, both at once. Dr Ed was keeping the car close in towards the crater wall, for whatever shelter that could give, and even so: the dust in the wind was like a living, vicious thing, slamming the car like a fist or coiling around it like a whip, pushing and tugging. Charm couldn't forget how close the edge was, just the width of the road away, and the road had never seemed so narrow. It seemed as though the storm were determined to drag the car over and watch them fall.

She glanced sidelong at Dr Ed. There was no joking now; he was staring fixedly ahead, thin-lipped with concentration, one hand flying between the levers while the other twitched the steering wheel fractionally this way and that. He could be seeing the way ahead only in glimpses. Unless doctors acquired their own X-ray vision, through constant contact with their machines? It could seem that way sometimes, when he gazed down at her with that same fixed expression and apparently saw right through bedclothes and pyjamas and all. Saw her thoughts, sometimes, marching through the privacy of her head.

At least he wasn't looking now. Not at her. Everyone was fixated by the storm, by the way the dust meant you could actually see the shapes of the wind as it battered and swirled against the rock of the crater wall. A particularly brutal gust bounced off the wall just ahead and got underneath the car, so that her bonnet lifted right off the road for a moment.

Mamma's arm came tight around Charm's shoulders. Dr Ed muttered something under his breath and worked the controls frantically. Heavy as she was, the great Armstrong Siddeley still bucked and veered across the road before he could bring her back to a proper sense of duty.

"Perhaps," from the back seat, "perhaps we should stop at the San to sit this out, and not make that last dash around to the school?"

That from Rowany, who was not famous for being faint of heart.

"Perhaps we should," Dr Ed said, through gritted teeth as he wrestled the car around another corner. "I'll see how things look when we get there. Sometimes these storms slacken off, before they build again. I'd like to see you kids home if we can, but I'm running no risks, that's for sure. Mrs B, I'm afraid goes for you too, you'll have to be our guest for the duration."

Mamma laughed lightly. "Well, at least you have plenty of beds—and of course there was never any question of your ferrying me back down again. I'm just as glad, not to be parted from my girls at such a time."

"I'm sure. Not far now; here's the last corner, and the San—"

"What's that?"

That was a pinnacle of rock from the crater's rim, or it had been. Now it was a jagged boulder lying sprawled across the road, just at the turn that would have brought them to the relative calm of the Sanatorium courtyard, and the shelter that great institution offered.

Dr Ed had no time to brake. He hauled mightily on the wheel, and even above the storm's blast, Charm could hear protesting squeals from the car's abused tyres.

Nevertheless, she came around sweetly, like a well-trained hunter in the field. They missed the rockfall by a distance too close to think about, and abruptly they were bumping along the rougher, less-used road that led all the way around the crater.

"School it is, then," Dr Ed cried cheerfully. "Everyone hold on, because this may be one bumpy ride, if there are rocks coming down. Enough to shake your fillings loose. Though hopefully it won't shake a tooth right out of your head, which seems to have happened to the poor Devil's Teeth today..."

Charm was the youngest in the car, and even she knew the sound of an adult trying to make light of something momentous. But she knew her duty, too; it always falls to the youngest to sound believing, to comfort the grown-ups in their anxiety.

So she giggled appreciatively, and asked if the Devil had a dentist, who could fit the tooth back for him after the storm was over?

"Without ether!" Dr Ed insisted. "The Devil deserves no anaesthetic!"

The back seat produced a volley of sympathy for the poor Devil, because the teenage girl does not exist on any of three planets who does not wholesomely fear and loathe all dentistry. Even Rowany observed that it was unChristian to wish pain on any creature, be he immortally damned or no. "Hasn't he suffered enough," she enquired pithily, "without wishing him bad teeth on top?"

That led of course to a theological debate of great matter and import, as they tried to sort out what suffering was due the Devil; and whether that had been Rowany's intent or not—though certainly no one in the car would put it past her—the heat of that discussion all but distracted them entirely from the jolting of the car and the howling of the storm, the grim relentless batter of dust flung hard as hailstones against the roof and windscreen.

Lise had just declared with the utmost satisfaction that if it fell to her, she would dock the Devil's tail and whip him with the pointy end, *while* Mr Messenger was drilling all his teeth in order, when Dr Ed interrupted her.

"We're here," he said. If his own voice held more relief than satisfaction, he was hardly to be blamed for that. These last miles he had been nursing the car far more than he hoped anyone else was aware, against both her slackening steam and an uncomfortable knocking in her engine. Not even a mighty Armstrong Siddeley was altogether proof against Martian dust on a Martian wind.

"Where?" Charm asked, a little bewildered. Nothing outside seemed familiar at all. Indeed, there seemed to be almost nothing outside, only blank walls on both sides, as though he'd pulled into a cave. No, not a cave—a tunnel. The storm's savagery showed ahead as well as behind. But what tunnel, where...?

"Oh—this is the back of the Castle!" Tawney declared. "The archway between the chapel and the library. Clever Dr Ed! Only, I thought you'd be taking us to our houses? We can't possibly walk down in this."

"No. Nor can any girl, nor any staff," he agreed. "Anyone caught in one of the houses when this blew up will be staying there until it's over. If you're to get schooling, never mind food, over the next few days, it's my betting that everyone has been marched up here to the Castle. Though why no one thought to close that gate we just came by, to close this archway off to the storm, I cannot imagine."

"Can't you?" Mamma said. "I suspect they were waiting for us. Blow them a blast on your horn, if there's any steam left in the boiler, and let's see what results."

It was as well, perhaps, that they had no goal beyond this, that they had reached safe harbour and were stopping now. Dr Ed's hand on the horn produced one rapid fantasia, a great raucous blast of sound—and then a dying gurgle, and then nothing at all when he tried it again.

"Well, that's it," he said, not sounding too dismayed. "It's good practice anyway, to let the steam out before you leave the beast to cool down—but how if we're wrong, Mrs B? How if they've decamped to one of the houses, or transported everyone across the water to the San for the duration?"

"We're not wrong," Mamma said with a confidence that Charm tried valiantly to believe in. "Why would they leave the Castle, for any accommodation else? Stone walls and a drawbridge too, heavy gates fore and aft and high towers to watch for what's coming: this is the perfect spot to weather any storm."

She said it, and then she folded her hands and sat like Patience on a monument, to see what would transpire.

Charm just had time to realise, with something a little less potent than surprise, that she hadn't felt sick at all, ever since she started feeling frightened. Then a shape appeared, almost formless in the whirling dust ahead. She nearly considered feeling frightened all over again, but didn't need to because the shape came rushing towards them into the somewhat-shelter of the archway, where it resolved itself into a person with a macintosh over their head. And then she flung the macintosh aside and straightened up, and was Miss Leven herself, come to welcome her stray lambs home.

Mamma thrust open the car door, and Miss Leven put her head in, visibly counting off her pupils.

"Good," she said, as soon as she was satisfied. "I hoped you'd have the sense to come straight to the Castle. Dr Ed, Mrs Buchanan, you're here for the duration now, I hope you realise. Not to worry, you'll both be very welcome. We've stores enough for an army, you can depend on Mrs Bailey for that. Now: everybody out and form a human chain, hand in hand. I'm not risking losing one of you now, after you've come all this way home. Yes, Tawney, I know we only have to cross the courtyard, but nevertheless. You don't know what it's like out there. Charm, I'm going to bundle you up in this mac and put you in the place of honour, between your mother and me. Dr Ed, will you and Rowany close those gates, please, and then join the end of the line? ... Splendid. Everyone ready? Out we go, then. Heads down, everyone. Follow the heels of the one ahead, and remember why the good Lord gave you eyelashes."

It was wise advice, Martian advice, born of a century and a half of pioneer experience, handed down like this from one generation to the next. They might blithely call it "dust", but the Martian regolith ran its natural gamut from the finest powder through sand and gravel to rocks too heavy even for this wind to lift. Anyone who ventured out into the Dry had a mask or a veil or some way to cloak their face; even city rats who'd never dream of facing Mars in the raw knew to shield nose and mouth in the crook of their elbow if nothing better, what time the wind brought the dust to town. But nothing could truly shield your eyes, if you wanted to see your way; and nothing had yet been devised that was better than eyelashes, for filtering out the worst of the dust while you squinted reluctantly ahead.

Truly, it wasn't far to go; and none the less, Charm was deeply grateful for the firm grip of her headmistress ahead and her mother behind, as they took those two dozen paces across the Castle courtyard to the nearest door. The wind stole her breath, while the dust in it was vicious, pinching and nipping and wanting to steal her skin. It was in her eyes, lashes or no; it was in her nose and ears, and threatening her tight-closed mouth, despite the mac wrapped tight about her head.

One foot after another, following the tug ahead: surely they'd gone too far already? Miss Leven couldn't possibly see her way, without the mac's protection. They were lost, and would wander in circles and die here in the midst of shelter, an awful warning to future generations of schoolchildren. Perhaps someone would build a monument of their sand-bleached bones...

But no, wait, here was a step up; and here were other hands, welcoming hands, drawing her in. Here was a place to stand where no wind battered at her, no dust tried to insinuate itself into her throat and lungs. She coughed none the less, and gasped a deep, wheezing, comforting, much-needed breath; and hadn't realised till this moment just how tight-shut her eyes were, and couldn't remember at what point she'd actually closed them.

It took an effort now to force them open. But there were warm, familiar hands on her shoulders that were not her mother's, and so it was absolutely necessary to stand straight and look up and say, "Liv! All serene?" in a concerned, casual, I'm-okay-if-you're-okay kind of voice.

"All serene, kiddo." And then Liv grinned, and unusually hugged her, and said, "Wasn't that an adventure?"

"We've been in dust storms before."

"Not like this one—and not out in them, ever. Don't you try to sound blasé at me, Charm Buchanan. I know your whole life-story, remember?"

"Sisters are the worst," Tawney said, shamelessly eaves-dropping.

"Big sisters are worse than twins," Charm asserted, glowering and giggling both at once.

"Don't you believe it." That was Rachel, chiming in on her own account. "The thing about twins is, one of them always has to come out first. Which leaves the other one facing a lifetime of big-sisterisms, from someone who's not one hour older."

"Not half an hour," Tawney added feelingly. Those two looked at each other and grinned like a conspiracy of two. They must both be the younger sisters, Charm reasoned. Did that gift them another kind of twinship? And if so, were Tasha and Jess similarly linked?

Those were questions for later. For now, she peeled off Miss Leven's mac, shook the coarse, gritty dust out of it as best she could and folded it neatly before handing it back to her headmistress with a polite thank-you.

"Bless you, child. I think that needs to go to Miss Lowe, to see what she can do with it. There's a science lesson in there, I imagine. Feel how heavy it is now, with all the particles caught up in the weave? Whether those help or hinder the waterproofing, I can't tell, but perhaps she can. Now, I know Sister Anthony wants to check you over later, but here's Marigold waiting to tell you all the news. Why don't the two of you run off now, take my poor mac to the laboratory and then find your own people for a while? You can see your mother and your sister again after lunch. No, don't worry about your things, I'll see that they are taken to where they ought to be. Go on, shoo, the pair of you."

Two girls talking at once, at the tops of their voices, in the sacred corridors of the Crater School during term-time, might be supposed to be courting trouble. That was a realisation that came late to Charm, who was still half-new to this. Not too late, though, for no trouble had descended. She broke off her narrative mid-storm, nevertheless, and turned her head from side to side, listening to each room as they passed, no longer listening to her friend at all; and at last she said, "Why's it so *loud* in here? And on a Sunday, too?"

Marigold stared at her, the very picture of exasperation. "Haven't you been listening to a word I said?"

"No, of course not. I was speaking," haughtily.

"Well, so was I—and if you'd bothered to pay attention, you wouldn't need to ask." Then, relenting with a giggle, "The whole school's here in the Castle, and we're not allowed out till the storm's blown over. The prefects and the staff have been ferrying up mattresses and bedstuff all morning, and we're making dormies class by class, not by house. In our own form-rooms. I brought up your jammies and things with my own, and I've saved you the space next to mine for your mattress. It's going to be a terrible squash, though. And I expect someone's going to get tired of the noise, before we're all tired of making it..."

True to her word: even as she spoke, the school bell rang out warningly. Three strokes, and a pause; three strokes, and a pause; three more steady strokes. Every girl in school knew what that meant. In an English village, the nine tailors meant that a man had died; here, the message was hopefully less catastrophic, but no less weighty. *Stay where you are,* the bell said, *and wait for authority to find you.* It was meant for climactic events, the kind of unexpected urgency that Mars could fling up without notice. It hadn't been rung in earnest during this generation of school life, but it was practised unannounced at least once a term and often more, so everyone knew the drill.

Obedient to that brassy command, Marigold and Charm stopped dead in the corridor, speculating wildly as they looked this way and that.

At last a prefect appeared, frowning momentously at the sight of two Juniors seemingly astray.

"What are you doing here?"

Waiting for instructions, as we're supposed to would be the glib answer, but Marigold was too wise to offer it and Charm too new, too suddenly shy. "Please, Alis," Marigold offered instead, "Charm's only just arrived, on the, on the wings of the storm, and Miss Leven took me to welcome her back. We were on our way to where we belong, as she told us to, when we heard the nine tailors. So we stopped."

"I—see." Alis Rasmussen's lips twitched, just a touch. "Very well, then. On the wings of the storm, were you, Charm? That must have been something. Everyone all right?"

"Yes, thank you. Only Miss Leven's mackintosh is a bit knocked about." She held it up for evidence. "We're to take it to the laboratory for Miss Lowe to experiment on, before we go to our form-room."

"Hurry along, then. If nobody's there, just leave it on Miss Lowe's bench; she'll know why. You're what, Lower Third? Good, you can save me an errand. When you get there, tell your crew to settle down quietly. That's what the bell's for, it's an awful warning. Everyone's getting excited, and there's too much rumpus. The staff are losing patience. Someone will come to supervise you soon. If you're lucky, if you're being quiet and getting organised, she'll read you something fun. If not, it'll be the riot act. Vamoose!"

They stood not upon the order of their going, but vamoosed.

The poor ravaged mackintosh was deposited as per instructions on Miss Lowe's scarred and stained work-bench in the Chemistry lab. Duty done, they skipped hurriedly on to the Lower Third form-room, where the door stood slightly ajar and an eye peered out watchfully.

"Cave—oh, no! As you were! It's Marigold—and she's bringing Charm! At last!"

"For a lookout," Marigold observed, "Andi has a *devastatingly* loud voice."

The door was flung wide and the volume rose alarmingly, as a cluster of girls came pell-mell to greet the new arrivals. Charm was sucked into the room as by a whirlpool, with a bevy of last term's new friends about her; she lost her hat and her breath simultaneously, trying to say hullo and to explain her sudden arrival and to tell the story of the storm all at once in half a dozen different conversations.

At last it was Marigold who brought some peace to the room, by dint of leaping onto the mistress's desk and hammering her feet on the wood until everyone stopped what they were doing—yelling, largely, or else tugging at Charm, or else both—and stared up at her.

"That's better, you goops! Do you *want* to bring wrath down on our tender necks? We've already been warned; that's what the bell was for. Alis told us. Someone's going to come any minute, and they need to find us quiet as mice, getting our beds set up and so forth. And give Charm some space, can you? She's been sick, you all know that, and she's just had a horrid journey up here. Look at her, she's as pale as a lilyflower. Charm, you come and sit here," her foot beating a tattoo on the desk again, "for there's no chairs left, we had to clear them all out of the way to make room for the mattresses."

Indeed, to poor Charm—who was indeed feeling giddy now as well as breathless, and would be glad of the chance to sit down—the room looked to be floored with one giant mattress, so close were they all squeezed together.

Someone folded their blazer to make a cushion for her, against the hard mahogany of the desk. Someone fetched a glass of water and pressed it into her hand. Someone asked if perhaps they should go in search of Sister Anthony, for truly Charm did look a little peaky.

She felt almost regal, sitting in solitary splendour with Marigold standing guard over her and so many anxious courtiers in attendance. Some of the girls she didn't even recognise. Her saying, "I'm sorry, I don't think I know you?" was Andi's prompt to fling her chest out like a sergeant major and cry, "New girls! Fall in, line abreast!"

The magisterial effect of this was slightly spoiled by the volley of disapproving shushes from all around the room. Still, eight unfamiliar faces did line up to be inspected and introduced.

"Recruits of the Lower Third, this is Charm Buchanan, who last term was as new as you are, but is now enfolded in our loving bosom, as you yourselves will be before too long has passed here in our beloved alma mater. Charm, these lucky individuals—some might call them blessed, indeed—are, from left to right, Lauren, Agnosia, Elana, Janna, Chrissy, Maeve, Evangeline and Cate. Their full names and lineages will be vouch, voucher, oh, what's the word?"

"Vouchsafed," offered a helpful voice from the back of the room. That was Yolanda, known to one and all as Laney, or simply The Brain.

"Thanks, Brain—vouchsafed unto you at a later date. After lights-out, prob'ly, because nobody imagines we're going to sleep tonight, do they?"

"You don't imagine the Powers That Be are going to leave us to talk all night, do you?" countered Marigold from above. "There'll be someone in here with us, a pree if not a staff."

"Oh—yes, you're right, of course. Not a staff, though. They'll split the prefects up between us. And won't they love that? No Sixth Form dorm for them. Well, then. We'd better get all our wickedness planned quick, before anyone does come. Because we are going to be wicked, aren't we? This is too good an opportunity to miss..."

CHAPTER EIGHT

A Pause for Breath

"Those infants are plotting something."

"Well, of course they are." Thus Melanie, reclined at her ease in the Prefects' Room, in the chair that by long custom belonged to the Head Girl and to her alone. "What self-respecting infant wouldn't turn her mind to thoughts of mayhem, at a time like this?"

"Honestly, I was hoping that the times would be exciting enough by themselves."

"Mary dear, were you really? For Lower Third?"

"How did you know I was speaking of Lower Third, specifically?"

"Well, let's see, now. For the Seconds, you're right: camping in the Castle while a dust storm hammers at the windows is excitement enough for those kids. They'll have a lovely time, and cause no trouble at all. Meanwhile, Upper Third wants to avoid trouble at all costs, because they've got their beady little eyes on promotion to the Middle School, and no one wants to be kept back an extra term in Juniors for mischief-making. Lower Third, though: they're poised between, and ripe for anything. And besides, they've got all those new kids this term: almost half the form, isn't it? The old hands will be feeling the need to do something outrageous, just to impress the fledglings."

Mary Holmes groaned, and sank into a chair at the table. "That sounds depressingly likely. Why did I have to draw the short straw, and be their dormitory prefect?"

"No straws involved, my love. I was there at the staff meeting, *ex officio*. You were selected by unanimous vote. It was felt that you were most likely to keep their feet on the ground and their little minds focused on their work. Flights of fancy they can manage by themselves; they need a steady hand and firm guidance. That's you."

"Well, I suppose." Mary knew quite well that she was a candidate for the school's least imaginative prefect ever. "I'll do my best, at any rate, and saints couldn't do more. But I still don't see why we couldn't have kept them in their house dormitory groups, with their dorm prefects to keep them in order. Putting the whole class together is just asking for trouble."

"It is, of course—but it's also an opportunity for the older girls to spend time with their own cohorts, the fifth-formers and so on, rather than having to be constantly chasing after their juniors."

"So all the work devolves onto us instead?"

"I'm afraid it does. Just until the storm blows over. Don't worry too much, Mary. The staff'll be patrolling, and every-one's alert. What tipped you off, anyway? That your little dears were plotting something?"

"Oh, they told me so. In so many words. At least, that little demon Andi Staddon did. For some reason, she couldn't make her bed without actually crawling inside it, and she was just backing out from under the blankets as I went in. I heard her clear as day. She must have heard the door close behind me and thought it was one of her little pals. She didn't even look around, she just said, 'Do you know who's got the Plotting Book? I've just had the most amazing wheeze for after—' and then she glanced over her shoulder to see who she was talking to, and blushed bright scarlet and dived back under the blankets again, muttering something inaudible. I say, you don't think that was eavesdropping, do you? I mean, she didn't think she was talking to me, but I was the only other one in the room, so…"

"I don't think you need to worry, Mary." Melanie smiled reassuringly. "About anything very much. Of course it's not eavesdropping if she spoke directly to you; any wrong impressions are of her own manufacture, and nothing to do with you. And if they're writing all their evil machinations down in a Plotting Book, chances are none of them are actually too wicked. I would dearly love a look at that book, mind you, if it can be contrived… No, you just do what you do best, and try to save them from the worst excesses of their own imaginations. You know the kids all love you, that's why you got that job. Don't prose at them, but try to guide their feet down all the ways of virtue. And help us think up ways to send them to bed too tired to be sinful. If they're plotting, then we need to plan."

In the Staff Room, meanwhile, a full council of war had come more or less to the same conclusion.

"It is not to be supposed," Miss Leven said in summary, "that two hundred girls may be mewed up withindoors for an uncertain period of time without ructions breaking out. We know it will happen, unpredictably and without warning; we must all stay alert, and stand by to put out fires as quickly as we may. I fear we will need regular patrols after lights-out, to catch the inevitable malefactors. Miss Bartlett, will you draw up a schedule? Thank you. In the meantime, our best form of defence, as so often, is attack. If we keep them busy from sunrise to sunset, we stand in better case for the hours of mischief. Miss Whitworth, you are both our best hope and our least provided for: I am not sure what games or exercises you can safely organise within these walls, but I can promise our full support for whatever you may manage."

"In that case," Miss Whitworth said, "I'll lay claim to the dining hall as my own territory between meals. The little dears will get mighty tired of clearing all the tables out of the way—and then setting them all up again—but that space is next best thing to a full gym, and I can run them ragged in there."

"Splendid. And after dinner, we can clear the room the same way and have dancing, theatricals, whatever our most inventive minds may devise, what time they would usually be in their houses. We might share the responsibility for that among the years, don't you think? Second to Sixth, Monday to Friday; Staff on Saturday and a quiet evening on Sunday. Planning and preparing for that will help to keep them within bounds. Go light with preparation for them, people, and leave them time to write skits and make costumes and so forth."

"What of tonight?" Mlle Latour asked, in her pretty accent. "*C'est Dimanche, oui,* but nevertheless. They are too excited to sleep, *les enfants*. But we have nothing prepared, and no time."

"Yes. I think tonight we must let them fling a little, Sunday or no Sunday. Miss Llewellyn, this falls to you, I think: can we manage an impromptu concert? With dancing afterwards, for the older girls…?"

"**Y**ou'll rally round, won't you, Rowany?"

"Yes, of course, Miss Llewellyn. *If*," she added with a twinkle, "you'll let me play my squeezebox."

"Oh, my dear!" Miss Llewellyn's face fell catastrophically. "I was hoping that you'd sing."

"I know you were, and of course I will—but let me bring the accordion out after. The kids do love a sing-song."

Miss Llewellyn suppressed a shudder, and even managed something close to a smile. "Very well, Rowany. We'll put that at the end of the programme, then. And have dancing after."

"To wipe the memory from everyone's minds?" Rowany laughed.

"Oh, if only. You know it is my least favourite instrument in all the panoply."

Of course Rowany knew, which was why she delighted in tormenting her poor music teacher with it. She also knew that she was right, though. The youngsters would sit through a formal music programme such as Miss Llewellyn delighted in, and some of the more gifted among them would enjoy it—but everyone would brighten up with the first appearance of her raucous instrument. Bach had nothing on a button accordion, when it came to a young girl's heart.

Speaking of young girls, her route from Miss Llewellyn's music room brought her face to face with a bevy of them, milling in the corridor to no apparent purpose. With the ease of long practice, Rowany picked out the faces she knew, and greeted them by name. "Marigold, Andi, Charm. My favourite trinity of sinners. You others must be new girls, yes?"

"That's right," Marigold confirmed, ahead of the other girls' shy nods. "Rowany, these are Elana Grey—like the tea, really truly, the Earl was her uncle of many greats—an' Maeve Denney, an' Agatha St Clair, only we have to call her Cate."

"Do we? Why Cate?" She could totally understand not wanting to be known as Agatha.

"Because my middle name's Hecate," that damsel vouch-safed, blushing. "Which is even worse, really. But at least you can shorten that."

Rowany firmly suppressed uncharitable thoughts about the unfortunate girl's godparents, and moved the subject along briskly. "Well met, all of you. Now, what are you up to?"

"Nothing," Andi replied, all innocence. Which of course meant precisely the reverse—but the question was also a trap, and Andi had been at school long enough to know better.

"Excellent," Rowany declared. "In that case, you won't mind running an errand for me, will you? Skip off and find me the twins, please. I want them."

"Which ones?" Marigold asked.

"Both. I mean, all four. Both sets. As many as you can turn up, at any rate. Tell them to come to—no, better not the Prefects' Room," as she belatedly remembered that she no longer had any rights there. "Send them to my study, please. It's number one, on the East staircase. If you scatter to the four winds, you'll stand a better chance than hunting them down mob-handed. Pair up, one new girl to each old hand, and hop to it."

In honesty, she wasn't entirely sure that she still had the right to summon, or to send; but these Juniors took it for granted. She was still Rowany de Vere, and her legend still held good, whatever her authority. Or lack of it. Certainly she had no right whatever to enquire further into what they had actually been about, this far from their form-room and any proper business. No right, and no intention either. She was feeling a fine fond detachment, finding herself neither fish nor fowl nor any real part of the school. She could join in as she liked, on either side or any; perhaps she'd redis-cover her old sense of mischief, and make common cause with the wicked...

Or perhaps not. Probably not, if she were honest. If school had taught her only one thing, it was a due appreciation of a proper sense of order. Her days of mischief, through Junior and Middle School, seemed terribly muddled, almost chaotic, looking back. She wouldn't choose to revisit that younger Rowany, never mind to relive her.

Oh, heavens above—did this mean that she was growing old? Young Rowany would have said so, surely. Regularity and order were the defining sins of adulthood—old age, young Rowany would have said—and not to be tolerated, never mind sought after.

Pensively, this older Rowany made her way to the eastern tower of the old Castle, climbed the stairs and came to a door with a pretty namecard, handwritten in Miss Bartlett's neat copperplate. *Rowany de Vere*, it said, blessedly omitting her long list of middle initials.

The rooms were a gift, quite unlooked-for. As soon as the school's reorganisation was explained, she'd assumed that she would muck in with her old friends, act as an extra prefect, sleep in whichever makeshift dormitory she was most needed to supervise.

She might yet do that last, if she felt it necessary—but it would be her choice freely made, and no kind of obligation. That was what adulthood meant, she thought, at least to her, at least at this point in her life. Nothing to do with growing old, young Rowany: it was about acquiring the freedom to make her own decisions about what was best for her and for those in her charge, if any.

Right now there were none, unless she chose. She could isolate herself entirely, here in this neat little suite, where she had a study, a bedroom and a bathroom to herself. She could do as she'd been told, work hard, all but ignore the school around her. Focus her mind on the future, and get ready to move on.

Or…

A tap on the door interrupted her thinking. Sitting at her desk, she called, "Come!" and a small troop of schoolgirls filed in uncertainly.

Rowany couldn't resist a smile as they shuffled into line, standing before her like delinquents. Only last term she had been their Head Girl, any summons from her a source of dread. Not much of that had rubbed off, seemingly, with the change of regime. She knew all the signs of hasty washing, newly combed hair, anxiety about quite what to do with their fingers.

She was tempted to keep them in suspense, just for a moment longer—but instead she said, "Oh, for heaven's sake, twins! I'm not a power in the land any more, remember? I want your help, not your humility. Sit down on that sofa there—I think it'll take all four of you if you squash up—and help yourselves to biscuits from the tin."

She waited until the tin had made its way all along the line of puzzled but grateful Middles. Then she took a digestive for herself and said, "Now is when you work for your supper. Sing for it, rather. I want you to teach me a Russian folk song. Something I can learn in an afternoon, and bring to the concert tonight."

The twins glanced at each other, then turned back to her. Facing two identical sets of identical expressions, she almost lost her composure and her credibility all at once. Especially when Rachel was first to find her voice, and said, "Seriously?"

"Absolutely seriously," Rowany confirmed. "I told you I wanted your help to learn Russian; this is the first step. I've a jug of Mrs Bailey's lemonade to lubricate our throats, there are plenty more biscuits in that tin, and I've got the squeezebox to give us a note. Now, what are you going to teach me?"

Each pair of twins shared a look between themselves, then turned to each other. As one, in a kind of four-way telepathy that anyone in authority would have found deeply worrisome, they said, "Kalinka!"

"It'll have to be," Tawney added. "That's all we've time for. If you'd only given us some warning, Rowany. There are some lovely carols that we know, but those take work."

"Carols—that's an idea! And this is Christmas term, even though it's a summer holiday this time around. Of course we'll sing carols. We'll talk about this further, girls. But for now, tell me all about Kalinka. Why that song, and who's going to sing it for me...?"

It barely seemed humanly possible, but girls who were there confirmed it in later years, that the dining hall that evening was noisier even than usual, noisier than it had ever been known. Nor could the storm be blamed, at least directly. The only windows looked inward to the courtyard, where dust and wind were muted and contained. Nevertheless, almost in vain did Miss Leven strike her little bell to moderate the rumpus. Each time she did, the volume would fade a little, only to swell again too soon. Two hundred over-excited girls simply could not manage to be quiet, when there was so very much to say, so much to speculate about, such fascinating things to discuss. Time and again their prefects warned them, "She'll have us all in silence—or worse!— if you don't stop shrieking," and time and again they forgot, because something urgent occurred to them that simply had to be said, and it stood no chance of being heard if it wasn't yelled, so...

At length, the penetrating tone of the high-table bell sounded out again, this time a merry little rhythm rather than the single monitory tone of before. That brought every girl's head around to see—and what they saw was not Miss Leven in her wrath.

No, it was Rowany de Vere, looking more amused than wrathful: standing before the high table with her arms folded, surveying the gathered school. Her head turning slowly from one side of the hall to the other, while she so clearly waited to be heard.

This time, when the prefects shushed their tables, the tables shushed. Staff glanced at each other wryly—why was it ever thus, that the girls gave more respect to their own kind than to their mistresses?—and then shushed themselves, the better to hear Rowany.

Who waited one moment longer, stretching out the hush until you could have heard a pin drop; and then spoke thoughtfully, her voice carrying effortlessly to the furthest corners of the hall.

"That's better. The youngsters among you are too new to know how awful it is to be put under silence even for a meal, never mind a day or longer; but if you ask your seniors, most of them will remember Mute Week, with all the horrors that entailed. I know I do.

"Seriously, people. Miss Lowe can tell you all about the damaging effects of sound-waves magnified too greatly; Miss Llewellyn can speak movingly of great musicians driven deaf by too much noise. Don't do it. Especially tonight, when we have a concert to look forward to. You know how the school orchestra struggles to keep in tune, never mind in time; imagine how much worse it would be if half of them had lost their hearing."

This outrageous slander raised cries of protest all around the hall, and from Miss Llewellyn too, who nurtured in her secret bosom a great pride in the school's musical achievements. Rowany grinned, and raised her hands for hush, and won it once again.

And said, "That was payback, for many insults hurled against my squeezebox. I'll do due penance later. But listen,

I do have a proper announcement to make. No one knows how long we're all going to be pent up in the Castle here, before the storm blows over. It's going to be strange, and difficult in many ways—but hopefully some parts of it are going to be fun too. I expect you've all heard by now that we're having an impromptu concert in here, as soon as we're done with supper and the tables have been cleared to the sides. What you may not know yet is that entertainments of one sort or another will be a nightly affair now, for so long as the storm blows on. We'll pass the baton up from year to year, starting with the smallest—so Second Years, it's your turn tomorrow."

She beamed down at the smallest girls, and laughed at their faces. "Don't look so stricken! I happen to know you've been secretly rehearsing something—it's all right, I won't say what!—to surprise your teachers with; well, now you can surprise the whole school with it tomorrow night. See me afterwards, and I'll do whatever I can to help. For I have been appointed Mistress of the Revels, and this is my task, to make all your dreams come true. Third Years, you need to be thinking about Tuesday; appoint a spokesgirl between your-selves, and she can come and talk to me too. The rest of you, start working up ideas for your own evenings—but quietly, please. Quietly!"

It was no true penance for Rowany to sing anything in public, but she loved Bach best of all. For the sake of the youngsters in her audience—and the orchestra, who had been worked hard under Miss Llewellyn's baton—she lim-ited herself to "Sheep May Safely Graze". And in English too, which was something close to heresy in the mistress's mind, she knew.

Then she held up her hands to quiet the applause, grinned wickedly towards the middle of the hall—for the girls were seated hierarchically, front to back, Juniors to

Seniors all in order, with prefects and staff lining both sides—and said, "For my next trick, I require the assistance of four young ladies from the audience. Two matching pairs. … Oh, come on, twins. Did you think I was going to brave this alone? I need you here, to keep me on track if I get lost."

It was possibly not possible for four girls to blush any redder; but two stepped forward from the orchestra, two from the audience, and she lined them up behind her like a chorus. Then she strapped on her button accordion, played a few opening chords, and led them into the measured first verse of "Kalinka".

Once over the first shock, all four of the twins played up like troupers, as she'd been sure they would. With every round of verse and chorus the tempo speeded up, and soon enough it was a competition, the twins gasping for breath at her back as they struggled to sing faster than her flying fingers could keep pace.

The school caught on quickly enough, and started clapping in time with each other, just a little ahead of time with the music, to draw them on faster yet. It ended as it had to, in stuttering catastrophe, with the performers too short of breath and laughing too hard to carry on. The applause was riotous; and when she could speak again, when she could silence the delighted hall, Rowany said, "Very well then, one more time—and this time you all join in. One verse, one chorus: it's simple enough. Twins, step forward and teach them, as you taught me this afternoon."

This time through she started more sedately, playing the melody through while the twins called out the words, helped by a dozen other girls throughout the hall for whom too "Kalinka" was a treasured family song.

Once they'd started, of course the school didn't want to stop singing it. Around and around they went, faster and faster, until at last Rowany's frenzied fingers slipped off the keys and she held her hands up in surrender.

"Enough, enough! You've defeated me. And what's more, I'm getting signals from the staff. Little ones, I'm sorry, but that's the end of your fun for tonight. All Juniors should go to your form-rooms—I suppose I should say your dormitories now—where your form mistress will show you which bathrooms to use and see you settled down. I know you'd rather stay and dance with the big girls, but it simply can't be done. We're past your proper bedtimes already, and it's going to be such a squeeze with all of us living here in the Castle, we have to stagger the exodus or we'll all be jamming up against each other in the corridors and fighting for the towels. If you're quick and quiet about it, I'm told that your mistresses have all promised to read you a story before you sleep. Go on now, off you scoot. Everybody else: let's get these chairs cleared away to the sides, shall we...?"

CHAPTER NINE

Look What the Dust Dragged In

The storm blew on and on, day after day. The fun of camping out in the Castle began to fade, as new school routines began to settle in.

Meanwhile, the rage of the Juniors only grew deeper, day after day, like the whirling shrouds of dust trapped in the courtyard. Every night—*every night!*—they were packed off early to bed after the evening's formal entertainment, while their seniors danced or played games in the hall. Even the Middles were allowed an extra hour. The Juniors felt as though they were being hustled out of the way, and they resented it bitterly.

"'Tisn't fair," Charm remarked to her mother, after spending ten minutes reciting just exactly how unfair it was, in every particular.

"Well, no, dear. Life isn't. Especially when you're the younger—barely by a year, I know—and you see your sister winning privileges that don't yet come to you. Should I have had you first, I wonder?"

"Don't *joke*, Mamma!" They were alone in the rooms allotted to Mrs Buchanan for the duration of her enforced stay, and the Castle walls were thick. Even so, Charm should probably not have objected so loudly, or so forcefully.

Her mother shushed her swiftly, and went on, "And don't tell me you young ones haven't been making your own fun, and planning more... Now, what have I said to make you blush like that?"

Charm mumbled something anodyne, hoping desperately that her mother would not pursue that particular line of enquiry. Her mother was kind on this occasion, changing the subject briskly, wondering how their new house and garden were enduring the storm.

"Well, we did shut the house up carefully before we left—but, oh, I hadn't thought about the garden! Andi says that Mr Felton had the whole Third Year out in the Mistresses' Garden, wrapping everything in sacking. You wouldn't think that would help very much, but some of those hedges have survived fifty years of storms, he says. We didn't know to do that, though. Did we?"

"No, indeed. I've never had a garden before, here on Mars. We were always too busy moving," chasing her inspiration and at the same time keeping one step ahead of the children's father. Charm knew that now, if she had never quite understood it before.

"Now," her mother went on, as the dust-muffled school bell thudded its awful warning through the Castle, "don't you have somewhere else you have to be? Somewhere supersecret, that you can't even tell me about?"

"Hush, Mamma! I never told you that...!"

"It has been determined," declared Marigold, once she'd called the meeting to order, "by, by dint of careful experiment on the part of several dutiful and honourable members here present, that Mary Holmes is a very solid sleeper, bless her heart. Which means that if we can draw her to bed early, we should be able to slip out of the dorm room without waking her. And then, you know, the school is our oyster.

"It has also been determined," she went on, stoutly ignoring expressions of disgust from those of her cohort who were not fond of oysters, "that most of you are frivolous creatures without a bare-bone thought in your pretty vacant heads."

That, of course, brought instant vilification from the gathered luminaries of the Lower Third. Marigold danced her impatience on the mistress's desktop, gesturing wildly until the room was tolerably quiet again; then she said, "Keep it down, you fatheads! Do you *want* to bring a staff thundering in here—or even worse, a pree?"

Needless to say, they did not. Thoughts of retribution were set aside for later. Satisfied with the silence, Marigold returned to her point. "Every suggestion in the Plotting Book has been read and discussed in committee"—by which she meant herself and Andi, the acknowledged leaders of their year, plus Charm acting *ex officio* as their new best friend, their inseparable adoptee—"and a more hopeless set of duffers never breathed the good sharp air of Mars. Half your ideas are copied straight out of books—if you ask Charm, she'll give you chapter and verse, 'cos she knows them all— and the rest we just can't do, for reasons that should've been obvious to anyone with the brains of a, of a cabbage white butterfly. Or a cabbage, come to that. Luckily, there is one more idea that never made it into the book, because we've been talking it through and making it better every day."

"Who's 'we'?" Hilda Rathe demanded.

"The committee. Charm an' Andi an' me."

"I thought so," with a nod at her bosom companion, Christine Elphinstone. "Who put you in charge?"

"Does anybody else want to *take* charge?" Andi asked dangerously. "No? Well then, stop fratcheting and listen up. We'll be a legend for this, it's really good."

"The issue before us," Marigold resumed with all the dignity that twelve could possibly muster, "is that the Middles and Seniors are staying up late every night, dancing and enjoying themselves, while we have to go to bed. It is beyond peradventure"—she had learned the phrase from her adored elder brother Michael, who was at Oxford to study the law—"that we need to resist this tyranny." Michael was also fond of feeding his kid sister lines that would inevitably lead her into trouble with the Powers That Be. "What's sauce for the goose is sauce for the gander, I say: the best way to, to restore the scales of justice"—another of Michael's pet phrases—"is to pay them back in their own coin."

"Please, Marigold, I don't know what that means?" One of the new girls, uncertainly raising her hand to interrupt.

"It means that we have to dance and have fun after they've all gone to bed. Only we'll have to wait for the staff too, and make sure that Mary's properly asleep. So the proposal before the house is that we hold a Midnight Ball in the dining hall, this very night. Do I hear a second?"

Again, the room erupted into noise; again Marigold danced her frustration as she tried to silence them.

At length, there was quiet enough for people to start raising the inevitable objections. The chair rather grandly recognised Cate St Clair, who said bluntly, "You're potty. All three of you. How can we have a dance? What will we do for music?"

"Well, *obviously* we can't have *music*." Marigold's scorn was a magnificent achievement, for someone who had needed this very flaw pointed out to her not twenty-four hours earlier. "That would bring everyone running; half the school is sleeping above the dining hall, remember. But you don't need music to dance. All you need is rhythm."

That flummoxed her auditors, at least for long enough. Charm tossed a broom up to her, smuggled from Mr Fenton's cubby for this very demonstration; then she and Andi dragged a couple of mattresses aside, to clear space enough. The owners of those particular beds objected, and were swiftly hushed.

"Waltz time!" Marigold declared; and while she pumped the broom handle up and down like a conductor with a silent orchestra, Charm and Andi came together, bowed—and waltzed, as they had practised, taking their time by sidelong glances at the compelling figure on the desk above.

"We're going to call it 'A Dance to the Music of Shadow'," Marigold announced, "and it will go down in Crater School history, in Mars history, maybe even in historical history. This may be the first time ever that a ball has been held in complete silence. It'll be amazing. People will be amazed. Vengeance will be ours. This very night…"

That very night, then, Lower Third prepared themselves and their form-room for sleep—for apparent sleep—in a state of excitement pitched so high that they were almost mute, almost breathless with anticipation. No one remembered to complain as they were sent away early from the evening's entertainment; no one dallied in the bathroom, or couldn't find her pyjamas where they were supposed to be. It is possible that hair-brushing and prayers were both skimped. They were so quiet, their arriving form mistress wondered aloud if they were all sickening for something, and whether she should perhaps send for Sister Anthony.

The urgent denials which that aroused from all corners of the room had her laughing and covering her ears.

"All right, all right! I'm convinced! Settle down, you wretched children—or don't you want a story?"

In honesty, they did not. They wanted to lie awake in the dark and whisper to one another and imagine how much fun they would have at their secret midnight ball. But they liked Miss Tarleton, and the wisest among them were uneasily aware that they might need her support in the morning; so they wriggled down beneath their blankets and lay unnervingly quiet and still while she read to them from *Penelope of Mars*. They all knew and loved the book, of course, and she read it well, investing the characters with real life and urgency. Nevertheless, even the funniest moments raised barely more than a titter of recognition tonight, and at chapter's end nobody begged for another one.

Miss Tarleton gazed around the silent room and said, "Are you all really that tired? Very well, then. Good night, people. Sleep soundly, and I'll see you all at breakfast."

A murmured chorus of "Good night, Miss Tarleton" herded her out of the door; breaths were held again, as the whole room listened intently. Miss Tarleton was new to school, but like any mistress she had quickly picked up some of the prefects' nastier habits, like closing a door behind them and then just standing there, waiting for people to start talking when they weren't supposed to.

They heard the firm click-click-click of her heels, though, as she walked along the corridor and down the stairs; they heard a brief and distant whisper of music, as she pushed open the heavy dining-hall door on the floor below.

"She's gone back to join the dancing," Andi said, in a low but carrying murmur. Any other night there would have been a growl of outrage at this blatant flaunting of privilege, but not this night. This night, everyone knew that they themselves would be having more and better fun, illicitly, later.

Time passed: slowly, lingeringly, as time does when it's in the mood to tease. The Lower Third lay awake, murmuring softly to each other until at last Mary Holmes came sliding in to join them, stepping awkwardly between mattresses with the help of her pocket-torch, apologising in whispers to anyone she thought she had disturbed.

By school tradition, the dormitory prefect always took the bed furthest from the door. Perhaps it was a gesture of trust; perhaps it only put her in a convenient position to chivvy the slowcoaches out of bed. Certainly this night it was a quirk that the whole dorm was grateful for. More awake than ever, they lay silent in the dark and waited for Mary to fall asleep, for Sister Anthony to make her regular round of every form-room dormitory, for the last of the staff to go to bed. They hoped.

And then for half an hour more—the longest half-hour in the history of the world!—until at last Marigold whispered, "Now...!"

Then one by one, in due order from closest to furthest away, they crawled across each other's abandoned mattresses towards the door. First girl there was one of the new girls, Maeve Denney, but they had drilled her through the afternoon and spent a full vial of Lauren Ipsun's hair-oil on the hinges besides. The door smelled oddly, but it swung open in silence and one by one they all crept out undetected.

Breathless with excitement, two dozen girls tiptoed along the corridor and down the nearest turret stairs. They weren't allowed there, but they were breaking so many rules already, one more didn't seem to matter. Andi inched open the door at the bottom, and Charm peeped out.

"All clear!" she whispered.

They slipped through, and here they were in the dining hall—and here was their first disappointment, because the prefects and Seniors had helpfully put all the tables and benches back in place, ready for breakfast.

"At least they haven't laid out the cloths and cutlery," said Marigold, determinedly optimistic. "We can shift all this out of the way again, so long as we do it quietly. No dragging!"

"And so long as we remember to put it all back again after," added Andi. "We don't have to worry about turning the lights on," she went on, suiting the action to the words, "with those great heavy storm-shutters up on all the windows; nobody's going to see a glimmer across the courtyard, even if anybody's up and about at this hour."

"We'd better take it in turns to keep cave at the door, though," Charm said warily. "I wouldn't be surprised if they patrol, what with the whole school being camped out here."

"Good idea," quoth the insouciant Marigold. "We can knock all the lights off and hide in the chapel, if anybody does come around to check that all's quiet. Open the chapel door, somebody, so we don't have to grope for it in the dark. There's always that little light burning on the altar; that'll be enough to see by. Like a guiding star."

Charm wasn't the only girl there to feel not quite comfortable about using the chapel as a hideaway, but nobody quite wanted to say so either. Besides, the whole form was accustomed to following where Marigold led. Mistresses had spoken to them about that, more than once, after she'd led them all into trouble on earlier occasions.

Any trouble tonight would be worth it, though. They were all quite clear about that. This wasn't mischief for mischief's sake, this was justified by all the laws of fairness.

They lifted the furniture and carried it to the sides of the hall with exaggerated caution, leaving just one table for Marigold to stand on, to conduct her invisible orchestra and give them all a beat to dance to. Nobody had remembered to bring the broom handle they'd secreted so carefully in their form-room, but there were long poles used to open and close the windows, when the shutters weren't up. One of those made an excellent substitute.

They stood poised in their chosen pairs, eyes on their conductress, ready to spin into the opening waltz—and just as she raised her staff to start them off, there came a tremendous thumping sound that startled her into dropping it with a clatter.

The girls all stared at each other with a wild alarm. Paulina, who was standing watch by the cracked-open door, shook her head emphatically and came scuttling back to join her friends.

"Nothing out there," she murmured. "But oh, what *was* that...?"

No one had an answer for her. Then the sound came again, more imperative even than before.

"It, it sounds like someone's knocking," Charm said hesitantly.

"It sounds like Death knocking," said Marigold, looking strangely pale as she slid down from her table. "And it's coming from the chapel."

She was right, and they all knew it. Bold Andi took a step in that direction, then glanced back over her shoulder.

"Come on! We have to go and see, of course—but I do think we should all go together."

Perhaps she was not quite so bold after all. Nevertheless, they pressed in behind her, much like the sheep their form mistress had called them. Andi, Marigold and Charm all caught hands together and edged first through the open chapel door.

The great high space was full of gloom and shadow, with an echo of incense in the air. Unconsciously, they were all on tiptoe as they sidled in.

"Do you, do you think it's an angel?" someone asked on a breath. "Come to summon us, because we were sinning so badly?"

Marigold snorted dismissively, but didn't answer. In honesty, no one there was quite sure that the answer was no. After all, what else could be raising such a thunder, and in the chapel of all places...?

One more time the sound came, and now it was quite clearly a knocking; and with a gasp of relief Charm said, "It's the other door. The one we're never allowed to use, that leads outside the Castle..."

Now that she'd said it, they all realised that she was right. They called it the priest's door, because Mr Hartley—the chaplain at the Sanatorium, who came over the water every week to hold Sabbath services at the school—liked to come in that way on a Sunday morning, making an entrance before the gathered school. It wasn't ever locked, but it was absolutely forbidden for the girls to use it to come and go. The chapel was a sacred space, never used for shortcuts. Except by the most wicked of Middles, of course; there were stories, legends of girls gone by breaching that most rigid rule. And always getting caught, of course, because how else could the stories ever be told? No Crater School girl would be crass enough to boast about such a thing. These were tales of shame and confession, nothing to aspire to.

And now here was a whole classful of Juniors—not even Middles yet!—where they ought never to have been, creeping towards a door they never ought to open. Mischief was the last thing on their minds, but they all knew that that was no excuse.

"It must be someone caught out in the storm," Hilda Rathe said, in possibly the most sensible speech ever to pass her lips in all her years as a Craterean. "We have to let them in."

"Of course we do," Charm agreed. "Shouldn't we go and fetch a mistress, though?"

"Are you batty?" Marigold demanded scornfully.

"This is an emergency," Andi said, with a little more tact. "By the time a mistress came, something terrible might have happened."

"If a mistress came," Marigold muttered, "something terrible really would happen. To us."

So the three of them set their hands to the great iron ring that raised the latch, paused only to take one last determined breath, twisted the handle and heaved at the heavy door.

A blast of wind ripped it out of their hands and slammed it open. A cloud of dust blew in, making them cough, making them stagger back; when they could open their eyes again, they saw a figure coming out of the absolute dark of the night, stepping over the threshold, laying hold of the door and hauling it closed against all the force of the wind.

It was a figure barely taller than they were themselves, dressed in a desert robe and hood. Two slim hands brushed back that hood, and it was a boy with cropped dark hair, matted now with dust. He blinked at them and said, "Is this the Crater School?"

"Yes, it is," half a dozen voices answered him at once. Only Marigold was forward enough to go on, "Who are you?"

"My name is Ellen-Stephanie, and I've come here to learn how to be a girl. First, though, can someone show me where I can shelter my camel?"

CHAPTER TEN

Ellen-Stephanie Causes a Stir

The Rowany of Crater School legend never slept, saw through walls and girls' skulls with equal ease, and was able to manifest silently wherever she wished. The true Rowany, of course, had none of those advantages. She was used to sleeping sweetly and deeply, and to waking swiftly at need—especially if that need was occasioned by the wickedness of her juniors. Long years at school had given her almost a sixth sense for detecting trouble in the making; often she couldn't actually say what had roused her, or what had guided her to the particular place or the particular malefactor. Training and familiarity together had combined into something that was not quite instinct, and could seem almost supernatural.

Since her time at Oxford, though, easy sleep had been evasive. Nor had the searing embarrassment of coming back for an extra year of schooling helped with that. Tonight she had entertained the prefects with a late supper in her cherished sitting room, seducing them away from dancing for an hour or so, until they had to go to their assigned dormitories. She'd washed up their cups and plates, then sat reading for a while to settle her mind. That hadn't at all reconciled her to the notion of sleeping, though. She was havering between two equally unattractive notions—sitting down at her desk for some serious work, or else going to Sister Anthony for a sleeping-draught—when she was blessedly interrupted by an unexpected tap at the door.

An unexpected and *hesitant* tap. Immediately she was all Head Girl again. "That's certainly a youngster out there," she thought, "or more likely more than one; they tend to travel in packs. Especially where they really ought not to go. They're supposed to be all tucked up and dreaming by now; what on Mars are any of them doing loose at this hour?"

There was only one way to learn, of course. She opened the door to the stairwell, and found no fewer than three Juniors on her threshold, in pyjamas and a high state of excitement.

"Andi, Charm and—Janna, isn't it? What trouble are you in now, and how can I help?"

"Please, Rowany, we think someone ought to wake a staff," Andi said carefully, "and we, we don't *quite* like to do it ourselves…"

"I should imagine that you don't," Rowany said, "since your very presence out and about at this hour is a confession of your having broken any number of rules. But why do you need a mistress—is anybody hurt? Or sick? No, surely not, or you'd have gone straight for Sister Anthony. What is it, then?"

"There's a, a visitor at the back gate," Charm said carefully. "And they need to bring their camel in from the storm."

"Their *camel*?"

"That's what he—she—they said. We haven't seen it, we haven't been outside to look." Andi clearly wanted to impress her with the virtue of that restraint.

"I should think not, indeed, in your pyjamas during a dust storm! But if you need a mistress—and I suspect that you're right, you most certainly do—then you must fetch her yourselves. Partly to face the consequences of your own choices, which is a lesson everyone learns here at the Crater School sooner or later, and partly because I for one am going to the gate to see this mysterious visitor. And possibly that problematic camel."

"Oh, but—Rowany...!"

The conversation so far had been conducted in a decent murmur. The protests and pleading that followed, not so. The frantic girls made noise enough that they brought another temporary resident to her door, unless it was simply the sound of her own daughter's voice that Mrs Buchanan responded to.

"Charm? What's to do?"

"Oh, Mamma! Please come, there's the most peculiar person at the gate. With a camel. Only the gate's too high and heavy for us to manage on our own, and we didn't quite think we ought to without a grown-up, so we came for Rowany, but..."

"But Rowany is not enough of a grown-up for the situation," that damsel asserted, having absolutely no intention of missing the fun by needing to act adult and responsible, "so I was sending them on to fetch a proper member of staff, while I went to recce the situation."

"Of course you were," Mrs Buchanan murmured, with the air of seeing directly through her disingenuity. "And so would I, if I weren't alas irredeemably grown-up. All right, girls, off you go. I'll bring someone with actual authority here, just as soon as I've put a dressing gown over my nightthings. Which apparently none of you little ones thought of doing. Nor slippers, neither. For shame, Charm! You'd best pray Sister Anthony doesn't see you dashing about barefoot at midnight..."

The youngsters weren't noticeably chastened. They seized hold of Rowany's arms and hustled her through the darkened corridors, down to the dining hall. There around a table like an island in the centre of the room sat an unlikely number of their cohort—was it really *all* of the Lower Third?—and one more, who was most emphatically not of their cohort.

Dust-smothered robes and dust-smothered hair, skin tanned almost to leather beneath its coat of caked dust; piercing bright blue eyes that were oddly confident and barely anxious at all, despite the bizarre circumstances of this meeting. The stranger stood to meet Rowany's gaze and said, "Are you a teacher here?"

"Me? Oh, no. I'm barely more than a pupil. I just came to see who you were and how you were. A refugee from the storm, I take it—but how can you have survived it this long, and what in the world brought you here?"

"Oh, a dust storm's easy enough to live through, if you have the right gear. And a camel, for her shelter and her strength. We all live in the shadow of our camel, my dad says, when we're out on the high plains. And I came here because I was looking for it, of course. Looking for you. We had a doctor come through the settlement last winter, a lady doctor. I didn't know that was allowed. We don't see many women that far out in the Dry. Nor doctors either, come to that. No blame to Dad for raising me as a boy, after Mum died; it was easier all round. Only she told me about this place, the doctor did, and ever since then I've been wanting to come here and have you teach me how to be the girl she named me, Ellen-Stephanie. I'm tired of being Steve."

"I can well imagine." The voice came from behind them, abrupt and austere. The Lower Third startled as one, then stood up and put their hands behind their backs as guilty schoolgirls have done since time immemorial.

With Mrs Buchanan following, Sister Anthony bore down upon them like a tall ship in full sail, but the newcomer was all that held her eye. "Red skies above us, child, how old are you?"

"Eight. Nearly eight," added with a curious mix of stubbornness and inveterate honesty. "Seven and three quarters."

"I don't believe that for an instant. Tell me truly, now."

"Sister," Rowany interjected, "I think she means in Martian years."

"Of course I do. We're on Mars, aren't we? What other way is there to count?"

Sister Anthony ignored that outburst, and went on, "Very well. That would make you, what, fourteen? That seems right. So tell me—without havering, if you please—however far have you come?"

"From Cydonia, please..." No living creature, however self-possessed, had ever maintained their insouciance in the face of Sister Anthony's determined interrogation. Rowany herself was no exception to that rule, and neither was poor Steve, never mind the nascent Ellen-Stephanie.

"On your own?"

"Well, my camel..."

"Your camel is not germane. You'd best come with me. A hot bath, a cup of warm milk and a night's sleep in my sanatorium, I think, before you interview Miss Leven in the morning. She'll get to the bottom of this. No, don't speak any more, it's nobody's business here. Come along."

And to nobody's surprise except perhaps their own, Steve or Ellen-Stephanie went along. Watching with interest, Rowany half thought that she detected a hesitation at the door, perhaps a swallowed mutter about "my camel"; but a gaunt hand caught hold of a young shoulder, the high door swung imperiously closed at their backs, and the moment was gone.

The moment, but presumably not the camel.

All eyes turned inevitably to Rowany, even though Mrs Buchanan was the adult there. She too was waiting on the former Head Girl, acknowledging experience if not authority. Rowany wasn't quite sure how she felt about that—it still seemed to her that the adult world was a step ahead of her, and a long step at that, university and more—but she did at least know what the situation required.

"I do hope no one here is going to suggest that you heard knocking on the chapel door all the way from your form-room at the other end of the school," she said sweetly. "Or that you knew instantly that the situation required every single one of you to sneak out of bed without waking up your dorm prefect. Who is that, by the way? Mary Holmes? Very well. I choose to assume that none of you knew that Mary has been prescribed a sleeping-draught this term, for reasons that are nothing to do with you, and so could be depended on to sleep through anything milder than a Marsquake. No, don't bother me with your excuses now. As Sister Anthony said, explanations can wait until the morning. You all troop back to bed now, and creep in as quietly as you crept out, please. There's no reason to disturb Mary at this stage. Who are your form prefects? Andi and Marigold? Yes, well, no surprise there. Very well, you two: herd everybody back, and keep them quiet. And come and see me in the morning, the pair of you. No, the three of you: I know you two never do anything without Charm in tow these days. Off you go."

When Rowany spoke like that, whether or not she had any right to do so, no Craterean born or raised could resist her. The Lower Third positively slithered out of there, "like snakes upon their bellies," as Rowany vouchsafed next day in the privacy of the Prefects' Room.

That of course left Rowany and Mrs Buchanan, gazing at each other in a suddenly empty aftermath.

"Thank you for including my daughter in your dire prognostications," the elder said unexpectedly, startling Rowany to her core. "The more trouble she finds herself in alongside her classmates, the more she'll feel that she belongs. I do believe that I was wrong to keep my girls so close to me all these years, when really they needed the company of their own kind."

"I don't think you need to worry, Mrs Buchanan. Your girls are doing exceedingly well here, landing on their feet and making friends and—yes, getting into trouble. As they should. Lord only knows what they were up to tonight, but they've shifted all the furniture around in the hall. Properly I should have made them put it all back, but I thought bed was best for them right now. And in the circumstances, I may have to plead amnesty for them in the morning, to avert the wrath of Caesar. By the time they come to see me, they will already have apologised to Mary, if I know anything about that crew; and she'll have set them some dreary task, dusting all the books in the library or some such, which will eat up their minimal spare time and make them duly penitent. I think that's enough. If they hadn't been out of bed in their wickedness, no one would have heard that child hammering back here, and who knows if she would have survived the night?"

"Oh, I think that one is a survivor," Mrs Buchanan murmured. "As presumably is her camel. Do you have any experience with the beasts, Rowany? Because it is still out there, and the child is right, it does need tending to."

"As it happens, I do," Rowany admitted, on a groan. Her own bed seemed suddenly luringly attractive, and horribly far away. "I've a cousin in the Camel Corps, who loved to turn up for Christmas in full regalia, with a train of camels in his wake. Which fell to me to groom and water, because of course he never brought his batman with him and I did more or less live in the stables, so I was in no position to complain."

"You mean you loved it, yes? Just as well, because there's only you and me to deal with this one and I haven't the least idea about the creatures. On the other hand, I do know a little about dust storms, from painful experience; I think I can guarantee to see us out and home again in safety."

Rowany had her own experiences in that regard, probably equally painful, and she knew full well that she could get out and in again, with or without a camel in tow. But another lesson well learned said that it never hurt to give charge to an adult, if you were confident in their ability. So she acquiesced, and let Mrs Buchanan organise their dash out into the storm under cover of a tarpaulin liberated from Mr Felton's store.

They found the camel, moored like an abandoned ship to a convenient decorative railing, lying apparently content with its rump to the wind and its cud in its mouth, its ludicrous long luxurious lashes closed against the dust.

Rowany urged the beast to its feet, with a confidence that was half remembered and half entirely fake.

"Well, that's a blessing," she bellowed through the storm's noise to the hovering Mrs Buchanan. "She's a queen, so at least she's likely to be sensible. Come on now, best beloved. I don't know your name, but you won't mind that. There's a good safe stable just over here, and you'll have ponies for company and warm mash to eat..."

Queen or otherwise, that camel does not exist which will not protest at being obliged to move once she is settled. Dust storms worry her no more than abandonment, so long as she has cud to chew and water in her belly.

Still, as Rowany had foreseen, she was more of a clown than a bully. She bellowed her outrage into the howl of the wind, but rose to her feet anyway, back end first, after the manner of her kind. She didn't so much as offer to bite her one tormentor, nor to kick the other. And once up, she needed little more urging than a haul on her headrope to follow Rowany at a slow sway into the stable's shelter, while Mrs Buchanan did her best to keep all three of them under the cover of the flapping, tugging tarpaulin.

Once under cover, it was off with her harness, her blanket and her saddle-bags. Mrs Buchanan hefted those last and raised a significant eyebrow. "I'll say this for the child, she travels light. If she has one change of clothes in here, that's as much as she can have."

"A prospector's daughter, raised out in the Dry; I don't suppose she ever had much of anything," Rowany said thoughtfully, bringing a bucket of water to the camel.

"No, but it's more than that, though. A prospector's daughter raised as a boy, and finally rebelling against it: likely whatever she had was Steve's, and Ellen-Stephanie didn't want it."

"Yes, I see. I'm sure you're right. But—oh Lord, Mrs Buchanan. How is the school ever going to manage this?"

"Turning a boy into the girl she was meant to be? I have absolutely no idea," the older woman confessed. "But I'll tell you one thing, Rowany: I'm delighted to be here to see the trick performed. Assuming that it is performed, that Miss Leven will accept this particular new pupil."

"Well, she's not the first to run away to the Crater School. As you know: we had Jessica Abramoff, only last term. But I don't think we've ever had anyone quite like Ellen-Stephanie. Oh, Miss Leven will take her, I've no doubt of that; she really has no choice in any case, with this storm blowing. The creature may know better than any of us how to survive it—unless that wisdom is all the camel's—but we couldn't conceivably turn her away and let her go back out in it. She's here for the duration, at any rate; and by the time this blows itself out, she'll be a settled Craterean, or else I miss my guess. We like the bold and the unpredictable, hereabouts."

CHAPTER ELEVEN

Cameelious Hump

"I don't suppose there's any doubt that the creature is actually a girl?"

"'Course not, no. Not once Sister Anthony has vouched for her. I b'lieve she rolled up her sleeves and tubbed the poor thing herself, with Monkey Brand and a stiff brush."

"Pity she couldn't scrub off the, the boyishness, then. I s'pose it's just the way she was raised, but honestly, she's worse than Pete."

"No, she's not. At least Ellen-Stephanie *wants* to be a girl. Pete really doesn't."

"No, that's right. Though at least Pete knows how to wear a skirt, even if she'd really rather not. Ellen-Stephanie's never been out of trousers in her life, except for that jelly-baby thing she wore to get here."

"Djellaba. The Arabs wear them in the desert, so of course we brought them here for the Dry."

"How can you know that when I don't? Shouldn't we both know exactly the same things, if our brains are identical and we've been to all the same lessons and read the same books and everything?"

"I've read twice as many books as you have."

"You have not. Not more than three to two. Anyway, never mind: that, yes. Djellaba. Which looks like it was woven out of what her camel moulted, if you ask me."

"There's a reason for that. It was."

"Really truly?"

"I asked her. She seemed proud."

"She would."

The Mishkin sisters, Tasha and Tawney—"Mishtwins" to their friends, who largely comprised the wickeder half of the school—were watching Ellen-Stephanie walk slowly back and forth with a book balanced on her head, under the sharp tutelage of Bob Tucker, their classmate and authority on all matters etiquettical. The book in question was "Every Girl's Guide to Deportment", which no right-thinking Martian girl had ever taken seriously, until now. This copy came from the school library, a gift from an Old Girl with a legendary sense of sardonic humour, and it had probably never been borrowed before, unless to be giggled over by a mess of Juniors.

Ellen-Stephanie took it seriously, though. She had fallen upon it with delight, determined to absorb its every lesson. Bob—never Bobby, and absolutely on pain of death never ever Wilhelmina, her actual baptismal name—was only too happy to help. Her mother had been writing the "Martian Manners" column in the Arean-Messenger out of Marsport for longer than Bob had been alive. Inevitably, the growing girl child had absorbed the nuances of polite behaviour almost by osmosis, and was revelling in this sudden opportunity to practise what she knew. Never was a pupil both so ignorant and so eager to learn.

"You have to admit Ellen-Stephanie is trying, though," said Tawney, ever the peacemaker.

"Very trying," returned Tasha, as she was morally obliged to do.

It had been three days since the Lower Fourth had woken to find their number increased by one—and what a one she was! Here only on sufferance until her father could be contacted, which would surely not be this term; a hero perhaps, certainly an object of admiration for the long solo journey she had undertaken; but still a girl only by courtesy, at least as far as some of her new classmates were concerned.

She might not look the part, but then neither did stubbornly tomboy Pete, and Pete had been welcomed none the less into the very heart of the Crew. The difference was that Ellen-Stephanie had barely ever even seen a girl, raised as she was in an all-male settlement out on the far frontier. Quite what her father had been thinking, first to take a baby girl that far and then to raise her in trousers, the Lower Fourth could not actually imagine. Popular rumour had it that he had been driven mad by grief at the death of his wife, and so forsook the sight of any woman else. Even his daughter was too painful a reminder of what he had lost, and thus Ellen-Stephanie had become Steve, and grew up barely knowing that she was not a boy.

Popular rumour might be far astray, but certainly she still looked like a boy, walked like a boy, talked like a boy. More than that—worse than that, as far as the Crater School was concerned—she talked like the frontier brat that she was, coarse and direct and heedless seemingly of normal manners, never mind the niceties of community life. In three days she'd contrived to alienate half her form and half the staff besides, not to mention most of the prefects.

"I still think that Pete is our best hope, for persuading her to behave like a, like a rational human being." It had often been said—usually in a despairing tone of voice—that Tasha held both twins' ration of stubbornness in one slender frame. This had been her idea, and she was sticking to it.

"They almost came to fisticuffs last evening, Tash."

"I know. My shoulder still aches, from where I thrust myself between them. There's going to be the most tremendous bruise, and how I'm to hide it from Sister Anthony, I can't imagine. That Ellen-Stephanie has a punch like a mule."

"I don't think mules do punch, do they? I know what you mean, though. It was very brave of you to hurl yourself forward, when you saw it coming."

"Well, I couldn't let the two idiots get themselves into an actual brawl, could I? Though if you ask me, the only brave thing I did was not to punch her back. Do you remember that sermon we had last term, where the Bishop said that true courage meant turning away from conflict? Well, it sounded idiotic at the time, but I do think he might have been right. And now, speaking of which..."

"I know," Tawney said on a dramatic sigh. "Now we get to exhibit our courage all over again, and not punch her for a whole hour on end."

The dust storm was still raging around the Castle and across the lake, the wind howling at the boarded-up windows and snatching at every open door. Everything at the Crater School had been turned topsy-turvy—but some things never changed, and one eternal verity was that the ponies had to be fed and groomed and watered. The ponies and the sandkits, and now Ellen-Stephanie's camel too.

The little girls were forbidden to do it—that was another of the Juniors' grievances, their protests led by Charm at her loudest—but Middles were allowed, under supervision. There was a rota drawn up by Miss Bartlett the school secretary, three girls each morning with a mistress to watch over them. One of those girls was always Ellen-Stephanie, at her own insistence; she would allow no one else to tend her camel. Some of her friends suspected that she was the prime source of the rumours which held Mabel to be as bad-tempered and unpleasant as the worst of her breed had ever been, just to keep others away.

This morning the Mishtwins were to be Ellen-Stephanie's companions. It was one of the rare school duties that they were allowed to do together. Generally staff and prefects both preferred to split them up and deal with them separately, but there seemed to be an unvoiced sentiment abroad that dealing with Ellen-Stephanie called for everyone's best effort, and—like the Abramoffs—the Mishkins were never stronger than when they were together.

They stepped forward in unison, as the school bell rang its dust-muffled peal.

"Sorry to interrupt," Tasha said, "but that's our signal. We'll need to dash, if we're not to keep the mistress waiting."

Ellen-Stephanie's mobile face twisted into a scowl. Tasha and Tawney both held their breath, anticipating a flood of invective; this peculiar new girl could swear as fluently as any prospector in a pioneer settlement out in the Dry. Which was of course exactly where she'd come from, and how she'd been raised, and even so. It had been a shock the first time, to girls so very unaccustomed to that kind of talk; and even now, when they thought they knew what was coming, they had to brace themselves to hear it.

Ellen-Stephanie's nostrils flared, as she drew breath—but then she laughed unexpectedly and shook her head hard enough to send "Every Girl's Guide to Deportment" tumbling. Bob saved it with a squeal, and clutched it protectively to her chest.

"I can only take so much of this, anyway," Ellen-Stephanie confided. "How anyone manages to be ladylike twenty-four hours a day is beyond me. Maybe it always will be."

"I s'pose it gets to be second nature after a while," Tawney said, a little doubtfully. "But it hasn't happened to us yet, either. If that's any comfort. Nothing's going to be very comfortable if we don't run now, though. I don't know who's on stable duty this morning, but there's not one staff who can't flay you alive for keeping her waiting."

They duly ran, leaving Bob Tucker to flourish her manual despairingly. There was probably nothing in that whole book about how to run politely; well-brought-up young ladies didn't do that sort of thing, except perhaps on the tennis court. Ellen-Stephanie, meanwhile, ran like a gazelle: head high, with long springy strides, making the twins work hard to keep up with her.

"Wait till Melanie sees her—or, no, I suppose it's Alis now, isn't it?" Tawney grunted as they went. "Either way, she's a natural for the lax second eleven, if she can catch and throw."

"That's two big 'ifs'," Tasha replied. "And neither of them matters at the moment, when we don't have a lacrosse court to try her out on."

"Even so, though. D'you suppose we could mock something up in the dining hall, with lax sticks and a, a rag ball? Just to keep in practice?"

"You're loopy. Can you really see anyone letting us do that? You know how Mr Felton feels about ball-games indoors, and even a rag ball is going to break windows, hurled that hard..."

Happily neither one of them had breath enough to argue further; and besides, their honour was at stake. They couldn't let a new girl—any new girl—show them a clean pair of heels. They put their heads down and sprinted as God and Miss Whitworth intended them to, hauling in that lead yard by effortful yard until they were practically neck-and-neck with Ellen-Stephanie as they all three came hurtling around the last blind corner—

—And hurtled plumb into Rowany de Vere, or would have done if she hadn't taken swift shelter behind a bust of Ada Lovelace on a stout marble plinth.

"Steady, you giddy young Amazons!" she cried, laughing as they blundered to an apologetic halt. "There really isn't that much hurry, the creatures won't starve for having breakfast five minutes later than promised. It's lucky that I heard you coming, or you'd have flattened me entirely."

"We, we didn't know it would be you, Rowany," Tawney gasped, doubled over, hands on knees but still and always the responsible one, finding excuses, or at least searching for them.

"So you think it would have been all right if you trampled Miss Llewellyn—or Mlle Latour?" Rowany named the two lightest, most delicate members of staff.

"No—no, of course not! We just, we didn't want to keep you waiting. Whoever you were..."

"Well, who I am is me; and if you've got your breath back, all three of you, then buckle up and let's be at it. Mr Felton is promising some miraculous device to let us walk through the dust untouched, a kind of giant umbrella as I understand it, or else a mobile tent; but that's not ready yet, and in the meantime you know the drill."

They did indeed. More specifically, they knew the heavy cotton drill overgarments that Miss Leven had decreed they had to wear, if they were to go out—however briefly—into the storm. In vain did Ellen-Stephanie protest that her desert robes had seen her safely this far, through worse than this; she was a Crater School girl now, if only pro tem, and she must follow this rule along with all the others.

Garbed, then—or not so much garbed as smothered, according to the muffled grumbles emitting from beneath their all-engulfing hoods—and as ready as they ever would be, they lined up by the door, while Rowany wrestled back the bolts.

"Stand by," she said cheerfully. "Three, two, one…"

Three breaths drew in as one, and Rowany hauled the door open.

Was it a blast of wind that struck them, woven through and through with frantic dust? Or was it a wall of dust, heaved in by manic winds? More than one girl had asked the question, after stable duty. Overhearing one such conversation, Miss Whitworth had laughed, and murmured "How can we know the dancer from the dance?" And then of course sent them away to trace the quotation to its source, read the entire poem and write an essay about its meaning and their response. Sullen girls had called down imprecations upon her name—when they were safely private—but any Crater School mistress would have done the same. It was a school tradition, to encourage the girls to hunt down knowledge beyond the classroom and outside the curriculum. In her own rebellious youth, Rowany had once declared that Crater School notions of encouragement came closer to whips and scorpions than seemed entirely Christian. By the time she reached prefecthood, though, she was perfectly happy to crack the same whips and bottle up the same scorpions in honey, smilingly assuring Juniors that it was all for their own good, and that they would believe her later in life and feel grateful for the breadth and range of their understanding, even if it felt like cruel tyranny now.

No such thoughts for the moment, though, and no questions either. No thoughts at all, in this maelstrom of wind and dust. Holding their breaths and bowing their heads, each girl groped in turn for the guide-rope slung between chapel door and stable yard. Rowany saw each one firmly attached— "Both hands, now!"—before she pulled the door closed at their backs and seized the rope on her own behalf.

Mr Felton had strung the rope out like Ariadne's thread, three days ago. Before that they'd had to make this march like little children, holding hands in an unbroken chain, with a mistress fore and aft to be sure that no one let go and was lost.

Rowany had been careful to put Ellen-Stephanie between the twins, on the principle—the rather brilliant principle, she felt—that Tasha and Tawney would be so watchful for each other, they couldn't help but watch over the girl in the middle at the same time.

Not that Ellen-Stephanie needed watching, particularly— she who had come so far on her own, and found her way in the midst of the storm—but she was new, and still very much an unknown quantity. And by no means integrated with the other girls yet, and by any definition independent to a worrying degree. Rowany was hardly the only one who felt that she merited a careful eye being kept on her doings and her whereabouts, at least until she showed some signs of settling in.

Hand over hand along the lifeline, feeling the coarse rope against her palms but never looking up to find it, keeping her eyes fixed firmly on Tawney's heels ahead. That was about as far as she could see with her head shrouded, blinking frantically against the whipping dust. Perhaps she should have set Ellen-Stephanie directly before her after all, rather than shift that responsibility onto the twins. It was too late to change now. And where else did she imagine the girl would go, anyway, when her precious camel waited at the end of this ropewalk...?

Step after step, trying not to worry: feeling the three lives ahead of her fragile as eggshells in her palm—which was ridiculous, when they were three robust Martian girls, and Crater School girls at that. And she worried nevertheless, until the soles of her feet told her that she was walking on the cobbles of the stable yard, until the rope led her into the comparative calm and safety of an open loose-box, until she could rub the dust from her eyes and gaze about her in the dimness and count off one, two, three figures as strangely draped as herself.

Their first move was to shrug off those cumbersome outer garments, even before they lit oil lamps to drive back the shadows. Whickers of welcome and the thuds of agitated bodies came from the stalls to greet them; with the stable doors closed and bolted against the storm, and no one willing to risk leaving lamps unattended where there was so much dry hay and straw, the animals had to live in near-darkness except for these brief visits from the girls.

Happily, whoever designed the stable knew the risk of dust storms, and other Martian dangers; it was as solidly built as the Castle itself, and a broad aisle gave them access to every stall without their needing to go outside again.

Ellen-Stephanie headed straight for the far end, cooing to her camel as she went. Rowany stayed with the twins, probably helping more than a mistress would or should—but of course she had her own favourite pony just as the younger girls did, a stalwart and elderly gentleman who'd been at the school longer than she had; and of course she'd brought carrots from the kitchen; and after an exchange of compliments, of course she was going to clean out his stall for him and see that he had fresh hay and water and rather more than a handful of the horsenuts that he liked so well.

At the same time, she carried on a steady dialogue with the twins, while they were doing the same work in other stalls.

"What's the Russian for a bridle? ... for a bucket? ... for a broom? Can you put that into a sentence for me? How's my accent now?"

When she moved on to see how Ellen-Stephanie was coming along in the loose-box at the far end of the aisle, where her camel had been bedded down in its own space, the girl looked at her curiously and asked, "Why do you do that?"

"Why do I do what?"

"Ask people to teach you things all the time. You're not at school any more."

"I'm going to college soon, I hope. This will help. And after that I'll be going out into the worlds—this world mostly, I expect—and the more you know, the better you can manage whatever life throws at you. It's all about being ready. And there's nowhere like the Crater School to teach you to be prepared. Don't waste your chance, Ellen-Stephanie. I know you came here to learn how to be a girl—but a Martian girl can turn her hand to anything at need, and you never know what'll turn up next. Especially on Mars. By the way, are you seriously going to insist on your full name, on every occasion? If so, of course we'll do as you ask; but there's nothing unfeminine about a nickname, or just a short. People have been known to call me Ro at need, and most of them have lived. I quite understand that you don't want to be Steve any more, but you might like to come up with something else. If you don't, I expect your friends will, and so I warn you."

Ellen-Stephanie worked on in silence for a while, forking soiled straw into a wheelbarrow; and when at least she did speak, she spoke mostly to her pitchfork.

"I don't have any friends," she muttered.

"Really? Let's see, you've been put into Lower Fourth, haven't you, pro tem? They're a pretty friendly gang, by and large. And I believe I've seen you out and about with Bob Tucker, more than most. Incidentally, she's a fine example of what I meant, about the name: there's no more, more *girlish* girl than Bob, to be found here or anywhere; and yet she's 'Bob' to all comers, be they staff or school. Even Miss Leven calls her nothing else, unless she's in deep, deep trouble. And don't tell me she's only spending time with you because she's your sherpa, for I won't believe it."

"But she's not!"

"That's what I said."

"No, I mean, she's not my sherpa."

"Not? That's a shame. You seem a perfect blend, the two of you." Every new girl was allocated a sherpa, a more experienced partner to act as guide and mentor through her first half-term, to ease her way into school life. "So who is sherping you, and why haven't I seen the two of you together?"

Ellen-Stephanie stood mute. Finally, exasperated, Rowany went on, "Look, I can't help you if you don't tell me what's going on. It's not tale-bearing if I ask directly—and this must be common knowledge anyway. Your form mistress will know, so will your housemistress. And your dorm prefect, and, oh, everyone except me. Speak up, now. Who is it?"

"Pete," in a sullen growl.

"*Pete*? Oh, Lord." Rowany sat down abruptly on a convenient bale of straw. "Whose bright idea was that?"

"Everyone's. They all thought we were made for each other—even the staff, which is why I was put into her dormie, and the next bed. But it was Mary Holmes who said it."

"Yes. That makes sense." Rowany would have expected better of the staff, perhaps—of Miss Leven, at least, who must surely have had a say—but of course Mary would look at those two and see them as a matched pair. And of course they would pull against each other, and refuse to learn how to work in harness.

She sighed a little and said, "Well, I don't know if it's possible to change your sherpa—or your bed, or your house: Bob's in Butler, isn't she?—but I'll see what I can find out. And in the meantime, do your best to make the current arrangements work. It's in your own interest, you know. Friendships take effort, you don't just fall into them as to the manner born. And if you can find your way somehow onto Pete's good side, then the whole Crew will welcome you in, as like as not." It occurred to Rowany, a little belatedly, that Ellen-Stephanie probably had as little experience in making friends as she did in being a girl. There wouldn't be many children of any kind out in a prospectors' camp, nor likely any time to play together. She knew something of the pioneer life; even the smallest would be put to work, from dawn to dusk as soon as they could manage it. "Also, you might try working your way around Pete's blind side. Spend time with one of the twins—try Jessica, she's almost as new as you are, though of course so is Pete if it comes to that—and there you are, hey presto, snug up against your sherpa whether she likes it or not. Now, enough of this. Let's talk about Mabel. How did she come by her name?"

"I named her after my aunt. My mother's sister. I've never seen her, I only know that she exists somewhere on Mars. An aunt you can't talk to is no manner of help—so I talk to Mabel instead. Not that she's much use either, but still—"

Any further confession was cut off by the sudden irruption of two furry solid bodies hurtling into the back of Rowany's knees, hard enough to make her stagger. Someone had injudiciously opened the sandkits' stall, and after so long pent up in the dark they had not unreasonably decided that Out was better even than breakfast.

Rowany bent, laughing, and scooped up the nearest by his armpits. Holding him dangling at head height, she said, "If you knock me flat, then how are you ever to ride about in your favoured position, hey? Didn't think of that, did you?"

Then, relenting, she slung him across her shoulders, where he settled like a living tippet, if tippets were desert-hot and restless and weighed two stone already and purred

loudly into your ear about the urgent need for food and milk
and company.

CHAPTER TWELVE

A Rehearsal to Remember

"**G**ood King Wenceslas looked out, on the feast of Andy
While the dust blew all about, thick and red and sandy.

Barely shone the moons that night, and the wind was cru-el..."

Whether Pete's inventiveness would have held up for even one more line, one more rhyme, was fated never to be known. The infant posted at the hall's high double doors to keep watch shrieked a sudden "Cave!", loud enough for whoever was coming to hear clearly all the way down at the far end of the corridor. That was inevitable; her alarm-call needed to be heard by a dozen different groups, all making noise on their own accounts, and the traditional hissed whisper would never have been enough.

A mad scramble ensued, as all through the hall those diverse bands abandoned whatever wickedness had occupied them up till then and scuttled to their seats. Miss Llewellyn would expect to find them quiet and prepared, each in their proper place; and no one wanted to risk being sent out of this crucial first rehearsal, never mind being exiled from the carol concert its very self. Pete swallowed down her improvisation as she and the rest of the Crew slithered out of the deep window-seat where they'd been massing, and made a dive for those chairs marked out for themselves by their own blazers and satchels. The boarded-up window had offered them no actual view of the dust storm, and this wasn't actually St Andrew's Day—but then neither was Pete a good king, or any kind of king at all, so actual literal looking out wasn't really called for; and the window-seat made for a pleasant sense of clubbishness. Lean as they were, they'd have struggled to fit one more girl in there, even if anyone had offered themselves up as a candidate. It would be a bold soul who did so: the Crew was already acquiring a reputation for exclusiveness, even unattainability. They were perfectly friendly towards other girls, individually or en masse—which was just as well, as the Crater School frowned on anything that looked like cliqueishness—but left to their own devices they would come together as a coherent whole, as now, and leave no space at all for any stranger.

Pete's conscience was being troublesome in that regard. Sidling into her seat, she couldn't help but glance to the far end of the row, where Ellen-Stephanie was sitting with Bob Tucker. It really wasn't Pete's fault if they just didn't like each other, if everything about each of them rubbed the other the wrong way—but even so. Pete was officially her sherpa. That didn't oblige them to be best friends, or any kind of friends at all—but even so. It ought to be Pete sitting there with her, explaining things. Not that Pete knew anything about carol concerts; all this was new to her too. And Bob had been at the school for ever, and somehow even seemed to like Ellen-Stephanie, unless she just liked to have someone to practise etiquette with. And even so...

The high door swung open, to find school and orchestra all sitting dutifully if a little breathlessly in their places, displaying an ostentatious if unconvincing virtue, waiting for someone to take charge—and here they were. Footsteps sounded on the parquet flooring, echoing sweetly from the high beamed roof. Not a head turned, not a whisper disturbed the silence that embraced that steady beat—until the new arrival was halfway down the hall, and those behind could see her quite clearly, and a single incautious voice cried out "Oh, it's only Rowany!" in tones of deep disgust.

Only Rowany? *Only Rowany?* Had those words, those two brief words, ever been said before, in that order, in this school? Perhaps they had, but not in living memory. There was a communal sucking in of breath, and a sudden ripple of movement all through the hall as every girl but one turned her head, or else twisted right around in her seat—the younger half of the school, sitting far forward of the drama—to see exactly who the idiot was, and exactly what was going to happen to her now.

There was no mistaking who had spoken. Her friends seated either side were staring at her in horror; she herself had clapped both hands across her mouth, as though she were trying to push the words back down her throat again.

Too late for that. The footsteps had paused already in response; all eyes moved to Rowany, where she stood in the centre of the aisle, the only still point in the entire hall.

Slowly, deliberately, she turned her head to find the speaker; slowly, deliberately, she smiled.

"Only me, Izzy," she confirmed. "Sorry to disappoint. I'm not much of a pianist, but I can manage carols; and Miss Llewellyn asked me to act as accompanist, so she can give all her attention to your singing. *All* her attention," she repeated meanly, for Miss Llewellyn was famous for being able to hear every single voice among two hundred, and Izzy was notorious for striking firmly either side of any note that offered.

The hapless Izzy sank even further into her seat, her small form vanishing entirely behind her big friend Brigitta. Who met Rowany's gaze with a look that was trying to be both defensive and apologetic at once, and managed only to look comically belligerent. Rowany gave her a friendly nod in response, walked to the far end of the hall and started to arrange her music on the piano's lid.

With her so seemingly disengaged—and not strictly staff, and certainly no longer a prefect, though of course still and always Rowany, a name writ large in legend—a buzz of conversation worked its way up out of the silence. In deference to that legend, though, and their sudden lack of anyone keeping watch on the corridor, it was a low buzz, easily to be muted at need; and not a girl left her seat again. Most of them, indeed, were so fixated on Rowany that they wholly missed the sound of a new arrival, brisk footsteps coming up behind them; and it was their former Head Girl—revered and feared in almost equal measure—who gave them the cue by rising politely to her feet as Miss Llewellyn came busily down the aisle.

A moment later, the whole school was standing. The music mistress came first to Rowany, and shook her formally by the hand, much as a conductor shakes hands with the first violin. The handshake was accompanied by a private murmur, "You no longer need to stand for me, Rowany."

"Perhaps not—but I think I should, Miss Llewellyn. I am still officially school, and here to learn—at your feet, among others. Besides, someone had to act as prompt for this vile mob. Beware, they're not so much brewing mischief as boiling over..."

"I know it. They'll be good this afternoon, though: most of them love to sing, and no one wants to be turned out of the carol concert."

"Not even Izzy?" There was still a wicked schoolgirl lurking somewhere in Rowany's heart.

"Izzy knows that if she behaves, she can be in charge of selling programmes on the day. Anything, to keep her out of my choir! But last year I promised that any ill-discipline would see her rolling bandages all day for Sister Anthony instead. That settled her down."

"It would!"

Rowany tried her piano stool, finding it sturdy but too low, as every piano stool ever made was doomed to be. She touched fingers to the keys for the first time, cherishing the soft sweet response of a true Tiedemann, made of the finest high pine timber right here on Mars; then she improvised lightly while Miss Llewellyn turned to the gathered throng.

"Thank you, girls. Sit down now, and listen carefully. I've excused the prefects from this assembly, as they have other duties on the day and so don't sing in the concert, so I depend on your honour to keep good order through this afternoon. We've a lot to get through, and I can't waste time with misbehaviour. Don't whisper and giggle with your neighbours, don't tilt your chairs; obviously don't pass notes. Sit up straight, pay attention and enjoy the music. I've some carols here that I doubt any of you have ever heard before: some old traditional songs that I collected in the Tyrolean mountains on my last visit to our sister-foundation, and some that had their birth right here on Mars. You'll be hearing those, and learning them, soon enough—but let's start with one that you all know, just to warm up those voices. 'Once A Family', everybody. Give us the note, Rowany, and we'll plunge straight in..."

Once a family travelled on the old canal
- Cold canal -
Many days they travelled on the still canal
- Chill canal -

Not a girl but knew this, even the youngest of the babes. It was Christmas fare in every household, in every community the length and breadth of Charter lands, wherever humankind had lawfully set foot and settled down. It was in their bones, in their blood, words and tune together; and even the youngest of the babes understood that while it was the story of a pioneer couple, caught out in the winter freeze by their duty to Authority, at one and the same time it was the story of the Christ-child, transposed to their harsh and beloved home planet.

They joined in with a will, one and all, and the rafters rang with their voices. Rowany felt herself all but unnecessary, and abandoned the melody altogether, strumming a descant with one hand while she plumbed chords with the other. She watched Miss Llewellyn watching the girls, because she dearly loved a masterclass, and there was much to learn here about pulling a disparate group together into a single purpose. So it was that she saw the moment of Miss Llewellyn's utter startlement; she saw the intent focused look that followed, and the determined stalking down the aisle, the head that turned like a redbat's to find its victim.

Briefly, Rowany worried for poor Izzy, who really couldn't help it. Then she stopped playing entirely, and listened on her own account. She didn't have Miss Llewellyn's notorious ear, but she could sing better than she played, and she played better than she knew; and she loved music of all kinds and sung music above all others, so she did know how to listen. It took her a moment to tune out the clumsy, the mechanical and the merely loud; but then, yes, there it was. One voice in a different register, startlingly low, the true contralto: rare anywhere, as rare as hen's teeth among schoolgirls not yet come into their full growth. Rowany's own voice had settled eventually into mezzo soprano, her last years here, and there had been no one then singing a lower line than she could reach.

Now here was someone, as much a surprise to Miss Llewellyn as to anyone else; and that meant a new girl, a very new girl; and that meant—

Ellen-Stephanie had her eyes closed as she sang, and her mind a long, long way away. A long, long time ago. Somewhere in her memory, a woman's voice sang this same song just for her. It was a moment out of context, no notion where or when: only a sense of warmth and comfort, a gentle rocking in time with the music, a feeling of being held close to the body and closer to the heart. She had always believed that it was her mother's voice that sang to her, her mother's arms that held her. It was the only memory she had, the faintest possible contact with that long-gone woman who was only otherwise a name without a face; she treasured it, and so this song, and in the privacy of her own head she was always singing it back to her mother.

Lost as she was in yearning and grief and music, she had no awareness of the room around her; and so she was startled when a hand closed on her elbow, and she let out a wretched squawk when the hand tugged her out into the aisle.

Her eyes sprang open, and she was doubly startled to find herself in Miss Llewellyn's grip. She couldn't think what she might have done wrong. She hadn't been paying attention, perhaps, but with this song of all songs she knew her way, she knew the words, she knew she'd been in tune. That squawk of hers had silenced everybody, piano and chorus alike, but that was hardly her fault.

Blushing furiously, she faced the mistress—stared down at her, indeed, for Miss Llewellyn was a slight figure and born on Earth to boot, with none of the native Martian height.

"Ellen-Stephanie, isn't it?"

"Yes, Miss Llewellyn."

"Why didn't you tell me?"

"Please, I'm sorry—tell you what?"

"About your voice, child, about your voice!"

Helpless under interrogation, confused beyond measure, horribly aware of the entire school listening in fascination, Ellen-Stephanie could do nothing but shake her head meaninglessly.

Salvation came unexpectedly to her, predictably to almost everyone else in the hall: in the form of a figure so tall even Ellen-Stephanie could look up with a sigh of relief as Rowany came down the aisle in a hurry. "I don't think she knows, Miss Llewellyn. I don't suppose there's much music taught in the prospectors' camps, is there, Ellen-Stephanie?"

She shook her head again, but firmly this time, feeling herself on slightly more solid ground. She still didn't know what they were talking about, but at least this was a question she could answer. "No, not at all. Of course we have sing-songs, the men love to sing after supper; I know all their songs. And an old claim-miner taught me to play his harmonica. But truly, I was lucky that I learned to read and write, from the Franciscan brothers when they came through on migration. There really weren't any lessons else. That's why I had to come here. But—please, I don't know what I've done wrong?"

"Wrong? *Wrong?* Child, you've done nothing wrong. Only, your voice... No, never mind explanations. They wouldn't mean anything anyway. Come up to the front, and let me try your range."

She had been embarrassed already, with this all too public catechism; now she was ready to die, sooner than sing solo in front of everybody. Rowany gave her a look of sympathy, but no help else; and she played the notes and chords that the music mistress called for, and there was no help for it, Ellen-Stephanie had to sing.

Sing she did, note for note, from the highest note she could reach to the lowest, in careful scales; and then Miss Llewellyn asked her for a song, something she knew, something she'd grown up with. "Anything at all, I just want to hear words rather than la-la-la."

So many sing-songs, with the men passing her physically to the front while she was still tiny, where she could sit in the fire's glow and pipe along with their growling chorus. She barely hesitated, she didn't think at all: she only pitched straight in with "The Ballad of the Lost Nellie Martin".

"The bell rings a warning or a fond farewell
As we pull from the roads it's goodbye to Pell
There's a nymph in the water but it won't touch us
When we kissed the vicar's daughter there was much more fuss
And we're not scared of the bosun with his knotted rope
We're more scared of the parson with his promised hope
He can ring his bell for ever and we won't look back
The wind's on our quarter and the current's slack
We're the men of Nellie Martin and we're on our way
From Pell to New Victoria."

S he paused then, expecting everyone to join in with the shanty chorus. Instead she heard gasps, whispers, titters, all laid over a general shocked silence that she didn't understand.

Miss Llewellyn seemed almost as bewildered as Ellen-Stephanie was, caught somewhere between wrath and wonder. She frowned momentously, opened her mouth, closed it, shook her head, was clearly baffled how to proceed; and again it was Rowany who came to the rescue, again saying, "She doesn't know. Ellen-Stephanie, you must not sing that song here. Or anywhere else, come to that. It isn't fit for a decent school, nor for decent girls."

"But, but it's a true story. It commemorates a tragedy. Shouldn't we—?"

"Not with that song, dear, no." Miss Llewellyn had recovered herself, and took charge again. "You have a lovely voice, a unique voice; it's a shame to sully it with coarseness. What else do you know?"

"Umm…" If the school objected to *Nellie Martin*, it was hard to think of anything in her repertoire that would pass muster. The men she had grown up among were very fond of singing, yes, so she knew a lot of songs—but even she recognised that most of them were likely to make any well-brought-up young lady blench.

Even mistresses were human, of a sort. Ellen-Stephanie thought she could see an understanding twinkle of amusement in Miss Llewellyn's eye as she said, "Well, never mind. We don't really have time for this now in any case; there is much to do today. I'll see you at another time, Ellen-Stephanie—soon!—and we'll see what we can do to exercise that voice of yours. There's some wonderful music I can introduce you to. Go back to your seat now, dear, and sing out as much as you can. You'll find your friends know little more than you do, of these carols; you'll all be learning together."

It would have been a long and lonely walk, under the eyes of the entire school; but Rowany came with her for moral support, all the way to her chair. And leaned over her to murmur to her neighbour, "Bob, if you could just help Ellen-Stephanie to understand *why* we don't sing *Nellie Martin* here, you'd be doing her a greater favour and being a greater help even than you are already."

"I, I'll try, Rowany." And in the honour of that trust Bob sat straighter even than before, and tugged Ellen-Stephanie up too when she would rather have slid beneath her seat and stayed there all afternoon.

And if, as she straightened up, Rowany happened to glance along the row to the far end, where Pete was watching all of this transpire, no doubt that was pure happenstance; and if Pete felt those chill blue eyes pierce her to the very soul, accusatory and justified—well, no doubt that was only her own guilty soul nudging her, because not even the former and legendary Head Girl was actually, could actually be all-knowing and all-seeing and a mind-reader to boot.

CHAPTER THIRTEEN

Obstacles, Of Course

The next morning, Miss Whitworth and the prefects took over the dining hall as soon as breakfast was over. Any girl finding an excuse to pass by before classes started—and the excuses were many, and almost as unconvincing as they were extremely various—could hear the sounds of effortful voices, and the shifting of heavy things. Those bold souls who tried to inch open one of the doors, just to see, found them locked; and more than one Middle reported to her cronies that the key was in the lock, on the inside, so she couldn't even squint through the keyhole.

The banging and thumping continued until the mid-morning break, which the girls had grown accustomed to taking in the dining hall, where they did so much else these locked-in days. No one had told them otherwise, so they filed through the corridors, curious and excited—and found the doors still closed against them, only now they were adorned with a poster declaring, *'THE GREAT DUST OBSTA-CLE COURSE! ENTER AT YOUR PERIL! PRIZES FOR THE BOLD, AND LESSONS FOR THE FOOLHARDY!'*

Beside the notice, leaning casually against the door with her arms folded, was Melanie Fitzwalter, Head Girl and subject of almost as much awe as Rowany herself.

"Please, Melanie," asked a little, a very little girl at the front. "What does it mean?"

"It means what it says, Dolores. We've made you an obstacle course—and I'm your first obstacle. Nobody gets inside, until invited. But don't worry, you little ones have the chance to try it first. Trot on back to your form-room now; you'll find milk and biscuits waiting for you. Tell all your friends that the first hour is reserved for you, and we have some very special surprises waiting. Your mistress will bring you along when it's time. Third-formers will have the next hour, and so on up through the school."

"What about lunch?" a voice called from the back of the gathering crowd.

"Was that you, Christine? Calm your anxious stomach. Lunch will come to you, as you can't come to it; Mrs Bailey has made up picnic hampers, and you'll eat them in your form-rooms. We're hoping to have everything straight again by dinner time, but if not, something else will be arranged. Don't worry, you won't miss a meal." Over the chorus of soft laughter—for Christine was known to be fond of her provender—Melanie made great shooing gestures with her hands, as though she was herding a flock of chickens. "Go on now, run along. Make yourselves scarce. There's no point hanging around here like a bunch of nuisances. Your turn will come—and until it does, you will learn nothing useful. Except that the wrath of a Fitzwalter is not to be lightly sneezed at. Begone!"

They fled, in a laughing mob that diminished as girls peeled away to this form-room or to that, to find their particular mistresses waiting for them with trays and jugs. The staff proved as unforthcoming as Melanie, despite all the wheedling their favourites could come up with. "I'm sorry, girls, but this is a prefects' affair. I don't know any more than you do," was the best response that anyone could get, and that was no use at all.

The Crew, being fourth-formers, were obliged to wait till after lunch for their turn in the hall. Worse, they were obliged to sit through two hours of lessons—ordinary, boring lessons—beforehand; and then, eating as they must in their own form-room, they had no opportunity to interrogate the younger girls about what they could expect.

"Of course that's deliberate," Tasha growled to the rest of the Crew. "The prefects are teasing us, just because they love to be provoking."

Still, it was quite fun to clear all their desks and chairs to the side and picnic in one big circle, sitting on the floor. Even if things did get spilled, and needed mopping up, and more than one gym slip would have to go to the laundry tonight.

Pork pies and salad and scotch eggs, with a slice of lemon cake to follow: it was as much lunch as anyone wanted, and more than one girl had to be called to order for bolting her food, as though that could make the time pass faster.

After they'd cleared up and washed hands and faces and tidied themselves as much as was in their nature or their training—which for several meant "as little as they could get away with"—they still had to set the room straight, with all the furniture back where it belonged. Only then, only when their form mistress agreed that both girls and room looked as trig as could be expected, were they allowed—at last!—to change shoes for plimsolls and march in line astern down to the hall again.

Halfway there, they met the girls of Upper Fourth heading in the same direction. Sometimes they were rivals, sometimes they were friends; today it was hard to be sure. Both forms were curious, puzzled, excited, almost in equal measure. They marched on side by side, eyeing each other a little askance, sharing tentative smiles and wary whispered words.

This time, when they reached the hall, gatekeeper Melanie greeted them with a smile and opened the door wide. The Fourth Years advanced two by two—and found themselves in a broad clear space curtained by sheets, so that they still couldn't see the hall proper. Tasha nudged her sister, and nodded upwards. They could at least see much of the hall roof above the curtain-rail, and there were gym ropes hanging down from the exposed beams of the rafters.

"Fourth Years, welcome!" The voice boomed at them out of nowhere, deep and gravelly and oscillating strangely, as though it rose from the bottom of the crater lake. One or two of the more nervous girls gasped; Florimel embarrassed herself and all her classmates by shrieking.

Rachel snorted. "It's only Fidelis," she said loudly enough for her voice to carry through the sheets to whoever waited beyond, "playing with that thing she built in science lab. You remember, that microphone-and-speakers contraption we were shooed away from, in case we broke the valves or knocked something out of alignment? She calls it an echo machine, but really all it does is distort her voice till she sounds like, like—"

"Like that," her twin Jessica put in helpfully.

"Like a newt with a megaphone," Rachel persisted.

"Or a bull bellowing through a hose into a bucket of water," suggested Lise.

"Mortals, attend!" The sudden breathlessness in that awful voice suggested strongly that Rachel was right, and that Fidelis was struggling not to laugh. Struggling almost in vain, to judge by the curious gurgling noise that overtook her briefly. Still, she recovered fast, and the fell voice continued after a short break. "I am your judge. Before you lie many challenges; only the good will triumph. Virtue lies in helping those who fall behind; the race is not to the swift, nor the battle to the strong. Ecclesiastes 9:11," she added, rather spoiling the impression of some deep mythical creature.

"But that's not fair! Why shouldn't the race be to the swift?" objected Levity, the long of leg and fleet of foot. "What's the point of racing, else?"

"In this case, my love, the point is that old-fashioned thing called teamwork." This voice came from behind them, a purely normal human voice, familiar to every girl there. They turned as one, and there was Melanie, smiling at them knowingly. "We want you to divide into teams of eight—and the winning team will be timed by its slowest member, so if you leave anyone behind, you're doomed. You have to help each other, Levity. Even at the cost of not personally coming first this time."

Levity blushed, furiously unhappy at being called out this way. She had perhaps caught something of Lise's hero-worship, where Melanie was concerned; it really stung her, that Melanie in particular might see her competitiveness as selfish. Before coming to school, she'd only ever had her younger sister Charm to challenge, and even one year's gap in age and growth was enough to give her an inbuilt advantage. She'd relished the opportunity here to pit herself against girls her own age or older, bigger, better trained; she loved the strain of going all-out for the tape, and she did relish the victory when it came. If Melanie thought that was wrong—worse, if Melanie had seen it in her and disliked what she saw—then Levity would have to mend her ways. Though not trying, not competing must be equally wrong, surely? That would be dishonest...

Hopelessly confused, Levity resolved only to become the most helpful member of her team imaginable, today and every day, in every sport or game. Even if Melanie wasn't watching. She'd pass the ball whenever she had the chance, rather than go for glory herself; she'd play defence instead of attack; she'd be the very best back-up imaginable. First among the second fiddles...

Some part of her knew she was being ridiculous. Before the rising bubble inside her could burst into a giggle, though—or make her blush again—a hand seized hers, and that was Rachel saying, "We're a team, of course. All of us."

"Well, I hope so..."

"Of course we are," the twins said in unison.

"If nobody tries to break us up," Tasha added, scowling as she peered suspiciously around at Melanie.

For once, authority seemed inclined to let them go their own way, without interference—until Melanie reached out a long arm and snagged Ellen-Stephanie by the elbow, leading her over to where the group stood watching, staring, appalled.

"I take it the Crew is sticking together?" she said blandly. "Splendid. There's only seven of you, isn't that right? You need an eighth, to keep things even; and Ellen-Stephanie needs a team. Besides, you're her sherpa, aren't you, Pete? Well, then. You really should have asked her yourself; she's still too new to be left to fend for herself, in this kind of scrum. I know you're newish too, but even so: you've found yourself a solid bunch of friends, and it's time to reach out and be considerate of others not so fortunate. The sherpa programme's a lesson for you youngsters in learning to share your time, as much as it is a helping hand to new girls who don't know our ways. Now you eight line up over there, next to the Uppers' first team..."

Upper Fourth and Lower Fourth, in alternating lines: muttering back and forth to each other but not side to side, because that might be fraternising with the enemy. At last, at long last, unseen hands tugged the curtains down, all at once, and suddenly they could see the hall.

At least, they could see ten feet into the hall, where a wall built of gym horses and benches rose up before them, ten or twelve feet high. Beyond that—well, there were ropes hanging from the roof-beams, but they knew that already. They couldn't see anything more.

"You went for a hike," Melanie said behind them, "in your teams, and the dust storm blew up unexpectedly. You've just seen it coming over the horizon, and you have to dash madly back to school before it hits. We know how long you've got—but you don't. You'd best be quick. Your first obstacle is to scale the crater wall; there's no time to go around by the path. You have to get all eight of you across, remember, before you can tackle the next task. Think of the team, not of yourselves. Ready?"

"Ready!" The chorus was perhaps a little uncertain, but every team had at least a few determined characters in it. The Crew—plus Ellen-Stephanie—was possibly more famous for its stubborn determination than anything else, including mischief.

"Set—go!"

Almost without discussion, three of the tallest girls in the team ran to the wall, set their backs against it and made stirrups of their hands. Three of the shortest ran in, leaped, set one foot in that stirrup and sprang upward, scrabbling to catch hold of the wall's rim. This was something they'd practised in gym, time and time again.

That, inevitably, left short Pete glowering up at Ellen-Stephanie, who had never seen any such move before.

"Go on, then!" Pete snarled. "I'm not doing it for you, that's for sure."

"I, I didn't know..." But she knew now, and their team would fall behind if she dithered, while Pete stood no chance of making it over the wall without help from someone. Already the tall girls were making their own run-and-leap, snatching at arms that reached down from the top to haul them up.

Ellen-Stephanie ran up in her turn, set her back to the smooth polished wood, made a stirrup of her hands. Almost before she knew it Pete was there, hurtling at her and bounding high, her front foot aimed at Ellen-Stephanie's midriff.

It was hard not to flinch, not to fend her off; but Ellen-Stephanie set her shoulders, caught that questing foot in both hands, felt the smaller girl's weight and momentum, and flung her high. Ellen-Stephanie put all she could, all she had into that heave.

She heard a squawk above her, and looked up in time to see Pete's legs almost disappearing over the top of the wall. Rachel and Jessica grabbed hold of her, just in time; the Mishtwins beamed down and cried, "Come on, your turn now! Take a running jump, and we'll grab you as you come…"

Ellen-Stephanie backed up a few steps, concentrating hard, trying to block out everything happening on either side of her, where other teams were tackling the wall in their own ways. There was a lot of yelling involved, but she knew how to ignore that; the men in the camp were noisy from sun-down to sun-up, seven nights of the working week. If she could sleep through a prospectors' ceilidh, she could shrug off the incidental screaming of fifty excited girls.

There was the wall, here was the ground between: not much of a run-up, but if there was one thing Ellen-Stephanie had learned to do out in the Dry, it was jump. The hills her father tramped, seeking his fortune—the hills she had grown up tramping at his heels—were broken, savage ranges, no use for farms nor industry. They were torn by sudden gullies, and seamed by rocky upthrusts; if you couldn't leap or scramble, you might as well turn back to wherever you'd come from.

So she sprinted forward, judged her moment, and thrust upward with all the spring in her long slim legs. She was aiming for the top of the wall, and sure that she could reach it by herself; but as she reached, just before her fingers could claw over the edge, she felt strong hands seize her and haul her up by main force, the twins working together in an easy harmony.

"Welcome to our perch," Tawney said, which to Ellen-Stephanie's ears almost sounded like *"Welcome to the Crew"*. Which almost warmed her heart, until she looked over Tawney's shoulder and saw Pete's face. Than which nothing could conceivably have been less welcoming.

No matter. There was no time to think about that, no time to revel in the warmth from the others. Tasha said, "Tall ones down, and stand by to help the others," and led the way herself, dangling by her hands and dropping down the further side of the wall.

The rest of the team did the same a moment later, even the shortest of them—Pete, of course—spurning the notion or need of any help. A short whistle-blast marked the moment she touched down to ground, and there was a prefect—Elise van Buren, Ellen-Stephanie thought—with a clipboard and a stopwatch, making a note.

"Well done, girls. You're running second. Stand quiet now while the other teams finish"—there were whistles further up and down the wall, even as she said it—"and we'll tell you what you have to do next."

"We'd have been first if Ellen-Stephanie hadn't dithered about like that," Pete grumbled, as soon as Elise was out of earshot.

"We might have been first if you'd explained to her what she needed to do, rather than waiting for the chance to show her up," Tasha snapped. "You two need to work together, if we're going to win this. Now be quiet, keep your eye on the prees and your mind on your work."

"Your eye on the prees and your mind on the prize," Jessica amended, grinning. "Is there a prize? No one's said."

"I suppose we'll find out at the end," Tasha said. "And I don't want to be clapping someone else, do you hear me? Shush now, everybody. They're ready."

The prefects had been standing in a huddle, comparing notes. Now Melanie stood forth and called out, "We should have made you pick team leaders first. Sorry about that. We'll just have to do what we did with the little ones, and name your teams after the prefect who's looking after you. So: Fidelis' team finished seven seconds ahead of Elise's, so they'll start with a seven-second cushion. Arie, your team was thirteen seconds behind them..."

And so on, down through all six of the teams; but the Crew had stopped listening. They knew only two things: first, that they had to stay ahead of Arie's team; and second—and far more important—they had to overtake Fidelis'. What else could possibly matter?

They waited in an agony of impatience, until at last Melanie said, "So now you all know where you stand. What's next, you ask? You've made it safely over the crater wall—but the merlins have risen from the lake, as they are known to do in dust storms. Maybe they just can't breathe the water when it's full of sand; we don't know. But anyway, up they come, and you see a nymph's shadow through the storm. You have no chance of speaking to it; it wouldn't see your fingers move, and you wouldn't see its antennae. You have to get away before it senses you. Happily, here's a stand of high pines," and she waved an elegant arm towards the ropes that hung from the roof-beams. "There's one for each team, as you can see. You need to get all eight of you into the tree, high enough that a passing nymph can't reach you. In this scenario, I will be playing the nymph, and the reach of my claw will be exemplified by this broom." She waved it cheerfully above her head. "If I can swat you, you're dead—and if you're dead, your team has to carry your body the rest of the way around the course. And I'm looming at you right now. Ready? ... Go!"

On the word, they went: dashing for the nearest rope, leaping to scramble up while their individual prefects stood watchfully by, occasionally calling encouragement or advice.

"Me and Tawney first," Tasha called down, from halfway up already, "and we'll sit along the beam to make room. Sort yourselves out, and send the weakest climbers up after us, so we can help them at the top. Best climbers last."

Ellen-Stephanie and Pete looked at each other, and neither one of them made a move towards the lashing tail-end of the rope.

"I suppose you grew up in a mineshaft, climbing up every morning to milk whatever it is that miners milk," Pete growled.

Ellen-Stephanie smiled thinly. "More or less. And you must be half monkey, after spending half your life clambering around the rigging of your uncle's airship."

"Right."

"Right, then. We're last," she declared, turning to the rest of the Crew. "Does anybody need a boost up?"

Lise was already helping Levity, who had barely met a rope before she came to school. The Abramoff twins were following on, comfortable and competent; that left only the two antagonists still on the ground.

"After you," Ellen-Stephanie said, determined to yield nothing to this short, difficult girl.

"No, you. I'm your sherpa; it's my job to tag along behind, not to scramble up ahead of you. Besides, your legs are longer, you'll be easier for Melanie to reach. Look out, she's coming! Go on, quick...!"

Sacrificing pride to emergency, Ellen-Stephanie leaped for the highest grip she could achieve, and swarmed upwards.

Climbing a rope was easy, enjoyable exercise. There was no need to look down; just from the way the rope grew suddenly tauter below her as she climbed, she knew that Pete was following on behind. She didn't think to look up, though, she thought she had plenty of headroom—until her reaching hand closed not on the thick coarse rope, but on a slender and elegant warm ankle twined about it.

"That's me," Jessica said, bubbling with laughter. "I mean, you can climb me if you want, I'll hold on like a trouper, but—"

"Sorry," Ellen-Stephanie said, hastily letting go of the foot and gripping lower down instead. "Move up higher, can you, though?"

"Can't," was the brief answer. "Levity's stuck. She can hang on, but she can't make it any higher, and she didn't get far enough for the twins to haul her up onto the beam. So we're stuck below her. We're scrunching up as much as we can, but..."

But here came Melanie with her broom, swishing it cheerfully above her head—and Ellen-Stephanie might be safe, but Pete below her certainly was not. She looked doomed, indeed, unless—

"Pete!" Ellen-Stephanie yelled. "Climb up me! I can take you on my back!"

Wiser voices above them told her to wait, to stop, not to do anything so rash—but Pete was oblivious to common caution, with the fate of their team in her hands. Ellen-Stephanie barely had a chance to draw breath before she felt those hands seize her legs, then her waist, then her shoulders.

Pete's lithe body followed, snaking up until her head was suddenly on a level with Ellen-Stephanie's. The smaller girl's knees locked around her waist, while her arms reached over Ellen-Stephanie's shoulders to grip the rope. They met each other's eyes for a moment, from an inch away; then both looked down.

There was Melanie below them, reaching up, wafting with her broom. Ellen-Stephanie squawked, and tried to retract her feet; she felt the bristles just stroke across the sole of her plimsoll.

Melanie laughed. "I'll let you get away with that one, Ellie—though you should probably limp over the rest of the course, just to placate me. Try to remember, your foot's been nipped by a nymph's claw..."

There followed half a dozen more tests: tasks to complete, races to win, challenges to survive. It was close all the way, but the Crew won through in the end. Melanie presented them with a bar of chocolate, "and I hope you like it bitter, for that's the only kind I buy, and we haven't exactly had much chance to shop"—and then she went on to add, "though really I should have broken you up at the start, it's not fair having all the year's best athletes in the same team," which made seven out of eight girls beam delightedly at the compliment. Ellen-Stephanie wasn't sure she was included anyway, as she'd had very little chance yet to demonstrate any athletic ability; and besides, she was still working through how she felt about being called Ellie. It had never happened before, because nobody in her memory had ever called her anything but Steve before she came here, and since then she'd always insisted on the full mouthful.

Now, though, she remembered Rowany's advice, and she noted how much respect everyone around her paid to Melanie, and—well, she wasn't sure. Should she be offended or flattered or delighted? Or any combination, or all three? She had never thought that choosing—or accepting—a name could be so complicated. She had come here determined to claim the one her mother had given her at birth, hold to that and nothing more—but suddenly she was uncertain.

She was still awake when the dorm prefect came to bed, still thinking things through; and she was still awake an hour later, when she heard a hiss that startled her eyes open.

"Psst! Ellen-Stephanie!"

"What do you want?"

"Put your dressing gown on, and come down to the hall with me. I want to try something."

Ellen-Stephanie wasn't sure that she wanted to try anything other than going to sleep, or anything at all with Pete— but she was suddenly intensely curious, and knew from a lifetime's experience inside her own head that that itch wouldn't go away until she scratched it. What on earth could Pete want with her—Pete, of all people!—in the middle of the night?

So she dragged herself out from under her warm covers, wrapped her dressing gown around her and followed Pete between the mattresses of sleeping classmates and into the corridor beyond. Neither one of them had thought to put on slippers.

They found their way to the hall by torchlight, with not a word spent between them. Once they'd dragged the door closed behind them, Pete switched on all the lights, in a gesture of defiance to rules, authority and Fate itself; then she said, "I want to race you. So we can find out who's best."

Ellen-Stephanie just blinked at her. "What? I'm sorry, I don't—"

"That obstacle course this afternoon," Pete said, with an exaggerated patience. "We weren't allowed to compete, you and I, they put us in the same team. But it's obvious that we're the best in our year, even when we're helping each other." Her mouth twisted as she said that, as if it were the most revolting thing that had ever happened to her. "Now I want a real race, just you against me. Let's find out who's best."

"Pete..." Ellen-Stephanie shook her head helplessly, then fell back on the simplest, most obvious reason why they couldn't conceivably do that. "Look around you. Everything's in place for breakfast. The prefects demolished the course before we had supper in here. Don't you remember?"

"Not everything. See?" Pete nodded upwards—and to be sure, there were the gym-ropes, all six of them still tied to their beam. The middle four had been looped up high out of reach, but the ones at each end had simply been tucked behind convenient statuary. "I noticed, at supper-time. My guess is that whoever went up there didn't have time to undo those gruesome knots at the top, so they just left them like this overnight. And didn't loop up those end-ropes because they had to get down themselves somehow, and up again tomorrow morning. Which means that we can make a real race of it. Look, it's easy. We start on opposite sides of the hall. Climb one rope, balance along the beam to the next, let that down and climb down it. Then up again, and along the beam to the third. Same again—and then all the ropes are down, and we can just climb down and up each of them, and the first one back to ground at the end is the winner. What do you say?"

"You're crazy," Ellen-Stephanie said.

"What, you mean you're too much of a goodie two-shoes? Or are you scared? I bet that's it. You think we'll get in trouble, and—"

"I'm not scared." How many challenges had she faced down, how many fights had she faced up to, all prompted by that simple accusation? The hot denial came to her lips unthinkingly. "We'll do it. You call go."

And with no more preparation than that, she slid her dressing gown off her shoulders and stalked to one side of the hall, where the rope-end was twisted around a bust of Caroline Herschel. She uncoiled it from the great astronomer's throat, let it hang naturally, and peered up into the shadows high overhead. Gave it a tug, just for reassurance, though she knew intellectually that it was entirely secure; how many girls had been up it and down again today? One-sixth of the whole school, give or take, though the babies must have had some help from watchful prefects. It would take a couple more.

She glanced across the hall to where Pete was standing at the foot of her own rope. Ellen-Stephanie raised her arm, to show that she was ready; Pete did the same, to be perfectly fair; and then she cried, "Go!"

On the word, both girls were climbing. Neither was gym-trained, so they had poor form and technique; but both had grown up swarming from rope to rope, unthinkingly. If Pete was a monkey, nimble and lithe and heedless, Ellen-Stephanie was an ape, all strength and confidence. They reached the beam almost at the same moment, balanced casually along to the next rope and let that fall.

Down and then up again, the moment that their first toe touched the ground; still neck and neck.

Along to the last of their own ropes, face to face at last, barely six feet apart; side by side as they slid down, stretched a leg to ground—not quite cheating, either of them, but almost, just the barest hint of contact—and powerered back up the thick slow swing of the rope to the dark ancient beam above.

Where they were face to face again, climbing up onto the beam almost at the same moment, and needing to pass each other; and there wasn't much light and the beam seemed suddenly much narrower, as two pyjama'd bodies struggled not to touch as they inched by. Ellen-Stephanie found herself rising up on tiptoe, as if that could possibly help. Pete glowered up at her, and she suddenly wondered if the shorter girl took it as a slight. That wasn't what she meant at all, and she brought her heels rapidly down to ground again—except that there was no ground, because she and Pete were sidling past each other and all that lay behind Ellen-Stephanie was open space. Space that she was falling into, toppling backwards, and there was nothing for her hands to catch hold of except Pete's slim body, and she wouldn't do that, she wouldn't take another girl down with her as she fell, as she fell and fell.

CHAPTER FOURTEEN

Deep in the Darkness, Something Stirs

Ellen-Stephanie opened her eyes to a wide, white world.

Where on Mars was she? Nowhere she had ever been before, she was sure of that. A high ceiling, no walls in sight, and so much light, she might almost be outside...

No, not that. There was no outside: not any more. She remembered. Wind and dust, the air turned solid, lethal, like trying to swim through turbulent sand. She was blasé about it after, but at the time it was monstrous, cruel. She couldn't breathe or think, she could barely move. One foot after the other, step by step, hour by hour, day by day. She'd made light of it to her classmates, but in truth she never would have survived it, but for her camel...

After. Survived. Classmates. She had survived, and this was after. She had reached the Crater School, which was the point and purpose of it all; but now what? Had she died after all, and was this Heaven? She'd never imagined that God might have a sense of humour—there was no sign of it, at least, in anything the Brothers had ever taught her, no hint of *Jesus laughed*—but He might perhaps deal in irony. He might love that.

She could hear a voice, she realised: very softly counting: "...nine hundred and ninety-seven, nine hundred and ninety-eight, nine hundred and ninety-nine, one thousand. Un, deux, trois, quatre..."

The voice sounded weary beyond measure. Ellen-Stephanie had almost, *almost* decided that she was dead indeed, and that was a clerk-angel at the Pearly Gates counting in a thousand English folk, followed by a thousand French to keep things even.

Then she turned her head to look.

Oh. That was no angel; that was Pete, sitting on a hard chair with a bundle of fabric in her lap and plying a needle relentlessly, counting her stitches as she went.

Not Heaven, then. Categorically, not Heaven. You couldn't be dead and in Heaven and wake up to Pete. That was beyond imagining, far beyond irony.

"Hullo," she said—or tried to say, but nothing came out. Ellen-Stephanie frowned, and licked dry lips with a dry tongue, and tried again.

"Hullo?"

This time she managed a croak, at least. That was enough. Pete's head jerked up in startlement; she dropped her needle and bounded to her feet, amid a great slither as all her sewing rustled to the floor in reckless abandon.

Having achieved that much, it seemed that she could achieve nothing more. She didn't speak, she didn't stir; she only stood there, staring.

"What are you doing?" Ellen-Stephanie asked, after a while. Sewing didn't seem likely to be high on Pete's list of pleasures. Any more than sitting with Ellen-Stephanie did, awake or otherwise.

"Old sheets," Pete said briefly. "Stitching sides to middle, and then hemming. There's a cupboardful, and I have to do them all. It's my punishment. And sitting with you, that too."

"I'm a punishment?" Ellen-Stephanie came close to a smile then. She could feel it twitching at the corners of her mouth, though it was a little too much effort actually to let it show.

"While everyone else does fun things, I mean. All my spare time, I have to be here. With you. Now that you're awake, I suppose that does mean you're my punishment too—oh! You're awake!"

"Well, I hope so," Ellen-Stephanie said. "I certainly wouldn't want to be *dreaming* you."

Pete paused just long enough to pull a face at her, then hurried on, "I mean, I'm supposed to dash and fetch Sister Anthony, the moment you wake up. And not talk to you first. She did kind of underline that bit. 'Don't sit there gossiping with your friend,' she said. So I'd better scoot. You know what she's like."

"I do. Go on, then. Thanks..."

For a moment they gazed at each other, in a kind of mutual bewilderment. Then Pete turned on her heel and scooted, as fast as the laws allowed: and if she clung closer to the law of gravity than the laws of the Crater School, she had the perfect excuse at hand. *Please, Sister Anthony told me to hurry...* That would get her out of any trouble she might dive headlong into, on her way.

Which left Ellen-Stephanie alone for this little while. It wasn't likely to last, so—as soon as she had recovered from the notion that Sister Anthony of all people considered that she and Pete might somehow be friends—she looked about her swiftly. And felt stupid, recognising at last that this was the school sanatorium, and nothing like Heaven at all. All that light was coming in from all those windows, with their long view out across the crater and the lake. Here all the walls and the curtains and the bedding were scrupulous white, nothing like the bright attractive colours in any of the various houses; no wonder she'd not known it at first. Apparently no one else was ill at the moment, either. All the beds but hers were stripped and empty, all the cubicle curtains thrown up over their rods while hers were merely pulled back to the wall.

That was as much as she could see, turning her head from side to side on the pillow. The next obvious step was to sit up—but she tried that, and her legs and arms were like dull dead weights with no interest in moving, while a shock of pain ran up and down her spine.

She subsided onto her pillows, with time enough to picture every moment of her appalling future before Sister Anthony came bustling in, with Pete awkwardly in her train.

"Please, Sister Anthony, am I—am I paralysed for life?"

She got that out on one breath, in one short burst, because otherwise she knew she'd never ask it. It was the worst possible question, the sort of question you never ask unless you're already dreading the only possible answer. She'd been raised to confront life's terrors, and so she did; and she half expected a blunt and affirmative response, half a non-committal "we'll see what the doctor says in the morning," not at all the derisive snort that actually greeted her bold front.

"Paralysed for life, forsooth! Child, whatever put that into your head? It's your wits that have been knocked astray, not your limbs."

"But I, I can't move..."

"Oh, and indeed you can. Haven't you turned your head since I came in here, even? You'll not be sitting up for a while, because you've bruised yourself every inch and wrenched your back into the bargain, but you've the Devil's own luck, young Ellie. You didn't even break a bone in that ridiculous plummet. I know you're too sore to move right now, and serve you right; but you'll be up and about soon enough. Not soon enough for you, I'm sure. Now open your mouth and put this under your tongue, while you give me your wrist."

Her temperature was taken, her pulse counted by Sister Anthony's cool, strong, reassuring fingers. Notes were made on the clipboard that hung at the end of her bed. Various questions were asked: was she dizzy? No. Did her head ache? Yes. Did this hurt? Ouch!

That last part of the interrogation, the actual literal torture, went on rather longer than Ellen-Stephanie might have wished. Apparently each separate one of her limbs and joints, every separate one of her vertebrae had been individually bruised or wrenched or both. And each separate one had to be poked, prodded, turned and twisted now, until she yelped each separate time.

Desperate to take her mind off this, she turned to Pete— Pete, of all people! but Pete was all she had—and saw her surreptitiously trying to draw up the fallen sheet that she'd been sewing, that she'd abandoned on the floor, and fold it neatly. Behind her back, yet, while her face was all virtue and concern, in case Sister Anthony should turn around.

Suddenly Ellen-Stephanie was frantically trying to concentrate on the pain instead, to stop herself bursting into laughter and giving Pete entirely away.

"Yes, well. Dr Penberthy said he didn't think you'd broken anything, and you've given me no cause to disagree. He'll want to check that head of yours again, now that you're awake; I'll send someone to find him straight away. Not you, Pete. The carol-concert rehearsal will be over any minute now, and you'll need to rejoin your class. I believe you have Scripture next, isn't that right? When you've put your work away—tidily, mind, so that you can find everything and start again without wasting time—you'd best go straight to Miss Warren's classroom and busy yourself with your books until she comes. That'll take you past Miss Leven's study; knock on the door and tell her—or Miss Bartlett, if she answers—that Ellen-Stephanie has roused. I know she wants to speak to you too, young lady. Not before the doctor sees you, and not until he says that she may: but she'll want to hear the news right away. You two have caused her a great deal of concern, with your ridiculous antics. This will be a great relief to her mind—though you shouldn't expect kinder treatment, Ellen-Stephanie, just because you've been hurt. She's equally angry with the pair of you, as Pete can bear witness. I'm sure you'll share her punishment hereafter. Now, I expect you could manage a light meal, so I'll just warm you up a little bread-and-milk. Hurry along, Pete—but do tidy yourself up before you go. You resemble an urchin more closely than a schoolgirl, after all that heedless dashing about..."

Left alone at last, if only for a minute, both girls pulled faces at each other.

"I hate bread-and-milk," said Ellen-Stephanie; and

"I hate Scripture," said Pete, both in the same breath.

They both checked, and giggled a little; but Ellen-Stephanie had heard something worse than either bread-and-milk or Scripture lessons, and the gloom settled broad across her shoulders.

"Oh, Pete—are you out of the carol concert too?"

Pete nodded emphatically. "We both are. Everything that's any fun at all. Miss Leven will tell you. And I'm sure she'll want me there too, so she can tell me all over again, just to watch me squirm. It's miserable. She says, she says they can't trust us unsupervised," and clearly she found that devastating, a terrible blow to her honour.

Ellen-Stephanie had never had much cause to worry about her honour, before she came here to the Crater

School. Bob Tucker had done her best to explain just how important it was, or ought to be, to any right-thinking Martian girl in general and to a Crater School girl in particular. She still wasn't sure that she wholly understood, but she was willing to allow that it was something her new companions held very dear, very close to their hearts, and that she should therefore respect it even when it didn't seem to make any sense. She and Pete must have broken any number of rules, sneaking out of the dormitory to challenge each other at something that was so very obviously not safe; of course the staff couldn't trust them any more. Ellen-Stephanie thought that was so obvious, it really didn't need saying. What on earth was Pete so upset about? You could break rules, or you could be trustworthy; she didn't see how you could manage both. Not getting caught didn't make you any more deserving of trust, only better at cheating your deserts, and hence if anything less trustworthy than people who messed up or didn't bother to try to hide what they were doing. Or of course those idiots who did something wicked and then immediately stepped forward to confess what they'd done. Ellen-Stephanie didn't see the point of that at all.

Still, Pete really was upset, and Ellen-Stephanie hadn't needed school to teach her when to be quiet. She and Pete couldn't stand each other, and even so: she didn't want to make the girl feel worse than she was already.

"We could learn the music anyway," she said carefully. "Not for the school, not for the concert, just for ourselves. The other girls would help us."

"What would be the point of that?" Pete didn't sound aggressive, so much as purely baffled. It seemed to be something they did to each other a lot.

"Didn't you think that some of those carols were beautiful?"

"Of course I did. Nobody could think anything else," Pete asserted, with all the certainty of fourteen. "But if we don't get to sing them, then—"

"But that's just the point. We absolutely would get to sing them. There might not be anyone else to hear them, but carols aren't performances, they're, they're something you do together, something you share. I don't need an audience. Do you?"

She didn't mean it as a challenge, still less an accusation; it was only a question. For a wonder, that seemed to be how Pete heard it, too.

"N-no... It would be fun, I think, the way people have talked about it, with all the parents and the San folk there. But I do see what you mean, Ellen-Stephanie. If we have to be hemming sheets while they sing, at least we can sing along with them. We'll probably be able to hear it, even up here..."

Just at that moment, what they heard was brisk foot-steps in the corridor, and then a snappish Sister Anthony, "Pete, did I not tell you to tidy yourself up? And to be about your business, rather than lurking here gossiping with your friend?"

"Yes. Sister Anthony. Sorry, Sister Anthony."

"Go into my office there and make yourself presentable. You will find a mirror and a comb convenient to hand. Then let me see you, and then be off. Meanwhile, Ellen-Stephanie, you are to eat this—and pull no faces, please—and then close your eyes and sleep if you can. That's the best cure for any headache. I'll wake you when Dr Penberthy comes. Pete, are you *still* standing there?"

"No, Sister Anthony. Honest, I'm not. See, here's me, all gone already..."

Take two girls who have both been more or less raised as boys—more in the one case and less in the other, as nobody except herself had really intended Pete to grow up quite so laddish, while quite the reverse was true of Ellen-Stephanie—and toss them into a deep pit of trouble at a school devoted to the raising up of fine Martian women, and on the one hand you will have two tough characters determined not to show any emotion, any weakness of any kind; while on the other hand you will find an expert—in Miss Leven, a past master of the art—at finding her way through a girl's most stubborn and intransigent facade to the tender soul beneath, to be sure that she entirely understands the magnitude of her own fault and the school's disappointment.

Had they been asked, or had they spoken about the possibility between themselves and before the event—which of course they did not, it would have been quite impossible—both Pete and Ellen-Stephanie would have been quite clear on one point, one common ground: that there was absolutely no chance, no possibility whatever of either one of them being reduced to tears at Miss Leven's interview. It simply couldn't happen. They might not be friends in any way, but they could recognise their own grit when it was reflected in another's steel.

It was not in fact Pete's first time through that particular mill, but even so: she had faith none the less, in herself and in her partner in crime. This time she was not, she was *not* going to cry. In front of Ellen-Stephanie? Unthinkable!

Ten minutes after they passed the fateful study door, both girls were sobbing in earnest. Miss Leven stopped talking then—for 'twas certain neither one was listening any more— and let them howl until the hiccups came; then she passed them both clean handkerchiefs from her drawer and told them briskly to mop up and pull themselves together.

"We're all pleased to see you up and about, Ellen-Stephanie, after that ridiculous escapade, but Sister Anthony says you're to do nothing but rest yet, for the next few days. No schoolwork, and certainly no physical exercise. Oh, don't look so alarmed!—you don't have to go back to bed. I do want you back up in the san, though. Go out and sit in the sun while it lasts, you're an uncomfortably pallid creature yet. Don't worry, Pete can come with you. She still has a mountain of sewing to do, I know—and so do you, of course. You may as well make a start, and we'll see what kind of needlewoman you are—*now* what's got into you, child? We were bound to discover sooner or later how poor your stitchery is. Pete can show you the minimum that Sister Anthony will accept, and you can undo and start again as often as you need to."

"Please, it's not that. But how can we sit in the sun, when—ooohhh..."

"Great heavens, girl, haven't you looked out of a window since you roused? Or have you just forgotten how to think? The storm passed over, while you were unconscious. Which is not to say that it won't flare up again, or that another may not follow in the tracks of the first; but for now at least we have clear skies and sunshine, and I mean to make the most of it, on everyone's behalf. Even two sinners condemned to a lifetime of stitching sheets. Off you go, now. Pete, you can stay with her until supper; you're excused preparation for today. And Ellen-Stephanie, if the close work gives you a headache at all, you're to stop immediately and tell Sister Anthony. And ask Pete to find her for you, I won't have you dashing about all over the school in search."

"**H**ow's your head now? Not too achey?"
They were sitting out in the air, on the battlemented gatehouse roof—was "battlemented" even a word?

She'd have to ask someone, if she remembered, when there was somebody to ask—with the sanatorium's high glass doors flung wide open at their backs and the lake and the view spread out before them. Once again, it was only Pete and herself; Fate seemed determined to toss the two of them together, even though they disliked each other so very much.

Fate could go jump in the lake, as far as Ellen-Stephanie was concerned. Especially right now, when the lake looked so strange. She'd been assured—by Pete, inevitably, so she believed it absolutely; sworn enemies don't lie to each other—that ordinarily the water was dark but clear, like a deep tawny glass, like every other crater lake that Ellen-Stephanie had seen. Pete said you could see the merlins coming when they rose.

Now, though? Now the lake looked like brickdust soup, thick and red and curdled. Properly, of course, it was curry paste soup she was thinking of, but no one called it that. Curry paste came in bricks, hard and dry and not heavy, easy to carry; it was sold in every general store out on the frontier, and you would find it in the pack of every shank's-pony prospector, in sacks in every pioneer wagon, in every camel-bag, on every claim. You could break off a chunk of it—who didn't have a hammer, out in the Dry? A dead man, that's who—and boil it in water and that was brickdust soup, spicy and hot, doubly warming. Mix it with real food and you had a real meal: which meant that everything ended up tasting of curry paste, whether you'd actually cooked with it or not.

One of the most startling things about this short time Ellen-Stephanie had been at the Crater School was the food. So far, nothing at all had tasted like curry paste. She'd had no idea that food could be so various, so interesting, so delicious.

Even here in the san, even Sister Anthony's dreaded bread-and-milk had been nothing like she'd ever tasted before. There was nutmeg in it, and sugar, and other spices she couldn't name that had lain on her tongue like a blessing. Every meal since had been the same, new tastes that excited and delighted her, as though the otherwise austere school matron believed that good food and swift healing should go hand in hand.

Perhaps they did. Certainly Ellen-Stephanie was feeling better, day by day. She'd be back in classes tomorrow, perhaps, if Doctor Ed allowed it. If she was well enough to be so harshly scolded, surely she was well enough for school? She'd be back up here every day in any case, whenever Lower Fourth was having games or gym or free time, anything fun: she and Pete both, to continue this relentless punishment under Sister Anthony's strict eye.

Right now, if she were honest, she did have something of a headache; but it wasn't too terribly bad, so she could legitimately say, "Only a bit, thanks," in response to Pete's question. And then, "It's this sewing that makes it ache, so many tiny stitches, white thread on white cotton, it's awful."

"Especially when you know that she'll make you rip half of it out and do it again," Pete agreed ruefully, surveying this afternoon's handiwork with a jaundiced eye. "*We* know these stitches are too tiny for human skin to feel, but that means nothing to Sister Anthony. She is *inhumanly* sensitive."

That thought reduced both of them instantly to a state of paralysing giggles, which ended only and abruptly when the object of their mirth strode out of the ward and stood gazing severely down at them from her lofty height.

"Do I need to remind you girls *again*—that you are not here for your amusement, neither for my own? Ellen-Stephanie, you look flushed. Let me feel your brow. ... Yes, well. I don't detect a fever, but you are certainly over-excited. I will fetch my own work out here, and while we sew I shall recite to you. Scriptural verses and meditations, such as sustained me throughout my long solitude. Quiet attentiveness will be a useful skill to practice, for both of you. Wait in silence now, until I return."

"I'm counting the moments," rebellious Pete muttered under her breath, as soon as Sister Anthony's back was turned. That almost reduced Ellen-Stephanie to tears of laughter once again; but she was too much in awe of the school matron to give way this time. Besides, Bob Tucker had stressed how important it was for a girl to respect authority; and no one, not even Miss Leven herself, could represent Authority more convincingly than Sister Anthony. Silence she had called for, and silence she should have, if Ellen-Stephanie burst for it.

She gazed out over the water, hoping for something to distract her mind—and saw it, in a slow bubble rising through the murk and bursting at the surface.

They had been placed on their honour, as Bob would say, not to talk while Sister Anthony was gone. Ellen-Stephanie reached out a leg to nudge Pete's foot; when she had the smaller girl's attention, she nodded briefly at the lake. Pete turned her head, just in time to see another bubble rise and break.

The water might be thick with dust, it might look airless and dead, but something was still living down below.

CHAPTER FIFTEEN

A Hare's Unexpected Encounters

"**B**ut why can't we join in? It sounds the most tremendous fun. I'm sure I'd catch you, Rowany. I can run like the wind, Miss Whitworth said so..."

"Can you, Lauren? That's excellent—though you probably shouldn't say so yourself, even if you did hear it from a staff. It sounds a little too close to boasting, and that's ungentlemanly. But the point is, could you run all the way around the lake? No? That's why you can't join in. It's not how fast you can run that matters in Hare and Hounds, but how far. And I won't be following the lake path, either; I'll set a really hard trail, uphill and downhill and everywhere except my lady's chamber. You Juniors don't need to feel singled out; the Middle School can't join in either, today's run is strictly for Seniors. I'll tell you what, though, I will talk to Miss Whitworth about setting a shorter course for the younger girls, one afternoon this week. And I'll volunteer to be the hare again, so we'll see if you really can catch me. Will you be happy with that?"

Lauren nodded ecstatically, while her friends grinned and nudged each other in excitement.

"Good. Now, back to your tearing, minions! I need a lot more scent than this."

It was the third day after the storm's end, the sky was clear and the sun was warm, and the school was devoting itself to outdoor pursuits of all kinds while this weather lasted. Miss Hendy was taking one class after another on long nature rambles; Miss Whitworth had all the school pitches in constant use, to the despair of Mr Marks the groundsman; even regular lessons were being held outside, in groves and gardens and shady corners, wherever the mistresses preferred.

Rowany had claimed and corralled half a dozen of her favourite Juniors, and now had them tearing used exam paper first into strips and then into squares, for her to scatter and the hounds to trace. In truth, this was really a cross-country run, rather than a genuine chase; with half an hour's head start over ground she knew so well, long-legged Rowany was entirely confident of getting home before even the swiftest of the Seniors could catch her. But calling it Hare and Hounds added zest to everyone's afternoon; it was always more fun to hunt—or to be hunted—than simply to slog over rock and turf with no goal except endurance to the end.

To placate the Juniors for being burdened with an onerous task for a game that couldn't include them, Rowany told them stories while they worked; to placate the mistresses from whose classes she had stolen them, the stories were tales of Martian history, of the first bold men to ride on the first aethership when they couldn't talk to the merlins and had no idea where they might be going or to what end. She spoke quietly, almost reverently, and a dozen fascinated ears strained for every word; these were their heroes and more, they were the first fathers of their world. Some girls here still carried those famous names, Illingworth and Carter and Berowne. Rowany had watched them through all her years at the Crater School, and seen something of the same spirit in each, as though a descendant of the First Ship pioneers was obliged to try a little harder, stretch a little further, be the very best they could achieve.

Rowany herself was a military brat through and through, raised to an idea of service; perhaps it was much the same thing, or at least had much the same result. Her father wasn't famous, exactly, though anyone who studied the records of the Great Triplanetary War must inevitably know about then-Major de Vere and the heroic retreat he led from Deimos to Phobos to Mars, bringing almost all his men home safe against insuperable odds. *Almost* insuperable odds, odds insuperable to anyone except a de Vere, to whom all things were superable...

Still: she too had always felt obliged to exceed, it was only that she didn't have the legendary name to mark her out from birth. Something to live up to. She'd had to make her own legend, here at the school; whether that could carry on into the worlds beyond, she wasn't certain. Even little Mars was very big, compared to the Crater School that had been her world entire for so long. And then there was Earth, unthinkably old and huge and complex; and Venus too, which was merely unthinkable.

She shook her head against darkling thoughts and hopes and dreams, and tried to force her attention back to the here and now.

Her narration had obviously faltered to a halt. One of the kids took advantage of that to ask one more of their inevitable questions. "Isn't this bag going to be impossibly heavy to carry, while you run?"

"It gets lighter as I go, you know." As opposed to most of life's burdens—but they didn't need to be told that, not yet. "Having said which, mind you, that is probably enough. Don't want to scatter too much scent and make it easy for the hounds."

"Oh. All right, then."

"If you're sure."

"We wouldn't want you to run out halfway."

Rowany laughed aloud. "What you mean is, you want me to go on telling you stories, and you'll bury me in paper if you have to, to keep me here. Is that right?"

Six heads nodded as one, quite unabashed.

"Please, Rowany?" Lauren wheedled. "You haven't even mentioned the Long Winter yet, or how the colony survived..."

This time, Rowany hid her smile. Everyone there knew that the leader most spoken of during that dreadful time was a woman, one Constancy Ipsun by name, and Lauren's direct ancestress. They all knew the story, and nevertheless: they all wanted to hear it again, as much as Rowany wanted to tell it.

"Well. 'Vast tearing, then, and sit up straight. It's more respectful to the memory of our forebears, and more sparing of your elbows. Some of you already need to change your blouse before the lunch bell rings. Yes, Elana, don't worry about it now; I promise I'll chase you off in time. Now, what you need to understand about the Long Winter and the famine that followed is that everyone knew it was coming, and there was absolutely nothing they could do but wait it out, and stay alive in any way they could. Sometimes that's what heroism means, just gritting your teeth and bearing terrible adversity, in hopes of a better life to come for your children or your community, if not for you. Constancy Ipsun may be the finest example I know..."

Lunch came and went. Rowany changed into the traditional Hare's summer running kit—stark white, to stand out against any landscape Mars could offer—and hefted the old worn canvas bag full of paper scent onto her shoulder. One third of the school—the elder third, that third which would shortly be chasing down her trail—had gathered in the courtyard to see her go. Precisely at the stroke of two, she trotted easily down the steps from the main door, gave everyone a cheerful wave and ran through the passageway to the gatehouse and the drawbridge beyond, over the moat and down through the Mistresses' Garden to the lake path. Tradition all the way: Hare and Hounds always started this way.

This time, though, and totally against tradition, there were staff posted left and right, on watch for any unusual activity from the merlins in the water. That ought to be unnecessary—there was nothing they could do, after all, but usher the girls back into safety, and any Crater School Senior should be self-ushering in that respect—but Rowany could understand the impulse. Nevertheless, she was so busy thinking about that, wondering if she should be perhaps a little insulted, she almost forgot to scent her way, to show that she'd chosen the right-hand, anticlockwise route around the lake. Among Hare and Hounds aficionados, it was held to be the tougher course; the school would expect that of her, and she could expect nothing less of herself. Besides, they'd been pent up withindoors so long, they all needed a hard run, hunters and prey together.

She didn't honestly feel much like prey. It was her task to lead the hounds a merry dance, and leave them gasping at the end: a task she relished, like a nymph tempting mortals from the path, purely for the game of it. She might have lost a little condition in these last weeks, but the same was true of her pursuers. She didn't expect that even Melanie could catch her. Certainly she had no intention of allowing it, so long as there was breath in her body and power in her legs.

She stretched those long legs out in a steady lope, and briefly considered climbing up the cliff-face to Sister Anthony's Step and the high path to the ridge. That might be deemed unfair, though, or even unsafe; even at the Crater

School, not every girl was a climber. So she turned along the narrow path at the edge of school property, which led around the playing fields and onto the open slopes outside the crater wall. She'd double back up to the ridge later and give the hounds some rocky scrambles; there were a few out-crops she knew that would call for hands and feet together to surmount. That would do.

It felt so good, so very good to be running free at last: the spring in her legs and the breeze in her face, the weight of her ponytail swinging at her back. She loved to read and listen, she loved to question and challenge, she loved to think and learn and stretch her mind—but sometimes, often, she did just yearn to be moving.

Moving fast now, for the sheer pleasure of it, she plunged through the gap in the hedge that divided school property from the heath beyond—Ball's Gap it had been named since time immemorial, for reasons that no one could ever remember—leaving a scatter of scent behind her for the principle of the thing, even though everyone would know that she was sure to head out this way. A good hare always got away from school at the earliest opportunity; a wild run around the crater was the point, up hill and down dale, leaving a trail that was fair but foxy, to have the hounds casting about for scent but never entirely bewildered. It was reckoned a disgrace to the hare if the hounds lost her trail altogether. On one famous occasion, the entire pack had pointedly turned around and come back to school, so that when the hare came pounding in an hour later she found all those who should have been chasing her waiting instead in the courtyard, a silent condemnation of what should have been her triumph.

With that in mind—and perhaps the present, the ever-present weight of the satchel on her shoulder—Row-any left a conscientious trail of scent all the way up the slope as she headed towards her first landmark, an abrupt outcropping of rock that everyone called the Drowsy Lion, partly from its weathered shape and partly because it was such a good place to lie and doze after Sunday lunch, when quiet was mandatory and the sun seductive.

Up and up, and here was the warm rock-face at last. She tossed a handful of scent upward, to scatter over the cracks and ledges, hopefully to fool at least a few girls into thinking they had to climb it; then she doubled around to the shady side, where—

—Where she startled herself almost as much as the couple she interrupted, where they sat perched on what should have been the privacy of the Lion's hind-quarters, holding hands. Rowany wasn't entirely sure, but she was almost certain, almost mortifyingly certain that she had caught them kissing.

What was worse, if anything could conceivably be worse, was that she knew them both. Of course she did; she knew everyone on the crater. But these two weren't just crater folk, some random shepherd-boy and his lass. They were closely allied to the Crater School, as well as apparently to each other.

"Dr Ed! Miss Calomy! I—I'm so terribly sorry, I didn't—"

The two grown-ups seemed just as flustered, just as embarrassed as herself. If anything, poor Miss Calomy had blushed even redder, though Rowany could feel the fire in her own cheeks.

"Hullo, Rowany." Young Dr Penberthy could at least find his tongue, though otherwise he didn't seem quite to know what to do with himself. He came awkwardly to his feet, fussed a moment with his hands, then turned to help Miss Calomy down from her perch. She thanked him with a dis-tracted smile, glanced back to Rowany, could find no words at all.

Dr Penberthy made an uncomfortable gesture towards her satchel. "Paper chase, is it, Rowany?"

"Hare and Hounds, sir, yes."

"Ah. It was Fox and Hounds at Shrewsbury—and the hounds had license to do whatever they wanted to the fox, if they could catch him. I don't suppose you girls are quite that bloodthirsty, but perhaps you should get a move on, eh? Just in case?"

"Um, yes. Of course. Thank you, Doctor. Um, 'bye, then..."

And she could turn and sprint away, almost forgetting to scent her trail in her relief, barely remembering not to push too hard too early, not to exhaust herself before first sight of home.

It took her a while to find her rhythm again, to settle back into the easy stride that eats miles, that she could keep up half the day if she needed to. By the time she did, she could hear a distant tolling behind her, the school bell's warning that the hounds had been released. It was meant to help the hare, but all too often it made anxious girls speed up; once again Rowany had to stifle the urge to stretch out. *Swift but steady wins the race*—that was the rubric she'd been raised with, and it was never more true than now.

Swiftly and steadily, then, she ran on, allowing herself not so much as a glance back to see when the Upper School would come pouring through the hedge. Not for a few minutes yet, at any rate, and she was likely out of sight already, though she was absolutely not going to look back to check. A good hare kept her eyes forward and her mind on her task, worrying nothing about the chase.

Nevertheless, she couldn't help but keep her ears open for the *view-halloo!* at her back, long before she could ever actually expect it, if indeed it ever came. More than once she'd been chased home when she was younger, abandoning the scent bag and sprinting for safety with the hounds hot on her heels. She had always made it home, if only just; and she truly didn't believe she was in any danger now, inches taller and years wiser as she was, as wily a hare as ever ran this ground; and nevertheless.

On and on: upslope and down, over this crag and around that; now trotting up to the Devil's Teeth themselves, those great skewed rocks that lined the rim, and now plunging almost to the valley bottom; always keeping the crater's height on her left hand and running widdershins around it, a path that however winding and obscure must eventually and inevitably bring her home.

Here now was the rising coach road, a smooth and easy run that no girl would ever deign to use except right here, where it opened into the broad courtyard of the great Sanatorium where Dr Ed worked—but she wasn't going to think about Dr Ed—and so many like him, confronting all the worst of the many diseases that Mars flung at its new colonists. Sometimes she wondered if the planet hated this occupation, and wanted them all gone.

One simpler thing was certain, though: that Crater School girls were always welcome at the San. The reverse was also true, that San staff were always welcome at the school—but that also led back to thoughts of Dr Ed and Miss Calomy, which she was not going to entertain. She hated to hear gossip in the corridors, and would stamp on it every time. Even more she hated to hear it in her own head, and know there was nothing she could do to wipe it from her memories.

Still: here she was, and here—the San—could be a major distraction. She jogged slowly between the two wide wings, scattering a little honest scent here and there and waving wildly at everyone she saw, patients or staff, whether she knew them or not. In honesty, the scent was probably not necessary. Every hare came here as a matter of course, as a matter of honour. If you were laid up in San, whether you had the marthambles or the Red Dot or worse, any distraction was welcome. Girls from the school came over as often as ever they were allowed to; for seniors and prefects, that could mean almost every week. For the hare in Hare and Hounds, it meant every run, without fail. Patients would wave from their balconies; doctors and nurses come out to cheer her on from the steps. Rowany had often thought that if a hound wanted to cheat, the trick would be to run directly to the San, ignoring any scent-trails wherever they led. She might not beat the hare, but she'd be ahead of anyone else and in prime position to pick up the hare's trail.

Happily, the Crater School had never spawned anyone inclined to cheat that way. Which was probably just as well, because the repercussions would be appalling as soon as the story broke, which it inevitably would. Someone would see, someone would know. No one would tell a staff, of course, or—worse!—a prefect; but she'd tell her own cohort, they would pass it on in their turn, and the news would sweep the school. It didn't bear thinking about: everyone looking at you, everyone knowing what you'd done. A few idiots might admire you for it—that kind of lazy cleverness always has its fans, and its allure—but you'd be in disgrace with anyone who troubled to think it through. The school as a whole admired honest effort almost more than achievement, and generally had no time for slackers. Slackers who tried to win applause by fraud—ugh! That would not sit well.

Fraud was an uncomfortable word for Rowany just now, though, so she decided not to think about that any longer. She would put it firmly aside, along with Miss Calomy and Dr Ed.

Coming through to the San's long frontage, she found the two great eminences of Lowell Crater standing in quiet conversation on the forecourt, overlooking the calm, eerily dust-stained waters of the lake. As she hesitated, they turned to smile at her in greeting, so she trotted over.

"Miss Tolchard! Uh, I mean, Mrs Mackenzie," as her husband was standing right beside her and glowering momentously, as he loved to do whenever a Crater School girl made that inevitable slip. "And Dr Mac!" Reading their faces she went on, a little anxiously, "This isn't a coincidence, is it?"

"More like an ambush," Mrs Mackenzie confirmed.

"The Upper School telephoned, and asked us to delay you by any means necessary," said the great doctor, who had played host to her that week before term began.

"Oh, do be quiet, Mac!" scolded his wife. "Rowany, we won't hold you up; I do understand how important school games are, even if certain dimmer folk never did catch on," with a laughing glance sideways at her man, who had both rowed and played stand-off half for school and college before coming back to Mars: *home from Home*, as people liked to say.

"What can I do for you, Mrs Mackenzie?" She still wasn't going to look behind her, despite this sudden halt; she wasn't even going to listen for sounds of pursuit, no. She was going to attend to the school's onlie begetter. Miss Tolchard was owed that much, and more. Much more, in point of fact, but it was the kind of debt one never really got to repay.

"Yes, well. A ... situation has arisen, that may well lie within your interests. We'll talk more about it later, once it's had time to settle in your mind, but in brief: a Martian woman studying at Cambridge formed, let's say an unwise alliance with a military attaché from the Russian embassy. They married, and there was a daughter; and when he was recalled to Moscow, she and the girl went too.

"The whole affair was most unsatisfactory, and handled very poorly by the family and the authorities combined, in my belief. At least she had the sense to keep their citizenships, and the child was raised in a clear understanding of her dual nationality. Her mother made sure that she kept up her English—"

"—Or else her father did," Dr Mackenzie put in flatly. "Here's the thing, Rowany. The marriage collapsed in the end, as it was bound to do. I understand that she felt her daughter was being weaned away from her by Tsarist interests; certainly the girl was exposed to Russian propaganda all day at school, and at home from her father too. At length her mother brought her back to England, ostensibly to visit family, at a time when her father couldn't accompany them; and once there, of course, she simply refused to return to Moscow. A divorce was arranged swiftly, with the help of officials at Whitehall, and that might have been that."

"That should have been that," Mrs Mackenzie said, picking up the narrative again, "except that ever since she came to England, the mother has been agitating to bring her child to Mars. Authority would never allow it—and rightly so, in my opinion: you know how careful we have to be here, and Lord knows the girl has no reason to love us; indeed, she knows nothing of us—but at length the mother went over Authority's head. Somehow she got a letter through to the Regent. That man has always had a tender heart, and of course a fondness for Mars since his own service here as a young officer in the Double Reds. He ordered them to let her through, and her daughter with her."

"And so they're here now," the doctor again, "under some very careful restrictions. The mother has to live with relatives in Marsport; she's been found a job where she could do no harm if she wanted to, and she's being kept under discreet observation. In my opinion, though, they're watching the wrong one. It's the girl who has uncertain loyalties, very much her father's daughter as I understand it. She may have been reluctant to leave Russia, reluctant to come here; or she may have been instructed to seem reluctant."

"Either way, she's here now." Were they playing a deliberate kind of verbal tennis, to keep her off-balance? Rowany didn't really think so; rather they were trying to support each other, in something they both found difficult to discuss. "And of course her mother wants her in a good school, and the day-schools nearby are hopeless; so it's been suggested that she might come to us."

"Was her mother here?"

"A Craterean? Oh dear, no. I like to think that none of our girls would behave so ... injudiciously, let's say. No, this is coming from Authority. The girl seems eager, from all that we've been told; I gather she's finding the confines of her family's flat—well, confining. And cramped, of course, there are far too many of them squeezed into far too little. On the face of it, I think we should take her. She's sixteen now, so it would only be for a couple of years, and after first Moscow and then Marsport it would do her the world of good to stretch her legs and her wings too, find out just what kind of creature she actually is."

"That's just the question, though. What kind of creature is she? A couple of years here would stand her in very good stead for a place at the university in New Victoria; and then she's settled here, she's apparently one of us, with every opportunity to make her way into government circles. I don't want to be melodramatic, but the Russians have had years to win her heart, if they didn't have it already by virtue of her father's influence."

"We could be nurturing a viper in our bosoms, you mean?" Rowany was trying to lighten the tone, at least a little, but the effort fell very flat.

"Yes, I mean exactly that," Dr Mackenzie confirmed. "You may think she's too young to be any kind of a spy—but the young can be deeply passionate, and deeply attached. If she thinks of Russia as home, and this as an alien land where she's separated from everything and everyone she knows and loves, then she could be fertile ground for the Tsar's agents in the Okhrana. She might hardly know that she was helping them: just a meeting in a tea-shop every now and then, a few insidious questions, a little deeper every time. Or, as I say, she may already be under direct orders. She might do anything to protect her father, for example. I don't say that he's under threat—to all appearances, he's the perfect Imperial servant, a loyal patriotic soldier through and through—but even so. Older wiser heads than hers have been deceived, and the Okhrana are masters of the art."

He seemed to speak with a particular passion, and Rowany wondered how he knew, what history was there; but more even than that, she had another question, and one that she could actually decently ask. "I see, I think. But I'm not clear how this involves me?"

"We've said that we'll take her for the rest of this term," Mrs Mackenzie told her, "on approval, as it were. What we'd like you to do is stand by her, watch over her, make an effort to learn who she is."

"Lawks," said Rowany.

Mrs Mackenzie's lips twitched, at this sudden unexpected reminder of the fourteen-year-old Rowany and her occasionally disreputable friendships. Had she picked that up from the boy-of-all-work, or from squaddie devotees in the hols? Well, never mind. She went on determinedly: "You're a little old for sherpa duty, and it wouldn't really be feasible in any case; but she's coming into your house—your current house, I should say; I know your heart belongs to Stokes, wherever you may presently reside—and she's older than our normal intake too, so it won't seem particularly strange to her. I'm not asking you to spy on her, mind," though to Rowany's mind she very clearly was. "Just spend time with her, get to know her, see if she seems honest to you. We'd trust your instincts on this, Rowany, above anyone else in the school. Which includes ourselves, as a matter of fact."

"It won't go unnoticed, if you do this," Dr Mackenzie put in. "It's an opportunity for you too; it'll look very well on your curriculum vitae, when you come to move on. That was, ah, pointed out to me, in no uncertain terms, by one in a position to know."

"Oh, was it? And how is the old codger?" If there was one thing Rowany was deeply familiar with, it was offhand or indirect references to her beloved father.

Dr Mackenzie spluttered into the pipe he had not yet got around to lighting. Mrs Mackenzie said only, "We'll talk it over more this evening, Rowany. We want you and Miss Leven to come to dinner with us. I expect Dr Penberthy will pick you up; it's his day off, and he never seems to mind an excuse to drive over to the school."

"Um, actually I think he might be there already," Rowany muttered, her mind tripping back to the Drowsy Lion unwillingly once more.

"Indeed? Well, so much the better." Not by the flicker of an eyelash did Dr Mackenzie give away whatever he might be thinking. "I'll telephone Miss Leven, then, and ask her to detain him. Meanwhile, should you not be sprinting away for all you're worth? Those hounds can't be far behind you."

"Oh, lor'! I, um, I'll see you tonight, then, Dr Mac, Miss Tolchard, I mean Mrs Mac..."

In the midst of that desperate scramble of words she was abruptly gone, and never knew that she left two previously sombre adults laughing behind her.

She needed to cover ground quickly now, so she kept to the lake path, dropping scent only at those points where she might have turned up a goat-track to the ridge again. If she occasionally scattered as many paper scraps on that track as on the path she actually followed—well, it wasn't exactly cheating. Running some way up the track to drop scent before doubling back would be unfair, but there was nothing wrong with being occasionally misleading. Nor with hoping to mislead. And they knew she was sneaky; with any luck at least some of the hounds would think she was trying to mislead them the other way. When did Rowany ever take the simple, level course? Of *course* she'd lead them back up into the crags as soon as possible...

Instead, she kept to the lake path for another half-mile, only hoping that no one was close enough behind that they'd actually catch sight of her. Her feet wanted to fly, but her mind kept straying back to that conversation and everything it implied for her future; and she'd realise at last that her pace had dropped almost to a dawdle, and she'd press on again, and her thoughts would drift, and...

But here at last was the little lakeside Catholic chapel, which served the country folk as well as some patients and staff from the Sanatorium, some pupils and staff from the school. Rowany herself was fond of the pull across the lake of a Sunday morning, and then a service that she felt was almost within reach of her understanding, only to find it slither away at the last. She knew what all the Latin meant, and even so: there was something inherently numinous in the ancient words, that Cranmer couldn't rival nor the human mind entirely encompass.

Just now, though, her thoughts were not on the simple whitewashed building nor the complex mysticism it bespoke. Here was one more gap between the Devil's Teeth, a chance to run swiftly through to the outer slopes of the crater again, with endless opportunities ahead to evade her pursuers. She tossed a dutiful trail of scent and drove her legs deter- minedly through the gap, her mind on her task once again—

Only to be hauled up short once again by a sudden unexpected person doing something she could barely fathom, never mind explain. Against all her better instincts, almost against her intent, her legs stammered to a stop once more.

"Mrs Buchanan? What are you—no, I'm sorry, that's rude..."

"But you still want to ask it anyway, am I right? What on Earth—I'm sorry, what on Mars—am I doing? Well, as you see: I'm chalking lines on this boulder. Asking it questions, trying to learn what it is inside. What it has to tell me. I'm probably wasting my time, though. Do you suppose there's any way that we might get it back to the school? Intact?"

The question took Rowany aback, all too literally: one abrupt pace to the rear. Then she forgot everything else and stood arms akimbo, surveying the rock. It wasn't really so very large, all things considered. And it was appealingly round, and the right side of the crater wall...

"Actually, I think there is," she said at last. "A couple of husky chaps with poles could dig it out and roll it down the slope to the coach road; and then Mr Jenkins from the funicular station would be happpy to oblige, I'm sure, with his steam-wagon. He drives that thing the length of the road every day anyway, making deliveries to the San and the village down below. And he's always willing to help out the school, for an extra shilling or two. But—I'm sorry, I do have to ask after all. Why this rock? There are so many rocks, so very much closer to the school..."

"This one speaks to me, in ways that others don't. And I owe the school somewhat, for giving me shelter through the storm; and I owe the girls rather more, for making them sit through my lectures about sculpture. I think they ought at least to have the chance of seeing me put my words into action; and I know just the place, down in that glade with all the other work."

"Are you, are you saying what I think you're saying? That we could have an actual Isobel Buchanan in our Sculpture Garden?"

"Well, you've had an actual Isobel Buchanan in situ for weeks now—but I do know what you mean, and yes. I'd like to make something as a gift for the school, and I'd like the children to see me make it. Do you suppose we could make that happen?"

"Mrs Buchanan, believe me: there is absolutely no doubt that we can make that happen. I will see to it myself. I do know just who to speak to." Of course she did. She'd been called Head Girl of Lowell Crater for years now, and even though she was no longer Head Girl of the Crater School, that older broader title still held true. Her life had been here—for holidays didn't count at all—since she was eleven years old. Seven wondrous years, and now this golden bonus time, when she could pay back at least a little of what she owed the school. She knew everyone hereabouts—and she knew whom to tease, whom to pay, whom to wheedle. She knew herself locally adored, and lived with that like any other fact; and tried not to exploit it too badly, and worried about it not at all, when it clearly made her idolaters so happy.

"Thank you so much, Rowany. What a blessing that you came along when you did." Only now did the renowned artist drag her attention away from the boulder, sufficient to look Rowany up and down and say, "But why did you, what are you up to? You look very hot."

"Oh, heavens!" Startled once again back into her proper role, Rowany glanced feverishly over her shoulder, saw no one coming through the gap and drew no comfort from that, none at all. "Sorry, Mrs B! Hare and Hounds—paper chase, you know—I have to run, or they'll be on me..."

A nd run she did, no time to be wily now: it was all about distance and focus, head high, legs pounding, her breath coming hard and fast. She seemed to hear Miss Whitworth's voice in her ear, "Concentrate on form, Rowany! Keep those arms working! Never mind what's happening behind you, don't even think to look. Everything that matters lies ahead. Stretch out now..."

She stretched out, she drove herself as only she could do, the whip of her own will stronger than any coach's words; and there was the Castle at last, in its broad declivity where the Devil must have had several of his teeth plucked out.

Now she could relax, now she could let all that speed slip away from her as she idled to a trot, as she hauled in great draughts of air, as she thought longingly of a cool bath and fresh clothes and a comfortable chair. A banana, a mug of cocoa and a book.

She had to run one last lap of the Castle, tradition demanded that, before she could go through the gate into the courtyard and declare herself the victor once again, the hare who always made it home. Not a problem, and she still wasn't even going to favour the hounds with a glance behind. No matter if they were in sight, even, they couldn't catch her now.

She came jogging up the road towards the drawbridge, turned right to go widdershins once more along the path that ran all around the great red structure, hearing a muted cheer already from the central courtyard, where the Junior girls who would have gathered to hail her home in her triumph must just have glimpsed her through the passage-way—

—And was brought to an abrupt halt one more time, by something else she could hear.

Something clear and present and unmediated, striking, beautiful.

Two voices, lifted in rare harmony: soprano and contralto, picking their way carefully through a tune still new to both. It was still new to Rowany too, one of those unusual carols Miss Llewellyn had brought back to the school from her European tour. Two girls, quite invisible: they must be up on the gatehouse roof and singing to the sky. Singing for the pleasure of it, and nothing more. Because she could certainly put a name to one, Rowany was confident of the other too, and was privately delighted that they were rebelling this privately against the diktat that kept them from the carol concert.

She stood quite still, listening, enraptured—until she felt a hot sticky arm come around her neck, and heard a hoarse gasping voice in her ear, "Miss Hare, you are thoroughly jugged," and startled around to find the sweaty, laughing, victorious face of her oldest and closest friend, Melanie Fitzwalter, new Head of School and—of course!—leader of the hound-pack.

CHAPTER SIXTEEN

A New Leaf

Melanie Fitzwalter came to a meditative pause between one long athletic stride and the next, almost without realising that she had done so. She'd always been a girl of action rather than deep thought, and what lay in her immediate future—about thirty seconds ahead, if she was any judge of the carrying-power of giggles down corridors— required no thought at all at this stage. Still, thirty seconds was thirty seconds, and she did hate to waste time, especially at school, where there seemed so precious little of it available; and this particular corridor was lined with photographs, generations of former pupils drawn up in rank and file.

Another girl's eye might have been caught by the uniforms of the early years, so much less chic than today's; but Melanie had never cared much for clothes, so long as she looked smart and kempt. An earlier edition of Melanie—actually any edition previous to this term's, this very version—would have looked for the sports teams on the opposite wall, and pictured herself among them, because the game had never yet been invented that Melanie could not play or did not want to try.

Today, though, with time to fill and images of yesteryear before her, Melanie's gaze strayed across the faces of staff, familiar and unknown, and fell upon the girl seated at the right hand of Miss Tolchard her very self, revered founder and first headmistress of this great institution. That was the Head Girl's position as by right—and this year, later this term, when the photographer came and all the chairs were lined up in front of the Castle steps, it would be Melanie herself who occupied that position, although Miss Leven would take the seat beside her.

Melanie Fitzwalter, Head Girl. She could see the faintest possible reflection of her head in the glass of the frame, and there on her beret was the badge to confirm it, and even so. Inside every Senior, it was said, was a shy Junior and a wicked Middle, both wondering what on Mars had happened. The same was true in spades, she was learning, inside a Head Girl. She felt a complete impostor, and only wanted to hand that badge back where it rightfully belonged, to her best friend Rowany, of course. Who hadn't even had the decency to go away and leave her to it; she lurked at Melanie's shoulder like an *eminence grise*, a ghost at the feast, a beloved and ridiculously helpful uninvited guest.

Besides which, had any Head Girl in all the history of the Crater School had to deal with such an extraordinary term? Six years a pupil had taught her that every term was extraordinary, and nevertheless: a dust storm, a runaway—complete with camel!—and Rowany turning up like a bad penny and talking the most ridiculous evasive tosh about somehow being sent back to school and having to resit Oxford Entrance next year, which couldn't conceivably be true. That girl would have walked into any college fit to take her, sight unseen. And she seemed more excited than upset by the delay, even with the cost to her reputation in the school. And she really didn't want to talk about it, but that was nothing to do with embarrassment or failure. No, the truth was that

Rowany hated to tell lies, especially to her oldest and closest friends, but something in this situation obliged her to do it. And given all the possibilities that a trained and strategic mind could dream up to justify such a scenario—well, Melanie would neither jump down her friend's throat nor try to ferret out her secrets. If she was remotely close to being right, the best way to help Rowany was to accept what she said at face value, cross her fingers tightly and hope, nay, *yearn* for the best.

In the meantime, here she was, Head Girl in the midst of sudden duty. What she'd been listening to all this little while resolved itself into four very grubby Juniors crossing the head of the corridor, walking almost on tiptoe as they hauled along a burden almost too big and awkward for them all, so anxious not to drop it in its bundled blanket they actually forgot to glance this way in case of trouble looming. Melanie stood entirely still, not to catch the corner of anyone's eye until they were almost across the junction, almost out of sight and away; then,

"Yes, well," she said crisply. "What exactly do you have there, may I know?"

The four girls startled comically, twisted around to find her, and froze abruptly with their hidden load sagging bulkily in its blanket.

"Well?" she snapped, Head Girl to the very core, no doubts now.

"P-please, Melanie, it's for art. For Miss Calomy."

"No doubt. Many an article of contraband has been smuggled in under the name of art. And I didn't ask who it was for, Lauren, I asked what it was. Answer the question, please."

"It, it was meant for a secret. For a surprise…"

"…And not at all for me, Janna? No, I quite see that. Nevertheless. Here I am. And I'm still waiting."

Was she being too hard on them? They were young, they were new this term, they'd barely been here long enough to learn what trouble meant; and here they were, caught doing something that they clearly shouldn't. Caught by the fearsome Head Girl, no less. More than one of them looked close to tears.

Also, more than one looked close to dropping her corner of the blanket, which would no doubt spill whatever-it-was all over Mr Felton's polished floors. At that point, the trouble would become very much worse, with very little that Melanie could do to mitigate it.

In a softer tone, she said, "All right, let's try this another way. Set that thing down—carefully, mind!—and tell me what you're up to. Elana, what did Miss Calomy set you to do?"

"Please,"—and oh, why did little girls in trouble always start that way? Melanie had done it herself, she knew, many and many a time, and it never helped at all—"we were talking about the carol concert, and she said we were to help her come up with ideas for the staging. She told us we should use nature as our inspiration, because she needed a, a, a..."

"A bosky glade," the last little imp put in, when Elana faltered.

"That's right! Only I didn't know the word, so it was hard to remember."

"Well, I only know it because of Papa's beard."

"Yes, all right, Maeve. Thank you." Melanie was mildly anxious that she might explode, either with unseemly giggles or else with unsatisfied curiosity, because of *course* she couldn't conceivably ask about Papa's beard. Still: she sucked air in through her nostrils, breathed it out slowly, decided that she was in control after all, and said, "Go on. You were to think of a bosky glade."

"Yes, so of course we went down to the sculpture garden, because that's the, the boskiest place we know."

Except for Maeve's father's beard, Melanie thought, on the very edge of losing all her hard-won ground in one wild moment of hilarity. She couldn't speak; she nodded briskly, and hoped the infants would take that as encouragement to carry on. Meanwhile, *breathe: in through the nose, out through the mouth. And again. Perfect calm, perfect stillness,* and never mind what it looked like to these poor scared children, seeing her nostrils flare like a dragon's while she glowered at them unmoving, unspeaking...

"So then," Lauren went on uncertainly, picking up the trailing edge of the story, "we saw how all the trees from England had dropped their leaves after the dust storm..."

"Miss Henty says they'll be all right," Maeve said earnestly, "and you can see, they're already starting to bud again, some of them..."

"...So we thought there's nothing more bosky than leaves," Lauren went on, annoyed at the interruption, "and we remembered that Miss Calomy has those screens in her storeroom, which would just be perfect because they're only that fine lawn muslin and if we had lights behind them and pinned leaves all over them then the light on the stage would be all dappled, just like it should be in a glade—so we thought we'd just do that, it's such a good idea, and present her with a, a fat accomplice, all the work done for her..."

The fat accomplice was nearly too much for Melanie, despite all her rigorous breathing. Nearly. Happily, just in that moment she saw a spider wriggle free of the bundled blanket and lower itself indignantly to the floor. She had better sense than to point it out, but the blessed creature did give her a cue.

"So you gathered up all those leaves," she said, with as straight a face as she could manage, "although as far as I recall most of them had already been reduced to skeletons by the dust on the wind—and now I understand the state of you, your gymmers and your persons, Elana, your *hair...!*— and you never stopped to think that you wouldn't just be importing leaves into the school, but all the bugs and beetles and creepy-crawlies that naturally found shelter in those leaves...?"

At least one had already found shelter in Elana's hair, but she wasn't going to mention that either. Just the general warning was enough: these girls might have blithely borne it all inside without a second thought—heavens, without a first thought, as far as she could tell—but now they were backing warily away from their abandoned bundle. Any moment, one of them was going to spot the spider, and then any hope of keeping charge of the situation would just be straws in the wind. Dry leaves in the fire...

"Oh no you don't," she said swiftly. "You brought that in; you can take it out again. Carry it straight down to the vegetable garden; I know Mr Felton has a bonfire there today. Burn everything—what's that? No, Janna, not the blanket, obviously; beat that clean and take it back to the stables. Then scurry off to your houses and get yourselves cleaned up; you'll want to be looking smart for when you have to apologise to the duty mistress for being late to lunch." Then, relenting at the woe on their little faces, "After lunch, come and find me in the Prefects' Room. If you add us all up, all we prefects, we must have put in fifty years or more at this school, with needlework lessons every week of that time. I know we all have bags stuffed with oddments. You can cut out all the leaves you like, in all sorts of different shapes and fabrics, and sew those onto Miss Calomy's screens. *After* you've asked her permission first, of course. All right?"

"Oh yes, Melanie. Yes. Thank you so much..."

"Go on, then. Scat. If you're really quick, you might make it back in time for lunch after all. Just don't come in smelling of smoke. Or singed. Check with Mr Felton before you touch the fire. Run!"

First you wither them, for the good of their little souls; then you give them a penance to help them remember, hopefully even to make them *think* before they act next time; then you hand them a sweetie to take the sting away and chase them off. It was a technique she'd learned—of course!—from Rowany; she had a deep suspicion that she should have learned it when Rowany did, when the same justice-with-mercy was being handed down to them by the goddesses who had led the school in years gone by. Even while she was being castigated, Melanie knew, Rowany had been taking notes internally, identifying patterns, absorbing lessons.

Melanie had just never had that kind of brain. Truth to tell, she wasn't sure anyone but Rowany had Rowany's kind of brain; that girl was *sui generis*.

She wondered mildly what Rowany would have done differently—but of course, there was no point in trying to imagine. By definition, her own brain could never go where Rowany's would lead her. It was better, she had found, to set-tle for being Melanie and following along in her best friend's wake. No telling where you might end up, but there was safe to be an adventure along the way.

Rowany was adventuring alone this day, gone down to Terminus to meet a new girl off the Marsport train and see her safely up to school. That was odd in itself, just one more oddity in this strangest of terms. The school was always reluctant to admit girls mid-term, when any new pupil must be inherently disruptive; the rule was that they should always arrive with a parent or guardian, but this one appeared to be travelling alone; on the rare, the very rare occasions that Melanie had known such a thing before, a member of staff had always gone down to collect them. Rowany was making such a point of *not* being staff in any way, it seemed beyond strange that she should take this on. Or that Miss Leven should have asked her to.

Of course one couldn't exactly interrogate one's headmistress, even when one's best friend was being so remarkably unforthcoming—but blunt and practical Melanie was fighting an urge to do exactly that, in her incurable state of itchiness. She felt like a Middle again, consumed by curiosity, desperate to learn just exactly what was going on.

Rowany, meanwhile, was standing on the platform at Terminus watching a coil of approaching smoke curl redly up above a not-yet-visible locomotive, and feeling oddly reluctant to see the train arrive. She wasn't ordinarily daunted by the tasks life flung in her direction; indeed, she was more inclined to snatch at them two-handed and wrestle them gleefully into submission. And this, after all, was what she had signed up for—and nevertheless. There was something uncomfortable in being set to spy on a schoolgirl, on her own old stamping-ground yet, in her beloved Crater School.

And nevertheless. Here she was, and here came the train, rushing forward unfairly fast, it seemed to her; and here it was at the platform: doors flying open all up and down the carriages, passengers stepping down, porters mobbing the baggage wagon and loading up their trolleys—and in the midst of all that noise and bustle, one slender solitary girl standing stock still, like a rabbit in the glare of a naphtha lamp.

In that moment, Rowany forgot her misgivings about her own task and all the official doubts that had set her to it. All she saw was a Crater School girl in need: immaculate in her brand-new uniform, both hands clutched tight to the handle of an equally new satchel, seemingly too scared to move either this way or that.

Taking charge was second nature. A brisk whistle summoned a porter—an old friend, as it happened: but then who in this valley was unknown to Rowany, and who that she knew could count as anything other than a friend?—and six quick strides brought her to the girl's side.

"Hullo. I think you must be Ekaterina, is that right?"

The girl's eyes opened wide, for Rowany had greeted her in careful, practised Russian; but she replied in softly accented English, "Please, I am to be Catherine now, my mother says. It was always my name in England."

"That's probably quite sensible in the circumstances," said Rowany, thinking that no girl she knew would have said "England" in quite that way, as though it were a place entirely alien to her. Even the most patriotic of Martians might rightly insist that everything was better here, but would still speak of Home even if they'd never called it home. "A new world, a new school, a new life: I do know how daunting that can be. Just as well to dive in head-first with a new name too, to remind you how everything's changed. I think your mother's very wise. So: I'll call you Catherine, as will we all, and you must call me Rowany. I'm a Crater School girl through and through, as you'll learn before you're very much older, so there's no one better to welcome you to our midst." *When in doubt,* her father had said of her, *Rowany will just bully you with kindness until you capitulate. Honestly, you might as well give up at the start. Resistance is meaningless.* At the time, she had merely stuck her tongue out at him—across her grandmother's dinner-table, yet!—but of course there was a truth in it. She could talk relentlessly at need, and why should she ever want to be unkind? "Now, here comes Joe with your trunk and your overnight case. You ought to have kept that with you, by the way; that's the point of it, in case your trunk gets lost. If you leave them together, they might get lost together, and then where would you be?" Actually, of course, she'd be at the Crater School, where they were well used to kitting out girls who turned up without essential items of uniform or personal care; but she'd learn that soon enough, no doubt. Rowany couldn't remember a new girl ever arriving with absolutely everything she needed. "If you'd been coming at the start of term, you'd have found half a dozen other girls in your carriage who could have told you that, but never mind: you're here now, and so are your things, all safe and sound. Off we go: just a short skip through to another platform, and then another train. This way now, step lively. Ever been on a funicular, Catherine?"

"Of course! In Russia, we—I mean, they have many such. I remember the one in Vladivostok very well, and also in Kiev. But"—she looked at the waiting train and screwed her head sideways to look up at Rowany, frowning mightily, as though she thought she were being made fun of—"that is not a funicular!"

"No, it's not," Rowany agreed equably. "What it is, it's a rack-and-pinion locomotive, as you'll realise when we reach the crater wall and the gears engage. But we call it the funicular anyway, it's an old tradition. There's a more famous version at Cassini—which if you've never seen it, you must try to persuade your mother to take you there in the holidays, if there isn't a school trip before then; it's a remarkable sight, the city high on the crater's rim, and the water spilling constantly from the lake to the valley far below. They do as we do, calling their train a funicular, and it climbs up beside the waterfall. On a windy day the spray positively batters against the windows, and in summer they run an open carriage, for those who enjoy getting wet."

"Do they?" The girl gave a thin, tentative smile, that was somehow encouraging and heartbreaking both at once. "And have you ever taken it?"

"Oh, I have indeed. I have three brothers, Catherine; staying cosy and dry with my parents in the other carriage was never an option."

Catherine the only child gazed at her in some confusion. "My father would never have allowed…" Her voice cut short abruptly, though, before it could find an end to that sentence. Rowany was willing to bet that she'd been told not to talk about her father. By whom, though: the mother, or the father? The answer to that question might make all the difference to this girl's life, and others' too. And it was down to Rowany to discover it. Had she ever felt so unprepared for anything, all her life long? Not that she could remember now.

Well, never mind. This was no time for introspection. "In we go," she said briskly, hustling the girl towards an open door. "There's never much traffic at this time of day, going up; they mostly run this particular train for the San visitors who need to come down. Do you know about our Sanatorium? No? That's a story I can tell you once we're settled. With luck we'll have the compartment to ourselves, and I can answer all your questions without troubling anyone else. You must have questions, I expect?"

"Oh—yes, but…"

"But you're not even clear what's smart to ask, am I right, or what's downright idiotic? Don't worry so, Catherine. That's half the reason I'm here to meet you, because I'm neither staff nor prefect nor proper pupil now, only someone who knows everything there is to know about the Crater School. You likely won't run across me much—if at all—in your own school life, so you can ask me anything, and I can answer you, without fear or favour on either side. The more idiotic the better, to be honest, while you have this chance. I shan't breathe a word to anyone," or at least she hoped not to need to, "so you just let it all out now, where there's no one to overhear. Because you'll find that is *not* the case at school.

Privacy is a rare beast, and almost impossible to track down. Am I right to suppose that you've never been away to school before?"

"I haven't, no. I was too small when we were in England, and in St Petersburg Mother always wanted to keep me close. She used to say that I was all she had, so she couldn't bear to part with me."

"I'm sure," though in fact Rowany wasn't sure about either part of that, the assertion of it nor the truth. The woman had her husband too, didn't she? That, after all, was why she'd gone to Russia in the first place. And taken her daughter with her. And had she actually said that, or had Catherine only been told to say it for her, to put words in her mouth...?

Rowany was beginning to think this task impossible. At every step, she was second-guessing herself. Did the legendary spycatchers of the past actually have more insight than normal folk, to see through all the layers of bluff and double-bluff, and uncover the buried truth beneath? Or had they just been the lucky ones, those who guessed correctly; was the history of their deadly trade riddled with many and many forgotten names, of all those who had failed?

One thing Rowany was determined on, amid all this confusion. If Catherine were innocent of any intrigue—if she were the shy uncertain schoolgirl that she seemed, neither the dupe of an ambitious father nor his willing co-conspirator—then a simple schoolgirl she must be allowed to be, with not a blemish on her reputation, free to blaze her own trail and write her own story in the annals as generations of Cratereans had done before her, with not a whisper of rumour dragging at her heels.

Which only made it all the more imperative that Rowany establish the truth, and sooner rather than later.

Oh, lor'...

CHAPTER SEVENTEEN

"The Strength of a Woman"

At least half the school—or so at least it seemed to Levity—must have seen her mother's rock arrive. It had been hauled slowly along on the back of Mr Jenkins' steam-wagon, up the coach road and through the stable yard and as far as ever he could take it down between the houses, ensuring a good view from the library, the science labs and most of the classrooms. Certainly Levity's own Lower Fourth had been scolded roundly by Miss Grüber for staring out of the windows instead of concentrating on their German; and judging by the occasional out-of-all-patience comment sharp enough to pierce even castle walls, the same was true in the rooms on either side of theirs.

Just as certainly, no one at lunch was talking about anything else. The whole dining hall was abuzz with excitement and speculation—such a boulder it was, so big and so awkwardly shaped, and what on Mars was Mrs Buchanan going to do with it? and would they be allowed to watch? or help? and where exactly had it been taken, anyway?—and of course everyone assumed that she could answer all their questions, which she *couldn't*. Every time she raised her eyes from her plate, it seemed to Levity that somebody else was watching her speculatively from another table. Even the prefects, even the *mistresses*.

The same had to be true for her sister Charm, of course— but as far as she could see, Charm was revelling in all the attention, soaking it up at the heart of her little coterie. She was still young enough to enjoy fuss, where Levity only ever wanted to flinch away.

She had her own coterie, of course, in the Crew—but the Crew was a little fractured at the moment, less certain of itself, not quite so cosily arm-in-arm against the world. Pete was still held in durance vile, allowed out of the San for lessons and walks but not for games or for anything fun at all, which apparently and absolutely included spending time with her closest friends. How would she ever survive being mewed up with no one to talk to but Ellen-Stephanie, her very worst enemy? They couldn't imagine. And in the meantime, they had had another stranger foisted on them, all unwilling; and it was mean to be incharitable, but even so.

Levity had never had a close circle of friends before. She had learned very quickly to depend on the Crew, and valued her membership above rubies; now she was badly missing the security it offered, the sense of being wrapped around and wholeheartedly accepted. They were still best friends, of course, all six of the survivors; but Pete's absence was like a missing tooth, and the newcomer was something they just had to keep chewing on because they couldn't swallow, and...

And even now, the twins—both sets—were ranged either side of that interloper, and talking desultorily in Russian, which might as well have been a secret code, a door slammed in her face, no use to Levity at all.

Lise was at her side, of course—but even Lise only wanted to talk about that wretched rock and her mother's intentions for it and surely Levity must know *something*...?

No, actually: Levity knew nothing at all. Mamma rarely talked about her work before she'd finished it. To her daughters no more than to anyone else, no. And there'd been no chance to talk anyway, she'd barely had a word with her parent in weeks; and she was so tired of people asking, and assuming, and not really believing even her most fervent denials, and *staring* at her across the width of the dining hall as if they could read some hidden truth revealed in her face…

She was close to snapping even at Lise by the time Miss Leven blessedly struck her bell and the whole school rose to hear Grace. Then there was the usual clatter of plates and cutlery as everyone stacked their own and stood ready to carry them to the trolleys, table by table, to make life easier for the maids; and while she stood waiting, there was suddenly a touch at her elbow and she startled around to find Rowany with a smile on her lips and a message to follow.

"Levity, your mother would very much enjoy your company just now, down in the sculpture garden. As soon as you've put your crockery away, just skip down there; don't worry about telling people where you're going, I'll see that everyone knows. And don't watch the time, either; you're not expected back for class. Okay?"

Levity nodded, mute and astonished. This never happened. It was understood that Mrs Buchanan's ongoing presence here at school was never allowed and never to be allowed to interfere with her daughters' education. Neither Levity nor Charm had ever asked nor ever expected any favours or special treatment. They snatched time with their mother when they could, when three busy schedules allowed; it was unheard of, almost unthinkable that time should be deliberately carved out like this, and officially sanctioned. Time out of lessons, even!

Shocked, she recovered her voice just in time, or at least a squeak of it, and at least enough wit to say, "Charm too?" even while she was already looking around for her sister, because of course Charm too, their mother would never single out just one of them for such a treat.

"No, not on this occasion. Just you." Rowany gave her a smile and departed, leaving more than one girl gaping after her.

"'Not expected back...'" Lise repeated breathlessly. "And it's Areography too, first period this afternoon. Miss Fanshawe at her dustiest. Lucky you, getting out of that!"

"Collect my prep for me, will you, Lise? She's bound to give me extra, as a reward for missing her class."

She filed forward with the rest of the Lower Fourth, when it came their turn to load the trolley; and then, true to Rowany's command, Levity skipped away. The others would spend half an hour compulsorily resting, reading storybooks or talking quietly or just lazing in the sunshine, forbidden to yell or dash; then they'd buckle up for an afternoon of lessons, starting with the dreaded Areology.

Meanwhile, what lay ahead for Levity? She didn't know, and couldn't guess—except that it must surely be something to do with that blessed rock. Her mother, in the sculpture garden: it was too much coincidence, else.

Unless that was just where her mother was certain to be this afternoon, and there was something else that Mamma wanted to talk to her about, just her, and the location was merely convenient for a completely unconnected conversation. That could almost be more likely, now she'd thought of it. There had been many such conversations in the past; she thought sometimes that Mamma found it easier to talk seriously with her children while her hands and eyes and half her mind were busy with charcoal, clay or stone.

What possible conversation could be important enough, though, to justify Levity's absence from class? Unless her father was planning to kidnap them again, or opening a court case to try to win them legally. But no, if it was anything like that Mamma would certainly have sent for both her girls together; she never tried to shield Charm from the truth of their situation. Besides, if she'd heard the least rumour of such a move, Levity couldn't imagine that they'd still be here at the Crater School. Promise or no promise, Mamma would whisk them away in a moment, if she felt they were threatened here.

Oh, there was no point trying to guess. She'd find out soon enough—and there was Mamma, her tall upright figure unmistakable as she strode along, only a minute ahead of her. Staff didn't have to clear their own table, of course. Levity sighed over the iniquities visited upon children, and then she did what she was strictly forbidden to do so soon after lunch: she yelled and dashed.

"Mamma, hullo! What's all this about? Why did you send Rowany to fetch me down here?" Rowany, of all people— used like a second-form messenger girl! "What's so important that I don't even have to go back to classes? Is it, is it something awful...?"

"Girlie, what a gloomy outlook! Can't a mother want to spend an hour or two with her elder daughter, uninterrupted?"

"Not at the Crater School she can't, no. It's impossible. You *know* that."

"Do I? Well, perhaps I do. And yet, here we are." Mrs Buchanan took Levity's hand and tucked it firmly through her arm. "*Not* dashing anywhere, *not* prone to being haled off to some essential duty, both of us with official approval to spend the afternoon together, on our own, in this charming space."

"Do you really like it?" Levity asked, looking around dubiously at the sculpture garden. It still hadn't recovered from the dust storm; half the trees had been stripped bare of all their soft spring growth, the pond still looked murky, and some of the sculptures themselves had suffered a vicious kind of erosion, twenty or thirty years'-worth of weathering all in a brief few weeks of sand and wind-blast.

"Darling, I love it! I recognise the hands that made half the work here, if not the works themselves; heavens, I ought to, because half of those have been pupils of mine at some point, and the other half are colleagues or mentors. The garden needs a little tender care at the moment, of course, and it can't be the top priority, naturally the vegetable gardens and the staff's roses must come first; but if there's one thing we know about Mars, it's that the land is robustly generous and that even Earth-plants recover quickly, whatever the planet may throw at them. For this little time, I get to see the bones of this place, and to add my own contribution; soon enough it'll all be green and clear and delightful once again, you'll see."

Levity glowered at Old Gaunt—who had lost his trailing ivy and perhaps a little of one eye, but was still a lurking malevolent presence, destined to be for ever unloved—and waited to learn why she was here.

And watched her mother move to something that had never been here before, a newly lurking presence, that ridiculous boulder which steam- and man-power had somehow heaved and rolled all the way to where she presumably wanted it, right there, neither by the water nor among the trees but halfway between, a thrusting expression of permanence new-come.

"Sit down there, girlie—over by the water, yes—and tell me what's troubling you."

"How did you—?"

"I have eyes in my head," her mother said drily. "When I see one of my daughters wearing a face twice as long as normal, I am often curious to know why."

With a sigh Levity sat as directed, turning her back ostentatiously to Old Gaunt, and said, "It's nothing much, not really. Only that things were so perfect before, and now they're not. I miss Pete, we all do; I even miss Ellen-Stephanie now, even though those two were squabbling all the time."

"They'll be back," Mamma said equably, laying out a box of chalks and charcoal atop the rock. "Squabbling as hard as ever, I make no doubt. And in the meantime, don't you survivors have a substitute to amuse yourselves with? Every time I see the Crew out and about these days, there seems to be a new member with you."

"Yes, that's another thing," Levity said gloomily. "Catherine. Ekaterina Popov. I wish she would pop off," she added fiercely, in an utterly uncharacteristic growl. "She can pop off back to Marsport any time she likes. Or back to her beloved Russia, that'd be even better."

"Darling!"

"Sorry, Mamma." But was she, though? A little surprised at herself, certainly, taken aback by her own sudden vehemence—but not truly sorry, no. Certainly not contrite.

"What's this girl done, then, to raise your hackles like that?"

"Nothing at all." Levity could be entirely fair and entirely unreasonable both at once, she was finding. "She's polite, she's quiet, she's trying very hard to fit in. But—well, it's *us* she's trying to fit in with, and she's ... just not. Not one of us."

"You weren't 'one of us' last term, Liv." Mrs Buchanan spoke quietly, all her attention apparently on the rockface that Levity couldn't see, her hand sketching broad arcs with a lump of charcoal.

"No, but—the others made room for me, they *wanted* me. Lise was my sherpa, of course, but that didn't mean she had to be my friend. None of the Crew did, it was their choice.

Like it was everybody's choice to drag Pete in too, when she turned up at half term. It's different with Catherine. She's being shoehorned in on us, and it's nobody's choice: not ours, and I don't think really hers either."

"Oh? Who's her sherpa, then, and why isn't she doing her job?"

"That's the truly weird thing, because if she even has a sherpa, it's Rowany. Which is all wrong. Rowany's far too old," said Miss Fourteen in critical consideration of Miss Eighteen-and-a-Half. "And of course she's not in any of Catherine's classes. We are, but honestly Catherine's too old for us; she's sixteen already, and she ought to be in the Fifth, only she's had all her schooling in Russia, and everything's so different there. She has the *weirdest* ideas about history"— Miss Mars speaking now, from the confident heights of a thoroughly British outlook and education—"and she knows no Areography at all. Even her maths is all askew; she comes up with the right answers every time, or at least as often as the rest of us do, but the way she gets there is enough to make Miss Tattersall rend her garment and scatter ashes in her hair. Her own, I mean, Miss Tattersall's. Though come to think of it, she might well do it to Catherine one of these days, she gets so *angry* with her. It's not that she can't learn our way of doing it, it's just that she won't. Or at least that's what she thinks. Miss Tattersall, I mean. Catherine won't. If you follow me."

"Faint, but pursuing. Do go on."

"So she's been put in with us—not even Upper Fourth— until she catches up. That wouldn't matter, except that it must be pretty grisly for her, having to work with girls two years younger; only Rowany seems to be doing her very best to put Catherine into the Crew as well. And I'm sorry, I know it sounds mean, but we just don't *want* her."

"You're right," her mother said judiciously, "that does sound mean. And nothing like the girl I've tried to raise. You're still quite new to school, Liv, and I know how much you love being part of such a tight group, but I don't like to see you growing selfish with your friendships. This Catherine may not turn out to be a lifelong pal, but you can surely make a little time for her now. It won't damage what you have with the others."

"It sort of does, though," Levity said, even as she felt her skin flush scarlet at her mother's disapproval. "It's not me she's looking to spend time with, for a start, it's the twinses; and she only wants to talk Russian with them, so Lise and me are cut out anyway. She's not driving a wedge between us, she actually is the wedge, and Rowany's the, the driver. The hammer, I suppose. And Catherine's being really odd about it, too. According to the twinses, she's always on about how marvellous Russia is and how much she loved life in St Petersburg, how much better everything was there than it is in grimy old London, never mind Marsport—but she never sounds convincing about it, they say. She shows them photographs where she's obviously happy as a lamb, but her voice goes all dull and dreary as she talks about it."

"Well, if she's homesick, of course she's going to sound sad."

Levity shook her head briskly. "Not like that. She sounds like she's reading from a textbook, the twinses say. In a subject she doesn't enjoy. It's like she's two people sometimes, twins herself, inside her head. Half the time she's really trying to fit in, paying attention in class, joining in with games when she can even though she's never played them before. She can be shy like any new girl," spoken with all the authority of a term and a half, "but she's learning to ask for help when she needs it, and that's fine. But then there's this other Catherine, I suppose we should call her Ekaterina then, who just wants to drone on and on about Russia being so much better than we are, but insists on doing it in Russian, to the only four girls who can understand her. And the twinses don't want to hear it, of course they don't; but Rowany keeps pushing her at us, and we just can't get away and this whole term is spoiled now, and…"

And she didn't know where to go from there, because she liked this sullen griping version of herself no better than her mother did; and it was a blessing then to see her mother's lips quirk with amusement, to hear her say, "I take it that 'twinses' is your new shorthand to encompass, what shall we call it, a plurality of twins? A multiplicity?"

Levity giggled. "Multiplicitwins. Yes, of course: once twins is twins, twice twins is twinses. We've added it officially to the multiplication table, we needed it so badly. Write it out a dozen times in your exercise book, to help you remember."

"Oh, I think I'll manage. And if I were you, I wouldn't let the staff hear you say it. I know one can't stop schoolgirls from slanging, and I think Miss Leven puts up with a lot for the sake of inventiveness, but that might be a step too far for her."

"Or for the prefects," Levity said, pulling a terrible face. "They're worse than any staff for coming down on slang. Don't worry, we're terribly careful. Oh—you're not saying I have to be careful around you, are you? Now that you're a staff? Because I don't think I can, not when we're alone like this…"

"No, it's fine when we're alone, girlie. I really shouldn't encourage you in bad habits, but sometimes I do still need to be Mamma instead of Mrs Buchanan. Besides, I'm not really a member of the staff; I started helping out because I was stuck here as much as you were, and one has to do something, and I've only stayed because I want to, because they tolerate me, because I mean to give back something consequential as a gesture of thanks. Hush now, darling. All this talk has given me an idea, better than I had before..."

And indeed she was suddenly running a cloth over the boulder, rubbing out much of what she'd sketched in. Quickly, then, before she could get so absorbed in her work that she wouldn't even hear a question—the daughter knew the mother's creative soul of old—Levity said, "Shouldn't Charm be here too, if you're planning to use us as models? Or couldn't you beg her off classes?" They had already been drawn in pencil and charcoal, painted in watercolours and oils, moulded in clay and cast in bronze, in pursuit of their mother's many projects and inspirations; it was almost a surprise that they'd never been carved in stone before.

It was more of a surprise when Mamma said, "Not Charm, no. Not this time. I only wanted you. Hush now, darling. Let me think."

She thought, of course, with her hands: with charcoal and chalk, rapidly now, much as she made her first sketches on paper or canvas or her early models in clay. Levity sat quite still, entirely accustomed to the practice, and let time like a river flow over her while her mind drifted from school to family to friendships to the mysterious unknowable future.

Long used as she was to her mother's trance-state when she was obsessed with a new piece of work, Levity didn't think of that as something she'd inherited, and was startled to be called back into herself by Mrs Buchanan's abrupt call, "That's enough, for now. Do you want to come and see?"

Like waking from a dream, it was impossible to recollect exactly where her thoughts had wandered; she shook her head bewilderedly, then replayed her mother's words to glean their meaning, and nodded vigorously instead. Of course she wanted to look! It was almost unheard of, to get a privileged early sight even of a work that she had modelled for. She and her sister, until now. Sitting solo was totally unheard of.

She scrambled to her feet, ignoring pins-and-needles from sitting still so long, and hurried around to Mamma's side of the rock before the great Martian artist could change her great Martian mind.

There on the rock-face, drawn in with strong black lines and a hint of colour to exploit the bumps and dips of the original surface, sat Levity herself. There was nothing new in that, but this was not a portrait, however lifelike it appeared. On either side of her image, and fading back into a blurred distance, sat other figures in the same pose: the nearest easily recognisable, rough images of the rest of the Crew, all the twinses and Lise and Pete. More girls beyond and behind those, not drawn clearly enough to put a name to.

"I ... don't think I understand?" Levity ventured.

"It's called 'The Strength of a Woman,'" her mother said behind her.

"But, but, I'm not a woman yet..." She'd been drawn very clearly as a girl, still in school uniform.

"Think about it. Then explain it to me."

Levity took her time then, recognising the tone of her mother's voice; this was serious. Not a test, but a time to learn something. What art was for.

At last she said carefully, "What you're saying is that, that the strength of a woman is built on the friendships she makes as a child, is that right?"

"That's exactly right. This is the time when you can reach out, when you can find and gather in the people who will matter most through later life. You have the opportunity now to lay broad foundations and build strong walls, to meet whatever will come to challenge you in the future. Of course you'll make adult friends too, once you're an adult yourself, but not friendships like this. There's nothing like school, to fit young minds together and teach them to hold fast; and once you're set together that way, nothing is going to break you apart.

"Now," she went on robustly, as though the one thing followed entirely from the other, "I thought I'd put Catherine here, just behind the Mishtwins. I can't so much as sketch her face in yet, because I've never seen her, but it seems a likely placement, yes...?"

CHAPTER EIGHTEEN

Step by Step and *"One*, Two, Three..."

Beyond doubt or question, there was a conspiracy afoot. Ellen-Stephanie suspected it, and Pete confirmed it gloomily from her vastly greater experience of school, two full halves of a term thus far. It was unheard of, almost unthinkable, that so much time could go by—weeks on end!—with no girls falling sick enough for San, no broken bones or feverish colds or marsles or the mumps. Day after day, night after night the two disgraced Middles occupied their two beds side by side at one end of the long ward, yearning for company, any other company; and days and nights went by and no one came to join them. They saw their friends in class, but couldn't talk; they were marched swiftly and silently from one class to another, from chapel to gym to the library, under guard of prefect or a staff; they ate break-fast and dinner in the San, and sat together at an isolated table for lunch, where the whole school could stare at them in their shame. On games afternoons while all the rest of the school was running and shrieking in vigorous games of cricket or lax, they had walks with one or another of the staff, who always made it plain what a dreadful inconvenience this was, and how much they would rather be doing something else than watch over naughty little girls who couldn't be trusted on their own.

It all made for long and miserable days, and they yearned and prayed to find someone new tucked up ready in the next bed down as they trooped reluctantly back to San every evening. And it never happened, and it had to be conspiracy, there was no explanation else. Either Sister Anthony was secreting all her other patients elsewhere on the grounds, just to keep Pete and Ellen-Stephanie isolated, or else all the girls of the school were in on it, concealing their illnesses from staff, struggling through with wrenched ankles and worse, simply to avoid being hospitalised alongside the reprobates. Some nights they believed the one thing, some nights it was the other. One or the other, though, was a cold and clear certainty.

Until that time they came in—together as ever, disconsolate as ever, feeling that punishment was one thing but eternal never-ending cruelty was something else entirely—to see that the next bed along was indeed made up and turned down, with someone's wash-things on the stand beside.

"Who do we know," Ellen-Stephanie said slowly, "who has chased silver hairbrushes with pretty mother-of-pearl handles?"

"Absolutely nobody," Pete said gruffly; and it didn't strike either of them as odd until after she'd said it that the two of them could be thinking of each other as "we" and somebody else, anybody else as an outsider. "Some of the older girls have ivories, I know," she went on, "gifts from godparents and so on, but horn or tortoiseshell or plain old wood are good enough for the rest of us," glancing contentedly at her own hairbrush and comb, as plain as plain could be, old wood with the varnish rubbing off, not even matching.

The newcomer's toiletries were a matched set all the way, including the gleaming case they came in. Both girls drew closer for a better look, not quite daring to touch for fear of leaving a smudgy fingerprint on bright-polished metal.

"Whosever it is, she takes care of it," Pete said, a little grudgingly.

"Well, you would, wouldn't you? I mean, actually even you would, if you had something this pretty. You might not want it, exactly, but that's not the same thing. You do take care of your things."

"Well, of course I do. Who wouldn't? When you don't have much, of course you look after what there is."

"Well, maybe it's the same for Mystery Girl. Maybe this is all she has. It might have been her grandmother's. Or her mother's, come to that. One last memento, that she'd never leave behind."

"I'd never bring it to school, though, in that case. Would you? If you had anywhere else to keep it safe?"

For a moment they were once again united, two girls with but a single thought, their own lost mothers heavy in their minds. They were hardly alone. The Crater School almost seemed to specialise in orphans and demi-orphans, as Rowany had once memorably described it. Perhaps that was inevitable here on Mars, where death could still lurk around any blind corner, unseen and inescapable; and especially so here on Lowell Crater, with the great Sanatorium always looming across the water. So many girls came because a parent or guardian was a patient over there. They could be orphans *de facto* for months, terms, even years before the true end came at last; the school always stood by to comfort, to nurture, to protect. Every year, there were some pupils whose only true home was here.

Pete herself had no one but an uncle to look to, and he no kind of homemaker. She'd be lost without the school.

Ellen-Stephanie did still have a father, but she'd sort of run away from him; did that make her a hemi-demi-orphan? Pete grinned privately at the thought, and decided not to pose the question. Not, at least, while there were much more important questions to be probed, like who on Mars this new girl could be, who carried such precious toiletries with her.

She'd barely drawn a breath, though, to break that awkward-but-companionable silence, when they both heard footsteps behind them, coming down the ward. They turned as one, and there was Sister Anthony, steering a girl down the aisle with one long hand firmly on her back.

"Ah, here you are, you two. Good." That was the most welcoming she'd been in all this time. Pete wondered briefly whether she and Ellen-Stephanie had been elevated out of the ranks of sinners at last, or whether the new girl had somehow achieved something so heinous that she could suddenly rank below even them. She was the very newest of new girls, though, the Russian girl, what was her name, Catherine?—and the Crater School was generally lenient for the first weeks, until you found your feet. Pete had reason to know that. And how often were sinners sent to isolation in the San, anyway...?

"You'll both know Catherine, of course," Sister Anthony went on, "since she's in your class. You'll have someone else to walk with now, to and from lessons; and someone else to talk with. No doubt that'll be something of a relief, after all this time. You're to talk quietly, mind, and not get rambunctious. I'm pulling Catherine out of regular school because I'm not pleased with her colour and I can tell that she's been sleeping poorly. Whatever she says," with a patent Sisterly glower at the unfortunate Catherine, who went abruptly paler than ever, if that was even possible.

"She needs rest," Sister Anthony went on crushingly, "not rumpus. I'm depending on you two, mind. You're not to excite yourselves, nor Catherine. Talk quietly, or don't talk at all. I know you've been murmuring to each other after lights-out"—guilty, astonished glances: how could she possibly know that?—"and that has to stop now. You'll be earlier to bed, all three of you, and I want absolute silence from the time I say goodnight until I wake you in the morning. I can't be here all the time to supervise, so I have to look to your sense of honour. You've both been well-behaved, since you were sent to me; I'm hopeful that I can trust you now, when the health of your classmate is concerned. Or am I being too sanguine?"

Neither one of them was quite sure what "sanguine" meant, and certainly neither one was going to ask. They stammered their reassurances, "Oh—no, Sister, of course, we'll be quiet as mice," all the while wondering what was actually wrong with Catherine, because it was an unwritten but absolute rule that grown-ups were never right about this sort of thing. They were good on diseases and broken bones and the like, but when it came to reasons for looking peaky and not sleeping at night, they did come up with the weirdest ideas. And they never thought to ask the people who were sure to know, the girls who shared the victim's meals and her out-of-school hours, her chores and her secrets, her dormitory at night. If they didn't actually share her nightmares, at least they'd know about them. But offering up helpful information like that was frowned upon as somewhere between gossip and tale-bearing, and being asked for it was somehow unthinkable too.

Strange people, grown-ups.

Strange person, Catherine, too. They didn't know her well—honestly, they didn't know her at all—but they knew that much. She barely talked in class, unless she was directly called upon; she never offered an opinion, which was— well, almost unpatriotic. Martian women should be forceful. The colony would never have survived else. Pete and Ellen-Stephanie hadn't had a chance till now to talk to her outside class, but they'd picked up rumours and whispers, of course they had. They knew that she was odd to the point of being dotty.

Maybe that's why she was being singled out of the herd now, because she really was dotty? Maybe the Powers That Be felt it better to risk infecting two wayward girls than the whole school else? If dottiness was infectious. That would have been a thing for Pete to discuss with Ellen-Stephanie—probably after lights-out, Sister, yes—except that it was impossible now, of course, now that it was needful.

Oh, well. If ever there were two girls born and raised to make the best of things, Pete and Ellen-Stephanie were surely they. Pete gave the new girl her best insouciant urchin grin; Ellen-Stephanie put her hand out as elegantly as she knew how. "Catherine, how do you do? I don't b'lieve we've had the chance to talk before." Except in French Conversation, where Catherine was something of a star, and both her new acquaintances appalling. "I'm Ellen-Stephanie Carew, and this is Pete Thorogood." As if she wouldn't know that already—but Ellen-Stephanie was putting her best foot forward, and all her newly-acquired etiquette to the test. Bob Tucker should have no cause to blush for her pupil, if she had anything to say to the matter.

A little startled, Catherine shook hands gravely, and then turned to Pete to offer the same. Pete gave the slim, shapely hand a gruff, embarrassed tug—and then couldn't keep from exclaiming, "Heavens, Catherine, your fingers are freezing! No wonder Sister wants you here under her eye. Are you sure you're not coming down with something grisly?"

"That'll do, Pete," Sister Anthony said sharply. "There's nothing wrong with Catherine that won't be cured by better sleep and less excitement. She needs peace and quiet, and I mean to see that she gets it. Am I understood?"

"Yes, Sister Anthony," in a dutiful mutter from both girls together.

"Very well, then. Catherine, put on your pyjamas and dressing gown, and then get into bed. That'll warm you up," with a beetling frown at Pete, who met it with her blandest butter-wouldn't-melt expression. One learned fast at the Crater School, or suffered much. "You're excused preparation for today. You other girls are not"—was it even possible to pin two separate girls at once, with a single steely glare?—"so you'd best take out your books and be about it. I will want to see significant progress before tea, and all done by supper. Catherine, there are story-books on the shelf there; you may choose one of those, to pass the time. Nothing more demanding," and—as Pete and Ellen-Stephanie well knew by now, after their long incarceration here—there was absolutely nothing demanding about Sister Anthony's choice of reading matter for her patients. If there was one good reason for escaping the San as quickly as possible, it was how dull those books were. Dull and pious too. Perhaps that was the point, though, to make convalescence so excruciatingly boring that any right-thinking girl would fight to be released as soon as possible?

That had been another whispered discussion in the dark. Pete didn't really believe that grown-ups could be that devious; Ellen-Stephanie insisted that even Sister Anthony had been a girl once, with all that that implied. Until then, Pete had rather supposed her to have been an immaculate conception, born out of the stones of her cell high on the crater's rim, a Martian saint emerging from between the Devil's Teeth. It was unimaginable that she should ever have had a girlhood, whispering in dorms and plotting mischief with her friends. Unimaginable that she might ever have had friends.

Like a pillar of salt, if salt were hard and chill as bitter ice, Sister Anthony stayed to see herself obeyed, to the very letter of her law; then she strode away down the ward to her own quarters. As soon as the door closed behind her, Ellen-Stephanie—not raising her head from her exercise-book—murmured, "She didn't actually say we couldn't talk, did she? I don't think she did."

"Prob'ly knew we were going to anyway, so she was just saving herself the trouble an' inconvenience of having to scold us more." Pete scratched her head over a problem of arithmetic, pencilled down something more hopeful than likely, and went on, "'Sides, we can talk and work at the same time. *They* never believe it, but we can. Though I s'pose it might be best if Catherine does most of the talking, at least up till tea-time. Where are you actually from, Catherine? Tell us everything. Oh, and does anybody ever call you Cathy or Cath or any short at all? Because 'Catherine' is quite a mouthful, and—"

"No, never." As staff and prefects had learned these last months, it was hard to crush heedless Pete, but the swift chill of that response snatched the very breath from her lungs, at least for long enough to allow Catherine time perhaps to regret it, perhaps to step back and try again: "My, my father calls me Katya. So did everyone else, in St Petersburg. But Mother says we must leave all that behind now, and begin again. So my name is Catherine, please. She insists on it."

"Ooh, tell us about St Petersburg!" So many emotions had followed each other across Catherine's face in that one simple speech, love and loss and longing and something else that Pete couldn't read, something deeper and more disturbing. It was instinct in Pete to try to turn her mind aside from sorrow, she might have stumbled in her urgency, but if Catherine was homesick for the Russian capital, at least that was a simple understandable kind of grieving. Maybe talking about it would help, even? In any case, Pete blundered on: "I mean, I've seen pictures of the Winter Palace, of course, and the canals, and all those bridges—Miss Harribeth says that as

Martians, of course we're all obsessed with canals, but actually I think it's her, she has a secret passion for them and she talks about them whenever she gets the chance, which is why we had a lesson about St Petersburg at all—but that's really all I know. Tell us something int'resting."

"Tell us about the court," Ellen-Stephanie demanded. "I heard someone say that your father was a cavalry officer, is that right? He must have taken you to court. Did you see the Tsar, or any of his children? Tell us—"

"I said something *int'resting*," Pete objected vociferously. "Like how they drained the swamp, how they connected all the waterways, how they control the water. Engineering. What their locks are like. Int'resting stuff."

"Tell us about the dresses," Ellen-Stephanie went on, not thrown for a moment by Pete's outburst. "Tell us about the *balls*. They must have let you go to a ball, surely, even if you were too young to stand up with any of the gentlemen? I've never seen a ball. Actually, I've never even seen a ballgown, only the plates in books—and only since I came here, of course. I barely saw a book, in all my life before—and all the Brothers ever had were terribly proper. Here we have dancing, of course, and I'm doing my best to learn—but oh, I would like a proper gown. I *crave* a gown. I want to *swirl*..."

Her own words were too much to contain her. She leaped out into the broad aisle that ran all the length of the ward, and swept into a full courtly curtsey, as best Bob Tucker had taught her, as best she could in a gym tunic and woollen stockings. It was an opportunity impossible to ignore, even if you'd been on the point of yet one more quarrel a moment earlier. Pete scrambled up, stood face to face with Ellen-Stephanie, bowed low, and held her hand out in open invitation.

The taller girl stepped forward, just as they had practised with other girls, though never ever together until this moment; a moment of settling, and then Pete counted carefully, "*One*, two, three, and—"

—and they whirled away down the long San in strict waltz time, Pete leading as a gentleman should, even though she couldn't actually see over Ellen-Stephanie's shoulder.

And they were still at it when Sister Anthony came pacing in to discover what all the commotion was about; and when she found that the core of the commotion was her newest patient, Catherine lying on her bed and howling with laughter at the other girls' antics, there may even have been the twitch of a smile on her own face, before she suppressed it sternly. She went on to suppress the dancers, seeking to be sterner yet; but even as she castigated them, the two sinners were well aware that she might have been worse. She might have been much, much worse. Taught as they were to reason backwards, from symptom to cause, it may even have occurred to one or both that she was being deliberately lenient with them, in view of the effect they were having on their audience. Catherine had barely been seen to crack a smile, had certainly never laughed this deep or this long since the day she came to the Crater School, and likely some aching-weary stretch of time before. It must have been with some deep sense of relief, then, that Sister Anthony found herself obliged to call the girl to order and scold her too, before she relegated them all to bed and silence for the rest of the day.

To all its pupils—and to their parents too—the Crater School promised discipline, health, and friendship, these three: and the greatest of these was friendship.

CHAPTER NINETEEN

Telling Tales Out of School

"Well, what I say is, it's not a proper Christmas until you've had your bones rattled by a really scary ghost story."

Thus Charm, laying down the law to her known associates in the criminal underworld that was the Lower Third. Truth to tell, this was a law that she had learned more from her beloved school stories than at her mother's knee; ghost stories had not really been a feature of her family Christmases thus far. She only felt that they ought to have been.

Still, her friends didn't need to know that; and a lifetime on the move all across the province and back again had at least left her with an inexhaustible supply of deeply scary tales, even if most of them weren't really very seasonal.

But then again, Christmas on Mars was not strictly a seasonal feast in any case. Overlaying a proper 365-day Church of England calendar on a year that ran to 687 days meant that any fixed celebration drifted from one season to the next. Sometimes, often, they'd have two Christmases in the same Martian year; sometimes, as this year, it would fall in early summer with no hope of snow or sledging. Of course they sang the same Earthly carols anyway—"In the Bleak Midwinter", "Good King Wenceslas" and more—and even their own home-grown variety all assumed frozen canals, dark nights and bitter winds.

Ghost stories, on the other hand, came in any season, with any weather. Whatever Charm's friends might think. Even now, they were glancing skyward, frowning, laughing at her.

"Isn't it a bit, you know, *hot* for spooky stories?" That was Lauren, breaking every rule in the book by taking her hat off to fan herself with it. They were gathered behind the sight-screen on the First Eleven cricket pitch, which was probably a breach of rules in itself, because the high white screen did its work splendidly, hiding them from any authoritarian oversight. Charm perched high on the roller by right of leadership, while the others sat around and gave not a thought to grass-stains on their skirts or stockings.

"Never. The chill of a ghost story comes from the character of the ghost, not the temperature outside." She had read that once—was it in *Polly Saves The Day*, or *Melanie Meets Her Match*?—and never forgotten it, and felt no shame in trotting it out now as though it were her own thought. It did match her own thoughts exactly, so what harm? "I could tell you a dozen right now, that happened in summer and in full daylight too."

"Go on, then." No surprise, it was Janna who challenged her. That girl would never let you get away with anything.

"What, now?"

"Why not? It's summer, it's daylight."

"And we've only got half an hour before tea. But all right, then. If I can, if we don't run out of time. You can't hurry a good story. Let me think... I know! D'you all remember that song that Ellen-Stephanie started at rehearsal, that she was roundly squashed for?"

Of course they did; they'd been intrigued at the time, and bitterly disappointed to hear no more.

· "Well, d'you know the story behind it? The *true* story of the lost *Nellie Martin*?"

The whole gang looked at each other, and shook their heads uncertainly. They had had nice upbringings, for the most part, and nice girls did *not* come across such stories.

Except at school, obviously, from a suitably wicked fellow pupil. Who had picked it up herself at a prospectors' camp out in the Dry, while her mother was researching. The old miner who told it her had had a gap between his teeth, which lent a strange unearthly whistling to his hoarse voice; she had persuaded herself utterly from that day to this that it was that sound that chilled and horrified her, not the actual story itself. Certainly not. She was no scaredy-cat, to be frightened by a silly story, however true he claimed it to be.

"This is a true story," she said, just as he had said to her. "It happened not so terribly long ago, not back in the olden times, oh no: just far enough past that we hadn't found red-coal yet, so all the traffic on the water was still sail. No steam engines, no motor cars, no airships. Just the wind, to take us wherever we had to go. You listen now, to where this story takes us..."

"Wait," Chrissy Godfrey interrupted. "Do you really think we should? You know how Ellen-Stephanie got yelled at, for singing about it. I'm sure Miss Leven wouldn't like it."

"Miss Leven isn't hearing it," quoth insouciant Charm. "You don't have to, either. Nobody's forcing you to listen."

Chrissy blushed and fidgeted, under the communal glare of her closest friends. "Well, I still say we'll get in trouble," she muttered. "But no, go on, then, Charm. I do want to hear it, I really do. You always tell such fabulous stories. I swear I don't know how you do it. I'm sure I never could."

"Well, then." Peace restored by this gross flattery, Charm beamed upon her defeated challenger and said, "Anybody else worried about it? No? On we go, then. Where was I? ... Oh, yes. Wind and water, the two truths of early Mars." That was cribbed directly from her mother; it was an artist's task, as Charm understood it, to weave her cloth from many threads. "Our tale begins in the town of Pell. Now you've all heard tell of the town of Pell, where it lies at the backside of beyond." ("At the back end of beyond" was how Mrs Buchanan had put it, the one time she took her daughters there; but little girls will giggle in whispers together, and twelve-year-olds won't trouble about the whispering.) "No, don't laugh," Charm went on, struggling with her own smile, delighted at having won such an easy victory. "This is a serious story, about a serious time. It was Christmas, and the best Christmas present for the crew of the *Nellie Martin* was that they were leaving Pell and heading back towards civilisation, to where their families waited to welcome them at the docks of New Victoria. They had easy weather for the journey, a steady westerly to fill their sails, and nothing more to worry them than the bosun's temper, and they were used to that.

"Even under steam it's a long journey from Pell to NV, a journey of weeks; in those days of course it was longer yet, a matter of months if the winds turned against you. Christmas would be come and gone long before they saw their loved ones. But no matter: their hearts were light, and they sang as they hauled on the mainsheet. Journeys are always shorter and quicker when you're going home." Charm had never really known a home before now, but this was an article of faith with her, something she had read once and clung to ever since as a hope, a promise for the future.

"Why do they haul on the sheets, though?" Maeve demanded. "I've never understood that. Don't they just have to make the bed again after?"

Charm had never really understood it either, only as a thing that sailors did, so she was glad for once to be fore-stalled. Elana gurgled with laughter and said, "That's what they call ropes, silly. And no, I don't know why, but they do."

"I always thought the sheets were the sails. I mean, that makes better sense than ropes, doesn't it? Sails do look like sheets."

"We made a sail out of a bedsheet once, for a raft my brothers were building. You wouldn't believe the trouble we got into…"

"Never mind all that! Do you people want to hear this story or not?"

The interrupters were severely shushed, Agnosia going so far as to put her hand over Chrissy's mouth to silence her. The exasperated Charm glowered at the offenders, took a slow deep breath and continued.

"*As* I was saying—the *Nellie Martin* slipped her moor-ings"—the old prospector had been a navvy in his youth and then a deckhand before the gold rush seized him up and carried him away; he had flourished technical terms as to the manner born, and Charm was proud to have remembered as many as she could, liking the shape and the taste of them in her mouth—"and sailed away from Pell, with a long straight run ahead of her, all up the Home Water and nothing likely to trouble her on the way. There was a nymph in the canal, we know, and it tracked them for days, but that was never going to threaten a three-master and there was no reason for the crew to take to the boats. No reason that we know of," she added meaningfully, with heavy stress. In an essay for Miss Peters' composition class—assuming that she ever dared write down such a story, which she never would—she would have underlined both of the last two words. Possibly twice.

"They dropped anchor again at Aberwylth, we know, to take on water and leave two sickly crewmen to recover. At the same time, three of the local farm boys signed aboard, eager to see more of the world. Everyone knew the *Nellie Martin*, she'd made this run time and time again; they'd be paid off and safe home again with their families before winter came to freeze the canal and stifle all its traffic.

"From Aberwylth, the Home Water cuts clean through the Ranges, where it's all broken rock and jutting crags; no one can farm there, and even the prospectors steer clear, for there's no hope of finding workable veins. You remember, Miss Fanshawe gave us a whole lesson about that; she thinks it's where the Makers dumped all the spoil from the canals, way back ago.

"Anyway, no one lives there, for hundreds of miles at a stretch. That's why the wise captains pause to restock, even now. These days we have coaling stations cither side of the Ranges; back then it was chandlery and cordage"—more of her treasured vocabulary—"and water, as I said. And men." Oh, drat—she should have said "hands". Never mind. Too late now. On she went.

"Long days and short nights, we all know what high summer's like; but at least the captain had the anchors thrown out every night while they passed through the Ranges, not willing to risk his ship or his crew where the canal narrows and cliffs can turn the wind on end and the starlight's just a ribbon too high up. So the hands could get some rest"— there, she'd worked it in—"and the lookouts would be alert and ready as soon as the sun came up ahead.

"And they had a crate full of turkeys for Christmas dinner, and plum pudding after; and every hand, man and boy, would have an extra tot of rum as the tradition was, and even the hard-hearted first officer might turn a blind eye to drunken shenanigans that night."

"Shenani-what?"

It was barely a mutter, but just loud enough for Charm to hear, and pause, and glare.

"Shenani*gans*. You'll learn. It's the staff's favourite word, for when we cause a rumpus in the form-room."

"Or the dorm. Only then it's the prees who come to chase down the shenaniganisers, and that's worse."

"It is—but it's probably worse even, aboard ship. Shall I go on?"

She asked it sweetly, and was reassured by the chorus of affirmative responses.

"Well, then." She was standing on the roller now, keeping her balance by holding on to the long handle, keeping everyone's eyes on her, trying to hold them spellbound as the best storytellers did, as she did too in her yearning imagination. If only they wouldn't keep *interrupting*... "Where was I? Oh, yes. The *Nellie Martin* sailed off into the Ranges, well manned and experienced, ready for anything that Mars might throw at her before she came back to civilised lands on the other side—except that she never did come back. She sailed into the Ranges, and she was *never ... seen ... again.*"

Charm paused, for dramatic effect: which effect was wholly spoiled by Agnosia suddenly crying out, "Wait, is that all? Well, I call that blue cheese!"—which was the worst insult you could offer in the Junior School that term, and instantly had Charm riled up again.

"No, of course that's not all! I haven't reached the ending yet!"

"How can there possibly be an ending, though, if the ship was never seen again? How can anyone know what happened?"

"If you'll only keep *quiet*, then I'll *tell* you! There are Further Revelations Yet To Come! You see, the ship may have disappeared, but—"

But just then she was interrupted one more time, and this time by the worst of all possible causes: the steady beat of the school bell clanging up in the Castle, its voice reaching out across lake and lands, calling all its wandering pupils home.

"Oh—*botheration!*" More than one mistress had recently found occasion to bear down on the Lower Third's language, particularly their choice of expletives in moments of stress. Finally one bold soul had asked Miss Hendy to poll the Staff Room for words that would pass muster—"for 'tisn't fair to expect us never to need to say anything cross, 'tisn't *reasonable*, and they must have had words they said themselves, back in the olden days, you know. Before. You won't let us use the words we hear at home, that we mostly learn from our brothers, so it's only fair to tell us what we can say instead. What you used to say."

The staff had enjoyed themselves thoroughly, drawing up a list of acceptable epithets and the remembered cries of frustrated girlhood. Miss Hendy handed that over—along with a mild lecture on the desirability of speaking softly, listening to others and practising humility sooner than wrath— so of course the girls had devoted themselves to memorising and employing the whole list as widely and frequently as possible.

Botheration was unexceptionable, and had been heard widely through the school for weeks now. It might never have been uttered with such passion, though, as the bell spelled an inevitable end to Charm's storytelling.

Her audience stared back at her, equally distraught.

"We'll have to go," Elana said. "Even if we *pelt*, we'll hardly have time to make ourselves tidy before tea. And then we'll just be sent out to do it properly, and *then* we'll have to apologise to the staff at High Table and the prees at ours when we come back in, and you know how awful that is."

Of course they did, they'd all been late before; but even so they hesitated. "How are we ever going to find out now, what happened?" Agnosia lamented.

"I'll think of something. I promise, you'll all hear the end of the story, one way or another. By tonight. 'Twouldn't be fair to make anybody wait." It was a vow, taken before her entire cohort; Charm was bound to follow through. And determined not to let them down.

"How can you possibly?" That was Chrissy, determinedly distrustful. "You can't tell us over tea, with the prees listening in; and afterwards we have prep in the form-room, with prees again, and then we're all back to our own houses."

"I said, I'll think of something. Now come on, you—you felonious wenches!" *Felonious wenches* had been Miss Leven's own contribution to the lexicon of legitimacy. It was possible that she hadn't expected the Lower Third to attach her name to her contribution, but her handwriting was widely known and she hadn't thought to disguise it. The girls had taken to that phrase above all others with a love beyond measure, and with the imprimatur of the headmistress thereunto attached there was not a thing that anyone else, staff or prefect, could do about it.

They sprinted up to the Castle, annexed the first cloak room they came to for the briefest possible splash of water and tug of a comb through rebellious locks, and hustled into the dining hall last of all the school, under the beady eyes of the duty prefects, just not quite late enough nor quite untidy enough—not quite!—to be called to order or chased out again.

All through the meal Charm sat silent, with such a scowly frown on her face that her sister Levity was quite worried about her. As soon as they'd cleared the tables afterwards, though, and before Levity could make her way through the throng, Charm's little friends had packed themselves about her and borne her away. There'd be no chance of snatching a word with her now till prep was over; the Junior form-rooms were strictly out of bounds to an invading Middle at any time, never mind during the sacred hour of prep, and the supervising prefect would swiftly send her away with a flea in her ear.

Had any other prefect been in charge of Lower Third that evening—or of course Rowany, if she'd only thought to step in and take up her old burden of duties—then all the events that followed and their consequences might have played out very differently. As it chanced, though, the girl who chivvied her lambs to their desks and their work was Mary Holmes, much beloved and widely acknowledged—by herself, as much as any other—to be entirely bereft of any imagination whatsoever.

The whole form knew, of course. They eyed their Charm sidelong, almost as anxious as her sister after her introspective tea, and saw her bent over a sheaf of impot-paper, scribbling madly. One thing they were safe to assume, that wasn't her Areography prep she was working on so assiduously, far less her mathematics. They heaved sighs of relief, turned back to their own problems and tried not to make too bad a hash of them, even while half their minds could not help but wonder what exactly bright-spark Charm was up to. Mary, meanwhile, saw no more than a girl trying hard, as she ought to do; and turned dutifully back to her own essay on the virtues and vices of Renaissance Florence, and thought no more about the girls she was there to supervise except for a mild feeling of gratitude that they made her task tonight so easy.

When the bell rang, she looked up and said, "Thank you, girls. Put your books and your work away now, and line up by houses, please."

There was a necessary, an inevitable amount of milling-about, before they were all sorted and ready. During that amiable chaos, Charm made the chance to sidle up to two of her friends, press a wad of paper into their hands and murmur to each of them, "Read this to your dorm at bedtime. After prayers, and before the pree comes up. Don't look through it first, just read it fresh. Understand?"

From each she had a stammered, startled agreement. In return she gave each a haunted stare and a little dramatic shiver, before sidling back to her place in line.

Obedient to her instructions, Marigold kept Charm's screed carefully folded up and hidden away, resisting all her fellow Joplingites' pleadings "just for a peek, just to know what it's all about..."

Through Herculean effort and self-restraint she preserved the document's secrecy until bedtime, and it may be admitted that both hair-brushing and prayers were scanted in Lady Hester dormitory that night. Girls were forbidden to talk after they'd said their prayers, but they were allowed to read for a while, each in their separate cubicle, until lights out. Reading aloud was still reading, surely, and hence entirely lawful. Marigold waited until the last breathless "Ready!" reached her, then she unfolded the sheaf of papers and began to pick her way through Charm's hurried scrawl:

The Nellie Martin *was never seen in this world again, nor no trace of her ever found—except that years later, a woman rummaging in a dockside bazaar found a leather-bound journal, severely scorched and water-damaged too. It was—or it claimed to be—the logbook of the* Nellie Martin.

How it had come to be there, on a squalid stall in Marsport run by a one-eyed and unlettered ragamuffin orphan boy with no idea what he had; by what sailor's kitbag or captain's chest it had made its way across half a world, no one could learn. Above all, how it had survived whatever calamity had claimed both ship and crew, nor how it had been recovered after.

The woman knew something of the story, enough to understand that it was well worth a sixpence even if it was a forgery, even if the boy would spend her benevolence on half a gill of gin and an opium pipe as soon as she was gone.

She carried it straight to the Mariners' Brotherhood, where she knew they kept a small museum devoted to a hundred and fifty years'-worth of Martian navigational history. Reverently, the man who oversaw their treasures teased scorched and wrinkled pages apart with a paperknife wrought from a nymph's claw, and read what lay within.

Of the ship's last days, and the horror that had engulfed her in the heart of the Ranges, where there was no help to be found and no hope except just to sail on. On and on, till at last they sailed out of all knowledge, into those last dread waters that men call Davy Jones's Locker...

The log is written in half a dozen hands, and much is missing or illegible, but still. A story of a sort can be drawn from what remains. It started with one cabin boy, high on the foremast and giggling strangely when he should have been serving the captain's dinner.

The officer on watch sent a couple of hands aloft to bring the boy down. When they were halfway up, he stopped giggling and started screaming. The closer they came, the louder he screamed. Frenziedly he tried to climb higher, but he was too high already and there was nowhere to go. When it was clear that he couldn't escape, he simply—let go. Before either of the hands could seize hold and save him. He plummeted to the deck so far below, and was dead.

He was the first, and they supposed he had been into the captain's brandy. But the next day, the log reports that two of the hands fell to fighting with marlinspikes, and it needed half the watch to pull them apart, both of them terribly injured and raving incoherently. The day after that, the second officer simply couldn't be found. They searched the whole ship, but there was no trace of him aboard.

And so it went on, day after day, disappearances and deaths and stranger things than either, men and boys running mad with visions and terrors they couldn't explain.

One morning the captain ate his breakfast as ever in his cabin, strolled up to the quarterdeck, nodded affably to the first officer— then hoisted a long gaff from below the taffrail, stepped up onto the rail and plunged directly over the side.

Aghast, the officers on watch ran to see, but the heavy iron gaff must have dragged him deep, too deep. They hove to and searched for hours, but he never rose again.

The first officer declared that the crew was being poisoned. He hanged the cook, and had all the stores thrown overboard. All of them. While the ship was yet a hundred leagues from any hope of salvation. Then he locked himself in the captain's cabin with a pair of pistols and fired at anyone who tried to go in and reason with him.

So then the crew was starving as well as terrified, and no one was safe.

In the end—after the first officer shot himself, and the bosun shot anyone who came near him, and the doctor killed all his insane patients and then himself—there was only one young midshipman left of all the officers, and half a dozen hungry hands. Not enough to sail the ship.

The boy's last entry in the log reads, "I have a pistol, but only one shot. I shall climb to the masthead, and wait. I know they will come for me. When they do—well. I do not know what I shall do."

And of course, no one does know what he did, and no one knows what happened at last to a crewless ship adrift in the dreadful Ranges—but prospectors and wanderers tell tales of seeing a ghost-ship go by in the night, with lamps burning and no one at the wheel, and one solitary slender figure clinging to the masthead, staring far ahead...

At the same time, in Merganeth Dormitory in But-ler House, Evvy Greenwood was reading this to her enthralled cohort:

Long years after the loss of the Nellie Martin, *when she was no more than a memory and already a legend, a one-eyed man with a twisted leg could always be found dockside at the Marsport waterfront, if you knew where to look. He had a room above the opium den, and a Chinese woman who looked after him, but he spent his days out on the quay, sitting on an upturned crate and watching the water, always watching.*

Anyone who stopped to listen, he'd tell them the same story with the same frantic urgency, clutching at their coat, trying to shake belief into them.

He had been ship's boy, he said, on the Nellie Martin, *on her fateful final voyage. He was the sole survivor, he said; barely made it out alive himself, sheer luck that let him get away. Though it cost him a leg and an eye, he still counted himself the most fortunate of men. And it was his sacred duty now, he said, to warn the world of what lay beneath the waters: what had mayhap slain the great canal-builders themselves, and then slept—until now, until men came to wake it once again...*

It came out of the blue on a crisp, clear morning, cold in the shadow of the great cliffs that loomed on either side of the canal. There was nothing to be seen, no warning, although the cap-tain kept lookouts fore and aft, high on every masthead; only that abruptly the bows dipped low to the water, as though a sudden sucking current had her. She veered out of all control, sails flapping helplessly. Four men hauled on the wheel together, trying to bring her back into the wind, but the tiller was useless against that dread-ful drag.

The bosun ran for'ard to see—well, what? Whatever there was to be seen. A vortex in the water, a forming whirlpool, a sudden leak in the canal. Something.

He leaned perilously over the prow, holding hard to the rail, as the ship tilted ever more precipitously beneath him. What he himself saw, none can actually know: was it an eye, perhaps, looking back at him? Or a mouth stretched wide to receive him, all teeth and terror?

What the crew saw, all who were looking: they saw a great grey-green tentacle flung up from below. They saw it seize the bosun and snatch him from the rail with contemptuous ease, despite his desperate grip. Just for a moment, they saw him almost seem to fly, spread-eagled against the narrow band of sky, still in the grip of that appalling tentacle—and then he was gone, snatched down below, and no one ran to the side to see what might become of him. No one dared.

Rather they were all running the other way, crowding to the stern of the vessel. The captain and his officers bellowed at them to return to their duty, but no man would. Even the lookouts were scrambling down the rigging, abandoning their posts, shrieking dire warnings as they came. No man heard, no man heeded; the ship was lost already, even before another vast writhing tentacle came over the taffrail to sweep away half the ship's command in one fell stroke.

Men had been struggling to free the boats, where they were stored on deck; now they abandoned even that last vestige of hope, stampeding from bow to stern and back again as tentacles flung up groping from below. Some leaped overboard, surely to their doom— but those who stayed must be just as surely doomed.

Most stayed none the less, while those terrible thick tentacles wrapped themselves around the vessel, fore and aft. Then there came a brutal groaning, rending, bursting sound—and the poor Nellie Martin *was hauled below the water entire, while her holds ruptured and her masts broke away.*

Now all the men were in the water, in so far as they could find water amongst all the heaving tentacles and all the flotsam the ship's ruin left behind, timbers and bales and barrels and more. Few sailors can swim, and fewer that day lived long enough to try. There were mouths among the tentacles, many mouths, even if there were only one malign intelligence behind them all.

Whatever it was, this creature, it had never been seen by man before—or at least, never by any man who lived to tell. Almost, that was true again. One lone boy, struck by a tentacle but not seized, not carried to any one of those dreadful mouths: one boy found himself floating on a barrel of flour, half blind and helpless, racked with pain but seemingly forgotten or ignored, adrift in a chaos of wreckage—but no bodies, none, and no survivors else—on water that gradually settled and was still again, except for the slow tug of current drawing him slowly and inexorably downstream.

He daren't stir, he barely dared to breathe for days. He drank canal water, and bored a hole in the barrel with his dirk; a body can live on flour and water, live for a while. At last, at long last he came out of the Ranges, and touched a bank that he could climb, although his smashed leg had set all wrong and twisted.

He found farms where he could steal food and clothing, towns where he could beg. In the end, as such lost souls do, he found his way to Marsport, and the docks. And now he never goes near a ship, never lifts his eyes to any craft of man; but he sits on his crate and watches the water, and you or I would suppose him to be watching for any sign of tentacles, or mouths. And we'd be wrong, you and I, because he's watching for something utterly other. He looks below the surface of the canal, and watches for the first sign of what he's sure must come at last, the Nellie Martin *as he last saw her, dragging along the bottom with her masts broken and her hull split and a single manic crewman still clinging to the prow, still keeping watch...*

A nd in Charm's own dormitory in Stokes, the authoress herself was telling this to her own hushed audience:

"**Y**ou'll hear tell of this theory and that, of the crew running mad or else of monsters underneath the water, but give those tales no heed. This, now, this is the true story of what happened to the poor lost *Nellie Martin.*

"She didn't break apart, she didn't sink, she wasn't swallowed whole. No, her truth is far stranger than any of the thousand guesses out there. They've never found a trace of her, from one end of the Home Water to the other, Pell to New Victoria, because there is no trace to find—nor no crewman either, no last survivor with a tale to tell, a tale of hell and high water. She can't be found, because she isn't there; her people never turned up, because they never left their ship. The poor *Nellie Martin* is truly, literally lost. She's out there somewhere, sailing far and wondrous waters, forever searching for a way back home...

"That's impossible, of course. You only have to look at a map. The Home Water runs across the province without a break, without a junction, straight and sure all the way. Once you're on the Home Water, there's nowhere else to go. How could any ship get lost, never mind one who knew her way so well?

"Well, the Home Water may seem straight by daylight, by chart and set-square, but it's another story when the moons are high and hunting. You can ask any sailor, anyone who's ever had business on the water; starshine brings up other roads, other currents, other ways to go. Songs to lure you astray, visions to chase, dreams of another world. And what sailor is ever not a dreamer?

"That's the other reason ships drop anchor at night in the Ranges, if their captain is wise. The canal may be more like a tunnel there, squeezed between walls of towering rock, but there is more than a touch of mystery in those hills. If the canal-builders live on, as people say, if they never left the planet but only avoid human ken, then that's where we'll find them. Meantime, some vestige of their power still lingers:

ancient knowledge, unless it's ancient spells. You'll find men in every port, and women too, all with tales to tell about sailing those waters, and the special perils that they met. Survivors all, and none from the *Nellie Martin*.

"She went astray, you see, in the worst way. Just this once, her captain was foolish, and chose to sail on by starlight; with the Milky Way asprawl overhead, even that bare deep slot in the rock can gather light enough to see by, on a clear night. Or a man can think it does. Exactly what it is that he sees, though: that's another matter. Or what he thinks he sees.

"Who knows what gateway opened that night, for the master of the *Nellie Martin*? Or what roads he saw, what promises, what lure? All we can say for sure is that he steered a course he never should have taken, and either the rock swallowed him or the sky took him, him and all his crew, and their vessel too.

"That and one thing more, we can say with certainty: that the *Nellie Martin* is out there yet, lost yet, and looking for her way home. Sailing strange waters and searching, always searching for a way that will lead her back. Her crew keeps a careful, terrible watch from every masthead; and now and again a prospector out in the Dry will catch a glimpse of a ship where no ship could ever be, a ship whose rigging is woven of light and shade, whose every timber glistens in the dark. Or he'll hear a drift of song, a high hungry voice calling warnings in the fog, *three fathom, aye, three fathom and a half*, though he's a long dry journey from any sight of water and he hasn't seen a fog in all the bitter months and years since then..."

CHAPTER TWENTY

Aftermaths!

"Well, what I say is, this kind of disturbance in three separate houses overnight is no coincidence. There's wickedness in this, you mark my words."

Thus Sister Anthony, at her grimmest, after a long and troubled night; but to learn what had driven her to such an utterance, we must look back to the start of it all, to one Senior girl climbing the stairs of Jopling House, facing one last duty before the end of her day.

Tired but content with the day's achievements—the school's goal for every Craterean, from Head Girl to the newest Junior—Arie Bunker trod softly down the passage in her house slippers, and eased open the door to Lady Hester dormitory. As a school prefect, she was actually entitled and rather expected to take on more difficult charges—such as the most sinful of the Middles, next door but one, where both sets of twins held court—but she had begged and pleaded to keep her role as dormitory pree for Lady Hester. After all, she pointed out, her official prefectorial job was to act as mentor and helpmeet to the Juniors, so *obviously* she should keep at least half a dozen under her direct care, shouldn't she?

Miss Peters, housemistress of Jopling, had laughed and agreed that she could stay with her beloved youngsters. "Heaven knows, they'll be as pleased as you are, and I'm just as glad to have one dorm happy in the house. There are other sacrificial victims I can offer up to those evil Middles. Or call upon to squash them, come to that."

"Oh, thank you, Miss Peters! Squashing never was really in my line, anyway. I'm much better at plumping up deflated little girls."

That wasn't strictly true, even Arie would acknowledge; but she'd always sooner try to head off trouble at the pass, detecting mischief in the early stages and deflecting those energies to some worthier cause or pastime. If she had to come down hard upon her errant lambs, she always felt it as a failure in herself, something a better shepherd would have helped them to avoid.

Drawing the door closed behind her, she began her last inspection, twitching back the curtains of each cubicle and checking on the girl within. Not every dormitory prefect did this every night, but Arie held it as a sacred duty: a chance to wish sweet dreams to her sleeping charges, and to discover any who were not. There was always light enough to tell on clear nights, bright starlight falling through tall uncurtained windows; and besides, Arie had an instinct for the wakeful, even when they tried to pretend otherwise. Those she would always go in to, to sit on their bed and comfort the sorrowing, soothe the anxious, ease the conscience of the troubled sinner, all in the low murmur that she had learned long since, that carries through a sleeping roomful far less piercingly than a whisper.

None of her charges was wakeful this night, but even so she wasn't quite happy. There was a restlessness that seemed to pervade the dorm. More than one girl was tossing and turning in her sleep; Agnosia's covers had slipped off altogether. While she did some brisk, firm tucking-in—fortunately without disturbing any of the sleepers, more than they were disturbed already—Arie became aware of a low muttering somewhere in the room. Briefly her vivid imagination threw up thoughts of witches casting a spell over all the slumberers—but that was ridiculous, of course. Clearly, it was coming from another cubicle. She checked swiftly, and found Marigold Kettle as fast asleep as any of them, and talking none the less.

The words were incomprehensible, and the voice hardly even seemed to be Marigold's own, low and hoarse and hissing. Worried Arie laid a hand on the small girl's brow, but there was no fever, only that fretful restlessness that had gripped all the dorm.

Marigold must only be having a bad dream. Arie dismissed thoughts of dashing to fetch the housemistress, or even Sister Anthony. She was half inclined to wake her troubled junior, but while Marigold was a blithe and cheerful soul when conscious, she was known to be a poor sleeper. Better to leave her until the nightmare came to a natural end and she settled into a more healthful rest, rather than risk having her wakeful half the night.

Even so, Arie drew back the curtain between her own cubicle and Marigold's. She undressed speedily, said her prayers—with a special appeal to her own beloved St Raphael, patron saint of sweet dreams and restful nights—and slipped into bed with no intention of sleeping yet. She meant to keep an eye on young Marigold, and be instantly on hand if the girl should wake.

It was a pity, because her bed was delightfully warm and cosy, and she was so very full of sleep herself. Perhaps she should throw the covers off, just to be that little less comfortable? St Raphael would scold her, though, and she wouldn't want that...

A rie woke with a start, from dreams more pleasant than any of her companions'. What time was it? She blinked through the starlight at her watch on the bedside table. A little after one o'clock. What had wakened her? She hadn't meant to nod off, but ordinarily once she had gone over she would sleep through until morning, unless one of her lambs needed her.

Not much doubt which lamb that might be tonight. She glanced towards Marigold's bed, expecting to see the little girl wide awake and sitting up, waiting for the night-terrors to pass.

Instead, she saw tumbled sheets and blankets, an abandoned pillow, an empty bed.

Alert but still not quite alarmed, Arie rose and wrapped herself firmly in her dressing gown. Marigold's she saw still hanging from its hook on the wall. Tutting softly, Arie retrieved it and the neglected slippers too from the foot of the bed, before she went in search. The little tyke might just be fetching herself a glass of water from the nightstand in the hallway, or she might have given up on her bed altogether and gone in search of better entertainment. Either way, law-abiding or otherwise, she should have bundled up warmly before she ventured out of her cubicle. That was an absolute rule. She was asking for trouble, wandering about at night in just a nightdress. Even in early summer, Martian nights remembered their desert origin.

Hoping to spare the girl worse trouble than chilly feet and a brisk scolding, Arie trod softly to the dormitory door, and found it standing wide. Really, had the child no sense at all? You'd think she was deliberately seeking to draw down wrathful authority upon her unabashed head. No sign could be more revealing of mischief at work than an open dorm door. Arie would leave it ajar herself, but only just: enough for a quiet return with her straying lamb, not enough to attract notice from any other wanderer out later than she should be. Miss Peters would notice, sure as eggs is eggs, if she happened by—but she wouldn't raise the house with alarums, as a random schoolgirl might.

Arie glanced towards the hallway table, where a jug of water and a tray of glasses stood waiting. No sign of the little wretch there. Had she headed downstairs, to the common room? Most likely, unless she was visiting in another dorm, which was also strictly against the rules. Just to be sure, Arie looked the other way, along the corridor, in case she could spot another open door—and what she saw almost had her raising the house with alarums herself, though she swallowed down her incipient yell just in time.

There was Marigold, a slender figure barefoot in a nacre-ous starlit gown, at the end window that lit the whole cor-ridor. That window was left wide open all night in season and—according to some girls, at least—out of season, in compliance with the school's belief in fresh air whenever possible, and plenty of it.

There was Marigold, with both hands on the sill—and one knee rising in between them. Did the girl seriously mean to climb out? Arie's mind was working overtime as she hurried down the corridor, but she was already quite sure there was nothing there to climb out onto, no handy jut of roof below, no fire escape. Only the fall, twenty feet straight down. Into a flowerbed, granted—or was this where the bench stood, between two beds? Either way, even on Mars, schoolgirls didn't bounce.

She daren't call out, for fear of startling Marigold over the edge—but did she dare wait until she was in reach, in grab-bing range? And what in the world was the child *thinking*...?

Lightly though she trod in her effort not to spook the girl, perhaps she made some sound in her hurry. Or perhaps Marigold reacted to something else, the breath of Arie's movement, the urgency of her stare; or else it might always have been a part of her inward story, that she should turn now to stare in her turn down the corridor behind her.

Her eyes were wide and blank, reacting to nothing. She gazed at Arie—or through her, rather—as though she had no more solidity than the air, no more meaning than the starlight.

Oh!

One thing Arie knew, the only thing that mattered now: you should never try to wake a sleepwalker!

On the other hand, she couldn't conceivably allow Marigold to climb out of that window, which the younger girl still seemed utterly intent on doing.

"Marigold, you need to come in now." She kept her voice low, that same voice she used in the dormitory, not to wake the sleepers. "It's time for bed, Marigold. Step back from the window now."

She'd grab if she had to, at whatever cost—but something imperative in Arie's voice seemed to catch at Marigold's awareness. She held stock-still for a moment, then her knee drew back from the sill, and she did at least have both feet firmly planted inside the house again.

That was something. Not enough.

"Turn around, Marigold. Turn around, and come with me."

Arie was being—she hoped!—gently persuasive, a soft voice that could work in the sleeping girl's mind without waking her fully, only enough to bring some measure of control over whatever it was that she was dreaming.

Marigold did turn as instructed, still with that strange absence on her face, as though her gaze and the thoughts behind them were far and far away. She was muttering to herself again, Arie realised now—or singing, rather, in a thin and reedy whisper. The older girl bent close to hear, and again understood how all her junior's senses were turned elsewhere.

"The wind ... the wind is the current and the sky is ice... Here underwater we can all live twice..." And then, losing the tune all in a moment, "There are dead folk all around us. Dead in the ship behind me, dead in the water, dead ahead. They didn't live twice, no. Only me. And I can't die, not till I spy our way home again. Got to keep hold, got to keep looking. So cold, I think my eyes will freeze. I think my hands have frozen, couldn't let go now if I tried..."

Arie slid an arm carefully around the girl's slender shoulders and felt her trembling in that sheer nightie. "You are cold, aren't you?" she murmured, though the night was warm enough and she was sure that what shook Marigold was some internal chill, nothing to do with the actual temperature. "Come on, I'll take you somewhere warm."

One other thing she was sure of, that this was too much for her to deal with alone. Mortal schoolgirl was not made for this much responsibility, no. Blessedly, Marigold seemed content to be steered back down the corridor. She was singing again, achingly deep in her throat, but this time Arie made no attempt to distinguish the words. Not her task. She was a little afraid, if she were honest; she wanted an adult, and as soon as possible.

Still talking softly, as reassuring as she could manage, she brought Marigold to Miss Peters' door and tapped.

Housemistresses learn to sleep lightly. Arie heard movement, a voice, "Just a moment!"—and little more than a moment later, the door opened. Miss Peters was in dressing gown and slippers, ready for anything. This particular thing took her another moment, a blink and a visible rethink; and then, just to be certain, she murmured, "Arie, why is Marigold out of bed?"

"Please, Miss Peters, I—I think she's sleepwalking. I found her trying to climb out of a window. And she's been saying things…"

"Very well. Now then, Marigold," talking to the girl much as Arie had done, softly but clearly, trying to reach through horror and confusion to the sleeping brain without actually waking her, "come along into my room. I've some milk here which I expect you'd like, once I've warmed it up—heavens, child!" in an abrupt interruption of her own narrative, barely remembering to keep her voice low. "Your hands are like ice! Arie, are those her gown and slippers? Splendid. Give them to me, and you run for Sister Anthony, will you? No cause for alarm; I expect Marigold will be fine come morning, but I'd like to be sure there's nothing worse has brought this on. In you come now, Marigold. Sit on my bed here, where it's warm…"

Like an automaton, Marigold did as she was told. After a speaking glance from Miss Peters, so did the enthralled and anxious Arie. She hurried back to her own cubicle, and flung a mac over her dressing gown and nightie. That should be enough. Outdoor shoes replaced her slippers, and she barely took the time to tie them haphazardly before she was off again, stepping as lightly as she could, not to disturb any more of her lambs any more than they were disturbed already.

It wasn't the first time she'd been sent for Sister Anthony in the night, in an emergency. There were only two rules for such a mission: first, that you understood she might be anywhere on school grounds, or even further afield (it was widely rumoured that she didn't need sleep, thanks to the peculiar properties of a Martian herb she had discovered during her long vigil in her bare bleak hut on the crater's lip, before the school had opened); and second, that you always tried her room in the San first before looking elsewhere. As often as not that was where you found her, in a nightdress with her bedclothes disturbed behind her (an obvious distraction, to fool the gullible; for reasons unknown but never mercenary, Sister Anthony had pledged to keep her discovery secret). If not, then you faced a long and lonely hunt all through the school.

Arie was already wondering whom she might disturb to help in that hunt—Rowany, surely; and Rowany might dare to wake a mistress, when Arie couldn't—as she came dashing out of Jopling House into the clear Martian night. As always, the stars gave light enough to see by—but there was more light somehow than the sky could justify. Blinking about, she saw bright windows upstairs in Stokes House, and in Butler too. Those were dormitories, she knew, from the lack of curtains. She didn't know whose, but one thing for certain, something unusual was afoot in both houses. Lights and disturbance, at this time of night?

She was already stepping uncertainly towards Stokes, in clear defiance of the Second Rule of Seeking Sister Anthony, when the house door opened and a figure appeared, briefly outlined against a lamp burning in the hallway behind her. A figure tall even for Mars, gaunt even for Mars, with a stern and well-known, even well-beloved bearing...

Arie gasped in relief, and ran headlong.

"Oh, Sister Anthony! I'm so glad to find you. Can you come?"

"What, another?" If it weren't unthinkable, Arie might almost have thought she detected a note of weariness in the astringent voice, as though even Sister Anthony were susceptible on rare occasions to merely human frailty. "What's the trouble in Jopling, then?"

"It's Marigold Kettle, Sister. She's been sleepwalking. I barely stopped her climbing out of a top-floor window. She's safe now, but Miss Peters would be really glad if you could come and see her..."

"Did you wake her?" No note of weariness in that voice now, only the familiar snap, as crisp as her starched habit.

"I don't believe so. At least, I really tried not, and so did Miss Peters. When I left them, Marigold was doing what she was told, but she really didn't seem to have woken."

"Very well. I'll come at once. Marigold Kettle is Lower Third, isn't she? Your dormitory?"

"Yes, that's right, Sister." No possibility of surprise; Sister Anthony was known to know every smallest detail of the school's domestic arrangements, and to forget nothing.

"Hmm. Three out of four, then; there's been some mischief afoot, it's all too clear. How are the rest of that crew— wakeful at all?"

"No-o, not exactly wakeful, but they all seem restless tonight."

"And I have an outbreak of collective nightmare in Stokes, and a child in Butler sobbing herself into sickness and hysterics. All Lower Third, which is a diagnosis in itself. I'll search every locker in the morning, to see what those children have been reading. In the meantime, they've had doses all round, and should sleep through the rest of the night. I'll see you take a dose too, Arie, after chasing about in the cold like this. You might have taken the time to dress properly, knowing that you had to leave the house." Sister Anthony herself, of course, was immaculately dressed. And as brisk in pace as she was in manner; here they were already back at Jopling, and Aric too slow to open the door for her elder as she should have done.

Briskly in, and briskly upstairs; and there was a light spilling through the open door of Miss Peters' room, and there inside was Marigold awake now, in floods of tears, her hands shaking visibly as they wrapped around a mug of steaming milk.

"Yes, well. You cut along to bed now, Arie. I'll check on you as soon as we're finished here. And the rest of those imps of yours, too. If any of them are awake, make sure they lie quiet until I come."

"Yes, Sister. What about Marigold, though—should I fill a hot water bottle for her bed?"

"No, she won't be back in the dormitory tonight. I expect Miss Peters will want to keep her close; if not, I've a truckle in my own room, and she won't be walking out of that, no matter what spirit moves her."

It may have been the first time in Crater School history that three entire dormitories, all in different houses, were allowed—indeed, under firm instruction—to have their sleep out and then lie quiet in bed until they were summoned.

The instructions were just the same for the prefect in each dormitory. Ostensibly they were there to ensure obedience from their unreliable juniors; in fact the older girls were judged just as much in need of as much sleep as they could manage, after the violence of their disturbed nights. Like any healthy schoolgirl, they disliked frowsting in bed while the true life of the school went on without them; but like any sensible Crater School girl, like the very newest of new girls, they lived in wholesome awe of the tyrant of the San, and would never dare disobey her.

The school clock had already struck nine, therefore, before movement came to Lady Hester dorm; and when it did, it came from outside. First the door, opening and closing; then footsteps coming down all the way to Arie's cubicle. It was the Head Girl herself, Melanie Fitzwalter, who popped her head between the curtains and said, "Good morning, sleepyhead! You're to get up now, unless you have a really good reason not to."

"I'll be delighted," Arie said, suiting the action to the word and springing out of bed. "Do I have any hope of breakfast?"

"Idiot. As if they'd let you start a day without. Hurry through your bath, get dressed and hustle up to Miss Leven's study. Coffee awaits you, I am told, and a plate of Mrs Bailey's very best buns and pastries. Which is better fare than the rest of us could dream of, this being a porridge morning for we mere mortals. Go on, off you scoot. I am to stand watch over your pet lambs here, until they are sent for."

Nobody actually groaned aloud—who would dare?—but it was clear somehow that all the girls in the dormitory were awake now, and listening in, and didn't take this to be good news in any respect.

"Thanks, Melanie. Any word of Marigold?"

"Not for you, my child. You have your own interests, in this unusual hour. I would recommend you be about them."

Arie hurried through her ablutions, for remarkable values of "hurry" in a school that already granted its girls the barest minimum of time for their toilette. Breakfast in Miss Leven's study was unheard of, undreamed of; she dursen't be late, but at the same time she dursen't have a hair out of place or the least wrinkle in her stockings, the merest fleck of dust on a blazer shoulder. She was grateful to have Melanie's critical, experienced eye to check her over, before she hustled on her way up to the Castle.

On the way, she encountered two other girls emerging from their own houses, as hurried and as carefully dressed as she: Charmian Falk and Sophie Amersham, her classmates and her counterparts, she knew, watchful guardians over their own dormitories replete with bright sparks of the Lower Third.

"Are you two summoned too?" she greeted them.

"We absolutely are. Coffee and buns. What on earth is going on? This never happens!" Thus Sophie; while Charmian added, "Does either of you have any notion what those wretched children have been up to? Half my babes woke screaming from what seems to have been more or less the same nightmare; and meanwhile Sophie's Evangeline apparently made herself *revoltingly* ill, just from the same nameless upset..."

None of them knew any more, though Arie could at least bring them up to date with her own night of drama. Sleepwalking trumped mere sickness, as being so much more exotic and unusual; but altogether this whole notion of infectious nightmare engaged them all the way from their houses to the Castle steps.

There, they remembered the nature of their summons here, checked each other over one more time for neatness and respectability, and hurried to the study door. A slightly nervous tap—because who ever came to this particular door without a twinge of anxiety, however clear her conscience?— and a brief pause, then a voice calling them in.

Later and in private, among friends, Arie would say that it was like being summoned before the Star Chamber. They walked in to find more people than they had expected, more than they had ever seen in Miss Leven's study; and more chairs even than people. Besides the headmistress, there was Miss Tattersall of maths and Butler House, Miss Hendy—natural sciences and Stokes—and her own housemistress Miss Peters, all looking solemn and stern. There was Sister Anthony, who always did look solemn and stern. And then there was Mrs Buchanan, which made no sense at all. A parent staying on at school to do some work in the sculpture garden, much beloved by all the girls—what had she to do with this? Whatever this was? And why did she look upset?

And then those three empty chairs, and there were three of them but not one made any kind of move beyond the mandated curtsey until Miss Leven gestured.

"Do sit yourselves down, girls, and take a bun. I know you missed your breakfasts. I have coffee here," which she was pouring with her own hands, "so let's see if I remember how you like it: milky and sweet for you, Charmian, I know; milky but *not* sweet for Sophie, I think—and plain black for Arie. How did I do?"

That really wasn't even a question. Miss Leven had never been known to be wrong about such matters. If Sister Anthony knew everything about the domestic economy of the school, Miss Leven simply knew everything, full stop.

They took their coffees and mumbled their thanks, balanced buns awkwardly on their saucers, sat in the proffered chairs and tried to efface themselves entirely. Sixth-formers they might be and house prefects too—a school prefect in Arie's case, highest of the high—and yet they still felt young and gauche and hopelessly out of place in this company.

Long-seasoned mistresses did their best to put them at ease, talking lightly about neutral matters while the girls ate rapidly, embarrassed by everything including their own embarrassment; but as soon as cups and saucers both were empty, and they had shaken their heads to offers of more, Miss Leven came to the point.

"Girls, I'm sorry to put you through this, because I know you'll find it uncomfortable—uncomfortable at best—but it does have to be faced, and you're old enough to understand that. And to sit through it. We believe we've discovered the prime reason for all the disturbance last night, across three houses. None of her cohort would give her away, not even the girls most upset by nightmare or worse—but Sister

Anthony searched the dormitories thoroughly, and turned up these." She gestured towards two scribbled manuscripts on her desk. "Those creatures have been telling each other ghost stories, fit to chill the blood—or rather, it seems that one particularly inventive creature has been doing that, and must have been interrupted. She appears to have spent her prep-time scribbling down alternative endings to a tale half told, and distributing those among her friends' dormitories, while she presumably narrated the final version herself to her own. We will *not* be applauding her inventiveness, please, despite all temptation, in view of the effects her horrors have induced. Rather, I am going to summon her here to apologise in person to each and every one of those whose nights she disturbed so wilfully."

All three girls protested, pleaded, squirmed in their seats at the awfulness of this doom—they were properly victims here, and they felt as though they were being punished too—but Miss Leven was adamant; this would happen, and it would happen now. They would each of them be apologised to, directly and personally, however much they might loathe it.

"Mrs Buchanan has identified the handwriting as belonging to her daughter Charm. Other evidence supports this identification, not least the fact that she seems to have been the only one across three dormitories to have slept soundly last night. Miss Hendy, I think it's time that you fetched her here, please. I know she and all her cohorts have had their bread-and-milk by now, and will be dressed and ready; I daresay she may be expecting the summons."

It would still take time for Miss Hendy to make her way down to Stokes and return with the condemned, ready or not, expectant or otherwise; and they all knew how slow a reluctant girl could be, walking to her execution. While they waited, Miss Leven passed the documents in question to the three sixth-formers. "We've all read these, and I think you should too, so that you know just what these children have been up to."

"One child, chiefly, and to my eternal shame she's my own," Mrs Buchanan murmured. "Mind you, I don't want to excuse her in the slightest, and I promise never to mention it to her—at least, never until she's left school, and matters of discipline no longer apply—but there are some lines in there that made me blink and read them again. Far be it from me to say so, especially here and now, where it would be wholly inappropriate—but I wonder if my younger daughter might not turn out to be a real writer, and make some impression on the worlds in time to come."

"If we don't scare her off altogether, this morning," Miss Leven said grimly. "Oh, don't worry, Isobel, we shan't scarify your young sinner—or not unreasonably, not out of sea-son—but I do mean to drive it home just how unacceptable this particular outbreak of her talents has proven to be. If she weren't so good with her words, perhaps the effects might have been less alarming—but no, please don't tell her that until she is well out from under our purview. Rules exist for reasons, and this is one of them. Girls of that age, even stout and sensible Martian girls, are far too susceptible to be exposed to frightening tales last thing at night. And so I shall explain to her, albeit somewhat fearsomely; and then we will bend our efforts to redirecting her imagination into more appropriate channels. As it happens, I know that Miss Peters agrees with your assessment, and has some ideas that she'd like to discuss with you before presenting them to your errant offshoot. Though we won't mention that either, if you please; she's not to feel herself at all rewarded. Not today."

There was really no question about that, from the first minute that Charm entered the study. She gazed about her, and swallowed visibly in the face of that gathered assembly in its solemnity; even her mother didn't crack a smile of welcome. It looked almost as though Miss Hendy's hand firm on her shoulder was the only thing holding her upright—and that was before she saw the evidence arrayed against her, those two manuscripts spread out on Miss Leven's desk, an ultimate and unanswerable accusation.

She went visibly pale, paler even than she had been already, and Miss Hendy was quick to push a chair behind her failing knees. She sank into it, and gazed at her mother mutely; Mrs Buchanan shook her head briefly, and nodded towards Miss Leven.

"Very well, Charm. It's clear that you know why you're here. You wrote these stories, or half-stories, for your friends to read in their dorms—no, don't worry, I'm not going to ask which particular girls read them out loud, although I could probably guess—and I suppose that you told your own story to your own dorm without troubling to write it down, is that right?"

She paused, and the hapless Charm could do nothing but nod.

"You do know, I believe, that you are not supposed to talk after prayers? You're allowed that time for quiet reading, to prepare yourselves for sleep, not telling penny-dreadful stories to each other. Never mind stories that you must have known were not permitted to be told in this school. I know you were present at choir practice, when Ellen-Stephanie was chastised for singing the opening verse of the song that tells the same tale. She knew no better, but you do not have that excuse."

Poor Charm gulped at that, but Miss Leven went on relentlessly.

"That's two offences—and I suspect that we will learn of more through the day, as it seems likely that you sacrificed your prep time to preparing these ... narratives, rather than doing the work set for you. That's another act of dishonesty, as you're effectively lying to the prefect who supervises you, giving her the impression that you're working diligently when in fact you're stealing her trust and your own time. I should have had her here too; I don't know whether I can trust you to find her and apologise to her unsupervised. In the meantime, though, I am going to require you to apologise individually to each of us gathered here, who have all had their nights interrupted to deal with sick and frightened children, all thanks to your rampant self-indulgence..."

Watching, Arie was unclear whether it was the accusation of dishonesty that broke Charm's tremulous self-control, or the prospect of half a dozen apologies here, in front of witnesses, and more to come. One way or the other, though, the girl was reduced to racking sobs; the apologies came in due order, but were each of them almost inaudible through her tears; and when at last Arie and her fellows were allowed to leave, with a courteous nod and a sympathetic smile from their headmistress, Charm was on her knees with her face buried in her mother's skirt.

CHAPTER TWENTY-ONE

A Farewell to Decency

Rowany de Vere, scion of generals and sister of subalterns, was deeply dissatisfied with herself—which was sufficiently unusual as to come as a surprise even to her own deeply dissatisfied self. She simply wasn't accustomed to letting people down this badly. As a rule, as a matter of habit and principle both, she met every challenge head-on, with never a doubt or a hesitation; that was the de Vere way, a lesson learned at her grandfather's knee and reinforced by boisterous brothers all her life. It was also of course the Crater School way, and to a great extent the Martian way, the way of all her people.

This time, though, she was almost defined by doubt, and hobbled by hesitation. She knew her task, she had opportunity aplenty—and yet, and yet. The mere thought of putting it into effect soured her stomach and her self-content, even as her constant putting it off made her feel that she had been badly misjudged, overrated by people who were supposed to know better.

Still, it had to be done, she did recognise that; and who better to do it than herself, such a transient now in school, with only this last snatched year left to her? Had the task fallen to a mistress, it might have tainted her entire tenure here.

So: no more dithering. She would sally forth—right now, while she was still determined—and get it done. And if she felt sickened by herself afterwards, so be it.

The highly unorthodox summer school she had attended in a draughty country house outside Oxford—well, it had been barely springtime there, a cold and blustery March that had seemed specifically designed to have them suffer indoors and out, but the name had stuck regardless—had sent her home equipped with both the skills and the tools that she needed. Her blazer pockets jingled as she walked.

It was midday, and all the school was busy: either in the Castle at her back, or else out on the playing-fields under Miss Whitworth's eagle eye. There ought not to be a single girl in the houses in between.

Here was Jopling, where Miss Peters was housemistress, but of course she was teaching; there ought to be no one at all within. Besides, Jopling was where Rowany had her own small private room. No reason for her to skulk in shadows and watch the windows for any errant prying face, when she was wholly entitled to be here.

And yet skulk she did, and watch; and finally scuttle through the door with her cheeks aflame, the very definition of shamefaced, like the very guiltiest of girls under the eyes of an all-seeing Authority. Which was ridiculous, of course, when she was bent upon Authority's own mission.

I'm not asking you to spy on her, Miss Tolchard had said, and even at the time, that had not rung true to Rowany's ears. And since then—well. Rowany had singularly failed to make a confidante of young Catherine, even when opportunity had presented itself, at mealtimes or during evenings here in Jopling. Since Sister Anthony had swept the girl away into the San, there'd really been no chance at all to pursue any kind of relationship. It simply wasn't possible to sherpa a girl you never saw.

The task remained, though, to test where Catherine's true loyalties lay: to her English mother or her Russian father. Listening to other girls' chatter and probing obliquely with delicate questions had served no useful purpose; the only image Rowany had been able to draw from that was of a girl impossibly divided, starkly British on the one hand and equally starkly Russian on the other.

With all the sympathy in the world, Rowany simply did not, could not believe in such divided loyalties. She thought it literally impossible to hold two such opposing views within the same mind. Therefore, the girl must be deceiving everyone about one or the other. Whether she was deceiving herself too, Rowany didn't feel herself qualified to judge. But was she truly Catherine, or truly Ekaterina? Did her heart turn east, or west? There was only one way to know for certain, and it was Rowany's task to uncover the truth. If that task was bitter to her, so be it. No one had ever said that a spy's life was decorous or tasteful. Here was her chance to learn whether she could stomach it or not.

Very well, then. Across the hallway and up the stairs, brisk and purposeful. If she turned left, the corridor would take her to her own little room; instead she turned right, and counted off the dormitories. Here in Jopling they were named after mathematicians: Ada Lovelace, Emilie du Chatelet, Mary Somerville. Catherine was a Somerville girl. Second cubicle on the left.

The bed was made, the curtains were flung up over the rails according to regulation to let the room air out; there was nowhere to hide, from any unexpected arrival or from herself. Nothing to do but get on with it, then.

The authorities at the Crater School had always kept a distant but watchful eye on their pupils' correspondence. Not to read the contents, heavens no, but to know how often the girls heard from home, how often from friends and relations, how often and to whom they wrote themselves. There had been occasions when that scrupulous record-keeping had proved more than useful, in diagnosing a girl's troubles and finding a solution to them. Rare occasions, to be sure, but enough of them to justify the policy and its continuation.

It had been no trouble, then, for Rowany to learn that Catherine received weekly letters from her mother, and replied dutifully every Sunday in the hour set aside for that purpose; also that she heard equally regularly from her father, but replied—so far as the school knew—not at all.

It was hard to understand how she could have replied in any case, as there was no direct postal service from Mars to St Petersburg, nor indeed any other contact. Her only clear recourse would have been a letter sent care of the Russian Embassy in London, who might have forwarded it in a diplomatic pouch.

Equally hard to understand, though, was how her father's letters could be reaching her so regularly. Aetherships came and went unpredictably, and mail from Earth might take months to arrive. A steady weekly delivery from off-planet was quite impossible—and besides, these letters were postmarked in Marsport. It was beyond impossible that the man himself could be on Mars, and Authority not know it. They had of course checked in any case, and he was reported clearly at home. Had he perhaps written a dozen letters in advance, and conveyed them to a hidden agent to mail one by one? As Catherine was apparently making no effort to reply, there needed no back-and-forth responses, nor any current content. Or perhaps he sent his messages by radio, via a relay on one of the moons, and whoever received them wrote them out and posted them on his behalf? All Rowany had been able to learn was that these letters were written in Cyrillic script; she could come up with no way of asking Catherine whether or not they were in her father's hand. Or indeed if they were truly letters from her father, rather than instructions from a spymaster.

With their source so mysterious, it had become imperative to learn quite what the letters actually said. If they were somehow innocent, then perhaps Catherine was no more than an unhappy schoolgirl torn between two parents. If they were clearly something else, then that was almost impossible to believe true. It was up to Rowany to make that determination, little though she wanted to. It might be a spy's first duty to intercept communications from the enemy, but she was barely yet a spy; she had been a decent English girl all her life, and it was an absolute rule that a decent English girl never read someone else's private papers, be they letters or diaries or secret family recipes or whatnot.

So: farewell decency, she supposed.

She knew this much, that Catherine kept her letters in a locked box in her nightstand. One of her dormitory-mates had let slip as much, in a slightly shocked whisper. Crater School girls did not keep even their most private possessions under lock and key; there was no occasion to, where every other girl was assumed to be as decent as Rowany had believed herself, until now. It might not be actually against the rules to lock things away, but it was very much against the spirit of the school. Miss Peters must already have had a word with Catherine about that, but the box was still locked. Which might again argue for a bad conscience, a bad conscience at the least...

Enough dithering. Rowany opened Catherine's nightstand, and lifted out a padded box upholstered in worn cream silk. It looked well-loved, perhaps a gift or an inheritance from a grandmother: a Russian grandmother, to judge by the silver escutcheon with its engraved double-eagle around the keyhole. Rowany sat herself on Catherine's bed, set the box next to her and fished the picklocks from her pocket.

She played them for a moment between her fingers, getting the feel again; it had been too long since she'd practised. Nevertheless: there could be nothing challenging about this lock, unless it was significantly more sophisticated than it seemed. Which again would be a black mark against Catherine, because what schoolgirl needed a complicated lock behind a simple-seeming cover?

Jingle, jingle, little keys,
How I wonder what will please?
This one, that one, just a twist,
Lift and press and use the wrist...

It was a little rhyme she had come up with on her own account, that helped to steady her mind and her fingers both, as she slipped the first and then the second pick into the lock and fiddled delicately, scritching and scratching until she felt the levers connect.

There was a solid click, and the lid was suddenly loose. That was supposed to be the difficult part over with, but actually it was much harder to lift the lid and see, yes, seven or eight envelopes in there, and lift them out and lay them on the bed.

Even the hand that wrote the address in plain English script was Russian by birth and training; she could tell that from the square, careful shaping of the letters. The pages within were covered with a brisk, confident Cyrillic script, unintelligible to any average Martian, and to most of the girls at school here too. Not all of them, though. Catherine might have good reason to keep these letters locked away. Not that she need fear snoopers—at least, Rowany hoped not; she hoped no Crater School girl would stoop as low as this, as she was now—but one casual glance over her shoulder might be enough to give her away. If there was anything to give away, if she actually had anything to hide.

That was Rowany's chief anxiety, that she would find good cause for her seniors' suspicions. She desperately wanted Catherine to be an innocent in this, an unhappy schoolgirl and nothing more, nothing worse. She must set that feeling aside, though. It was her task here to be impartial, to make a fair assessment and a true report: nothing more, but certainly nothing less. If she felt like judge, jury and executioner all rolled into one—or worse, like Judas, befriending and then betraying—well, she must simply set that aside too. Her feelings mattered not at all here. They shouldn't, mustn't sway her one way or the other.

She cleared her mind, then, as best she could, and sorted the letters neatly into chronological order. One a week, punctual to the day, to the very hour according to the postmarks from the Marsport sorting office. Unfortunately there was no way to tell where in the city they might have been posted, or a watch could have been kept on that box, and something perhaps learned of who was doing the posting, and how they had come by the letters...

Rowany caught herself up sharply, as her mind began to speculate. There must surely be some method for discovering into which postbox any particular item had been dropped—but that was a question for another day and another school than this. Here and now, she had a different mission.

Accordingly—though still reluctantly—she began to read.

Rowany the cool assessor, the impartial judge: try though she might to invoke that aspect of herself, it lasted only about halfway down the first page of notepaper.

Before and long before she had reached the end of the last letter, she was silently raging.

"The man's a monster!" she burst out at last, silent no longer. She had pulled herself grimly and swiftly across the lake in one of the school's beloved boats, hoping that simple effort would sweat the fury out of her. It didn't seem to have worked. She'd run her targets to earth in the garden of their pretty house on the lakeside, in the shadow of the great Sanatorium; Dr Mackenzie was taking his ease in a deckchair on the lawn, while his wife—"Mrs Mac" to any pupil that remembered, but still and always "Miss Tolchard" to most, though no one still at school had known her before her marriage—was grubbing with a hand trowel in a border of bright marguerites.

Rowany had held her tongue during the necessary preludes of fetching another deckchair, calling for tea and biscuits, exchanging family and school news. Now she could let go.

"What that poor girl has been going through, week after week... It's no wonder she's in San now, and not getting any better, as far as I can see."

"Just tell us, Rowany. What's the situation?"

"Sorry, Dr Mac. I'm just so angry still, I can't think straight."

"Take a breath, marshal the facts and lay them out for us. Remember, we know nothing, except that she's been getting letters. And not answering them, as far as we can tell."

"Oh, I'm sure she's not answering them. How could she? There's no way for a girl to mail anything except through her housemistress, and I don't suppose she's leaving secret messages tucked in the hollow of an old oak for some go-between to collect and send on. Besides, these aren't that kind of letter. They don't call for answers, they're not asking for news or reports or results. They're ... exhortations, rather. Work harder, try harder, do more. Any ambitious parent might say the same—but any other parent would have a different future in mind for their daughter, college or a career, a trophy, something... Something *decent*. There's no decency in this.

"It's bullying of the worst kind: sometimes hectoring, sometimes insidious, always ruthless and above all relentless... I wanted to wash my hands after just touching those letters. And Catherine's been hoarding them, rereading them over and over, living with them all term. Of course she looks so pale and ill. I'm surprised she hasn't run quite mad, to be honest."

"Tell us, Rowany," Mrs Mackenzie said mildly. "What do the letters actually say?"

"They say... Oh, they say it all. Anything you can imagine, they say that and more. They tell her always to remember that she's Russian, first and last and always. I suppose there's nothing wrong with that, at least in theory, if only there were a voice reminding her that she's British too, just as much and just as importantly; but she doesn't have that. Over and over again, the letters say that her loyalty and duty are owed to Mother Russia and to her alone. And that she should listen to her father and to him alone, in the matter of what that loyalty and duty demand of her; and that at some future point she will be called on to account to him—and perhaps to other authorities, he makes that bit sound really scary—for how she has pursued her task while she was here.

"As to what that task is—well, I suppose it's as we feared. She's to make friends, high and low—which of course you'd want any schoolgirl to do, except this isn't to her own benefit in any way, it's all for the glory of Mother Russia. She's to sing the praises of the motherland at every opportunity, the beauties of the Winter Palace and the Tsar's court, the strength and wealth of St Petersburg and the stoic power of her people, in an effort to recruit girls at their most persuasible. I don't suppose they seriously think she'd be able to build a network of schoolgirl-spies, but it does no harm to try. To practise. Certainly they intend her to go on, to university and beyond; and he appears both ready and willing to go on and on, badgering her non-stop all the way.

"I don't think she's a willing partner in this, I don't believe she volunteered—but I can't see how she can hold up against so much pressure. Especially from her own father, that's what's most wicked. The man's a monster, but he is still her father, and I don't know how we can protect her from him."

"Not in the long run, no," Mrs Mackenzie said. "We've no right to withhold his letters, even knowing the content as we do now, even if we think they're entirely harmful to her well-being and her state of mind. A girl's contact with her family is sacrosanct and must remain so, for as long as she is trusted to our care. In the short term, I suspect that Sister Anthony would be willing to issue a blanket ban on all mail, with the girl as disturbed as she obviously is at present. That would offer no more than a respite, though, and she'd have to be given her letters sooner or later."

"That might even be worse," Rowany murmured, "getting them all at once like that."

"As you did yourself, just now? The full blast of the tempest, unmitigated by time? Perhaps so. Lord knows, I'd sooner not stand between the girl and her mail. I know how you girls do love your letters."

"Well, when you're away at school..." Rowany said vaguely, and didn't need to chase that thought any further. She knew that Mrs Mackenzie did absolutely understand. A letter was a touch of warmth, of home, of a wholly other and less complicated life; it was a chance to catch your breath in the midst of all the flurry.

Or it should be. A letter for Catherine must be something else entirely. A brief feeling of dread, perhaps, before the yearning: would it be from her mother? Let it be from her mother... Then she'd glance at the envelope, before she even saw the handwriting, and know immediately. Her heart would sink—at least, if she were the decent girl that Rowany was still hoping to discover in her—and she'd slide the letter quickly out of sight, not to be opened till she could be alone with her thoughts, with her misery, with her torn conflicted dual self.

Rowany had no idea how this could be mended. If that was even possible at all. She was determined, though, that should there be any way achievable by mortal woman, she would find it out. No child deserved to suffer this way, and certainly no Crater School pupil should be allowed to. They came here to find their own path through life, not to be pressed into service as someone else's pawn. Neither someone else's mouthpiece. This could not and would not stand, not while Rowany had breath in her body and all the steel will of her forefathers to drive her, not if she had to go to St Petersburg herself and confront the monster in his own perilous den...

CHAPTER TWENTY–TWO

"She's gone! She's run away!"

"**P**ete! Pete! Oh, wake up, will you? Wake *up*...!"

This time it was Ellen-Stephanie's turn to be rousing Pete in the dead of night, in a hissing whisper, with a vigorous shake of the shoulder to boot. Pete had been deep in the throes of a most delicious dream, much to do with ice cream (always in short supply during term-time), and was fiercely reluctant to be roused. She growled as viciously as she knew how, and rolled over to her other side, pulling the bedclothes up to cover her head entirely; but Ellen-Stephanie merely seized her with both hands and rolled her back again, stripping blankets and sheets away at the same time.

"I'm serious, Pete! This is *important*!"

"It had better be," Pete snarled. But she sat up, pushed both hands through her tangled hair as if to chase the dream entirely out of her head, and said, "Well, what, then?"

"It's Catherine," Ellen-Stephanie said, and then said no more.

Pete sighed. "Of course it's Catherine. What, is she being all moony and weepy again?" To her certain knowledge, the older girl was still crying herself to sleep every night like a baby. "There's nothing we can do about that. We did try, and if she won't *be* comforted..." It might not have helped—and Pete was guiltily aware that it might not have helped—that her idea of comfort was to say "Buck up!" and propose a game of draughts or snapwhistle. But honestly, everyone in the school must know by now that Pete was the very last chap to come to in search of sentimentality and a shoulder to cry on.

The fact that Catherine *hadn't* actually come to her—or indeed to Ellen-Stephanie or anyone else, but was still trying to shoulder her private miseries entirely by herself—was something else that Pete preferred not to think about, really. She'd been at the Crater School long enough to know that a fellow ought not to let that go on. Sometimes it was positively the gentlemanly thing to interfere, by invoking a higher authority if one was rebuffed oneself. As of course she had been. But who on earth should she turn to? Sister Anthony was hardly a comforting figure herself, and they hardly had the chance to talk to anyone else outside of formal lessons, being held still in this strict isolation. Pete could find excuses aplenty for her inaction, and if she knew perfectly well that they were only excuses—well, she didn't have to think about that either.

"No, nothing like that!" Ellen-Stephanie said, in the steam-kettle whisper that comes so naturally to girls out of bed out of hours, which they fondly suppose to be entirely inaudible beyond their cubicle curtains. "She's gone! She's run away!"

"She's *what*?" Now Pete was thoroughly awake, scrambling out of bed and grabbing for her dressing gown, ignoring her much-loathed slippers as she squirmed through the curtains to Ellen-Stephanie's cubie and then one further, to the bed where Catherine should have been sleeping.

Where Catherine clearly was not sleeping, not there, not anywhere in sight. The high uncurtained windows gave light enough to see that, on a crisp clear Martian night.

"We, we should wake Sister Anthony," Pete said hesitantly.

"No, wait. Look." Ellen-Stephanie pointed, to where an envelope lay posed on Catherine's pillow. "Let's see what she said, first."

"We shouldn't, it's not meant for us…"

"Isn't it? She's written on the back, see? That must be for anyone to read. Wait a mo." Ellen-Stephanie slithered back into her own cubicle, to reappear a moment later with an electric hand-torch. She played the beam onto the envelope, and sure enough, there were half a dozen lines in Catherine's meticulous hand, slanting across the sealed flap.

I'm sorry, the note said. *Please forgive me. I can't stand this any longer. I never should have agreed to try. Don't bother to come after me; I'll just go home, and you needn't trouble any more about me. Forget I was ever here. Catherine.*

"We should *definitely* wake Sister Anthony," Pete muttered.

"She'll get into the most frightful row."

"I know. And of course they will go after her, they'll have to; and they'll catch her, too. She doesn't know the country. Lucky if she doesn't get lost, and then the whole school will turn out to find her…"

"She'll head for the railway station, won't she? That's easy enough to find."

"She'd have to, that or the canal head. But the train's easier, if she's got money. I expect she's got money; she never seems to spend any, and her things are lovely." Pete noticed suddenly that the silver hairbrushes had gone from Catherine's nightstand. Of course she would have taken those. They'd be as good as money, anywhere from here to Marsport. If she had the nerve to enter a pawn shop, at least—and she'd already shown plenty of nerve, simply by heading off like this, alone in the dark.

"Miss Leven's bound to think the same. She'll telephone the station first thing, and then send a staff down with the car," Ellen-Stephanie predicted. "The poor girl doesn't stand a chance, even if she gets that far. She must be in uniform, all our other clothes are put away; everyone'll be looking for her, and she'll stand out like a blister."

"I wonder if she'll struggle, or try to run? They'll catch her anyway, of course. And then they'll bring her back, just so Miss Leven can expel her."

"D'you think so?"

"Sure as eggs is eggs. Can't have girls running away when they're supposed to stay put. It's, it's dishon'rable, I think. How could they trust her again?"

They gazed at each other, rapt in the horror of inevitable fate—and then, as one, they said, "We'll have to fetch her back ourselves."

It was just as inevitable, really. Catherine couldn't be allowed to get herself into so much trouble, and they were the only two in a position to prevent it.

"If we can find her..."

"...then we can smuggle her back in..."

"...and no one will be any the wiser. But we have to find her first."

"She won't go to the funicular." Pete was quite clear about that. "Even though she's new and all, even she must realise that she'd just be fetched straight back. She'll try to get down to Terminus, to the main station. How, though...?"

"Well, not by the coach road. That goes all the way around the crater to the Sanatorium first. Maybe she'll just try to make her way down through the sheep pastures to the

Basque village? There's a road from there, I know, because someone told me. She probably knows it too."

"No. She'll take the pony path. That goes right from school here, and direct to Terminus. She must know where the head is, right by the stable yard, and she'll think she can just follow it down, even in the dark. I don't know if that's true, though, I haven't been."

"No, but I have. We have. It's the way we came up here, through the dust storm. We know that path!" In her excitement, Ellen-Stephanie almost forgot to make the least attempt at whispering. Pete reached up to gag her, hand to mouth, with an meaningful glance up the length of the ward, to remind her of Sister Anthony's presumed presence in her own rooms beyond; and then, warily, she said, "We...?"

"Me and Mabel. She'll take us down the path, and remember every step. We'll be twice as quick as Catherine, and catch her before she ever gets to town, see if we don't..."

The two girls dressed hastily—if pulling gym-slips over pyjamas, shoes onto bare feet and raincoats over all actually counted as dressing at all—and thanked their lucky stars and the Castle's original owner that there was a way out into the corridor at this end of the ward. They had already perhaps been more fortunate than they deserved, not having brought Authority down upon their heads with all their wild whispering; they really would not have enjoyed the prospect of tiptoeing past Sister Anthony's very door to make their escape.

Both carried torches now, though they risked light only in flickers as they slithered down the back stairs. Neither one was fool enough to suggest the front door; that was a vast affair of oak and iron, with noisy, heavy bolts, and Mr Felton the janitor slept right there in the gatehouse. Besides, Ellen-Stephanie's midnight arrival was already legend throughout the school, never mind its being a part of their own lived experience. Of course they headed directly for the chapel, and the priest-door by the vestry.

Hearts in mouths one more time, because who knew if the staff hadn't taken to locking the door, since that hectic night? Neither of them had any notion else, how to find their way outside. But then, Catherine knew less than they did; if she could manage it, certainly so could they...

The door opened easily, when they hauled at it: another reminder that the school trusted its girls to stay where they were put. Ellen-Stephanie and Pete were breaking that parole, but only to bring back another greater sinner. That must count in their favour, surely, if it came to judgement?

But then, the whole point of this adventure was to avoid judgement for anybody. They eased the door closed behind them, pulling it not-quite-to in hopeful anticipation of a swift and silent return with their errant cohort, and hurried quickly over to the stables. Under the blaze of stars, they didn't need their torches at all.

In by the grooms' door at the end, closing it carefully behind them—and now both electric beams shot out to pierce the darkness. No windows here to betray them, only the individual stable doors on every stall, all closed up tight now against the chill of a Martian night. Curious snuffles greeted them from dozy ponies—and from the loose-box at the end, one hypercritical camelian snort.

Ellen-Stephanie cooed at her beloved Mabel, and murmured, "Don't mind her. She's always a bit grouchy if you wake her up. She'll settle soon enough."

According to popular rumour around the school, Mabel was grouchy at any time, day or night, sleepy or wakeful or chewing the cud. Pete followed the taller girl down past the ponies, determined to keep a safe distance from any outbreak of grouchiness. Camels were dangerous in all directions, as far as she could gather. Though how she was to keep that kind of distance was anybody's guess, given that she was supposed to ride the thing.

At least she'd be riding pillion. Though come to think, she'd rather have a sidecar...

That thought made her giggle, which made Ellen-Stephanie glance at her askance.

"What's funny?"

"Nothing. Well—not nothing, actually. Tell you later." They had serious business in hand; this wasn't the time to share a joke. Especially when she was depending on Ellen-Stephanie to manage her notoriously wilful beast. When they both found something hilarious, the two of them could dissolve into a manic kind of laughter that would leave them both literally writhing on the floor. They'd learned that through the long days and nights on the ward, and brought the wrath of Sister Anthony down upon their helpless heads more often than they could count.

"I'll hold you to that." Perhaps they both felt they might stand in need of cheering up, if tonight's escapade didn't go as planned. "Meanwhile," Ellen-Stephanie went on, "you hang back here, where she can see you but you're not too close. She might just get fratchety when I start saddling her up."

Mightily relieved, Pete settled herself on a straw-bale and watched Ellen-Stephanie approach the camel. "I might get fratchety myself," she observed—perhaps not entirely helpfully—"if someone came and woke me up in the middle of the night and made me get up and go out in the dark when I really didn't want to."

"Isn't that just exactly what I did, though?" Ellen-Stephanie asked, with a giggle of her own.

"I s'pose it is, now I come to think. I'm not fratchety, though. Am I?"

"Not so's I'd notice, anyway."

"Well. It's because we're on a mission of mercy, I expect. I don't suppose saints ever felt fratchety, did they?"

"Don't see how they could. It's not exactly saintly if you're snappish."

"Well, she's never going to be Saint Mabel, then," Pete observed, seeing a definitely malignant gleam in the camel's eye, and even Ellen-Stephanie's wariness around that long jaw with the big yellow teeth.

Ellen-Stephanie laughed aloud. "That she isn't—though she does good work. When she's inclined, at any rate. She got me here, didn't she?" She bent to heave up the heavy wooden saddle from its place in the corner, and swung it over Mabel's hump. "Yes, yes, I know," she went on, as the camel hissed and roared in protest. "Don't wake the whole school, now. We're only going for a midnight saunter. Up you come, and let me strap it properly. C'mon, girl, uppety-up now..."

A mix of tender crooning and brisk taps with a riding-stick brought the camel to her feet—back legs first, which just looked peculiar to Pete—so that her mistress could fasten the girths and see to the rest of her harness.

Pete had not realised that Mabel would be quite so tall. It looked like a terrible long way from ground to saddle. "Um, how do we get up there...?"

"Well, you can clamber—but with two of us, it's probably best if I couch her again. Make her lie down," she translated, seeing Pete's bafflement. "Then we can get properly comfy. I've got a riding-strap for you; it'll hold you on in case you slip."

"What about you?"

"Oh, I won't slip. Mabel wouldn't let me. She didn't bring me all this way just to drop me at the end."

Mabel grumbled all the time that she was being har-nessed, and especially when Ellen-Stephanie tightened the girths beneath her belly. But she stood still—mostly—and she didn't try to bite. Nor spit, which was something Pete had been scared of; every time she'd ever read anything about camels, it always seemed to involve being spat on.

Finally, Ellen-Stephanie urged Mabel back onto her knees, and mounted with a kind of athletic slither that left her sitting cross-legged at the front of the saddle.

"Climb on behind," she ordered, "and buckle that strap around your waist."

"I, um, I don't think I can sit like that, I'll just slide off…"

"Oh, you don't need to. Just sit astride, as you would on a pony. This is comfy for me, but I don't think it'd work for a passenger."

Pete was sure it wouldn't, if the passenger was her. She scrambled up awkwardly, apologising to Mabel when her foot caught the camel's hip.

"Um, there aren't any stirrups…"

"No, there aren't. Just strap on, and hold tight if you don't feel safe. Me or the saddle, it doesn't matter; neither one of us will be shifting."

Pete wrapped her arms around the taller girl's waist—tight, as instructed—and yelped as the camel's back half lurched precipitately upward. For a moment she thought she'd be flung clean over Ellen-Stephanie's head. True to her word, though, Ellen-Stephanie was rock-solid in her seat, despite how precarious it looked. Pete hung on grimly through a second lurch as Mabel's front half rose in its turn. A glance down showed her how far away the ground had suddenly become. She gulped, and her grip tightened fur-ther of its own accord.

"Hey, let a girl breathe," Ellen-Stephanie objected, mildly enough.

"Sorry." Pete forced her arms to slacken, just a little. "Just, it's an awfully long way down."

"I thought you grew up on an airship?"

"I did, pretty much," and she missed it still, that life with her uncle. School was turning out to be tremendous fun—for the most part, except for having deadly enemies and so forth—and much less lonely, but even so; she'd grown used to the freedom of the skies, and rigid school rules still chafed her. "It's different, though."

"It's a lot further to fall."

"Ye-es—but an airship isn't going to try and *make* you fall. I don't trust that look in Mabel's eye, not one bit..."

Ellen-Stephanie laughed, and tapped Mabel's neck with her long riding-stick. The camel stepped disdainfully forward, and they were off.

The queer swaying movement took a little getting used to—well, a lot, perhaps, if she were honest—but at least the situation was distracting. Setting out in the dead of night to seek a runaway might have been enough to think about all on its own, to stop a girl feeling seasick—camel-sick, she supposed—but the path that Ellen-Stephanie found for them to follow seemed to plunge over a cliff-edge, the crater wall was so steep just here behind the castle. Pete wasn't a nervous girl, and she certainly wasn't afraid of heights, but even so: she found it reassuring that Mabel used that long neck of hers to peer over and examine the way ahead before she committed a single foot to walking it.

When she was satisfied—and nothing Ellen-Stephanie could do would chivvy her any faster—she stretched out that single foot on its impossibly long leg and placed it carefully, pausing to test the footing for a moment before she trusted her weight to it. Her body swayed as she brought her back leg forward; the second foreleg followed the first, again feeling its way, making sure; and then they were committed, on the downward slope, with Mabel apparently happy beneath them. She was still cautious, but even a cautious camel can lick along at a pretty pace with the encouragement of two girls atop her and the reassurance of memory. Like elephants, camels never forget. Mabel might not quite like going downhill in the dark, but she knew she'd trodden this path before.

The girls didn't know how much of a head start Catherine had—to be fair, they didn't really know that she was even on this path, only that it afforded their best chance of finding her, so they were just going to assume it—but they were sure they must be moving faster than she was. If a camel was cautious, a girl would surely be more so, even if she had a torch with her (and did Catherine have a torch? Neither of them knew that either), as the path turned abruptly this way and that as it plunged down the steepest and rockiest part of the crater wall.

As Mabel picked her way along, the two girls played their torches ahead, half to help the camel spot the next turn, half in hopes of spotting something—someone—else themselves.

Even so, they almost missed their moment. Looking too far ahead, they both failed to spot the little mound of misery hunched beside the path. It was Mabel who paused mid-step, who swung her neck aside to investigate, who nudged her head at something that raised a moan in response, and then a sob, and then a hiccup...

By then, the focused power of two torchbeams and six eyes had pierced the darkness and translated that lump of rock into the bent form of a schoolgirl in her blazer, with one leg stretched awkwardly out before her.

"Catherine! There you are!"

"What's the matter, did you slip? Are you hurt?"

Of course she'd slipped, of course she was hurt; her tear-streaked face attested as much, as she squinted into the double light. They tumbled down to help, but could make little of the hot and swollen ankle; they didn't have so much as a school tie to wrap around it.

During her lonely pain-filled watch, Catherine seemed to have abandoned any notion—or any hope—of running away from school. At any rate, she made no effort to resist as the other two helped her up onto the saddle of the couched camel.

"Mabel can manage three of us, no trouble," Ellen-Stephanie said breezily. "Catherine, you hold on tight to me, okay? We'll just buckle this strap around you, see, and Pete can sit behind and help to hold you on if you feel faint or anything, and we'll soon have you back safe..."

It didn't happen that quickly, or that easily; but Mabel took the path up more readily than she had the path down, and both the rescuers found time enough to wonder just how they were to smuggle their companion back into the San, when she couldn't take a step without crying out in pain.

As it turned out, they didn't have to. The path brought them up into the stable yard—which was a riot of light and noise, a steamcar being stoked into life by two mistresses while half a dozen prefects were busy saddling ponies by lamplight, preparatory to mounting a full search on every road and pathway.

They rode into that blaze of chaos, and seemed to bring a curious stillness with them, and a silence that was broken only after a terrible wait of time. Broken by a single voice, their dread headmistress, saying, "And just *where* have you three been, may I ask...?"

CHAPTER TWENTY-THREE

"Give them to me"

"**H**onestly, I think I'm defeated. I haven't the faintest idea what to do with them."

Thus Miss Leven, confessing her bewilderment in the Staff Room, to all who were free to listen. Supper was over; the various housemistresses had separated out their own particular lambs and herded them away towards books and games and bedtime; the remainder of the staff had forgathered on their own turf as their custom was, over coffee and cigarettes and perhaps an occasional wicked little *digestif*. The headmistress was there by invitation, if invitation can be perforce. She had manifested at the door, with a bottle of her splendid pear brandy in hand, and an earnest appeal in her eyes. Of course they had welcomed her in, given her the prime seat by the hearth, pressed a cup into her hands and relieved her of her bottle. This wasn't an officer's mess, with rules forbidding the talking of shop. It was perfectly common to discuss the school's most intractable problems informally this way, with every person's voice and ideas weighed equal.

"Heaven knows, I'm reluctant to come down hard on the girls," Miss Leven went on. "They've broken school rules wholesale, of course, and taken ridiculous risks—but two of them went in search of the third, which shows the kind of independent spirit that frankly I like to instill in our Cratereans. And I fundamentally refuse to punish a child for being unhappy, especially when it was her own father who was making her so. And yet, and yet. We can't let them loose among their cohort after this. At a boarding school this one thing must stand above all, that we depend on our pupils to stay where they are put; if we can't trust them that far, then we cannot trust them at all, and that is an absolute failure. It's our failure, of course, and not theirs; but even so. I'm half inclined to ask their parents to take them away. If any one of you has another idea, I'm willing to entertain it—I'd be delighted to entertain it, for I've never yet expelled a girl, and I truly don't want to start with any of these three, never mind all of them—but we either keep them under lock and key, or else we stand watch over them night and day, or else we pass the problem on to someone else. I don't see any other option. And Sister Anthony has reached the limit of her willingness and her ability to oversee them, and besides which it's looking like she'll no longer have the beds, because there's an epidemic brewing among the Juniors or else I miss my guess; and—"

"Give them to me."

The words came from both sides at once, from two separate mouths. Two pairs of eyes caught each other, just too late for either to hold back the words. Rowany subsided, blushing, waving away her claim, submitting instantly to seniority: which left everyone focused on Mrs Buchanan, who said it again.

"Give them to me. After school, I mean, after their lessons; and any time they can be spared through the day, as it happens. I could really use the help. Managing the art room for a whole school is more than one person's work, and how Miss Calomy has contrived this long on her own is more than I can fathom; and then there's all the sets to be painted for the carol concert, for to be honest it's more of a Nativity play, with all those changes of scene that Miss Llewellyn has asked for. Not to mention the incidentals that come with that event, hand-painted invitations and so forth. Believe me, I have plenty of work to distract those sinners' wicked little minds and occupy their time. And much of it they might enjoy, so it won't feel exactly like punishment; but at the same time the school will be very well aware that they've been separated out from the herd, and that they are being kept an eye on. It's not as strict as Sanatorium isolation, but it's still a kind of internal exile."

"That's all very well, and thank you very much for the offer; I take your point entirely. But it only addresses one part of the problem. We can watch them during school, of course, and through daylight hours, one way or another, yes. But it was night-time when they slipped away, and Sister Anthony no longer wants the responsibility even if she has the room, and we can't ask their dormitory prefects to act as, as prison guards, that's not their task."

"Give them to me." Rowany, surprising herself as much as the room at large, repeating herself much as her elder had done. "I'll take charge of them after supper, and through till breakfast. Separation again, supervision, but not quite punishment. You gave me that set of rooms, here in the Castle; I haven't been using it since the dust storm passed, because I like the life of a busy house better, but it's perfect for this. We can fit three into the bedroom, with a bit of squeezing and shuffling about. I'll move my own bed out into the study, and then I'm between them and the only way out, if any of them should feel inclined to wander once again. Not even the most rebellious soul is going to try that window, three floors up and barred besides. And if I have the three of them together,

I'll bring them to a better understanding of their state of disgrace or my name's not Rowany Angelica Marten de Vere. Which it is, as a matter of fact."

"More than that," Miss Leven said musingly, "under those conditions, I'd be astonished if any one of them didn't feel happier about their lives, their futures and even their wretched families, come the end of term. Given that your name is indeed Rowany Angelica Marten de Vere. This might actually prove a solution, if you're both truly willing to take it on. We'll decide nothing binding tonight. They can bide where they are till morning. Then I have promised them one of my finest scoldings, and if any one of them emerges from my study with a dry handkerchief, you will know that I have lost my edge. After that, we three will have a talk," catching both Mrs Buchanan and Rowany within her gaze, "and see what we can contrive. Thank you very much, both; thank you for your hospitality, all. I'll be away now. No, no: keep the bottle, by all means. Keep it, don't hoard it. It's meant for drinking. Good night, now."

Rowany went to bed, inevitably wondering just what she had committed herself to. The offer had been unthinking, instinctive, spoken almost before she knew that she would speak. Mulling it over in the quiet of a sleeping house, she still believed that she had been right to do so; but what would come of it, she couldn't begin to guess.

Well, well. At least she'd have something to write home about. If she made the tale lurid enough, perhaps she might even draw her family up here for the carol concert and the end of term, her parents and any of the boys who happened to have made it back for Christmas. She'd enjoy that—and so would the school, most likely. Presentable young males in full bib and military tucker, each of them ready to be co-opted into any adventure, and the more wicked the better? The poor boys wouldn't stand a chance. They'd be gobbled up alive. And love every moment, or else she missed her guess.

Next morning, making her way towards Miss Leven's study—and trying not to feel trepidatious about it, still less to think of it as a council of war—she did indeed notice three very sorry objects huddled on a single bench in the courtyard. Apparently Miss Leven had not yet lost her edge.

Come to think of it, that was the very same bench she and her cohort used to flee to under similar circumstances, after similar excoriations. However many generations of school-girl misery had those wooden slats absorbed...?

Rowany shook her head briskly. Those were not the memories she wanted to be carrying into this meeting. She tapped on Miss Leven's door—firmly ignoring a rising tide of memory, how very many times she had done this same thing, usually trembling inwardly under a burden of black guilt and bleak expectation—and went in at her summons, to find Mrs Buchanan installed already with a cup of coffee and a plate of Mrs Bailey's famous ginger nuts.

"Rowany, good. Sit yourself down and help yourself. I don't suppose you've lost the taste for these?"

"Um, no. No, I haven't. Though I'd appreciate it if you didn't bring that old story up again in present company." Her nerves fled, in favour of the giggles. She poured herself a coffee and took a very moderate two biscuits, sat down and found Mrs Buchanan gazing at her musingly.

"Well, after an introduction like that, this meeting can go no further until you have divulged every detail of that old story."

"It's a Crater School legend," Miss Leven said. "Not mine to tell, though. Rowany, if you will kindly oblige?"

"Brute." Giggling yet, Rowany launched into the story of what might have been her greatest humiliation (*thus far,* she reminded herself sternly), that time when she and her Middle School cronies had elected in their wisdom to invade Mrs Bailey's sacred domain in the hours of darkness and bake a full batch of ginger nuts, as both a midnight snack for themselves and a surprise breakfast treat for the school at large. After all, they had the recipe by heart; their whole class had baked a trayful each with splendid success only that very week, and served them out for tea to general acclaim. They could certainly do the same again. All they needed to do was multiply the quantities they'd memorised by the twenty-four girls in their class, and then divide the mixture across the same number of trays, and they knew from experience they'd have plenty for everyone. They might perhaps get into trouble for the illicit nature of their adventure—nowhere in the school was as thoroughly out of bounds as the kitchens, except on authorised and strictly supervised occasions—but a delicious crumbly tangy biscuit was certain to melt the stoniest of hearts and soften the steeliest of glares, oh yes...

By the time she'd recounted all the many disasters of that never-to-be-forgotten night—the jug of what they had taken to be buttermilk, which turned out actually to be soured milk set aside for the pigs; the impossible labour of stirring that horrible stodgy mass of dough; the catastrophic failure of their attempts to divide the lumpy, off-smelling result into two hundred and eighty-eight equal pieces; their helplessness in the face of Mrs Bailey's massive iron stove, and the rank idiocy that had had them forging forth regardless, welding the mixture irrevocably to the trays, filling the Castle with smoke and bringing down wrathful authority on their miserable heads—Mrs Buchanan was in tears of laughter, and even Miss Leven was chuckling, despite her knowing the story backwards, and its consequences too. She had of course been the wrathful authority in question, and Rowany gave her a rueful smile.

"We were condemned to cleaning everything, from the stove to the dining-hall windows, wherever the smoke had reached. How the school hated us that first day, with the stove taken to pieces and no hot food all day long! And how we hated those wretched trays, that we scrubbed and soaked and scrubbed again for a week, and then still had to take a note home to our parents asking them to pay for replacements the following term."

"Yes, that was my master-stroke, I think," Miss Leven said, beaming on her former victim. "School punishments are all well and good, but making you take it home for the holidays brings a whole new level to the affair."

"Oh, it so very much did. That was sheer cruelty. Especially in a household beset with brothers. But," determinedly, "we didn't come here to rehearse my childhood misdeeds," as though that childhood were far and far behind her now. "Not mine," she repeated, to make her point more firmly.

"Quite right." Miss Leven seemed to gather up all the levity in herself and dismiss it, and with it any more that might remain in the room. "What are we to do about the Terrible Threesome? That's our subject now. You've both had time to repent your rashness of yesterday; is either one of you wishful to withdraw? With your conscience clear and no blame attached?"

"Absolutely not," quoth Mrs Buchanan; and "You know me better than to ask," said Rowany, flushed and defiant.

"Yes, well. I expected that; but I did have to ask." Miss Leven laughed, and waved Rowany towards the biscuits once again. "I worry that it'll prove an unreasonable burden, for both of you. Especially as you both have your own work to occupy you, without committing so much time to a trio of sinners."

"Oh, I plan to enlist the girls in my own work," Rowany said cheerfully. "Catherine can join my little after-hours

Russian class, there's nothing more useful than an accent straight from the source; and it wouldn't hurt the other two to join in, either. I don't know if either one of them does anything with languages at present?"

"No more than she has to, in Pete's case, at least," Miss Leven said. "Ellen-Stephanie might have a yen to speak French, but that would only be because she's heard it's a ladylike accomplishment. I don't believe Russian features in her ambitions."

"Well, they can sit and listen, at any rate. Perhaps something will soak in regardless. And those two both have more … physical skills, that frankly I can learn from." Rowany caught Miss Leven's eye with a meaningful glance; they couldn't talk about it directly with Mrs Buchanan in the room and in ignorance of her private curriculum, but it was much on her mind at the moment. "Don't you worry, I believe I have ways to keep all three of them occupied without detriment to my own interests."

"As have I," Mrs Buchanan averred. "There's no end to the usefulness of three tolerably competent girls, in and around an art studio. And if a mother of schoolgirls and a former Head Girl are incapable between them of bringing those miscreants to a better understanding of what's expected of them here, then we neither of us deserve the name of Cratereans. Which I don't officially own myself, of course," she went on hastily, "but I feel I've earned it by adoption this term."

"Or shall have done, at any rate, before Christmas," Miss Leven said drily. "Very well; thank you both once more, and we will set this in motion. With opportunities for review, of course, and withdrawal at any time if it proves too much for either one of you. Rowany, I believe you'll find the three little miseries still waiting their doom on the bench of shame; send them back in to me, will you, that I may break the news of their awful fates? While there are still a few ginger nuts left, to soothe their ravaged souls."

It would have taken harder hearts by far to send the girls— pale, sorry, heavy-eyed and headachy—into classes for the rest of the day. Besides, the hobble downstairs from the San to Miss Leven's study had been as much as Catherine could manage on her sprained and strapped-up ankle. Going back up again, she needed to lean on both tall Ellen-Stephanie and little Pete, and even so it was dot-and-carry-one all the way.

Sister Anthony took one look at them and condemned them to bed, with warm milk that perhaps hid a dose of something other; it was still mid-morning, but all three were asleep inside half an hour.

When they roused—one by one but in short order, each with a healthy schoolgirl appetite telling them it must be getting on for lunchtime—they found Rowany sitting quietly in a chair, watching them thoughtfully.

The first two she gestured into silence, until laggardly Pete woke last; then she said, "You can sit up now, girls, so long as you put on your dressing gowns. No, don't talk yet, I have things to tell you. In a minute I'll bring a tray of soup and bread, and we'll all have lunch together. In mugs, the soup, to make it easy and save spillage. After that you're to stay where you are, while we rearrange my rooms to accommodate the four of us. You can read story-books—but no schoolbooks, mind—or talk quietly. And I do mean quietly; if you disturb the sick kids at the other end of the ward, you will bring Sister Anthony down upon your unworthy heads like the wrath of God, and so I warn you. When everything's ready I'll come back and collect you. We'll get Catherine settled in, then the rest of us will gather up everybody's things from here and from your houses. By then it'll be tea-time,

I expect, so I'll run down to the kitchens and see what I can beg from Mrs Bailey..."

The afternoon was heavy labour, shifting furniture about with never quite enough space to make it easy; but at least there were hands enough, with Mr Felton making a strong foundation and a couple of leggy fifth-form volunteers. Gradually Rowany's little suite took on a whole new interior shape: two bunk beds and a singleton in the bedroom, with her own bed now dominating the sitting-room and her comfortable sofa relegated to a storeroom far below.

"Here we are, then, girls. It'll be a bit of a squeeze, but I think we can all manage. The single bed is for Catherine, of course"—indeed Catherine had already claimed it, easing herself free of the others' helping hands and sinking down in exhaustion—"and I'll leave the two of you to sort out who gets top and bottom bunk. Or you can swap them turn and turn about, if you can't agree."

"Oh, Pete had best have the top one," Ellen-Stephanie said, surprising perhaps everyone except herself. "If I sit up in bed, I'll crack my head something rotten on the ceiling."

"If you sit up in the bottom bunk, you'll bump your head on my mattress," Pete countered.

"Yes, but that'll be softer. And it'll help you wake up in the morning, if I give you a jolt. The good Lord knows you need the help. Sleeping Beauty."

"Beanstalk."

The two girls glowered ferociously at each other, and then spoiled it by bursting into simultaneous giggles. Rowany hid a smile of her own, then chivvied them off to trouble Sister Anthony for bed-linens. "I may have built these beds for you, at great cost to my fingernails, but you can make them up yourselves. And do Catherine's too, while you're at it; she's spent too long on her poor foot already, by the look of it. I'll put the kettle on, and by the time you're finished we'll have tea. Go on, scoot."

Tea they had, with egg sandwiches and slices of cherry almond cake. It was all a little elbow-to-elbow, but Rowany sat all three girls on her bed—"and *don't* tell Sister Anthony I allowed that"—while she took the only chair remaining to her, and they contrived to pass plates and cups back and forth without spilling.

"Now, then. It's not my place to scold, and I don't intend to; nor do I suppose there's any need. If Miss Leven hasn't brought you to a clear understanding of your many faults and errors, she's not the woman I take her for. The woman I've known, when she's done the same for me. Yes, Pete, and more times than you can possibly imagine. She makes you feel too low to crawl, doesn't she?

"Still, that's done with now. You still need to serve out your time, with Mrs Buchanan and with me; but I don't want you thinking this is punishment, because it's not. Call it ... supervision, if you like. Watchfulness. We need to be sure you're not going to fly off on another hare-brained adventure, and drag other kids along with you, as like as not. Therefore, you get to spend your time with us instead of your classmates; and therefore, we need to find ways to use that time. Mrs Buchanan has her own ideas, I know; she's hectically busy this term, and you three will be the most tremendous help to her if you just buckle down, building flats and... What is it, Ellen-Stephanie?"

"Miss—I mean Rowany, I'm sorry, but—building *flats*?"

"Oh—yes, of course, you probably haven't had much to do with theatres, have you, the life you've lived? Well, flats are what we call the elements of scenery—canvas, usually, stretched over a wooden frame and painted appropriately. If any of you have any skill in that direction, you can help with the painting too. And then you'll spend the evenings with me; and I promise, we won't be idle. We're all going to tutor each other. Catherine, I want Russian conversation classes with you and the twinses, and the other two can keep up as best they may. Pete, you know everything there is to know about airships and how to keep them flying; we can all learn from you. There's not a Martian born who won't need to understand the inwardness of engines, at one time or another. And Ellen-Stephanie, I mean to pick your brains about every last little detail of frontier life; I know you ran away from it, but none the less. I'm sure there's a wealth of knowledge there to be drawn on, however crude it may seem. And unladylike, yes. We're all going to practice the ladylike virtues, you'll be pleased to learn—Pete, don't pull faces, please, it'll do you no harm to acquire a little polish, whatever you look to do in the future—and while we're talking things over, we'll keep our fingers as busy as our minds. All that practice hemming sheets is going to come in useful, you two. I don't suppose it's occurred to you, but the carol concert is going to call for a great many costumes as well as sets, and Miss Tarleton's needlework classes can't possibly produce them all..."

CHAPTER TWENTY-FOUR

Rather More Lessons Than Carols

People commonly enjoy being asked to do something they know they're good at. Being well aware of this, and also of how a healthy sense of competition will drive the young to their utmost limit, Isobel Buchanan had no qualms about leaving Pete and Ellen-Stephanie alone with a heap of scavenged lumber and Mr Felton's set of second-best tools. She had asked them to build a manger for the Christ-child, "oh, and any other stage-furniture you think would suit the scene." They had set to with a will, Pete sketching ideas in charcoal while Ellen-Stephanie argued cheerfully over her shoulder, describing the kind of camel-trough she knew best.

Isobel laughed inwardly, and steered Catherine out of the workshop by one elbow.

"We'll come back to half a stable's-worth, unless I miss my guess," she said. "We may not be able to use it all, but that doesn't matter. They'll be happily occupied now until tea-time; which leaves us free for other matters."

Of course Catherine wanted to ask what other matters those might be, but of course she was too shy to do so. Isobel had known that, too.

Instead, Catherine said, "Aren't you worried they'll hurt themselves? Or each other? I've never been allowed tools without someone watching, and—well, they do quarrel all the time…"

"They do; but actually they quarrel rather nicely now. Like the very best of enemies. And those two were born and raised with hammers in their cradles and chisels at their feet, I never saw two girls more comfortable working with their hands; so no, I'm not worried in the least. Besides, Mr Felton would never have lent them his toolbox if he didn't trust them implicitly. It's good in you to be concerned, but truly, there's no need. Put them out of your mind, and then we'll both be nicely surprised by how much they've achieved by the time we go back to reclaim them."

"I—I do see what you mean, I think." Just for a moment, a smile tried to twitch the corner of Catherine's lip, before it was overwhelmed by her usual solemnity. *That's the way, my girl,* Isobel thought mischievously. *Stop fretting over others who don't need it, who are already a fair way to sorting out themselves and incidentally each other, and you focus on worrying about yourself…*

Catherine had time enough to do so quite thoroughly, as Isobel walked her down between the houses, between the playing fields and all the way to the quiet sculpture garden at the limit of school grounds. Catherine was limping a little at the start, still struggling with her twisted ankle; by the end she was limping severely, but still not asking for a rest. Nor did Isobel offer it, until they had actually arrived.

"Now, then. I know the whole school has sneaked down here when they've had the chance, just to see what I'm up to, and I don't suppose you're the exception. Even if you hadn't seen it in the working," and here Isobel made a grand gesture to encompass the half-carved rock, the tools and chalks laid out beside, the camping-stool that saved her middle-aged bones from having to crouch for hours on end when the creative urge overswept her, "I'm sure everyone's told you that I'm using my daughter and her friends as the models for this piece. But I've got their faces now, as you can see, and I really don't need them for the rest of it; any girl in school uniform will do, for sketching in their bodies, which is all I mean to do. Which means that today I can borrow you, and frankly talk to you like a Dutch uncle, while you can do nothing but sit there obediently—yes, there, on the edge of the water; and tuck your legs under you, please, and lean on one arm, yes, just like that—and not even squirm when I tell you what a silly goose you've been, and how close you've come to spoiling your own life and others' too."

"Oh, but—"

"No, hush; you're not allowed to talk. I know you girls, you can't talk without fidgeting, and if you fidget you'll ruin everything. I'll make a wrong stroke with my chisel here, and I'll have to start from scratch with another rock, and you don't want that, do you?"

Rendered mute, Catherine could do nothing but shake her head. And then regret even so much movement, and try to say so with her eyes. Isobel suppressed a chuckle, because of course nothing the girl might do could spoil her work at this stage. In honesty, she barely needed a model now. But Catherine did very much need a talking-to, and Isobel knew herself to be the best person to deliver it.

"Very well, then. That's perfect; hold that pose. If you're comfortable, nod your head. Good. Now, I'm sure you think you know everything I'm going to say, and perhaps you do, but I shall say it anyway, and I'm counting on you to listen, and to think about it. Another nod if you understand. Good.

"Now, your father is a Russian officer, and quite properly gives his loyalty where it is owed, to his own country. Likewise, your mother remains loyal to England and the Empire. All that is as it should be. But it does leave you horribly torn

between the two of them, any fool could have foreseen that."
Really, Isobel had small respect for Catherine's mother—but
never mind that. Not even a conversation for another day, it
was something the girl would have to think out for herself.

"What matters now is that you understand one thing
clearly: that while it is quite right for your father to remain
loyal to the Tsar, it is quite wrong for him to try to under-
mine your own loyalty to your mother and the country
that shelters you both. I know these are hard words to hear,
every girl wants her father to be perfect—but he has wholly
betrayed his own duty of care to you, by trying to enlist you
in his subterfuges.

"I imagine you have heard, from my girls or their friends,
how their own father turned traitor against his country, and
how he tried to steal them away from me. He wanted them
in the flesh, while your father is only trying to steal your
soul—but that would be the greater loss, and the greater sin.

"You're still only a girl, Catherine, and nobody expects
you to resist him by yourself. That was your own idiocy, to
keep this secret and let it prey upon you when you could
have gone to anyone—to your mistresses, or your prefects,
or your friends—for help at any time. Fortunately, we've
learned what was happening at no more cost than a twisted
ankle and an uncomfortable night for you, and a lot of
anxiety for everyone else; and now everyone knows, and
is standing by to help you willy-nilly. That's what happens,
you'll find, when you have friends; they step in when you're
in trouble, whether you ask them to or not.

"Also, of course, so do those in authority over you. So,
this has been decided: that you may no longer receive letters
directly from your father. We're still not sure quite how these
have been delivered so regularly, as he was certainly still
on Earth the last we heard; it seems clear that there's some
kind of trickery going on. At any rate, any further letters that
arrive here will be opened by your housemistress, who will

decide whether or not you should see them. I'm thinking not, at least for a while. Your mother will also be corresponding with him, to ask him not to write the sort of letters you've been struggling with since you came here.

"Meanwhile, we all feel that you still need a period of quiet, to think everything through; and you still have bridges to build, I know, with some of your classmates. And you still can't walk very handily on that ankle, can you? I probably shouldn't have brought you all the way down here; but you can rest for an hour or two now before the hobble home, and perhaps I wanted to test your mettle. Well done, for not crying off halfway. I'm not blind to the courage that called for, especially when you didn't know what awaited you once we got here.

"So, for now you and those other two miscreants will go on living under Rowany's watchful eye—but don't despair. It won't last for ever. Heavens, it won't even last for the rest of term. I'm going to leave Rowany to explain what comes next, as it was her idea. There has been some debate about that, I don't mind telling you; certain members of staff were in favour of ... well, let's say a quieter approach. But girls are fond of big dramatic gestures, and Rowany is still very much a girl at heart, however grown-up she may seem to you just now..."

I t was the day the whole school had been looking forward to and working towards all term, and never mind the weather. Christmas on Mars was a very moveable feast, shifting seasons almost willy-nilly, as the Calendar of Saints mapped so poorly onto the longer Martian year. Any Mars-born girl was accustomed to sun-hats and sandals as much as to warm coats and wellington boots, on the walk to meet Father Christmas at the parish hall.

This year would be warm and fine, though they would still decorate their cards and presents with snow and sleighs and all things proper to a Christmas spent in England, although most of them had never actually been there.

They would be going to their own homes and families soon enough, to parents and sisters too young for school and brothers—ugh!—and much-missed pets and local friends of long standing; but first came all the end-of-term fun and frolics here at school, and chief among them—last among them, the crowning glory—would be the Carol Concert. Which would be today, this very evening. Some fortunate hopeful girls were already casting yearning glances down the coach road, those who had any view of it, wondering how soon they'd see the parade of vehicles fetching in those same parents, sisters, brothers—ugh!—and friends to comprise the audience and make the party complete.

In the meantime, though, there was much to do. All the tables had to be cleared out of the dining hall—lunch would be sandwiches today, eaten from the hand and on the move if no staff or prefects were actually watching over their impatient, impetuous charges—and rows of chairs laid out from wall to wall, with the narrowest possible aisle between if everyone was to have a seat. Before that could happen, the hall had to be decorated within an inch of its apparently mediaeval life, with boughs of holly—no berries, alas, in early summer—and ropes of ivy hanging from the beams above, along with all the tinsel and paperchains and cotton-wool snowballs that the junior forms had been able to come up with, and some gorgeous tapestries and embroidery from their seniors. Their very seniors, in some cases: venerable fabrics that had endured long enough to have been made by girls then who were coming back as parents now.

By tradition, all this work was left to the girls alone, while staff kept far away. By special dispensation—and by dint of very special pleading from the prefects—both Rowany and

Mrs Buchanan had been roped in this year to help. Neither of them was quite staff, after all, not *quite*, not by the strictest definition; and they would both be very useful, in very different ways; and they were *here*, here above all, and there was so very much to *do*...

Rowany passed a few wickedly scathing comments about how she had never asked for adult help when she'd been in charge, nor any Head Girl before her. She might have gone on to develop her theme further, if it weren't for the various cushions flung at her head with more or less accuracy. Perhaps wisely, Mrs Buchanan only said, "Very well, I'll come — but I'll climb no ladders, and so I warn you. You'll have to do all the real work yourselves, you and your minions. I've no doubt you have minions, by the horde. I shall sit calmly by and criticise."

Of course no one believed her, and of course it wasn't true. Within a very short span of time, both Rowany and she were actively involved, arguing cheerfully, trying this here and that there. As it happened, Mrs Buchanan was not actually called upon to climb ladders; indeed, she was forbidden to do so. There were youngsters in plenty willing to scramble hither and yon with abandon, often with cries of "Oh, be *careful!*" following at their heedless heels.

The roll call of younger girls changed every hour, as one class came to take the place of another. No one was actually doing lessons on this day of all days, though Miss Llewellyn was ruthlessly rehearsing the orchestra, and the soloists when she could catch them; but there were countless other tasks that needed doing, if the whole were to be pristine and prepared before their guests began to arrive.

Also, this day, there was one extra treat in store. Mrs Buchanan's sculpture was finished at last, and due to be unveiled before the concert by Mrs Mackenzie herself, in the presence of the school governors and the parents duly assembled. There would be no room for the school as well;

not even the staff could be squeezed into the small sculpture garden without danger of someone toppling into the pond.

So, class by class and accompanied by their form mistress, every girl would troop down at scheduled intervals during the day to see the work and talk about it. Miss Calomy had nobly volunteered to stay throughout, to give the piece a context and discuss its place in Mrs Buchanan's oeuvre; the artist herself had shrieked with horror at the very thought and declined to go anywhere near it until the actual unveiling. If any of the girls had questions, she said, they could pose them later, during the last days of the closing term, and she'd do her best to answer.

If she'd thought she could hide in the hall, she was sadly mistaken. Of course the girls had questions; and by some malignancy of fate, or else—more likely, she suspected—deliberate conspiracy, it turned out that every class came to help with the decoration immediately after their session with the sculpture. So she was a captive audience after all, and helpless before the determined interrogation of massed and fascinated schoolgirls. Even her own daughters—even Levity, who had been the inspiration and the first model—chimed in with questions of their own, and encouraged their own particular friends to follow suit.

She had talked herself raw already before lunch offered any kind of relief. She and Rowany ate their sandwiches on duty, in one corner of the hall, still looking to see what further needed to be done. Rowany poured the older woman another glass of lemonade—her third!—and said, "Honestly, it already looks far better than it ever has in my time. It really does feel mediaeval now, even though we all know it's not actually a hundred years old. The kids are thrilled just to have been a part of this, and I promise you the parents will love it."

"Nevertheless." Perhaps the artist's eye could simply never be satisfied? Isobel still wasn't sure that she was quite done with her new sculpture; she gazed about the hall and saw the same thing, a work in progress, always falling short of her ideal.

Still, there comes a time when you have to walk away. Done with lunch, Isobel dusted her fingers and saw yet another file of girls heading into the hall, and decided that actually running away also counted, and was not at all craven in the circumstances. These were older girls, in any case; they could live with disappointment. It would be one more lesson on their path to adulthood. She was certainly doing them a favour, helping them grow. Yes.

Her own schooldays were long behind her, and on another world, and even so. She knew the perils of seeming to wander without purpose, on a day like this. Someone was safe to snare her: a mistress with a mission, a prefect with a problem, somcone. Something to do, somewhere to be, a new role: mentor, substitute parent, friend. And just for now she was done with doing, done with being anyone but herself. A parent in her own right, absent both her children; an artist tired of talking about her art. A woman of Earth, suddenly and unaccountably homesick for her own planet, her own landscapes, her own people, despite so many years of building another kind of life here, trying to help, to offer new hope to women on a whole new world.

People always said her work was rooted in the past, but they were wrong. Critics were usually wrong, she found, when they tried to attribute causes or messages to what was far better left to speak for itself. She looked to the future, always: aiming to speak to the lives her girls could live, what they could make for themselves, through the medium of what previous generations had made in their earlier turn. This whole experiment, this colony entire would have died long since, if it hadn't been for the heroics of those first settlers; and nevertheless, what mattered was what these children made of that, how they chose to build upon that sacrifice and effort.

Which was a stirring thought, and thank Heaven that she wouldn't be called upon to make a speech at any time this day—she had been very firm on that point, and in the end even Mrs Mackenzie had conceded it—or she might have been tempted to say all that, or something very like it. Some thoughts were very much better held to herself. Let her work be inspirational on her behalf, if that was how the public chose to view it. Sometimes it wasn't enough to inspire anything more than a weary self-reliance in herself.

Today—well, she could have got by with that. She could have got by. But the first relay of parents was just arriving at the front gate, fetched in from the funicular, with a bevy of staff waiting to greet them; and it was no effort at all to make herself one among them, to step forward and shake a stranger's hand and say, "Hullo, I'm Isobel. Welcome to the Crater School! We're hoping to give you a truly happy day here. Tell me about your daughter... Oh, daughters, plural? Felicity and Arabella? Those imps! I am obliged to tell you, they are both a sheer joy to have in my class, and a gift beyond measure these last weeks, when we've been struggling to get everything ready for tonight. I'm sure they'll tell you—no, I'm sure they'll *show* you—exactly everything they had a hand in, so I shan't spoil the surprise, but..."

This was a thing she very rarely did, introducing herself merely by her first name and letting those who were cognisant—or, in this case, more likely those who paid attention to their daughters' letters home—leap to their own conclusions. She was willing to listen to a compliment or two, if it came to that; she was willing to have an adult discussion about her work if push came to shove, but it almost never did, because a frontier society was a well-mannered society by and large. If she wasn't conspicuously on duty, she tended to find, people tended to let her reputation slide by in the pursuit of simple conversation. Besides which, everyone here today would be wanting to talk about their daughters, and that she could certainly do.

She was hiding in plain sight, then, as she steered parents towards the teacakes and sandwiches being served by the tennis courts, while the Seniors played exhibition matches and the Middles ran back and forth with plates and cups. Here was Levity, of course, bobbing a regulation curtsey—and when in the world did she learn to do *that*?—and fetching an array of delicacies that Isobel was willing to bet had more to do with Mrs Bailey than any fourteen-year-old this school had to offer. And bless the child, she served them simply and sweetly and then scurried away to her next table with no more than the glimmer of a wink at her mother, which must have called for superhuman effort on her part and should be rewarded in the hereafter.

Later she conducted another pair of visitors —"Melisande's parents? Ah, that child has been a revelation this term. So good for everyone in her class, so caring," and not a word about her any ability—to see the giant Nativity scene that the Juniors had been working on all term, with marionettes and an actual live lamb, complete with an actual live Basque shepherd boy to keep an eye on it. He was looking a little appalled by all the attention, but cynical Isobel thought he'd probably recover, under the constant ministrations—lemonade and biscuits, largely—from a circle of adoring youngsters. And of course her own Charm was there, with all her special friends about her; and they were a little too grand to be caught making a pet of a mere boy, given that theirs was control of all the puppets, which they had made themselves and were frantically eager to show off to everyone who came by. Isobel herself was singled out for no special notice; she understood her role to be meek amazement, with perhaps a brief acknowledgement, "Yes, indeed, that's my daughter. I believe the script they're following is down to her, too. Hasn't she done well...?"

And so the afternoon wore on: it wore on her feet as much as anything, so much trekking back and forth, so that they were aching already when a panting Middle came racing up to find her, to collect her, to march her briskly to Miss Leven's study as though—being a mere grown-up, and not properly School in any case—she really couldn't be trusted to find her own way there even after all this time.

Waiting with the headmistress were all the Board of Governors, along with various husbands, wives and the like. They were really too many for the room, so there was no chance for Isobel to sit down; they'd only been waiting for her arrival to begin their long processional. Through the courtyard and the rear gate, collecting gathered parents all the way; down between the houses and between the playing fields, all the way to the sculpture garden at the furthest reach of school grounds.

And there she was obliged to stand, solemn and a little singled out, while Mrs Mackenzie made a brief and gracious speech, before pulling away the tarpaulin which had cloaked her work for the occasion. And then there was applause, of course, and she had to make a brief and gracious reply, though not a speech, oh no; and then there were photographs, of course; and then there was too much polite conversation, and everybody's hand to shake, and compliments to field and try to shrug away, and of course the editor of the town newspaper was here and he seemed to want to interview her right then and there, except that then and there was a blessed hand on her arm and a warm voice murmuring in her ear, "Poor thing, I expect your feet are murder by now, aren't they? How these people do talk, to be sure. Come away, I'm going to put an end to this particular frolic. Someone has to, or they'll still be milling about here when the sun goes down, and the girls will be singing to an empty hall, and nobody wants that. If you and I step out boldly, I can promise that everyone else will follow, like the good sheep that they are; and then we can annex Miss Leven's study for a little while, just for ourselves this time, and you can take your shoes off and relax..."

As it was Mrs Mackenzie herself who stood at her elbow, there was really no doubt that all would follow as she had foreseen it. And so Isobel had just one more walk to face, arm in arm with the school's onlie begetter—its Founding Principle, her husband was inclined to say—and then at last she could sit down, with a very welcome gin and tonic in her hand and an equally welcome door closed at her back. Isobel found people fascinating individually, she enjoyed the company of her peers—and she found that as the number of those gathered increased, so her pleasure diminished. She was never really happy in a crowd, and today had been crowds from first to last.

Even now, she wasn't *tête-à-tête* with Mrs Mackenzie. They could hardly have excluded their hostess from her own study; so Miss Leven was there, tactically situated behind her desk, while Mrs Mackenzie was tactfully perched in the window-seat, leaving Isobel space to stretch out her weary legs in a visitor's chair before the hearth.

For a few minutes the other two women let her simply rest and breathe and relish the feeling of being no longer on her feet. Time, however, was never anybody's friend, especially on a day such as this. Miss Leven checked the clock, recruited her forerunner and co-conspirator with a glance, and said, "Actually, Isobel, I'm glad to have this moment of quiet together, before we must dive back into the mob. We both—by which of course I mean the whole school, but tradition dictates that it is embodied within the persons of the founder and the headmistress, so here we are—we both owe you a tremendous debt of gratitude, for the work you've done this term. We've loved having you here, staff and pupils both; and the girls have learned so much from you, either directly under your tutelage or simply from watching how an artist obeys her muse and applies her craft, meticulously and methodically, day after day."

"Oh, nonsense," Isobel managed. "If I've shown them anything of the grind of it, I'm glad, but really I did little but exploit your hospitality for weeks on end, entirely to my own purposes. As soon as I saw my Levity sitting in that rock, with her friends lined up on either hand behind her, I knew it was a thing I had to do. And of course I'm leaving it here for you, but believe me, it's no blessing. As the word spreads, I'm afraid you'll find yourselves beseiged by reporters and critics and art-lovers from all over Mars and beyond, wanting to see it for themselves."

"Oh, I'm sure we'll cope," Miss Leven said airily. "We've had a genuine princess here, remember, and we weathered that particular storm. But that wasn't really what I intended to say to you—or rather, it was only the preamble. We are grateful, and we have loved having you; but I'm afraid there's more."

"There always is," Isobel said, with a grin more suited to her fourteen-year-old than to a mature middle-aged woman.

"Yes, of course. That's one of the lessons of adulthood that we honestly haven't found a way to teach yet; girls always have to learn it for themselves. Bitter experience is the name of the game, and it never actually stops. But as I said, and as you can't honestly deny, the girls have learned from you in every conceivable way, in every day you've been here; and as you know, our Miss Calomy is leaving us at the end of this term, in just a few days now. Leaving to marry a doctor, as these young wretches will," she added, pausing to shake a fist in the general direction of the Sanatorium across the water.

"It seems to be a habit about these parts," Mrs Mackenzie said placidly, admiring the simple wedding band that gleamed upon her finger. "But that leaves us with a problem, Mrs Buchanan..."

"...And this is where you offer me her post, am I right?"

Isobel was secretly delighted by the brief pause, by the glimmer of startlement in both women's eyes before they laughed, before they acknowledged that she was.

"But how did you know, might I ask?" Miss Leven said, trying to sound stern.

"Oh, it's been all the talk for weeks among the girls. I had it from both Levity and Charm separately, and from the prefects too: Miss Calomy was leaving and I was so very much her obvious replacement, it couldn't possibly have turned out better, the whole school wanted me so *please* would I say yes when you finally made the offer? Truly, I've barely talked to a child since half-term without her making puppy-eyes at me and prophesying this entire scene. Except for the gin, that is. I don't think schoolgirls envision their particular grown-ups drinking gin." She took a defiant swig, and grinned again.

"Well. I ... am glad our girls are so percipient. I suppose. Though I could wish them to retain a childish simplicity per-haps a little longer—or else not to be so forthright with their views. They always do know first, of course; their networks are impenetrable, and appalling. But they really ought not to indulge in special pleading. That's putting their thumbs on the scale, when it ought to be left to mature reflection and individual whim. But they do have the right of it, Isobel. And they have effectively chosen you. You'd break a hundred young hearts, if you refused."

"As you see," Mrs Mackenzie put in drily, "Miss Leven is not above a little special pleading of her own. And nor of course am I. Suffice to say that we would love to have you, and the girls would adore it, and would benefit immeasur-ably from the experience. We're not asking for a lifetime commitment, of course; and we fully acknowledge that you have other responsibilities, to your muse and to your public both; and we are of course very out of the way up here. But we thought you might appreciate some distance and some quiet, to focus on your own work, perhaps; and your own girls are here, who are rightfully another part of your focus; and we'll do our very best to hold the press at bay, and—well, I hope you know that you've made some friends here, who would like to spend more time in your company. Is that enough?"

Isobel smiled, and said, "It might be. It might indeed."

Levity knew. It was a daughter's duty, of course, to know such things. As soon as she saw her mother walk into the transformed hall, not in any position of honour among the notables but rather with the staff—with the *rest* of the staff— she knew, positively and without a doubt.

Standing where she was, lined up with classmates against one wall and under strict instructions not to fidget, whisper or otherwise cause any kind of distraction while the adults filed in, she was hard put to it to convey the importance of this news to those who knew less than she did. Still, by dint of pulling extraordinary faces that would have brought down the wrath of staff or prefects on her guilty head if they had been spotted by anyone in authority, she did at least manage to attract her sister's attention. Charm was standing among her own cohort against the opposite wall; she stared for a moment, then followed the jerking aim of Levity's eyes, pondered a moment, and nodded gleefully.

That was it, then. That was their lives, settled for the next few years at least; which meant, of course, changed radically from what they had been before. Levity was glad of it. She thought she was glad. She'd miss the travelling, of course, and seeing all the new places; but not the turmoil, not the constant upheaval that life implied. It would do her mother good, she felt, to stay still for a while. Hopefully for a long while. And she and Charm could live something like an ordinary life at last, school and home and friends and *breathe*...

Meanwhile, she forwent trying to convey any or all of that to anybody else, and focused on the here and now. Breathed, yes: and stood upright with her feet planted and her head high, hands tidily behind her back, among so many others just the same, as uniform as nature and training and dress could make them. She had twinses on either side of her, one of each, and the rest of the Crew all close—well, all except poor exiled Pete, still locked away with her fellow sinners and forbidden to mix with her friends, forbidden even this Christmas celebration. Finally, Levity felt she had a place she could call her own: somewhere to belong, and people apart from her family that she belonged among. She was one of a tribe, claimed and adopted. She had come home.

The oboe played an A, and one by one all the other instruments of the orchestra tuned themselves to it. Levity could hear anxious girls up and down the line humming the note themselves, desperate not to be off-key. The last of the visiting families shuffled in and found places in the crowded hall. A prefect closed the doors; the lights were turned off one by one, from the back forward, until only the raised dais, their stage tonight, was lit. Miss Llewellyn stepped up onto her rostrum, to a scatter of applause; she raised her baton, nodded, and the evening began.

Good people all, this Christmas tide
Consider well, and bear in mind...

For the last, unexpected time—and she had sworn up and down that this really would be the last time, even if all her future failed her and she had to come back and work under Mrs Bailey as a kitchenmaid—Rowany's clear, pure mezzo-soprano rang out solo through the hall, in the old Wexford Carol that always began their Christmas concerts. It was said—and every generation of Crater School girls passed this down to the next, in tones of scorn and wonder—that back on Earth only men and boys were allowed to sing this carol. Which was why, of course, it was chosen to open every concert, because here on Mars no woman and no girl would be denied the right.

Rowany's noble voice soared through the first verse entirely unsupported, as it had for years before. Then the girls lined along both walls of the great hall joined wordlessly for the next verse, humming Miss Llewellyn's own harmonic arrangement, while the finest voices among the Senior girls sang a spiralling descant.

Finally, the orchestra was allowed to come in behind the words, soft and low and unobtrusive. All the musicality of this delicate arrangement was there to serve one purpose, the meaning and the message of those words. Even as familiar as she was after so many weeks of rehearsal, Levity still thrilled to the spare solemnity of the moment.

New-hung curtains had made the dais into a stage, with wings and backstage too. There was no room back there for massed schoolgirls, which was why the chorus lined the walls instead. Everyone's attention turned now to that stage. The scenery depicted a road through the wilderness—somewhat more reddish than the Holy Land itself, perhaps, but Levity's mother had encouraged the girls to paint from their own experience, and a very Martian desert was the inevitable result, with even a glimpse of a distant canal in the background—marked by a Roman milestone proclaiming that Bethlehem lay ahead, still many miles away.

Now came a thrill of another sort, as this scene's soloists appeared: Joseph (actually Melanie, whose costume included a delightfully full beard that tickled her nose and made it hard to sing, especially to keep her nerve and her pitch in the lower register that male roles demanded), leading Mary (Fidelis Carpenter, the most ethereally beautiful of the Senior School) mounted on an actual donkey, borrowed from another of the Basque families in the valley below.

They'd been waiting in the chapel behind the hall, having acquired special dispensation from both Mr Hartley the hospital chaplain who presided over school services too, and Father Ignatius the local Catholic priest—"Sure, and what could be more holy? Mary and Joseph, and their donkey too? If Our Lord can be born in a stable, then surely our chapel can stable his mount." Their appearance now was heralded by a tune played on Marina's unaccompanied violin and composed by the school's other musical genius, Lois Shannon of the pale skin, the raven tresses, the startlingly green eyes and the obscure and inexplicable devotion to the Russian Orthodox confession.

It was she who had brought not only this strain of music to Miss Llewellyn—it would be heard time and again through the evening, to cover all the necessary scene-changes—but also the Ukrainian carol that followed. Joseph lamented the long and weary way that they had come, and still no rest in sight; Mary feared the encroaching night, and the threats it brought from man and beast together. Just when body and spirit were weakest and most apt to fail, an angel came to encourage them—"Ride on! Ride on! It is the Christ you carry!"—and from the sides, all the school joined the jubilant chorus to echo the celestial being.

And so the tale unfolded, scene after scene and song after song: a tale intimately familiar to all, but its telling abidingly new. There were carols never heard on Mars until this; there were orchestral pieces never heard at all. Some of the sets had been painted by Mrs Buchanan's own hands, and all of them with her oversight. It made a difference. A carol concert at the Crater School had never been an everyday affair, but this year's was exceptional.

Slowly, piece by piece, stagehands built up the complexity of Pete and Ellen-Stephanie's stable around the Holy Family: walls and stalls and of course the essential manger. Some enterprising girls had offered to borrow a real live baby from the village, but Miss Leven had put her foot down firmly at last, and the traditional doll was in place. Angels and shepherds crowded around, some of the smallest finding a convenient perch on the placid donkey's back; the real live lamb of course made another appearance, accompanied by her real live long-suffering shepherd boy.

Everyone was there, it seemed—except the Three Kings. This was the last great mystery of term, Rowany's Secret everyone was calling it, because no one seemed to know who would play the Kings, or how they would appear. The orchestra knew their music, but that was all; nothing more had been rehearsed, nothing at all had been divulged. The school's finest spies—Tasha and Tawney Mishkin, that is to say—had been on the case for weeks, and even they had learned nothing. Rowany wouldn't talk, none of the staff admitted to knowing anything, no one had seen or heard so much as a hint let slip by accident or chance.

And now here they were, the school for once as much in the dark as the audience. Silence fell, silence and stillness engulfed them all—and gradually, from afar, voices found their way into the hall.

Rowany and Mary Holmes were standing by. They drew the tall doors open wide, and here came those voices more clearly now, singing a carol that no one there had heard before. Nor were the voices familiar: they belonged to schoolgirls, surely, but whose were they?

When the singers appeared, in the dark at the back of the hall, it was still impossible to tell. Impossible really to see anything except the camel that two kings rode on, while the third led it by a headstall.

Perhaps the penny started to drop then among the quicker girls. Or perhaps it was easier to pick the three voices apart now, and remember how strong and how strange one of them was. There was still no question of recognising any of them by sight, in their muffling costumes and exuberant facial hair.

The orchestra began to play softly behind the singing; a few of the more enterprising girls in the chorus began to hum in tune, as they picked up the melody. Most, though, were still trying to understand, or else whispering names up and down the line.

Frowning, Miss Llewellyn gestured to the orchestra to play a little louder; the three girls responded nobly, singing out as they came up the aisle towards the bright stable scene.

Now, there could be no doubt. That was tall Ellen-Stephanie leading the camel—her own camel, of course!—and leading the singing too with that rare deep voice of hers. There was little Pete, riding pillion on the camel's back, holding tight to the other girl in front; she must be, and yes, she absolutely was Catherine, the odd new girl who had tried to run away...

"The three Unwise Men," someone murmured, causing someone else to choke down a sudden laugh, causing several mistresses and—worse!—more than one prefect to scowl in their direction.

With that mystery solved, most others were simply held rapt by the music, so new to them, so touching and, yes, mysterious in itself. They listened, barely remembering to breathe, until finally the carol dwindled into silence.

Ellen-Stephanie nudged the camel into kneeling, jerkily, front end first. Pete slithered off at the rear, nimble as ever, and helped Catherine to dismount more carefully, onto her stronger foot. Then they all three bowed deeply toward the Christ Child and came forward to present their gifts. Catherine was conspicuously hobbling now, leaning on Pete's shoulder and trying to be inconspicuous about that.

Those near Sister Anthony quite clearly heard her mutter, "That child's been overdoing it again, despite my clear instructions." No one, neither staff nor prefect, scowled in her direction, however.

Another carol was sung around the manger, a mediaeval lay from Crusader times, about the meaning of the three gifts and their impact through all the centuries since. Then there was a merry peal of bells from the back of the orchestra, and Rowany's voice led all the school—and all the audience too, or as many as could remember the Latin words—in a vigorous rendition of "Adeste Fideles".

As they sang, the angels and shepherds and, yes, the Three Kings too, all backed away from the central tableau, to leave everyone's attention on the Holy Family.

At this same time, entirely unrehearsed and unauthorised, without so much as a whispered word or a glance aside, the entire body of the Crew stepped forward as one, to gather around their three lambs who had been lost and were found again.

There would be questions later—oh, such a slew of questions!—but for now this was all the girls knew, that the sinners were redeemed and released from durance vile. More than that, though, they too were claimed and owned. They belonged here, at the heart of this very particular group of friends. Levity's hand found Pete's, schoolgirl blazer pressed close against velvet robe; Tasha and Tawney had similarly attached themselves to Ellen-Stephanie; and the Abramoff twins were not going to allow Catherine to feel left out. The others all crowded round, singing lustily to hide the fact that something very different was going on between and among them all: a promise bound by touch, unspoken, very real for all of that. It felt to Levity slightly rebellious, and yet really Christmassy in a way she couldn't define, and very definitely and very deeply Craterean, the Crater School at its very, very best...

ACKNOWLEDGEMENTS

There's a rare craft in retrospect, looking back over the whole process of a book from first idea through creation to publication and bringing to mind everyone who helped along the way.

First and always, I am grateful to my Patreon supporters, without whom none of this would be happening (and oh, there is a great deal happening, so much yet to come...). At current count there are one hundred and twenty of you, and I love you all.

Also first and always, m'wife Karen, without whom ditto ditto. She's my criterion.

Next in line come Cheryl Morgan, longtime friend, now publisher, and John Jarrold, once my editor and now my agent, all the way between my friend.

Ben Baldwin is the genius who makes these covers so amazing.

Shannon Page—also a beloved friend—keeps me on the straight and narrow, copy-wise. Everyone should be this lucky with their friends, obvs.

Speaking of, I've a host of friends locally and elsewhere and far too far elsewhere dammit, without whom etc etc. Without some of them I would not even be here, so there's that.

Oh, and also the cats. Barry and Mac: I am tolerably sure that the Crater School girls would love you both, if they didn't have sandkits to adore. Oh, and a camel.

ABOUT THE AUTHOR

Chaz Brenchley spent his childhood in Oxford, one of four children. It was a rule of the household that he read everybody else's books as well as his own; from his elder brother he acquired a love of science fiction, and from his sisters a devotion to the Chalet School books by Elinor M Brent-Dyer.

In his adolescence, he was sent to boarding school. Unhappily, it was almost exactly nothing at all like the Chalet School, nor the Crater School neither.

He sold his first stories at the age of eighteen, and has been a professional writer ever since. His work ranges from science fiction to epic and urban fantasy, from mysteries and thrillers to romance and horror. He's published upwards of forty books, and many hundreds of short stories.

Ten years ago he moved from bachelordom to marriage, from Newcastle to California, along with 120 boxes (115 of which were books), two squabbling cats and a famous teddy bear.

http://www.chazbrenchley.co.uk/

@ChazBrenchley